Z

BY

GREGORY KEITH MORRIS

To Robert,
Read & Enjoy.
Thanks, for the support.

3TG PRESS
THIRD EDITION

PUBLISHED BY 3TG PRESS
6532 WICKVILLE DRIVE
CHARLOTTE, NORTH CAROLINA 28215

COVER ILLUSTRATION BY RICARDO KAYANAN

EDITORIAL ASSISTANCE BY CONSTANCE HALLAWAY / FINAL EDIT OF CHARLOTTE, NC

MANUFACTURED IN THE UNITED STATES OF AMERICA

FIRST SELF-PUBLISHED EDITION: FEBRUARY 1994
SECOND SELF-PUBLISHED EDITION: JULY 1994

ISBN: 0-9648617-0-4

* * *

Dedicated to my son, Este'von Teron Morris who inspired this novel.

Special thanks to Thal, my wife, for your love, encouragement, and support,

And to Nika, my Little Dancer Girl.

Many thanks to the many relatives and friends who supported me along the way.

AND MOST OF ALL, THANKS BE TO ALMIGHTY GOD.

1
VIRGIN MAN

"*Virgin! Virgin!*" Zon gripped his head madly with both hands. He sat alone in the misty night, a passenger on the deck of an old ocean freighter crawling over a tired ocean toward Africa. Though his hands clutched both ears, he couldn't block the maddening voice of his own mind, screaming from within— like a scratched record, repeating the word. Each refrain chipped away at what fragile sanity remained. His eyes bulged from the madness, fixed in a blind stare upon the cold gray steel of the ship's deck. Raising his head, he stared out into the murky darkness. A feverish sweat poured from his brow. Strong arms curled his thick black coat tautly about him. His mind was out of control, his life was out of control, and there wasn't a thing he could do about it. "What have I done to my life?" he sobbed quietly into the darkness.

Just a week before, he'd graduated with honors from North Carolina State University, having earned dual degrees in Metallurgical and Electronic Engineering. Sheer lunacy drove him to the Peace Corps on graduation day, made him turn down five lucrative career offers in the process. He'd turned them down cold— in spite of the loud and sane shouts of the few friends he'd come to trust in college.

"A real role model," he groaned, thinking of the countless references made of him by the staff at the Saint James Orphanage, where he'd been raised. But their bright beam of hope was extinguished, outdone by a hasty and career-less decision. Zon's thoughts wrenched harder at his gut. "All this brain— and yet, brainless decisions. Where was my mind? Where *is* my mind?" *Virgin* again rebounded off the inner walls of his head like a booming football chant, forcing him to relive the blunder that had pushed him over the edge.

A week before graduation, he and his two best college friends, Ken and Tab, were winding down on a Friday afternoon in their dorm room. Classes were over and the weekend was just getting under way. The three were engaged in their weekly session of The Dozens. The object was to smash the other's ego with facts (or facsimiles) of the past, future, or present. Truth was allowable, but unimportant. During this, the last session of their college life, Zon had innocently exposed his well-guarded secret; a secret far too sensitive to be played upon by even his best of friends.

"Man, that Wanda's phat." A wolflike gleam smothered Ken's face as he spoke of the short, cute light-skinned coed.

"She's a slut," Tab responded.

"Don't call that girl a slut," Ken grimaced, popping from his seat on the bed in mock anger.

"Man, that girl cusses like a sailor, and you know it," Tab continued. "She's a ho' . . . and I don't mean the gardening kind. You defending her 'cause you think she likes you."

"Just don't talk about the girl, all right?" Ken responded, face reddened and his fist balled tight.

"Yeah, she likes you--now," Tab persisted, "but that's cause she couldn't get Zon." Tab and Zon burst into laughter. Ken turned beet red with rage.

"She ain't never liked Zon!" Ken blurted back.

"Uh, huh. You know good and well she wanted a piece of him. Tell him, Zon." Grinning from having stung Ken so deeply, Tab turned to Zon for a confirming nod.

"Yeah. That loosey-booty wanted me . . . bad," Zon bragged as steam belched from Ken's ears. "Right in front of a crowd, she dared me to put the screws to her. Man, she wanted this so bad, she could taste it." He wrenched at his privates. Ken bit his lower lip.

"So what'd you do, big man?" Ken shot back, trying to ease the focus away from himself.

"What did I do? With everyone standing there watchin'? Shoot! I grabbed that girl by the hand, drug her back to my room, and gave her a big piece . . . of my mind!" Finishing the sentence, Zon collapsed across the bed in laughter. His buddies stood over him, laughing as well.

"You didn't get none of that?" Tab asked.

"Man, nawh," Zon answered. "She loud talked me, in front of everybody. Ain't no girl gonna loud talk me. If and when I pop some of this in a babe, he said as he wrenched at his privates, I'm gonna be the one to say when. And when I got her to the room, I told her so." This time, Zon laughed alone.

"If?" Tab popped back. "What do you mean, if?"

"Afraid it was too much for you, huh?" Ken asked, picking up on Tab's lead.

"No," Zon answered flatly.

"Tab," Ken said, ignoring Zon's response, "didn't he tell us the same thing 'bout him and Yolanda. Up in her room, alone, she all but ready, but he couldn't do it."

"Wouldn't do it," Zon corrected him.

"Wouldn't, couldn't. Point is, you didn't get none." Nervous laughter eased from Zon's lips.

"And Glenda," Ken continued, "he never did it with her either."

"Man, you're a fuckin' virgin," Tab shot at Zon, aiming for a scoring blow to his ego.

"Who? Who?" Zon wailed.

"Who, who, you, owl," Tab answered.

"Man, I'm no fu . . . fu . . . friggin' virgin."

"You can't even say it," Ken spouted, "so I know you ain't doin' it."

Zon looked back and forth at the two. Their eyes were cringing shut with laughter. He laughed along nervously, but inside, he could feel a meat cleaver whacking away at his gut. Now was the time for the focus to change, for him to pick up on the last line and hurl it onto someone else, but they'd struck a nerve. Unknowingly, they'd pried open the doors to his fragile ego, had loosed the beast that was engulfing his thoughts, not letting him think clearly.

"Unlike you," Zon stuttered at Tab, "I don't let my mouth do my lovin'."

"I knew that," Tab responded. "You're a fuckin' virgin. Oh, I'm sorry. I meant fuckless virgin. You don't let anything do your lovin'."

The roar of laughter pushed back the small room's walls, picked away at the fragile scab that held Zon's mind intact. Desperately he fought to laugh along, hoping for a quick passing of the accusation. It didn't pass. His smooth black face reddened. He was losing control. He lost control. Suddenly, a broad smile stretched across his face.

"I'm *not* a virgin! I *am* a virgin!" he shouted.

Surprised, Ken and Tab stopped laughing and turned to stare at their friend. "I'm not lying! Can't you see that?" Rushing madly up to Tab, Zon wrenched his bewildered friend's shirt collar into his fists. Streaming tears gushed from his red eyes, across his broad, mad smile. "F . . . f . . . fuck! There. I said it. See? Fuck! Fuck!"

"Nigga, what the hell's wrong with you?" Tab growled, tearing free of Zon's clutch and backing away. Gasping a quick breath, Zon turned his glance to Ken, who quickly threw his fists up in defense. "Man," Ken said, "are you all right?"

Zon looked again to Tab, then back to Ken, finally realizing that the deranged lunatic that he held inside had finally escaped. From deep within, his own voice began chanting the "V" word. Madly, he bolted out the door. His friends chased after him, out onto the dark campus, but the cock-strong madman easily outdistanced them. All night he ran: around the campus, down to the football stadium, around the field thirty times, then across campus to the unlighted activity field, where he ran until daylight. Only pounding footsteps drowned out the maddening cries from within. Each time he slowed or stopped for a breath, the voice within resounded, driving him onward. By daybreak, time and exhaustion had subdued the voice within, but for how long he didn't know.

Later that day, Zon found himself standing at the Peace Corps booth set up to recruit graduates in the Student Center. He'd seen it on television. What it held for him was of little importance; of utmost importance was escape. He needed to get away, to find himself. He needed time to heal his mind.

"How old are you?" came the nonchalant recruiter's voice. The young white male sitting behind the desk hardly looked up as he began filling in the form. Zon stood with his eyes fixed wildly on the top of the man's head.

"Twenty-one."

"Married?"

"No."

"Any major commitments in your life, like wife, kids, parents, jail, et cetera?"

"No, none."

"Why the Peace Corps?"

"I . . . I want to give a little, before I take some for myself."

Zon's answers calmed him. The recruiter's questions were aimed at gleaning information, more so to screen applicants for criminals and crazies. Zon knew what they wanted to hear and was determined to give it to them.

"Ever been abroad?"

"No."

"Do you fear flying or heavy seas?"

"No."

"We don't get many colored recruits. Would you mind an assignment in the Middle East or Africa?"

"No." *No colored recruits?* He wondered. *Why weren't there many blacks joining the Peace Corps? Was it greed, apprehension, or just plain ignorance of the need? Why did this little young white man call me colored? Was he a holdover from the fifties? Or is this a test to see how black I really am?* He handed the young man his resume. The recruiter's eyes bulged as he read.

"Get many job offers?" he asked.

"Five."

"Turn them all down?"

"Yes." The blond man looked up for the first time to take a long and deep look at Zon.

"Are you using, or have you ever used, illicit drugs?" Zon bristled as he peered into the man's eyes. The question didn't seem to come from the form, judging by the manner in which it was asked. Though it stung, Zon was committed (or needed to be) to getting away from himself. He answered coolly, forcing a more neutral face and body tone.

"I have never used any drugs at all, other than aspirin." He paused. "I want to be an electronics engineer, and know that I'll be a fine one, no matter when I begin my career. It's just that all my life, I've worked to that end, to be successful, to make it. Well, I've made it, only to realize that I've neglected giving a little along the way. I want to do that, give, for a year or so. I feel that I will be a better person for it." Zon beamed behind his innocence-stricken face. He wasn't sure where that line of hoot originated, but it sounded awfully good.

The blond man looked blandly back to his papers, unconvinced by the flowery speech. "Would you be willing to work in a jungle village in Africa? They have no electronics there, and I doubt that they ever will," he said with a chuckle that caught in his throat as he looked up into Zon's stern, dark brown face. "Just a joke," he grinned. Zon didn't smile.

"What would I be doing there?"

"There are already volunteer leaders there, helping the natives to grow food and secure a water source. They need help in digging, sowing, plowing, that kind of thing. Are you still interested?"

"Yes."

"I'll sign you up, then. When can you leave?"

"A week from next Monday."

"Good. There will be a boat leaving for Africa's northwest shore Monday morning. Here's your pass. It's a cargo ship, leaving from Wilmington. Be there by six A.M. They won't wait. Someone will meet you in Morocco." Zon nodded. "Take this down to the infirmary. They'll give you your shots, so you'll be all ready."

Zon hesitantly backed away from the recruiter, then headed for the infirmary.

* * *

Three days of cruise time on the ship, alone with his thoughts, was the last thing he needed. Alone, nowhere to go, nothing to do. Alone with his thoughts, alone with his memories, thoughts that he didn't want to think, memories he didn't want to have. All waited in silence, at the end of each breath, after every blink; the thoughts were there, armed, waiting to destroy him, from the inside out.

By this, the third day, his madness was back to a feverish pitch.

He'd relived what had happened a hundred times over, but he could find no flaw on which to blame the madness. Try as he may, he couldn't go back to undo what had happened.

"I can't win," he said. The moist sea air offered no reply. "Can't change what happened." With eyes glistening, he sang quietly into the darkness. "You can't win; you can't break even. You can't get out of the game." A thread of laughter eased from his throat. The song reminded him of the Scarecrow in *The Wiz* as he danced around Dorothy, but the humor passed as quickly as it had come. "Oh God," he sighed. A growing sense of hopelessness washed over him like a tidal wave.

Zon was virtuous. That alone, though embarrassing for a strong, modern day, straight, black twenty-one-year-old man, was not driving him crazy. Deep down inside he protected, even celebrated, his virginity, but his ego constantly and desperately fought to hide and destroy it. It was this battle that simultaneously generated extreme exuberance, extreme humiliation. Combined, these opposing emotions fueled his madness.

Suddenly, a shiver came over him. His hands fell away from his face. The dark foggy night now seemed eerie, unlike before, when it served as a heavy cloak to hide in. Bewildered, he looked around the deck, feeling as if he had just been mystically dropped on board for the first time. For two days he'd been lost to his troubled mind. Life-changing decisions had been made, life-changing actions followed. Queasiness grew in the pit of his stomach. His mind started to spin again, not from insanity this time, but from disbelief, as he finally grasped the plight he'd thrown himself into. As he shook his head, he slowly circled the ship's deck with his eyes.

"When I get back, I've got to have myself committed." Zon talked aloud while piecing together the means to get himself out of this mess and back to a normal life.

"Gotta problem?" The deep voice from behind caused Zon to bolt forward, but he gained control and stayed seated. His motion looked awkward, as if he were trying to stand up and force his rear end through the bench bottom at the same time. Slowly rising from his seat, he turned to face the gruff voice that had startled him. Had not he just scanned the deck, with perfect vision, and spotted no one? No footsteps were heard crossing the metal deck. Yet, a shadow talked to him from a space that, only a split second ago, was empty. Adrenaline surged through his heart, causing it to beat hard and rapid in his ears. His palms burst forth with sweat; his arms and legs tingled from the booster shot and excess of blood that prepared them for fight or flight. While his body reacted involuntarily, the shock centered his thoughts. For the moment, he dismissed his struggle with insanity. Instead, he started collecting, analyzing, as he'd done so often in the past.

It was he who was normally left standing to face a possibly threatening and unknown situation, while friends, mentors, and other adults jumped out of their skins. Such an asset often left him a hero, rescuing trapped children from dry wells, resolving hopelessly scrambled computer programs, stopping runaway cars, preventing would-be disastrous fires. The list of petty, yet consistent instances of his steady head seemed innumerable. He didn't keep count, but his confidence in facing the unknown grew with every experience. He answered the man in his own easy baritone voice.

"Ah, no, sir. I was just thinking out loud." Quickly, he scanned the black seaman and slyly slipped his hands deep into his pockets to raise a question of doubt in the stranger's mind, and to dry his sweaty palms.

The man stood about five feet nine. His clothes were all black, from the heavily scuffed and untied boots, baggy pants, and overcoat that hid any hint of his build, right up to the old oversized captain's hat sitting on his head. Though tall and erect, the man seemed old, unexplainably so, and very familiar. His face remained in a shadow. Zon couldn't see his eyes, which disturbed him. The first look at anyone, male or female, was always into the eyes. Through them, he could tell if the stranger could be trusted. While the stranger's body remained a mystery, his voice exposed much detail. His words were cocky, his voice, solid and bass.

"I've been watchin' ya fo some time," the faceless shadow said, slower this time and with a slightly altered voice. "You a mite tetched, ain't cha boy." It was still bass, but not as solid, sounding more flippant than arrogant. As he spoke, the dark figure raised his gloved right hand up to his right temple and tapped himself on the side of the head with a bent index finger, clearly suggesting that Zon had lost his mind. A snicker broke forth from the shadow.

The insult scorched Zon's ego. A normal fool would have backed off, not having full grasp of this stranger's origin, ability or intentions. But Zon was far more than an ordinary fool. Instead, he launched a nonchalant laugh back at the stranger, noting how close the very same thoughts were to his own. He answered the old man, matching his slower, lower, and jovial tone.

"How long have you been watching me?"

"Long 'nough to know ya tetched. Whas ailin' ya ana' how?" Zon stared at the old man, but didn't answer. He was insulted that a stranger knew that much about him, and even more so, now that he was confronted with it.

"Life must be kinda' slow here on this old tub." Zon attempted to alter the course of the conversation.

"Yep," the old man replied, "but id still don't tell me nuthin' bout yo' problem. Now, why would such a high-rollin' pup like you be so messed up?"

Zon tried to find malice or hate in the old man's words, but couldn't. Instead, he found curiosity and concern. Such traits, shown so sincerely, inexplicably melted his defenses. He relaxed as he thought of the old man. In spite of it all, he desperately needed to talk to someone else, besides himself. *Why not talk to the old black man of the sea*, he thought and dropped slowly back to his seat on the bench. The old man moved over beside him and sat. A passing thought told Zon to look into those hidden eyes that he'd missed before, but the thought disappeared as quickly as it had come. Instead, Zon's head dropped slowly, then hung loosely at the limit of his limber neck tendons.

"Ya turned down those job offas," the old man began.

"Don't need money if you don't have a mind," Zon replied.

"That won't no good decision."

"Best that I could come up with at the time."

"How long you been making 'dese bad decisions?" Instead of replying, Zon thought back to his early childhood at Saint James. There, he had little need to make any decisions at all. Life there had been extremely poor. Variety of any sort, including food, clothing, shelter, bedding, and friends, was nonexistent. The orphans used whatever was available. It made life simple.

"Not long," he replied to the deep voice, "Didn't need to. We ate whatever we had, wore whatever we found in the closet, believed whatever we were told."

"Ya all did?"

"No," Zon responded, looking about beyond his closed eyelids, deep into memories of the orphanage. All of them were different, but in many ways, the same. "I did. Charlie and NanaTuck, they told me the Bible. Took us all to Sunday school at the Baptist church. I learned there."

"Learned? Learned what?"

"How to live, what to believe." Zon beamed a broad smile. "All the teachers, even NanaTuck, they all liked the way I listened. All of them taught us, taught me, how to live."

"Quotin' the Bible," the old man sighed.

"Yeah, they all believed. And so do I."

"You neva axed no questions?" Zon's thoughts jumped again to NanaTuck, the orphanage matron. *You see somebody burn their fingers to a crisp on a stove*, she'd said, *no use in ya stickin' ya tongue to it to see if it's hot*. "No," he replied slowly. "I believed them and I respected them. Why waste the energy?"

"You all believed?"

"No. Some did." Though deeply involved, Zon listened to the conversation more so as an observer. He felt at ease being the observer, as if he had no choice or control over answering the old man's questions, of thinking his own thoughts.

"Wha day teach ya, these grown-ups?" the old man asked while sitting calmly by Zon's side. Zon thought back on the countless lectures and teachings by the Sunday school teachers, matrons, and even Charlie, the orphanage's groundskeeper.

"'Don't foul your body', Miss Jefferies, the schoolteacher said. 'It's a temple, not to be fouled with bad language, drugs, cigarettes, disease, unnatural acts or fornication.'"

"Forna-what?"

"Sex before marriage."

"Ya buy all that?"

"Every bit," Zon said with the innocence of a nine-year-old. "Cleanliness is next to godliness. Idle hands are the devil's workshop. Treat people the way you want to be treated . . . " Zon rattled off the laws of life into the night.

"You a regula' Boy Scout," the old man said. Zon grimaced. "But bein' a Boy Scout don't make ya crazy."

"That's what the other boys said," Zon replied meekly.

"What, you crazy?"

"No, that I was a Boy Scout . . . a scaredy cat . . . a nerd." His forehead wrinkled slightly. "They all outgrew me. All of them. They all got taller and bigger. They could run faster and jump higher. They all left me. I had to run with the younger boys." The wrinkles grew into a full grimace. Zon relived the insults and pains from the larger boys of his youth. "They all talked about their girls," he said with a small quiver in his voice. "How they made them howl 'cause they were so big."

"Noboda's that big."

"I know that now, but I didn't then."

"Ya just believed it."

"Television, the movies and those magazines, they all confirmed it."

"Yeah, bu'cha believed it."

"Just like I did everything else." Zon relaxed with that admission, though saddened. "They'd all rush off to the bathroom together, crowd around the single toilet bowl, eager to show their size. I and the other *little* boys would cower in a corner watching them, their chocolate sabers stretching out, slashing the air about, slashing our little egos, convincing us, convincing me of my inadequacy. With every slash, I grew more ashamed of myself."

"But ya was young," the old man countered, "ya grew up, didn't ya?"

"Not till I was eighteen. By then I'd had six years of feeling inadequate, afraid to show myself. While the other boys thought and talked about girls, the only thing that came to my mind was the laughter from any girl I ever dared to show myself to."

"Ya thought yourself right out of a life."

"That's about the size of it, forgive the pun."

"So thas' kept ya a virgin all these years," the old man recited. Zon winced at the mention of the "V" word.

"No, I mean, yes." Confusion knitted Zon's brow. "I don't know what I mean. I thought back then that I wouldn't let them, the older boys, get to me. The people whom I respected in my life, they'd taught me to refrain from all of that sexual nonsense, anyway. And that's just what I did. I refrained from girls because . . . because it was the right thing to do. Later, after I'd grown, that thinking persisted. Dating for me was merely a means to get married, so I could show myself, once and for all, without the laughter."

"But ya still was ashamed of ya'self."

"No! I was doing what was right."

"Ya was ashamed," the old man said calmly, "of doin' what was right."

Tears welled in Zon's eyes as he saw for the first time the root of his dilemma. "NanaTuck, Miss Jefferies, they made me ashamed of wanting to do wrong. I was ashamed of wanting to do wrong, and I was ashamed because I couldn't do wrong. I was afraid. I am afraid . . . of the laughter." Zon stood and clutched his head, his eyes slammed shut. "That's been my life! Shame, guilt, and laughter! Yeah, I got into the books! Did everything I could to stay out of life! It kept me sane!"

"Oh yeah," the old man snorted, "that bass-awkward thinkin' worked like a charm, too, didn't it?" Easing a heavy hand onto Zon's shoulder, he forced him back to his seat. "It's okay, boy. Ya done good. Cain't ya see that? Think of what it took to get ya here. The commitment, the perseverance, the pain. Ya made it."

"Made it?" Zon screeched. Now more than ever, he wanted to look into the old sea dog's face, but found it impossible to turn his head or open his eyes. "I haven't made anything; I've destroyed everything. I've an education and no means to use it! And a libido the size of Mount Everest that'd probably kill me if ever I sought to satisfy it. You call that, making it?"

"Look into the light," the old man said slowly.

"What?" Zon started to argue, but something gripped him from within. Inexplicably, he leaned back against the bench and again conjured up thoughts of his childhood. A wave of serenity engulfed him. He recalled the smell he'd expected when the old man sat beside him, that repulsive, foul odor that old sea dogs always kept about them, according to so many books he'd read. Taking a deep breath, he searched for it and smelled . . . nothing. Emptying his lungs quietly into the foggy night air, he leaned closer toward his companion and again expanded his chest to take in the stranger's aroma. As he breathed, he caught the smell, but it was wrong, not sweaty or fishy, but sweet and subtle, like . . . like NanaTuck's pies. Cherry pies, spilling over in her old iron oven. He took another long deep breath of those delicious pies, trying to inhale a slice from what had to be his imagination. He could almost taste the cherries as his tongue chased them between his teeth, smashing them into oceans of delightful red heaven, coating his taste buds with sweet sugar and tart. A broad smile eased across his face, the same old smile that NanaTuck had come to count on every time one of her little orphans bit into one of her culinary delights. Zon took a breath between each bite, chewing and breathing slowly, smiling broadly. Every mouthful seemed sweeter, every breath warmer. As he sat there consuming bite after bite, the sweet and warm feeling of being home consumed him. Biting into yet another piece, he gazed around NanaTuck's kitchen. Standing in each corner of the square room was a solid oak beam, hewn by hand. The floor in the corner where he sat was cool and slick. Broad hardwood boards fit smoothly together underneath him. All was peaceful, and yet, something was strange about it. He looked up into NanaTuck's pleasant, plump face. She smiled down at him as she stood there with the next pie. Zon had never eaten so many before. He reminded himself to say a prayer of thanks for allowing every bite to taste better than the last, even after he'd eaten so many.

Zon's head eased back to rest against the painted kitchen wall. Opening his eyes wide, he stared up into the ceiling as he chewed. Slowly, the ceiling dissolved before his eyes. Blue pastel ceiling turned into misty blue sky. He turned to look out the large kitchen window to the green yard. There, before his eyes, it too turned blue, then orange, then amber. Then, in a brilliant burst, the sun exploded into the first light of dawn. Zon shut his eyes hard to the brilliant sun rays. As he did, he shook his head to clear his mind.

"NanaTuck!" he screamed, then looked about. But there was no

NanaTuck, no warm kitchen, only the stark coldness of an old freighter's metal hull. Wrenching his head about, he gripped hard down on the chair rails. There he sat on the deck of that old tub. Fog and darkness had cleared away to reveal the most beautiful daybreak he'd ever seen. It had all been a dream, the warm and peaceful kitchen, the sweet, tasty pies, all fruits from his fertile mind. NanaTuck's kitchen had been the safe place, the secure haven for all the orphans during his childhood. It was the place that allowed no loud sirens, cussing drunks, or oversized bullies looking for an innocent victim. There, no harm entered, only harmony. It was filled with warmth from the two large stoves, soft melodies flowing on NanaTuck's alto voice, and so many delectable sweets to chase the worst of bogeyman away. Zon had escaped to his haven, lodged deep in his memories of long ago. He had spent the entire night there, in his dreams, but that dream seemed so real. *The old seaman!* Zon thought, remembering his companion from the night before. The bench next to him was empty and there was no sign of anyone having been there.

Was he real or was it all a dream? he thought as he calmly stared into the new morning. "It was a dream," he said solidly, "whether it was or not." Dismissing the thoughts, he rose to his feet, removed his jacket, and stretched his limbs to let the sun soak his bronze skin. "Dream or no dream," he said as he exercised, "that was the best night's rest I've had since high school. Just what the doctor ordered." He smiled as he felt the revived freshness in his mind and body. "And you can think a little clearer too, you virgin, you," he scoffed. "Right or wrong, I'm in this now." With calming resolve, he shouted toward the distant shoreline, "Look out, Africa! Ready or not, here I come!"

2
AFRICA - D.O.A.

Rusty cables uncoiled like dusty snakes, lassoing pylons, securing the ship to the dock. Zon, moving to the gangway, stood in line, waiting to get off the boat. The old black man was not in line. Slowly, he panned the view. The Moroccan harbor looked exactly like the one he'd just left back in North Carolina, except most of the people who worked here were dark-skinned. As he gazed from left to right, he thought of all the stories and anecdotes he'd heard of Africa, and wondered again of the old man. His language had been that of the classic Southern Negro, but why had he been on that ship?

Maybe he was African, Zon thought, *finally escaping from America . . . for a triumphant return to his roots.* The thought struck a funny bone. A huge laugh caught him by surprise, forcing its way out in one large snort. A short African crewman, standing in front of him, turned around and stared up into his face. Batting his eyes, Zon turned away. Laughter choked through his clenched teeth. It felt good to be laughing and conscious at the same time. An eternity seemed to have passed since he'd honestly felt like laughing.

The line shortened as the men shuffled through a checkpoint on the dock. There, two brown men checked for identification and destination. One's hair was straight and jet black, cut short with heavy bangs hanging to his brow. The other's hair was short and tightly curled. Both wore khaki brown uniforms. Two armed gunmen stood behind them with semiautomatic rifles.

On the dock, large cranes swung over the freighter, their booms lowered as men on the ship latched on crates and boxes. Forklifts and trucks scurried back and forth on a thin paved road that ran the length of the dock. Four other freighters were anchored; three were being loaded.

But it was brown and black men that fueled the activity. Men of different sizes, shapes, and hues, doing what white men did mostly, back in The States. Zon thought again of his preconceived notion of Africa. He'd come there expecting a continent full of wretchedly poor people. In this first look, he'd seen none. *O for one*, he thought, beginning a count of what he encountered versus what he expected.

The debarkation line inched forward. Zon's thoughts wandered as he waited, thinking of the tales he'd been told.

"Man, you must be crazy!" rang out the loud boisterous voice of Uncle Early from deep within Zon's memory. He'd talk loud and long during one of his many discussions on the Back-to-Africa movement. Uncle Early, as he was called by everyone at Saint James, was the maintenance man. He was always old in Zon's memory and had talked often of his service in the two world wars.

"Back to Africa, my ass! Man, them people over there hate us Negroes. They'd kill us if they had the chance. Why, I remember sailing on a Navy cruiser into port at Tripoli. Our captain warned us all of the danger for colored troops that lurked beyond the gangway. They just jealous, thas' all, cause you live in the U. S. of A. 'Take my advice', he'd say, 'Stay on board ship while we're in dock. The Navy won't be responsible if you leave.' And ya better believe I took his advice." Uncle Early always smiled at his own cunning when he'd finish a story.

Weren't they more jealous of white people, Zon thought as he stood in line? *They had far more to be jealous of than Negroes. Wasn't he curious enough to take a small look? And why did the white captain of the ship, who never saw any other reason to address the colored troops, make such painstaking effort to warn them? And if the warning was true and deadly . . . why was he so anxious to keep the black troops on board ship and out of Tripoli, Libya? And why did Uncle Early's matching stories of drunken white fools returning to the ship, some falling hilariously overboard, others missing the ship all together, why was there such a rip-roaring time for them among these bloodthirsty savages?* "All he had to do was look," Zon whispered. "I'm going to at least look. I won't be that gullible."

And NanaTuck was no better. She, too, had shared her wealth of hearsay and factless deductions of Africa with the Saint James kids.

"They stink," she said, "and I would trust 'em as far as I could throw 'em." She always talked of Africans with disgust, as if she could spit her distaste for them out with her words. "I remember that old Eubani. He smelled so bad, why, you could almost smell him comin'. The boy was musty--always musty. I don't think he even knew what a bathtub was. You boys," she'd say, waving away with her thick index finger, "whatever you do, always bathe--and use deodorant."

With head down and stare fixed to the ship's deck, Zon smiled again as he thought back to this kind wonderful woman and her hatred for a people she never knew.

"And maybe I'm just as bad," he said. He'd come to know Eubani as he grew older and always thought that he stank. But it was the same musty underarm odor he'd smelled on many Germans, Russians, Asians, and Africans he'd come to know during college. It was Americans who were the odd men out. America was one of the few *civilized* cultures of the world that found the musty odor of a man offensive. Most other cultures regarded the odor as a noble sign of a working man. Very few cultures desire sweet perfume under men's arms.

Close personal contact with Africans, or any foreigners, had truly been limited during Zon's youth. In fact, television had provided most of his exposure and that picture wasn't pretty. Africans were always shown as small, scrawny, and helpless.

I guess the same's true for all cultures, Zon pondered as he prepared to hand his papers to the debarkation inspectors. *Wonder what a Martian would report if he landed in the secluded West Virginia hills for a couple of hours, then just took off?* Images of space markers warning travelers away from the toothless inbred morons of earth coaxed another laugh from Zon's humor-starved mind.

"There is something funny?" the officer asked in heavily accented

English.

"Ah, no, sir," Zon replied. "I just had a passing thought, that's all."

"Over there. The officer will inspect your bag." He pointed to a lone, bare table with another armed agent standing behind it. Now it was the crew's turn to laugh as they stood in line watching Zon, and only Zon, being patted down while his bag was emptied onto the large wooden table.

* * *

The old B-52 bomber shook and rattled as it finally managed to leave the ground. Zon, along with eight other passengers, sat strapped to the floor as the pilot pointed the plane into the morning sun. A hasty departure from America had left him ignorant of what to expect on his journey to Zaire or of the country itself. He sat stiffly in the tail section with his legs stretched out in front of him. The lone black bag containing his personal effects sat propped behind his back and shoulders, providing a cushion against the plane's turbulence. Compared to the plane, the old ocean freighter with its rust, leaky pipes, and diesel smell seemed like a cruise ship.

The sickness in his stomach, which had passed during his dream of the night before, was back now, spawned this time from the wild motion of the plane. But it had started when he first approached the Peace Corps agent on the dock in Morocco. He'd gotten directions from the debarkation officer who'd frisked him. The officer pointed to a small booth, fifty yards down the dock, in front of an old warehouse. Zon grabbed his bag and walked briskly toward it. There, behind the table, stood three white men. Two of them were dressed in military garb. The third, and oldest of the three, wore a short-sleeved, white-collar shirt soaked with sweat. He stood listening and occasionally stroked a grimy handkerchief across his forehead. The other two did all the talking. As Zon approached, the fat white man pointed at him. The two men looked up, smiled, then walked away.

"Mr. ahh," Zon said as he fished through the folded papers in his hand for the agent's name. The fat man sat behind the table.

"Stevens," he said.

"Yeah, Mr. Stevens. I am Z . . ."

"I know who you are. Those your papers?" Stevens spoke gruffly and motioned for Zon to hand him the folded documents in his hand. Zon passed him the papers. Taking them, Stevens fished through the pile, found the one he sought, then stuffed the rest in his pants pocket. Signing the one remaining paper, he handed it back to Zon.

"You've made the plane late," he complained without looking up.

"Sir?" Zon replied.

"What are you doing here anyway?" he asked.

"What kind of question is that?"

"Oh, nothin'. It's just that we don't get many colored--least not comin' here, 'specially in the Peace Corps. What's your story anyhow?"

"Too long to tell," Zon answered in disgust. Two encounters with the Corps and both were with white men who couldn't believe that he was doing what he was doing because of his color.

"What did you say to the inspector?" the agent asked. "That's the first time I've seem 'em search anybody."

"Guess he thought I was laughing at him," Zon replied. "Where do I go from here?"

"Here. Take this to that boy standing over there on the dock." Zon looked over to see a tall black African leaning on the front of a tattered Volkswagen bus. He wore no uniform, but the khaki green of his shorts and shirt matched. "He's waiting to take you to that plane yonder." Stevens pointed off in the distance to a large plane sitting on a gravel airstrip. "It's headed to Zaire. Someone'll meet you there when it lands. The flight should take about, oh, three to four hours." Stevens turned to walk away. "Oh," he continued, pointing again at the man by the VW bus, "give him a dollar, too."

"I can carry my own bag to the plane, thank you," Zon replied insolently.

"I'm sure you can," Stevens responded, "but that's not the valet. It's your pilot." Zon paused in the tracks he was making toward the bus and turned to look into the smiling man's face. "Be nice to him. It'll be worth it in the end." Without another word, the fat man headed back to his office.

* * *

"I'm a racist. I'm a no-good racist," Zon chided himself as he rocked in rhythm with the bouncing plane. The pilot, the old man on the ship, all of the black faces at the docks--all had predetermined places in his mind that he was only now coming to realize. He shook his head as he looked around.

Six other passengers sat in odd array around the ex-warship turned cargo and passenger plane. Red and blue boxes filled the tail section. In front of them sat the two men who had been talking to Stevens. Both looked to be in their mid-thirties. They sat on a box end and were dressed alike, wearing old green T-shirts and camouflage pants tucked into army boots at the ankle. Both smoked. They talked quietly as one fidgeted with something down in a large duffle bag.

Zon swept his eyes along the rusty bulkheads to one of the two woman passengers sitting directly across from him. She too looked to be in her mid-thirties. Light wrinkles creased her face. Her flat brown hair was tied into a ball on the top of her head. She struggled to keep her eyes steady on an open book held tightly in her hands. The jolting airplane made reading nearly impossible, yet she managed to turn a page every five to six minutes.

On a bench up toward the front were the other woman passenger and her husband. Both were white, in their late fifties, and were dressed like the great white hunters so often seen in old Tarzan movies. They wore tan shorts with matching broad-flapped, pocketed, short-sleeved shirts. Each also wore wide-brimmed helmets with white bands tied around them. They held hands, sat with their heads close to one another, and talked excitedly.

The seventh and only other black passenger sat toward the front of the plane beside seven large suitcases. He apparently belonged to the great-white-hunter couple, like the luggage.

"How ya doin'?" Surprised, Zon turned around and looked into the face of one of the men who'd been sitting on the boxes, but had moved to the floor by his side. He'd brought the duffle bag that he'd been fidgeting in. The other of the two stepped passed them and proceeded to the front of the plane. Engine noise had prevented Zon from hearing their approach.

"Oh, fine, I guess," Zon responded. "To tell the truth, this trip has been quite a trip, so far." The turbulence and noise from the plane masked his natural inhibitions to strangers. He looked at the soldier, who stared down into the bag. His arms were submerged into it as well, up to the elbows. With a slight grin on his face, he continued his efforts in the bag. Small metallic clinks emanated from the oily pouch.

"On your way to Zaire?" he asked.

"Yes. I'm a Peace Corps volunteer." Zon looked for the same old surprise he'd received from the other white men he'd told, but didn't get it.

"That's good. First time to Africa?"

"Yes. And you?"

"Oh, no. I've been in and out of jungleland all my life." The jungleland crack disturbed Zon, but he dismissed it as tolerable racism.

"What have you got in that bag, if you don't mind me asking?"

"No, not at all. Guns, just guns."

"Guns?"

"Yep, wanna see one?" He lifted an Uzi machine gun from his pouch and shoved it heavily at Zon.

"Ah, no, thank you. Isn't that illegal?" The soldier set the weapon down on the floor between them.

"Heck no. Besides, I don't see any police around, do you?" Laughter cackled out of a crooked smile. Zon saw into his face for the first time. Closely cropped hair stood straight up on his head. His two-day old whiskers showed specks of gray. A shallow scar cut across his left eyebrow and cheek. His eyes were blue and wild.

A blade of fear slowly penetrated Zon's spine. "What . . . what are you going to do with that gun?"

"What, this gun? Oh, I've got plenty of guns. Ya see, me and my partner yonder are taking these guns to Liberia. There's a civil war going on there, ya know."

"Yes, I've heard about it."

"Ya have? Good! Anyway, ya see them blue boxes back there? Well, they're loaded with old M-16 rifles and ammo. We're gonna deliver them to the governor's troops. Ya with me?" Zon nodded his head as he gazed over the boxes, thinking that there must be enough there to outfit a small army. "Good!" the soldier exclaimed. "And they are gonna need 'em too, I tell ya, cause, ya see them red boxes back there? Well, they're slap full of Russian rifles and ammo that'll match the M-16s shot for shot. We're gonna give them to the opposition troops." The soldier chuckled boyishly. "Get it? They'll be shootin' and killin' each other with these babies for the next five months." Now the soldier laughed out loud, drawing a brief glance from the woman who read, ten feet away. She quickly turned back to her reading and didn't notice the machine-gun on the floor.

"You're a mercenary, aren't you?" Zon asked.

"I've been called worse," he replied.

"But I don't get it. If you supply both sides equally, then neither will win."

"Exactly. They'll just keep on fightin' and killin' each other."

"What will that do?"

"For them, nothing. But for us, it'll do plenty. The fightin' will keep them just where they are, underdeveloped and a threat to no one but themselves."

"Us? Who is us?"

"Why, Uncle Sam of course. I'm red, white, and blue right down to my jock strap." Again, the zealous soldier laughed aloud.

"Is Liberia that bad?"

"Nope. And it's my job to keep 'em that way. Why, if they managed to stabilize their government, they could join in with the likes of Libya, Egypt, Morocco, Iraq, Iran, or a couple other darky nations. Could you imagine, this United States of Africa, controlling oil, waterways, minerals, and on and on? Now, where would that leave us good guys, huh?"

Zon paused and pictured the African nations, united. Though he never considered it before, it didn't appear to be such a bad idea. But suddenly, while pondering the possibilities, a burning question rocketed to mind.

This guy was on an illegal mercenary mission, with illegal guns, all aboard an airship, not headed to Liberia, but Zaire. Everything was wrong and illegal, yet . . .

"Excuse me," Zon said, struggling to retain as much of the innocently curious voice that he could, "but, why are you telling me this?" The soldier smiled broadly and gazed back into his bag.

"Oh, it really doesn't matter that much," he said. Looking over at his partner, he nodded lightly. The other soldier pushed open the door leading to the cockpit and slid through. "Ya see, kid, neither you or any of your fellow passengers are gonna live much longer. So what difference does it make?"

Cold reality drained Zon's face, twisting his small intestines into fist-sized knots. Instinctively, he moved to stand up, but the soldier placed a solid hand on his rising shoulder and punched him hard in the rib cage. The blow knocked the wind out of him, bringing him back down to the floor.

"What's your hurry, son?" the soldier sang. "The fun's just startin'." Zon's eyes overflowed. He'd had many fights in his life, but had managed never to be hit that hard in such a vulnerable spot. Despite the pain, he rolled away from the soldier, toward the front of the plane. Once his feet hit the floor, he stood up, but leaned heavily against the ship's hull. Two shots rang out from the cockpit. The plane cut hard into a deep right bank. Zon fell across the plane, where he crashed into the other wall. Screams filled the cabin. Peering up, he spied the soldier still seated on the floor, smiling. His hand gripped a rope attached to the side of the plane.

Zon knew there was only one way to save himself or the other passengers. Pulling all the strength that he could muster, he leaped toward the seated soldier. The soldier smiled, then caught Zon in the groin with a karate kick as he neared. Again, Zon fell across the lopsided plane, this time onto the seated woman, who started kicking and screaming hysterically.

"Come on, boy, you can do better than that," the soldier yelled, rising to his feet. He held the gun in his left hand. The hijacked plane slowly righted itself. Zon's assailant stood smiling, goading him into another attack.

"I said come on, boy! Let's see what you're made of. Oh, oh. You need some incentive, right?" He raised his gun and shot multiple holes into the black guide seated by the older couple. Blood splattered all over the matching luggage and safari outfits. The old couple clutched each other and started yelling. Walking over to the large cargo door on the left side of the plane, the soldier slid it open. Zon struggled to his knees, but couldn't stand because of his crushed testicles.

"Come on, boy! Get up!" the soldier demanded as he walked over and grabbed the dead load-bearer, dragged him to the door, and threw him out. "All right, who's next?"

"Oh please, please," came the restricted voice of the lady hunter. "We have money. We can pay you."

"Now, ain't that nice. She can pay. You here that, Koonta? She can pay. Well, Missy," he said, grabbing the old lady by the shoulder and forcing her away from her feeble husband, "you can pay, but I wonder, can you fly?" He dragged her toward the door. Her husband grabbed her by the leg then threw a wild punch at her assailant. It landed on the soldier's jaw, but drew no reaction. Zon, seeing a new opportunity, darted toward the assassin. Jumping across his back, he landed a hard punch to his kidney. The soldier released the old lady, but straightened against Zon's grip. Zon pulled his left fist back for a better punch to the soldier's head, but the seasoned fighter countered with an elbow to his stomach. Zon wrenched over, but didn't lose his grip. His weight pulled them over as the old safari man jumped toward them. Spotting his approach, the soldier opened fire, cutting the old man nearly in two. The would-be hunter backpedaled, then fell out the open door. His wife ran to the door, arriving as he fell. She screamed his name while reaching for him and watched in horror as he fell away from the plane. The soldier grabbed Zon in a headlock and pulled him to the door. He smiled and talked as he wrestled control.

"What's a matter, honey? Can't reach him?" The soldier taunted the catatonic woman as Zon prepared to throw another punch. "Howse abou' a little hand, or should I say, a little foot?" Using Zon as a post, the soldier jumped up and kicked the old lady square in the back with both feet, blasting her out the door, ten feet beyond the plane. Her bloodcurdling screams cut Zon to the bone as he watched helplessly.

Releasing him, the soldier turned to fight. Overcome with fury, Zon threw a hard punch at his chin. The soldier blocked it with his right hand, then punched him in the nose. Zon stumbled backward, but didn't fall. Walking back to his assailant, he threw a left, then a right. Both were blocked and countered by the same right hand. All the while, the Uzi hung securely from the soldier's left hand.

Noticing the gun, Zon realized that the soldier was toying with him, taunting and using him as a cat would a mouse, for the amusement. Zon leaned on the far right wall of the plane, bruised and out of breath. Turning his throbbing head, he faced his opponent.

"What's the matter? You tired?" the soldier asked mockingly. "Heck. We just got started. Come on. I'll give you a shot. Aren't you gonna take it?" Zon stood there, beaten and silent. Whatever happened next, he was no longer going to get beaten just for this guy's amusement. The soldier jutted his chin out and closed his eyes. Zon didn't move. "Oh, well," the soldier sighed as he opened his eyes. "I guess recess is over." He raised his gun and took aim. Zon jumped at the gun with hands outstretched as the soldier opened fire. Hot lead ripped into his skin, his hands, then his chest as he fell. His momentum carried him into the soldier, who kicked him squarely in the stomach. Zon spun and fell to the floor, bleeding. Hot lead burned in his chest. Warm blood soaked his clothing. The soldier walked over and grabbed him by the collar.

"Come on, big boy. The jungle below awaits." But Zon's weight wouldn't allow him to be tossed about like the other passengers. As the soldier struggled to get the limp body off the floor, the other soldier emerged from the cockpit.

"She's on auto," he said. "Everything secure back here?"

"Just about. There's one alive and one stiff left. Which one you want?" The soldier-pilot walked over to the hysterical reading-woman. Dismissing Zon, the other soldier joined him there.

* * *

Zon slowly opened his eyes. He didn't know how long he'd been out. The bullets had badly wounded his hands. His chest throbbed with pain. Fire raged in his head and neck. He rolled over, saw the soldiers, then gagged. The woman who'd sat so serenely as she read her book now hung pale, nude, and facedown out of the open cargo door. Three gaping bullet holes interrupted the flow of clammy white skin down her back. Each of the soldiers held one of her legs, allowing her upper torso to hang from the plane. Her arms dangled limply over her head. The mercenary who'd killed the pilot held frantically onto the side of the door opening with his right hand. His left hand clamped down hard around the girl's left ankle as he wildly thrust his midsection toward her hips. The other soldier stood supporting their weight, preventing the three from tumbling out of the plane. Both were totally engulfed in their satanic rape.

With their backs turned and the engines roaring loudly, Zon painfully pulled his bleeding hands under himself, then shuffled upright to rest against the plane hull. His assailant still held the Uzi in his left hand. Zon looked out of the plane's window into the bright midday sunlight. Thick jungle lay a few hundred feet below. The sun was high, but to the right of the plane now, confirming a severe course change. The two soldiers had killed everyone and would surely kill him as soon as they noticed he was still alive. His only hope was to get out of the plane.

And what if I did, he pondered. *There was still the 300-foot drop to the ground, then thick jungle to face. Death or Bulla-Bulla,* he thought and managed a small chuckle in spite of his pain and impending doom. The line came from one of many jokes he'd heard about Africa, where a choice, of immediate death or rape then death, was given to three hunters by African savages. Momentarily forgetting about his wounds, he dropped his hands to his side, where they struck the plane hull. Instantly, throbbing pain shot through both and wrenched him back into his dilemma. As he clinched one wounded hand with the other, he accepted his doom.

If ya gotta go, ya gotta go, he thought, then stood. Collecting all of his remaining strength, he charged toward the unoccupied portion of the cabin door. Unknowingly, he roared aloud as he charged, startling the killers, both of whom turned to see this tall black, yet bloodied figure whirling toward them. Both released the dead girl simultaneously, allowing the body to fall mercifully through the door. The smaller of the two mercenaries, who'd been sodomizing the corpse, rose abruptly from his knees and stretched to block the opened door, only to have the soft flesh of his short stiff member lodge deep into the jaws of his pants zipper. The surprising pain wrenched him awkwardly back to the floor into a rolling heap, then barreling toward Zon's approaching feet. The floor acrobatics delayed the standing soldier's instincts for a split second. Coolly, he raised his gun, took aim at Zon's head, and fired. At that same instant, Zon tumbled over the rolling human lump in his path and fell backward through the door. The spray of bullets narrowly missed his temple, but ripped his forehead, cheeks, nose, lips, and chin. Had there not already been an immense loss of blood and nauseating numbness from the severe beating and earlier shots to his hands and chest, the new pain would have killed him. However, Zon was feeling no pain. The sight of those bullets exiting the gun barrel froze in his mind, the gun quaking in the soldier's hand as the powder lit, the smile across the mercenary's face as he fired, all froze and swirled into a blur as Zon floated free--and unconscious.

* * *

Wild birds flew overhead, singing loudly as if to wake the dead. The smell of the fresh earth and abundant greenery slowly tunneled its way through Zon's badly mangled nose and coagulated blood, arousing his deep and all but nonexistent consciousness. The ground underneath him was soft and warm. Sunlight filtered through the dense leaves, warming his limbs. Pleasant odors, feelings, and sounds encouraged him out of his deep slumber. Responding, he engaged his hefty chest muscles to take in a deep breath of air. As he did, the millions of damaged nerve endings in his hands, chest, groin, and face sprang to life, reminding him that the past few hours of his life were no dream. Tears welled in his eyes as the excruciating pain grew. Zon opened his eyes. The dense jungle leaves filled his sight. He lay silent, somewhat bitter about his pain, yet thankful. For in spite of the beating, shooting, and skydiving without a parachute, he was still alive. Raising his head slightly, he looked down over his body. His hands lay out by his side, jerking convulsively; he tried to draw them to him, but they didn't respond. Bullet holes were clearly visible. He looked down at his legs, then groaned with horror. They lay badly twisted beneath him, yet he couldn't feel them. After trying desperately to move them, he dropped his head back to the ground and sobbed aloud. The fall from the plane had broken his back, leaving him partially paralyzed.

"No, no," he sobbed hysterically as he rocked his head back and forth. The pain, the paralysis, the taste of his own blood upon his lips, all steadily combined and consumed him. The world blurred through his tears, then slowly darkened. But numbness of unconsciousness reduced the pain somewhat, momentarily allowing him to regain some composure.

"You are alive. You . . . are . . . alive," he repeated, trying to anchor his mind against the mighty winds of death that seemed to blow from every side. "You are live. There's no place to go but up. Got to keep fighting." Zon chanted his encouragements louder as he felt his consciousness returning. His eyes reopened and he blinked his ceiling of greenery back into focus. "You're gonna make it. You've got to make it. Maybe you're just weak, not paralyzed. Got to try." Encouraging as the words were, he managed only to move his head. Straining till drops of sweat appeared on his forehead, Zon again dropped his head to the ground. "Bulla buuu laaa, Bulla buuu laaa, Bulla buuu laaa, Bulla buuu laaa." He weakly sang the familiar college fight song and thought again of the old joke. He coughed, then laughed.

Smiling through the pain, he expanded a grin across his rippled lips until they, too, hurt. As he smiled, he heard something move to his left. Twisting his head around, he saw nothing. The movement was beyond the top of his head and out of sight. Zon cranked in the back of his head, stretched out his long bronze neck, then rolled his eyes upward till he saw the source of the noise. Not a foot from the top of his head lay a coiled viper, ready to strike.

"Oh, God. Oh, God," he sobbed through gritted teeth and stared into the snake's eyes. They consumed the horizon. There was no pain, no wounds, no earth, no sky. Only those eyes, those constricting tendons, open jaws, and glistening white fangs that sank deep into their victim's exposed neck. Zon's neck, the only muscular part that hadn't abandoned him, the snake had that now. Its body convulsed as it ejaculated stinging venom. Its cold body slapped wildly against open facial wounds. Zon's eyes rolled back in his head.

"For . . . give . . . me," oozed through pitiful lips as a mauled chest flattened toward a crumpled backbone.

* * *

"The boy does not move. Is he dead?" The three women moved toward Zon's motionless and maimed body. Lindi, the eldest, spoke softly as they made their way from behind the bushes.

"It is as Idrisi said. The boy lies asleep." The women walked up to Zon's cooling body. Glistening beads of perspiration lightly covered their exposed backs and shoulders, making the sun's rays burst into colors as it reflected off unblemished earthen skin. Zedra, the youngest, darted ahead, reached down, and grabbed the snake. It struck out at her hand as she approached, but she easily grabbed it just behind its head and squeezed its jaws open. Then, she hooked its fangs over a waiting cup and milked out the remaining poison. Lindi and Daisia paid no attention as they calmly moved in and knelt down. Quickly, they removed every stitch of Zon's bloody clothing.

"Men and women are as they are," Daisia said softly as she gazed innocently over Zon's body. Zon lay face up and motionless. A mixture of coagulated and flowing blood covered him. The last volley of machine-gun fire had all but removed his facial features, but his eyes were intact. He did not breathe, though his heart still pumped blood out the many round bullet and snake-tooth holes in his body.

"We have much to do, and you must go," Lindi spoke to Daisia without looking at her. She knelt beside Zon and placed her chocolaty brown thighs next to his head. Though untrue to her appearance, Lindi was not a solemn person. However, she approached her tasks with such seriousness that many viewed it as coldness. Such bleakness of manner in no way reflected her physical appearance. She, as well as the other two women, was beautiful. She wore her woolly brown hair close, preferring the sun and wind--rather than the comb and brush--to stimulate her scalp. She stood five feet eight in height and had bodily curves that'd make most models jealous. Her eyes were big, round, and hazel; their clarity seemed to reveal her very soul. Her features were soft with smooth round cheeks, high arching eyebrows, and full appetizing dark brown lips. Normally, she wore a wrap or halter made of silk or even spun gold on occasion, to support her melon-shaped breasts. But, because they were outside, she, Daisia, and Zedra wore nothing.

"Give me the cup," Lindi said to Zedra as she hoisted Zon's head upon her thigh. A year before, Zedra would have obeyed her older sister out of fear. Unlike Lindi, she was far more timid and serene. She and Lindi had the same general build, but Zedra was shorter, younger, and to some, prettier. Her dark hair fell down to her shoulders in natural curls. Zedra pulled a pouch from around her neck and emptied the contents into the cup with the snake's venom, swished it about, then handed it to Lindi. Lindi took the slimy concoction into her mouth, leaned over to Zon's lifeless face and blew her mouthful through his mouth, down into his lungs and stomach. She pinched his nose shut as she blew and noted a small sizzle coming from his ears and bullet holes. Her breasts cupped Zon's head as their lips united. Zon's chest heaved from the mighty blow, then fell motionless again as Lindi released his lips.

Daisia had moved into the jungle, where she used vines and leaves to fashion a loin strap. As she approached with it, she suddenly froze in her tracks, then looked knowingly to the sky. Lindi and Zedra simultaneously did the same, all but for a split second.

"We must hurry. The eye approaches," Daisia spoke calmly. Zedra grabbed Zon by the feet and lifted his legs, hips, and waist off the ground. Daisia stepped up and fitted him with the loin strap. She reached from the back and cupped his genitals with the quickly fashioned garment, then tied the vine straps securely around his bare waist. The bones in Zon's broken legs, though separated at the fracture, had not punctured the muscle and skin tissue. Once the loincloth was secure, Daisia grabbed Zon by the waist and folded him facedown over her left arm, exposing his back, legs, and buttocks. Lindi grabbed Zon's right leg, Zedra, his left. Both then artfully twisted the fractured bones back into place. Each leg snapped and popped as they slid back into their original form.

Daisia watched as she held Zon. She surveyed him, the parts that she could see, as the others worked to restore his body. *I wonder what he looked like,* she thought as she held him.

"He wonders the same of you," Lindi answered, taking Daisia by surprise. Her curiosity of this man made her forget momentarily of their way and their quest. Lindi was reading her thoughts and responding to them freely. Daisia looked at Lindi, who directed her eyes with a head nod toward Zon's face. Bloodied and distorted as it was, Zon's eyes were open and beamed bright through the torn skin and coagulation. As he stared, his chest suddenly thundered forth a cough that welcomed the long-missed life-giving breath of air. His eyes rolled, then slowly focused on the dark brown, coral-shaped birthmark on the back of Daisia's upper left thigh. It stood out against her caramel-colored skin. Zon had no idea what he was looking at, where he was, nor why he felt like he'd been run over repeatedly with a steam roller. His eyes drunkenly blinked, then his focus faded as he slipped back into unconsciousness.

Lindi felt for his back break with her right forefinger and thumb. "There is no fracture. His fifth and ninth bones are displaced. The ninth pinches the nerves." Skillfully, she pressed on Zon's fifth vertebrae until it slid back into place. She then did the same with his ninth, being careful to release the pressure from the restricted nerve. Then, using her forefinger, she lightly struck him in his lower back, thighs, shoulders, arms, neck, feet, and hands, carefully noting the involuntary responses to each strike. "He is as he was, but there will be much time until he heals," Lindi spoke in her poor bedside manner. "He is ready to go. Come, we must hurry."

Zedra, standing five foot two and weighing less than a hundred pounds, lifted Zon's 200-pound frame away from Daisia and draped him over her shoulder. Zon's feet almost touched the ground in front of her, his hands doing the same behind. Her small breast nested comfortably beneath his massive thighs.

"His hands and face still bleed," Daisia said as Zedra took him away from her. Lindi stepped behind Zedra. She used her forefinger to punched Zon in the soft flesh just under his chin. The trickle of blood from his cheeks and forehead stopped immediately. She punched each wrist, and for extra measure, punched him in each side, securing clots in the bullet wounds in his hands and stomach.

"We must be on our way," Lindi said as she turned to face Daisia. "We will miss you, my sister," she said and embraced her. Tears puddled in her eyes.

"Not as much as I will miss all of you," Daisia replied, her voice breaking with emotion. The ladies hugged for several minutes. Their embrace expressed to one another what words never could. Daisia then released Lindi and moved over to Zedra, who effortlessly held Zon over her shoulder. She touched Zedra's trembling cheek with her left hand and wiped away the falling tears. "Take care, little sister. I hope to see you again someday." Daisia spoke softly, hoping to comfort Zedra with her words.

"We will meet again," Zedra said, then turned to face the trail toward home. Without another word, Lindi stepped in front of Zedra, then the two ran off into the jungle. Daisia watched them disappear behind the fauna. She smiled, then turned in the opposite direction and ran off into the dense tropical forest.

* * *

Zedra had carried Zon at full trot for over fourteen miles before Lindi finally motioned her to stop. They stood in a grassy prairie. The sun was about to set. Zedra's body glistened with refreshing sweat that cooled her and coated Zon's body for easier hauling.

"The eye approaches," Lindi said. Just then, she smiled. Faintly, seemingly from afar, she heard a strong, rhythmic drum beat from afar. The beat was steady, deep, and hypnotic. It grew louder as human voices blended into the background. Suddenly, the air was filled with hundreds of voices singing in complete rhythm and harmony with the drumbeat. The singing was first in unison, then in three-, six-, then twelve-part harmony. The dense prairie grasses swayed with the rhythm. Lindi and Zedra stood smiling. The invisible wave of rhythm approached, expanded, and absorbed them. Then, all vanished in an instant. Only silence and the grassy prairie remained. It was as if they were never there. The eye passed over, oblivious to any life other than the jungle animals who stood calm and serene.

3
BORN AGAIN

Zon fought to maintain his balance as he ran along the wet concrete beside the public pool. The hem of his man-sized swim trunks hung to his knees. They sagged from his cheeks, though the safety pin prevented them from dropping off all together. He wiped at the sunlight in his eyes. He and the orphans rarely got a chance to go swimming. Even at public pools, you had to pay to get in. Swimming was a luxury that Saint James couldn't afford.

But today, the boys had gone to the city park with a church group that paid for everyone to swim. The orphanage director hadn't known about the pool, so no one brought bathing suits. However, a pile of abandoned trunks behind the pool attendant's counter, was kindly offered and gladly accepted. Zon's pair was colored wildly, the elastic, worn out and the drawstring, missing. He retrieved the safety pin that held up his pants and used it to pin the size forty men's shorts to his small, twelve-year-old frame.

Everyone laughed as he and the other orphans made their way out of the dressing room. But Zon heard only the rippling water, the splashing drops, the joyous laughter of children and adults alike, playing in the large Olympic-sized pool. A huge grin split his face as he emerged into the hot baking sun, moving swiftly toward the water.

He'd learned to swim when he was younger, but couldn't remember how he'd learned. Front strokes, backstrokes, crawls, breaststroke, he could do them all, but float.

By the time he'd reached the edge of the pool, Zon was in full gallop. He jumped as high and hard as he could into the air, grabbed his nose, and clamped his eyes shut. The shocking coolness of the water swallowed him. Blissful silence followed; the cool water filled his ears. Small toes lightly struck the bottom of the pool, where he coiled his legs, then launched skyward. As he broke the water's surface, he screamed with delight, then darted to the side of the pool.

Climbing out, he hurried to the high dive. A line of fidgeting children had formed there, small and large, black and white, mostly boys. Some shivered as they stood, dripping wet, in the summer breeze. Above, a large redheaded teenager bounced out onto the end of the board, bounced again, then soared into the air. At the zenith of his leap, the diver spread his arms, locked his knees straight and feet together, forming a perfectly angled cross, floating ever so gracefully to the water. Never breaking form, he held his arms extended as he approached, then slid gently into the glassy pool. Zon watched the clear blue rippling wakes spread from the diver to the pool walls. He pranced excitedly, imagining himself doing such a beautiful dive. He was going to do that dive, the same way, when he got his turn.

The small girl in front of him sprinted up the ladder. Zon reached for the handrail, but as he did so two young men with whistles approached him.

"Hey, boy! Did you shower before you got in this pool?" the larger boy yelled as the other kids turned around and started laughing.

"Huh? No," Zon answered sheepishly.

"Come on, Little Orphan Amos. Let's hit the showers." Each of the lifeguards grabbed an arm, lifting Zon off his feet.

"I can do it! Leave me alone!" Zon squirmed to free himself, but the two were too large and too strong. Everyone around the pool pointed and laughed. Unlike before, when he was oblivious to the taunts, laughter was all that he could hear now, the lifeguards laughing, the children laughing, swimmers, divers, sunbathers, even the water seemed to laugh as he was hauled away.

Inside the shower room, the larger lifeguard turned on the hot water, full blast. The other lifeguard stepped around to the other side as he firmly held the twelve-year-old by the arm. They stretched Zon out with his back to the shower, while positioning themselves out of its drenching spray. The water emerged cool at first and splashed down over Zon's head and shoulders, then quickly grew hotter as it poured. Zon screamed. The two lifeguards laughed all the louder, their grip remaining steady and rock hard. Hot water burned him all over. His skin crawled and twitched. His nerve endings pulsed as if coming alive for the very first time.

Zon tried to scream for help, but strangely, his lungs and voice would not respond. He couldn't move any part of his body. Everything was fixed--and burning. Unbearable pain squinted his eyes. Laughter still beat like a million drums in his ears. His skin, from head to toe, was on fire. His mouth stretched wide to attempt another scream. Desperate nostrils flared madly to pull in what seemed his last fresh breath of air. Hot, humid air, laden with steaming water, rushed into his lungs, delivering needed air along with drowning water. His life was over; he was dying, and he knew it. His skin, burning, on fire; his lungs filled with hot water that burned, that breathed like . . . air, refreshing air . . .

Still his lungs pulled hungrily, expanding his chest. His rib joints cracked as they fought to contain the engorged organs within. Then, just as they were about to explode, his throat contracted, blasting forth a mighty cough. As the cough rushed out, water rushed in and flooded his throat, cooling water splashing off his teeth and gums, dancing around his tongue, burning his skin like fire. Throughout it all, he could not move. His legs and arms were fixed, outstretched like the diver, forming a perfect cross, soaring like a bird . . . soaring . . . He was dying, was flying, was burning alive in a cool, refreshing cascade of water.

* * *

Zon's eyes popped open. Thick sheets of water poured over him. His head fell forward, allowing air to his face. He was suspended in water, in air, suspended above a pool in a small waterfall. Falling water roared in his ears.

The swimming pool, a dream, he thought groggily. Raising his head and craning his neck, he extended his face just beyond the rushing water. Cutting his eyes to the left, he saw his arm outstretched and bound at the wrist by leather straps to a wooden frame. So, too, was his right. The finely hewn wooden post glistened behind the clear sheath of water gushing over it. Looking down, he saw his ankles, crossed and bound similarly to a second thick straight wooden post.

Sheets of water poured over him by the barrel. It was cool to the touch on his face, but he could feel nothing of it upon his arms, legs or shoulders. He pulled at his arms; they didn't respond. Neither did his legs. Staring through the onslaught of water at his feet, he looked down on his nude body and tried to wiggle his toes. They remained deathly still. A cold emptiness bloomed in his stomach. His fingers wouldn't move and even though he breathed, he could balloon neither his chest nor stomach. Control existed only from the neck up.

I'm paralyzed, he thought, *but what about the wounds?* Staring through the water at his skin, Zon saw no scars from the gunshots. It appeared as smooth brown as ever . . . *as if the wounds had never been made*, he thought. *Don't know how long I've been here. What in the world could have fixed those scars? My face*, he thought, remembering the hot lead that shredded his features. *I want to see my face*. Craning his neck still further, he stared down into the pool below, but the clear water's surface was too turbulent to yield a reflection. Flexing his cheeks, he stared intently down on them and the sides of his nose. Wriggling his mouth into a bow, he stared at his lips. There were no scars. The movement caused no pain. His face felt as normal as ever. *If the wounds and scars are gone*, he thought, *then maybe this paralysis will pass as well.*

Dismissing his physical state for the moment, he peered out beyond the waterfall, which stood in a large shadow extending twenty yards across a large calm pool. The fall's reflection, as well as that of the steep mountain side over which it fell, floated serenely on the water. Falling, splashing water created a heavy, vision-blurring mist.

Greenery surrounded the pool, dark green of grass along the ground, above that, lighter and sparser shades of shrubbery to a man's height, then dense dark greenery of bountiful tree leaves, all capped off by Carolina blue sky. Scanning the pool's edge, Zon spotted two blurred, brown forms on the far bank directly across from the fall—people, who started instantly across the water as he caught sight of them. A third blurred form remained on shore.

Unable to hold his head outstretched any longer, Zon relaxed, submerging headlong once again into the falling water, though he continued watching the blurry forms moving toward him. They floated smoothly across the water, their paced steady, the black blur of their hair never veering.

Where're the boats?, he wondered and tried to extend his head again, but a large muscle in the back of his neck suddenly cramped. With his head tilted slightly forward, he calmly watched the two through the torrent of water.

Approaching the fall, the two separated, rose in the midst of the water, then passed behind him, never falling into focus. He tried to speak, but his lower jaw creaked open, then froze in the joint, as if it hadn't moved for years. The forms were nowhere in sight. Then, without warning, the wooden frame, with Zon strapped securely onboard, lurched forward, then glided out of the splashing water. Blinking his eyes clear, he watched the water surface cruise below him as he glided toward the far side of the pool. Twisting his neck, he tried to see the two who carried him, but they remained out of his sight except for the hands that wrapped around the cross's base.

As he cleared the falling water, Zon tried again to talk to his rescuers. "Hey, hello," he squeaked. There was no answer. *Probably don't speak English*, he thought, remembering that he was supposed to be in Africa, though he wasn't sure where he was. "Hey! Speak English! Speak English!" he yelled. Again, no reply. "Parlez-vous Francais?" Again, no answer. German, Latin, and Spanish also drew no response. The conversation remained one-sided as he glided the length of the quiescent pool.

Dismissing the carriers, Zon turned his attention to the awaiting figure at the end of the pool. There stood a man, old and nearly bald. He wore a single black wrap draped from his left shoulder, around his right hip then wrapped behind him. His face was hairless, his eyes large, but squinting slightly. His hair spoke of age, but his skin was dark and as smooth as the pool's surface. He stood oddly and motionless, like an ostrich, with one foot on the ground, the other clamped tightly to the inside of the opposite knee.

Although he had no idea where he was or what to expect, Zon was certain of one thing. He was glad to be alive, glad to breathe fresh air, glad to see such natural beauty before him, and especially glad that all of the horrid ordeal of mercenaries, murders, rape, falls, snakes, and shattered body was behind him. His body looked whole, and his skin, unbroken, at least as much of it that he could see. There was no feeling in his arms or legs, but he felt assured that this was, at worst, only temporary.

They must have found me, he thought. The memory of the viper flying over his face made him shudder. *Don't talk much, though.* Zon peered into the old man's eyes as he approached. Beyond the ancient African was a short grassy strip that bordered a well-manicured pathway, encircling a hill that was covered with short green grass and rose sixty feet into the air. Zon smiled as he got within earshot of the old man. The scene was so natural, so beautiful. *Africa*, he thought, cracking a grin, *'O' and two.*

"Hey, speak English," Zon rasped as he neared the bank. The old man didn't answer. At the edge of the pool, Zon's journey ended barely three feet from the bank where the old man stood. He felt the wooden frame sink two feet straight down into the pond's bottom, then lean back to where his weight rested on the wood, rather than hanging from the bindings. Looking down, he saw his toes not a foot above the water. Four small powerful hands were fixed about the base of the frame, pressing it down into the soft pool bed. Glimpses of brown skin bounced in and out of view until the wooden frame froze in place. Finally, the hands withdrew behind him and the bindings fell away from his feet and arms. He rested solidly on the frame. The two load bearers stepped around him, through the shallow water and toward shore.

Zon's eyes bulged. Before him walked two of the most beautiful women that he'd ever seen--at least, from behind. Both were deeply tan to a buttery caramel tone and covered with feminine bumps and curves, wearing scant loin and breast cloths that covered their bodies like a smile covers the face. Their motion sang in harmony as they stepped by him, up to the old man, to whom they bowed gracefully.

They then stepped behind him, turned, and stood serenely looking at Zon. They were lusciously beautiful. Slight smiles bowed their lips. Zon's eyes rushed up and down their bodies, jumping back and forth from woman to woman, not wanting to miss a single second of staring, a single inch of creamed-coffee feminine form. The corners of his mouth stretched toward his ears. His breath quickened. Though numbness possessed his arms and legs, the warm glow of desire ignited within, fueled by the vision that enslaved his eyes. As he lay gazing down his body, through the old man, and at the African women, a dark out-of-focus obstruction rose into view. But as he turned his head to stare around it, his eyes suddenly refocused.

"Oh . . . ah . . . " he gasped, realizing that his swelling manliness was appropriately reacting to the thoughts exploding in his mind. Though he could feel nothing of it, it stood there, throbbing with each heartbeat, joining the three on shore, all staring unblinkingly at him. Embarrassment flushed his face. Quickly he cut his eyes away and stared out across the pool, though he felt inexplicably drawn to look back toward shore. Slowly, his eyes panned back to the Africans. "No," he winced aloud, too ashamed to look at them, looking at him. Deeply submerged thoughts of size and laughter— virginity and laughter— lust and guilt consumed him. Closing his eyes, he strained to coil his lifeless legs up to hide himself, but to no avail. Thumping his head back to the wooden frame, he squeezed his eyes closed. Huge blood veins bulged in his neck, but nothing else moved.

He couldn't feel it, but he knew the monolith was still there. Raising his head, he forced his eyes to focus. He saw the two women, old man, and his one-eyed appendage, all of them, standing and staring. His head thumped like an overripe melon as he dropped it back to the wooden frame in despair.

Got to bake some bread, he thought, remembering the old tactic he'd used in high school to ease himself out of an excited state. It never failed during his senior year that, for no obvious reason, he'd get aroused just before the end-of-class bell, producing an embarrassing protrusion between his pockets that prevented him from standing up. To clear his mind, he'd conjure up pictures of NanaTuck making hoe-cake bread: sprinkling the flour, pouring the milk, kneading the dough. By the time she'd get the bread to the oven, he'd have flushed away the excitement, in time to get up and rush off to his next class.

"Paper covers rock . . ." he said slyly, thinking of the kids' hand game, "scissors cut paper . . . hoe-cake covers chocolate buns." A merciful chuckle eased from his lips. As his lusting subsided, the present predicament eased back to mind. Aroused or not, he was still helpless, paralyzed, and laid out like curing meat on a wooden cross by savages he knew nothing about. With thoughts refocused, he raised his head again to address the three. His arousal, and the two women, were gone.

"What are you going to do with me?" he asked the lone figure standing on shore. "I . . . I need help. I can't move. I'm paralyzed." Zon spoke softly, yet passionately. Still, the old man didn't reply. "Can you get someone to help? I need a doctor. Can't you understand?" The old man coldly stared. Zon dropped his head back to the wood and again shut his eyes. Shadows of swaying palm limbs flickered upon his closed eyelids. "Help me. Help me, please," he spoke again as he strained to move. "Oh God," he cried, "this has to be a dream."

"It is no dream," a baritone voice scowled. Zon's eyes popped open to see the old man, who had noiselessly moved to stand over him in the pool. "You are alive and here as you see," he said in perfect English with a slight twinge of disgust. Zon heaved to clear his voice. He had a thousand questions. But before he could speak, the old man cut him off. "And here you will remain." Turning abruptly, the ancient African walked out of the pool and across the grass.

"Wait! Wait a minute! Don't leave me here! Help me! Wait!" Zon yelled, further straining his neck muscles, trying to keep the Ancient African in view. The old man walked across the grass, then swiftly down the path. "Why are you doing this? What are you going to do with me?!" There was no reply. "Hey! Come back here! Please! Don't leave me! Don't leave me!" Only the birds answered as they flew back and forth over the water. Through tired eyes, Zon watched in disbelief as the old man disappeared around the distant bend.

"No! This can't be happening. It just can't . . . be . . . happening.

God, please," he prayed from behind clinched eyes, "make this a nightmare . . . and wake me up." He felt drained, exhausted. Sobbing pitifully, he repeated his desperate prayer over and over until he fainted slowly away into a long, deep, merciful sleep.

* * *

Chilly morning dew fell across Zon's face, drawing him back to consciousness. The trees above and about him were alive with singing birds. Sunshine slowly peaked over the trees beyond the waterfall. He lay outstretched and naked over the placid pool below him. Laughter abounded from the splashing water of the distant fall.

"It's no dream. It's no dream!" he shouted, trying to convince himself. A revived mind and fresh resolve made him think it all through again. *Can it all be real? There were bullets and broken bones, yet, no scars. My body looks fine and I can breathe. Everything above my neck works just fine.* Yet, my limbs are paralyzed.

"And I'm still in the Peace Corps," he said with a laugh. "Maybe they'll miss me and send someone." Pausing his solo conversation, he looked about. All was as it was the morning before, except him being alone. "That plane was way off course when I fell out," he continued. "Even if someone looks, they'd have a hard time finding me. These heathens probably moved me, anyway. And God only knows how long I've been here. Chances are someone's already come looking and have given up by now." The thought stung, but he wasn't going to dwell on it.

Looking his body over, he pulled at his paralyzed limbs again, concentrating intently on feeling anything, any movement or sensation. He couldn't feel the wooden structure beneath him, but could feel the healing warmth of the morning sun on his face. Yet, there was no sensation of it on his broad chest and shoulders. The contrast made him acutely aware of the gentle breeze on his face that didn't exist elsewhere. He strained to ball his fist. His jaw joints popped, but his arms and hands lay motionless.

Remembering the episode of the day before, he looked down on his groin and flexed at it, but there was no motion there either. "Oh. Now ya dead," he huffed in mock disgust at his uncooperative member. But the effort conjured memory of the two black women who had stood before him the day before. That was the first time in his life that he'd seen live women, so exposed, so close. The thought raised a smile, both above and below his waist.

The gentle breeze fluttered the hair on his legs. He noticed the small prickly bumps rise on his skin from their tickling motion. "Everything must still work," he reasoned, "I've just lost my control of it."

The wooden frame lightly cupped his arms, legs, torso, and head like a shallow spoon and held him at a small angle from the water. This allowed him full view of the surroundings if he wrenched his neck, but prevented his limp body from sliding into the shallow pool. His head felt cushioned.

"I need a haircut," he said, tapping his head lightly against the wood to gauge the thickness of his woolly curls. "Must have been unconscious for some time."

Thoughts of slow passing time and paralysis, permanent paralysis, sent a sudden shudder through him. But the night's rest had fully cleared his head. Turning from side to side, he examined the surroundings. Broad-leaf palm trees lined the pond's sandy bank. They'd provide shade during the hot part of the day, yet would allow healing sunbeams in the morning and evening. Beyond the pool on his right was a manicured forest of palms and bushes. Birds of every color fluttered from branch to branch. The grass before the path and on the hill was rich green and looked freshly mowed, though he was sure there could be no lawn mowers this deep in the jungle. The path down which the old man had disappeared fell twenty yards from the water's edge and encircled the hill. Its surface was sand-colored, but didn't appear to be loose sand. There were no obvious footprints on the path. The waterfall behind him sang steadily along with the birds as the sun rose slowly. Falling water sent huge circling wakes sailing smoothly across the pool. Beyond that, occasional small circles expanded on the pool as fish kissed the surface from beneath. Under better circumstances, this would truly have been a tropical paradise.

Zon dropped his head back to rest. He stared blankly into the treetops, struggling to make sense of his predicament. "Couldn't leave it alone, could you?" he said sarcastically, searching the palm trees for the answer. In a sing-songy voice, he lectured. "Top college grad, bright financial future, would have been good enough for some people, but not you. You had to lose your cool, lose your mind, had to become that noble volunteer, charging forth to save the Africans. But, nooo. That wasn't enough either. Had to add some flair to it. Had to battle crazy mercenaries, catch speeding bullets with your face, jump from airplanes without a parachute . . . " Zon laughed lightly, drawing strength in knowing that his sense of humor was alive and well. "But after all of that," he said soberly, "to end up dead. Yes, dead body, dead friendships, dead future, dead life. It makes no sense." For hours, he stared into the greenery, at times overcome with his situation, at others, contemplating what, if anything, he could do about it. The sun rose high in the sky behind the leafy palm roof above.

"Eat," a deep voice said. Zon jerked his head around to see the old man standing over him. He had two small white cups, one in each hand. After staring for a moment, Zon decided to cooperate in hopes of eventually befriending the native. Cautiously, he gaped his mouth wide. The old man put the two cups into one hand, reached behind his back and retrieved a white half-moon shaped piece of wood. He then stuck it under Zon's chin. The center was cut away so that the ends wrapped underneath his jawbone, around his neck and attached to the wooden frame, forming a tray below his chin. Then, instead of pouring food into Zon's mouth, the old man quietly set the cups on the tray, turned, then walked away. Zon watched on, his mouth standing open the whole time.

"Hey! Come back here!" His yell didn't alter the African's steps. "I can't feed myself! I need help! Hey! You hear me? I'll starve! I can't move!" The old man kept walking. "Okay, okay. I'll feed myself! Ya listening? Look! Come back! I'll feed myself and we can talk! Hey! Hey!" The old man disappeared beyond the path.

"Ahhhh!" Zon grimaced, then bit his lip in frustration. Taking a moment to calm himself, he raised his head and peered into the cups. The old man had delivered one containing three ounces of water, the other, three ounces of dark grain. "Bread and water to boot," he said. Though saddened and disgusted over the second unsuccessful encounter with the natives, hunger suddenly gripped his stomach. *Odd how I can feel hunger*, he thought, *yet nothing else. And what of my lungs, heart, and other bodily functions?* "Maybe that should have been detached, too," he said pitifully.

For hours he shifted his stare back and forth from cup to cup, then finally decided to eat. Using his head and lips, he managed to spill the water across the tray and down his neck. With his tongue, he tipped over the cup containing the grain and captured the bulk of it in his mouth. The remainder splattered about the wet tray. Slowly he chewed the tasty grain, then sipped at the spilled water. After his meal, he began formulating a better strategy to use for his next encounter with the natives. They had to talk to him sooner or later, he convinced himself. It was just a matter of time. Zon dropped his head back and stared out into the forest. He had no idea when the old man would return, though he reckoned that it would not be until feeding time again.

Though cruel, he couldn't help but admire the functionality of his *quarters.* The climate, day and night, was pleasantly warm. Combined with the shady palm trees, it eliminated the need for clothing and shelter. The cross on which he lay held him securely. He'd noticed dropping sounds during the day and deduced that it was his waste falling harmlessly into the pool. A light shower fell just before nightfall, cleansing his body and providing a refreshing nightcap. And he had bread and water delivered.

Yet, while functional, it was by no means humane. Natives occasionally passed by on the path during the day, totally oblivious to his existence. Each time they passed he yelled at them, doing all he could to gain their attention, concern, or pity. Nothing worked. Still, he reasoned that it was only a matter of time before they would do something with him.

"Just wait," he reassured himself, watching the evening sun slide behind the grassy hill. "Just wait." Above him, a small yellow bird, with a green head and red eyes, landed. Its eyes rapidly snapped open and closed. Its tail bobbed mechanically.

"What's the haps?" Zon grinned. "You come to help me wait?" The small creature pivoted on the branch to face the hill. "Oh, you're going watch for the natives too, huh, little birdie? Let's see. You look like a parakeet. I'll call you Keet. You like that?" The bird flew off. "Guess not." He caught sight of Keet, along with several other birds, flying back and forth across the pool. Keet then darted swiftly back to the branch. Zon smiled, but said nothing. Again the bird flew from its roost, across the pool, then back. Eventually, as the sun went down, Keet, along with three other birds, settled in on the tree above him. "I guess you guys are gonna have to do until the cavalry gets here." He stared up into the tree at the birds until the last of the daylight eased away. There was no other visit before nightfall.

"Only one feeding a day," he sighed. Slowly, darkness engulfed his immobile form as he stared and waited. As the night fell, so, too, did his hopes. The stars and moonlight reflected serenely off the water. The birds slept and Zon lay wide-eyed, helpless, and alone. "Could death be worse," he thought over and over until finally rescued by sleep?

* * *

The next five days were the same. One small meal of water and grain in the morning, yelling, ranting, and raving at the old man's silence and cold heart, followed by bird watching and star gazing until sleep reluctantly fell again. Out of his helplessness, hopelessness grew, then despair, then anger.

They are going to keep me alive and alone, he thought. *What pleasure are they getting from that? Maybe they've just put me up like some fattening hog, waiting till I'm fully cleansed and ripe before they barbecue me up. Maybe that's why they stared at me so hard that first day, trying to decide which piece of me they'd eat first. Well, if this is how it's going to be, I'm not going to help them.* Swelling emotion pulled at his throat. Raising his voice in the darkness, he yelled, "Do you hear me! Go have your fun with someone else! I'm dead! Do you hear? I'm dead." With this, Zon resolved to starve himself to death.

* * *

At sunrise, the old man did not come to deliver his food. Instead, Zon was awakened by drumbeats and music from over the hill, lively, upbeat music. At first, the sound set his heart to dancing, but then a deadly thought quickly overshadowed his mirth. "Those heathens are going to roast me as soon as they finish singing grace," he said, scanning the path for an approaching butcher and cook. "Gave me a whole week to season." He strained harder than ever to move from the cross, but he managed only to rock his head to and fro, not generating enough momentum to cast his body off into a liberating drowning below. He longed for liberation, but none came.

The rhythmic singing and drumming continued as the sun peeked over the horizon, but he saw no one. He gazed down his deteriorating body. His skin had grown ashy from inactivity. His limbs had shrunk to almost half their original size. The sight of his useless legs and arms, all lying deathly still, widened his eyes in sorrow.

After a few hours, he relaxed and stopped watching the path. Thoughts of being barbecued scared him. Thoughts of his degenerating body saddened him. Overall, the new day of music and no food had brought on a general state of depression. "Take that deep breath," he said to himself, pulling in as much air as he could, then letting it out slowly. "Good air in, depression out." Calmly he chanted, deeply inhaling and exhaling. His mind eased.

"Would you listen to that," he said. Relaxing reopened the ears of his mind. Deep, rich African rhythms gushed in. "That sounds almost good. Yeah, it sounds like . . . it ough'ta sound." Zon repeated the words he'd heard over fifteen years before, as a little boy, attending service with NanaTuck at the Tryon Street Baptist Church. The thought conjured up memories of his childhood: NanaTuck and Deacon Hughes, the eldest deacon and head of the Deacon's Council.

"Ya hear that?" Deacon Hughes had said proudly to NanaTuck. "That's the Hymn Choir, like it use ta soun'." Deacon Hughes was seated beside the choir of thirty-odd elder members. He didn't sing along, but stomped his foot rhythmically on the wooden box that stretched full length underneath the pew directly in front of him. "Y'all just had to have that new church, didn't ya?" Deacon Hughes spoke to NanaTuck, who stood by his side, but he wasn't looking for an answer. "Put in the big choir stand and more seats, wall-to-wall carpeting, and hard-as-the-devil concrete floors. Like to took the soul right out of this church."

"What do you mean?" NanaTuck asked the babbling old man.

"You know full well what I mean, woman. It was bad enough when ya put in that padded carpet in the old church. It liked to took away the choir's rhythm, but we managed through. But here, with the cement floor," he stomped hard down on the carpet, "you killed it completely. Listen to this. Listen!" he shouted quietly at NanaTuck, and stomped his foot yet again into the carpet.

"I cain't hear a thing," NanaTuck responded.

"Just my point," Deacon Hughes replied.

"What's your point?"

"All this carpet and concrete took away our drums."

"Now, Deacon Hughes. You know we don't 'low no drums or guitar in our worship."

"That's right, but this one's always been here, least until we moved to this new church. When the menfolk or hymn choir got to feeling the spirit, we'd all stomp like this." The deacon began stomping the stomp-box to the beat of the song the choir sang. The sound added a solid bass drumbeat to the singing voices. "In the old church, anybody who had rhythm and felt the spirit added in by stomping the floor. With a big, holy, and sanctified crowd, this church would thunder with the sound of praise. It pulled us all together in the Spirit."

"And how'd you make this wondrous discovery?" NanaTuck asked sarcastically.

"During choir practice, in the old sanctuary," the deacon answered. "Choir members gettin' happy all the time, the music seeming to sound better. At first, I thought it was just me, wanting to hold on to the old ways. But the more I listened, the more I knew the sound was different. And that's when Brother Earvin pointed out the concrete floors." Deacon Hughes smiled and switched stomping feet.

"So that's when the Deacon's Council voted in these . . . these boxes?" NanaTuck asked.

"Stomp-boxes," he said proudly. "And they get the job done. We special ordered the cedar ta build them. And just listen to that sound. It sounds like . . . it sounds just like it ough'ta soun'."

"Sounds like it ought to sound," Zon repeated hypnotically. "Never started church, prayed a prayer or opened a service without singing first. Maybe these people here aren't that different."

Thoughts of music and his younger days ignited Zon's natural appreciation of song. He hadn't notice until then how good the native's music actually sounded. Much of it was human voice with a strong complement of drums. There were plenty of instruments intermingled as well. And the bass dominated, not overbearingly, but yielding a solid foundation to the melody. The rhythms changed often, sometimes fast, sometimes slow. The occasional lyrics were foreign to him, but blended perfectly with the music. Listening intently, his eyes slid closed and his head instinctively began popping to the music. Movement breaks, joins, and blends all sent smiles of pleasure across his face as he listened.

But the sounds coming over the hill seemed different from others he'd heard. Like soul music, there was plenty of bass with a unique blend of human and instrumental voice. Then there were the drums, also strong, and at times, difficult to distinguish from the bass. But the rhythms were distinct, yet both familiar and strange. All together, Zon consumed a daylong concert that had him bursting at the seams with an unexplainable joy. Only the reality of his predicament kept him from floating right off into ecstasy.

* * *

Later that evening, Zon lay with his eyes wide, his head continuously bobbing to the rhythm. With a serene smile, he stared out at the birds. He'd named them and could identify each at a glance. Never before had his mind been so unoccupied, refreshed, and alert as it was now. Overload of simultaneous graduate and undergraduate work in college had vastly stretched his mental capacity. Now, because of his paralysis and abandonment, they stood as vast and as empty as the Grand Canyon, eager, even longing to be filled. Yet, for days, all that had occupied his thoughts were the birds, like a small babbling brook cutting through the vast emptiness of his mind.

Birds, as trivial and inconsequential as they were, stood as the sole source of life. Inspired by the music, Zon accepted it for what it was. "I'm gonna get to know you all," he said soberly to the birds. "I can neither move nor see beyond this pool, but I can see you. All of your colorful feathers, what you eat, even your bowel movements. They'll be . . . you all will be . . . my life."

He choked up from the unintentional summary of his pathetic situation. Sad as it was, it was also the truth. Except for the occasional heathen who passed by and his daily bread delivery, the birds were his only defense from boredom and insanity, the only thing that could occupy his mind and prevent chaos. Like it or not, the birds were his only salvation, provided he lived beyond the day.

Fortunately, he'd found them an easy study. Each day, they'd repeat the routine, leaving their roost, flying about, feeding, never changing. But today, with the music coming from over the hill, he had noticed a change. As he watched, Zon realized that today, they were dancing. Normally, after feeding, the birds settled in to rest. They'd perch on branches and chat with one another for hours, passing the hot day away. Today, they didn't perch, but darted back and forth, from one side of the pond to the other, in flocks. Back and forth, they flew, occasionally looping about, but always moving to the end of the pool, then back. Different flocks moved separately from others, disguising their pattern of flight. Able to identify the individual birds, Zon isolated their pattern and harmony with each other, and with the music.

"They're following the music," he said with amazement. "Must be a coincidence." Intent on finding out, he stared at them still harder. But after a few hours of uninterrupted stare, he was convinced that they were dancing. "Well I'll be," he said, not taking his eyes from them, nor his ears from the music. Every musical change coincided with changes in their flight. Even with drumming only, the birds continued. As deep bass joined in, the birds responded in kind by gliding lower to the ground, soaring in ever widening circles. With and without singing, they responded. With and without instruments, humming, or notes of any kind, with just the sustained beat of the drums or bass, they responded. "I wonder . . ." he pondered aloud. "Deacon Hughes needed the stomp-boxes. And NanaTuck had often commented after hearing a guest preacher, whether he managed to 'get in the groove' with his sermon. Church songs had to have it. Preaching, poetry, even jumping rope, all had to have it. "It's got to be the rhythm," he said curiously. "They understand it. It's there, no matter what." With knitted brow, he pressed inward to understand. "Maybe these are special birds. If they can learn to talk," he reasoned, thinking of parrots and parakeets, "then why not dance. Or maybe they're just ordinary birds, like all the rest, but the difference lies in me. Maybe no one up until now has had the chance to lie all day and night and just watch birds."

Zon spent the remainder of the day studying the birds and the music. By nightfall, he'd pleasurably exhausted himself: from the music, the revelation of bird dancing, and the relief of not being digesting in some cannibal's stomach. The music ended as the sun set and the birds flew off to nest for the night.

* * *

The next morning, the old man came as he had done before, leaving the cups of nourishment. As he sat them down, Zon did not speak, but with his outstretched tongue, quickly tipped over the cups before the old man could turn away. The African, caught by surprise, cast a piercing eye at him, then turned slowly and walked off. Zon smiled.

"I'm not eating anymore," he yelled after him. "I'll starve and you'll have to go find someone else to torture." There was no response. Not wanting to offer any further satisfaction by his taunts, Zon turned his head away toward the pool. The indignant stare he'd received told him that he'd hit a nerve in the old man.

* * *

Dumped grain began piling up as the old man continued to bring it and Zon continued to tip it over. Although determined to preoccupy himself with the birds, Zon was concerned over ignoring the food. And it was difficult to ignore, especially as his stomach emptied and his stamina weakened with hunger. However, he was committed to starving himself. And with the birds to occupy his mind, sooner or later, he would succeed.

Every day, he searched the trees. Bird watching would pass the time, but he knew that without contact with other interested people, it was all in vain. Deep inside, he knew that his only true escape was death, and starvation stood as his only means of escape. He'd never had such thoughts before, even when he was at the brink of insanity. But, under the current circumstances, it was the best of the few bad options he had. His life was over. He had accepted that.

Starvation came incredibly slow. The pile of soggy grain about his head deposited its aroma deep within his nostrils and on his taste buds, tempting him daily. Zon reasoned that his dormant body, requiring next to nothing to live, would take a long time to starve. But he expected it to take days or weeks, not months. As odd as it was, the time didn't really matter. He had no place to go. Besides, the grain and starvation were secondary now. Through the birds, he felt on the brink of discovery and realized that he was changing, too.

Music meant more to him now than it ever had. Study of the birds required heavy concentration on music and rhythm as well. He more thoroughly understood now why good music made him feel so good, made him want to dance, rock, sing, or shout. The sounds came into his ears, but the feelings emanated from deep within. His consciousness was completely unaware of the message in the music, and was more than content to receive it and the corresponding emotions that it generated. However, it was his inner mind, his subconscious, which he better understood now. It also received the music, but squeezed far more out of it. Weeks of meditation had taught him to exist in his subconscious as well as his conscious.

"Music is not just music. Through its rhythm, it's more like a language," he whispered. "Though I've spoken it forever, I've never understood it--until now." After some thought, he asked a passing breeze, "And if the birds and I both understand it, then why can't we understand each other?" An air of challenge filled his voice. A challenge. A goal, in the midst of such depraved conditions, conjured a wide smile.

* * *

Zon continued his meditations with greater conviction than ever, forcing his consciousness ever deeper into his subconscious, ever mindful of every rhythm. He experimented with the birds as he hypothesized on his newly discovered language, designing, executing, recording, and analyzing in his head with unimaginable speed and clarity.

During one of these mental experiments, he whistled the bird's good morning greeting as they prepared to nest for the evening, carefully matching the underlying rhythmic patterns always missed by the casual listener and bird watcher. Immediately, the birds within earshot sang it back, then proceeded to fly around in confusion, trying to leave the nest and go to it at the same time. Zon's heart leaped. For weeks, he hadn't talked with anyone or anything. Now, for the first time, he'd communicated with other living beings.

The soggy pile of grain overflowed into the pond as time passed. Still, it was delivered without failure, except on the seventh days when the natives sang all day on the other side of the hill. Though the music was wonderful, Zon grew to loath the song days as much as he did the old man. Every song reminded him of his loneliness as well as the joyous companionship of those on the other side.

During a particular seventh day, Zon followed the music and the birds as always. Toward the end of the day, he added his own raspy whistling to the sounds flowing over the hill. At first, his addition did not blend well, and the birds responded immediately by breaking rank and reverting back to their normal routines. Finally, Zon matched the rhythms, and the birds fell back into their dancing, but with an added twist. Their grouping changed. He changed his addition over and over and watched the reaction. By the end of the day and countless variations, Zon was choreographing the birds' movements. He started with a concert of flying colors. Flying sheets of yellow, then red, then brilliant blue swooped in synchronous harmony above the pool. He gazed skyward into the miracle of color. His lips quickly dried and chapped, so he switched to singing, then humming, and even grunting, all with the same delightful effect. As long as he delivered the correct rhythm, the birds responded.

The sun set, the singing from over the hill stopped and the birds quickly dispersed. As they flew home, Zon considered the obvious. "Delirium is setting in. I'm losing my mind," he concluded. But even if it wasn't real, the illusion of accomplishment made him feel more alive now than ever before. Despite his pitiful state, he had grown. He had shown progress against the odds. In spite of his circumstance, his life was growing by leaps and bounds. He had started with nothing, but challenge was borne in his life. With each passing day, his belly grew emptier and his neck and eyes, weaker, but his mind grew broader, his life, more fulfilled. He couldn't lose. Dying defeated the heartless old man and his band of heathens. They wanted him to suffer; he wouldn't. They wanted him to beg for mercy or starve in agony, surrounded by mounds of life-sustaining food. He would starve, but there would be no begging, no remorse, no agony. Each day also brought greater understanding of his finely feathered friends. If he lived long enough, he was going to talk to them. But how long was he going to live? He wasn't sure.

One morning after a song day, the old man came as always. He walked down into the water, planted the cups deep in the mound of grain, and retrieved the overturned empties. Small sprouts had formed on the bottom of the heap from the mixture of grain, water, and darkness. From behind the heap, Zon silently watched the old man. Then, as he raised his chin, he curled back his tongue, opened his mouth, and popped off a string of clicks that sounded like beans snapping. The old man paid no attention, but turned to walk away. Suddenly, from every direction, birds swooped down in one giant blur at Zon's head, each pecking, eating. The old man pivoted around and saw Zon's lifeless outstretched body crowned by a fury of flapping colorful feathers. As quickly as they had come, the birds flew away, leaving a clean semicircle tray with no grain and a smiling, starving Zon, casting his dancing eyes up to meet the surprised old heathen's. Zon grinned. The old man returned the stare for a moment, then walked away.

And it achieved its desired effect. In one gesture, Zon had delivered a message. To the birds, he'd said "All clear, come, eat," but to the old man and his people, he'd delivered a message that no words could more clearly have said. The tables were turning, and now they knew it.

* * *

Weeks passed, perhaps months. Death was crawling mercifully closer. Except for the singing days, Zon had lost track of time. He didn't know what pain or delirium to expect as he slowly died, but accepted it as a small price to pay for his freedom. One evening, with death close at hand, a bird landed on a limb just above him. In somewhat of a jovial delirium, Zon spoke to it in a weak and cracking voice.

"Oh. Hey, Keet. Where's everybody?" Smiling faintly, he closed his eyes and imagined all of the birds waking that morning, rolling out of their beds, getting dressed, then coffee, then making their way to rhythm analysis class, scurrying about so as not to be late. He pictured them sitting attentively behind desks awaiting roll call. "All here raise your hand," he said with his eyes closed and still smiling from this deluded vision. He laughed as he pictured all of the birds shooting their right wing into the air and yelling, *here*. "All of them, able to respond with live and working limbs," he weakly groaned. "All of them, but not me . . . not me. Best I can do, is die."

Zon stared meekly up at the bird as a self-pity-laden tear slid down his face. "Ya didn't raise your hand," he sobbed at the bird. "Raise your hand." Immediately, the right wing of the green-headed bird shot straight up into the air. Startled by the movement, the bird quickly flew off. "Wait a . . . " Zon rasped. The movement had shocked him as well as the bird. *Was I dreaming*, he thought, *or did I just make that bird's wing move--without the bird's knowing it? Sure, I can communicate with them, even semidirectly suggest some things to them. But there's no way that I could . . .*

Thinking it a fluke, he sought another bird, concentrated on it, then *thought* it off its perch, causing it to fall headlong onto the grass below. Once landed, it too darted away in shock. Zon was ecstatic, though extremely weak. *Could it be my mind?* he thought. "Oh yeah. It's my mind, all right. Or at least the one I use to have," he confessed. "Dancing birds, I'll buy. Even bird-talk, but I didn't sing or dance those birds away. I thought them away. How can it be? They understand rhythms, my thoughts, rhythmic waves . . . brain waves? Brain . . . rhythms? Could that be?" Zon weakly pulled air into his chest. "Could my thoughts be . . . " He paused. In his mind, he envisioned his head sticking up among the clouds, with thousands of encircling waves spreading out from it like a radio broadcasting tower. An inaudible chuckle escaped his lips. "Oh yeah," he croaked, rolling his head slowly back and forth on his wooden bed, "loony bird. You've finally made it. You're a loon." Again, he laughed. Keet returned to the branch above him. "But you were startled, too," he said to the bird. "If you were hearing my thoughts, then why were you surprised?" Zon lay in silence for an hour, thinking. Afterward, he said to Keet, who had come and gone several times, "If **I** made your wing move, then you didn't know about it until it happened. You didn't know about it," he repeated perplexed. "Come on, let's humor the fool," he encouraged himself. "You didn't know, you didn't consciously know, but your wing did." None of this sounded even remotely possible, yet he couldn't deny what he thought he saw.

Crazed by the idea, Zon began experimenting with every bird in sight. All responded, regardless of the command he sent forward. With each falling or backward-flying bird, growing excitement surged through his veins. Every thought and reaction was slowly convincing him of the impossible.

Fantastic ideas began exploding in his mind. "What if I could get them together," he whispered, "to pick me up and get me out of here? Or maybe I could send them somewhere with a rescue message. No, I'll send them to peck the head off that old man. Or . . ." Suddenly, his thoughts froze as a dazzling idea occurred, an idea that made his mind swell with anticipation, and his heart cower over the cruel disappointment if it failed.

Struggling against his self-inflicted weakness, Zon lifted his head from the cross. Steadying his gaze, he stared intently at the big toe on his right foot. He had paid little attention to his body as it wasted away, having come to grips with its loss months before. This first intense look startled him. His toe nail curled an inch over the end and was pale gray. His skin, too, had grown sickeningly white with ash. All muscle appeared to have wasted away, leaving his bones showing pitifully through his skin. Ignoring the grim scene, Zon concentrated on his toe. Silently, he screamed, *move*. If he could make the birds fall from trees, then he could make a muscle in his paralyzed foot contract. The birds had reacted unconsciously. And his toe was, in a sense, unconscious of the brain that had once controlled it. If he could reach around his own mind, beyond the nerve, into the muscle itself, would it not be like the bird's wing? Could he not deliver the signal to move, like his nervous system normally did, but using the new universal language that he'd come to understand?

Small beads of perspiration formed on his brow as he struggled to keep his head and thoughts steady on his toe. Nothing happened. Zon tuned his focus onto a single muscle on top of his toe that connected to the bone underneath the nail. *Contract,* was the message that he bounced about in his mind. The strain of holding his head up quickly sapped his strength. Slowly, it sank back toward its rest on the cross. Even so, he kept his gaze fixed on his big toe. Like the movement of the setting sun, Zon's head fell slowly back to the cross as his gaze was finally broken and his big toe . . . twitched.

4
THE BOLO

The old man knelt silently in the center of a large round field of grass. About him, on three sides, were thousands of people, all silent and seated in what looked like a giant horseshoe-shaped football stadium. The sun had not yet peaked over the tall hill that made up the fourth side of the bowl-shaped arena. Dusk-dawn light bathed the scene in dark, warm autumn orange hues. Though subdued by the absence of light, the assembly's clothing was distinctly African and dazzling, glowing in every shade of a leafy autumn rainbow. Women, seated randomly, wore headdresses of brightly colored cloth wrapped loosely about their heads. Their dresses covered them from neck to toe. The men wore shoulder and waist wraps. Many held instruments. They all sat silently, waiting with heads bowed, as did the old man in center field.

As the sun peeked over the hill, the men lifted their heads and began singing a low-pitched, steady note. A quarter of them moved their pitch up a third, turning the unison into harmony. As they reached the note, the women joined them, though an octave higher, then moved up another third where half stayed. The others continued up still another third, completing the major chord. The sound filled the arena in a continuous, well-tuned, hypnotic song. As they sang, hundreds began playing a fast and heavily syncopated rhythm on drums. One by one, all percussion, then, strings, then wind instruments joined in, creating the first song of the day. The sound was joyous, reflecting the freshness brought on by the early morning sunrise.

While the multitude made music, the old man sat like a block of ice, melting from the sun's warm rays as it toiled upward. Suddenly, the big red-orange ball peaked over the hill, filling the eastern horizon. Crisp, refreshing morning air dripped with heavy dew. Quickly, it heated and stirred, causing sunbeams to dance fervently about the horizon, echoing colors of blue, red, green, and yellow with its prismlike effect. Dazzling colors exploded from the crowd's apparel.

The song continued in sync with the dancing light, then with the sun's spreading warmth. A mild breeze blew about the arena, gently stirring the people's apparel. Children, all sizes and ages, sat together around the lower perimeter of the arena. The larger youths joined in the singing of songs that they knew. The smaller children calmly listened as the music filled the air like delicious cooking smells fill a busy kitchen.

As the sun's midpoint rose above the hill, the music changed, section by section, to a slower, more rhythmic pace. Singers formed words using very few consonants, yet plenty of long vowels that sustained the tune. The old man stirred, then took a deep breath. Slowly, deliberately, he raised his head and looked to the east. His eyes climbed the grassy slope to the hilltop, where the sun had just rested before leaping skyward. Reaching the top, he spied the peak. All music abruptly stopped in unison, as if a maestro had cut it off. Together, every head turned, every eye focused with his, fixed on the hilltop.

There on the zenith, beneath the brilliant sun, stood a frail, trembling human frame . . . Zon. He stood puppetlike, as if hanging by string from the mighty sun above him. But there were no strings, no props, no crutches. Only Zon--alone. His head trembled as he looked down onto the crowd. He could feel his emotions welling up inside as he paused on the peak. His heart pounded with triumphant jubilation that mixed with rage and amazement as he viewed the scene before him. But he couldn't afford any of the emotions, and concentrated hard to fight them back. His mind was working madly to concentrate and hold his body erect. Over and over, he commanded his knee muscles to remain locked, so too, his hips, ankles, and toes. His lifeless arms hung by his side. They had been ignored since they weren't needed to walk or stand. His back curled forward as far as the rack of his backbone allowed. The complexity of their control forced them to be ignored.

Together, the collection of locked joints and ignored limbs gave him the look of a standing mauled question mark. His shoulders listed heavily to the right, but his working neck muscles strained to hold his head erect. The months of inactivity had left his anemic body with ash-whitened skin and very little flesh. Imprints of his large knee and hip joints glared pitifully through his skin. The climb up the hillside had also taken its toll. Repeated falls had left bleeding cuts on his knees, thighs, chest, face, and back.

Zon had begun just before sunrise, determined to conquer the hill, that great monolith that separated him from the human contact he imagined to be on the other side. Lying there each seventh day, listening to the music, he conjured images of singing and dancing people, laughing, talking, eating, drinking, enjoying the music and the company of one another. People, enjoying one another while he remained abandoned and alone. To conquer that hill, on the day of their jubilation, was to conquer them, the same people who had so mercilessly kept him undead for so long.

Conquer the hill had become his battle cry as he worked feverishly day after day to develop control of his body. Once he'd discovered the ability to move his limbs with his mind, he began eating the grain immediately to regain his strength. Despite his efforts, he hadn't been able to return a sense of feeling to any of his numbed parts. Months had passed before he finally felt ready to throw himself off his wooden bed into the shallow, but deadly water below. It seemed ironic as he fell toward the watery grave, how he had often longed to cast himself down and drown. Now all he could think of was how he was going to keep his cool and concentrate below the water's surface, and stay alive.

Rolling off the wooden frame placed him facedown on the pool's bottom. With his face buried deep in the soft muck, Zon locked his elbows straight. Then, after what seemed an eternity, he focused his thoughts on his shoulders and cranked the muscles tight, forcing his stiffened wrists into the pool's bottom. He could tell his muscles to contract, but he couldn't tell them how strong to be, nor was he sure if they were going to be strong enough. Fortunately, they'd retained enough strength so that, combined with buoyancy from the water, they lifted him to the surface.

As the muscles contracted, his face rose out of the mud, up through the water. Blinking his eyes clear, he watched with grand satisfaction as the bottom fell away. Then suddenly, he stopped. His muscles had fully contracted, but his head was still below the water's surface. Panic broke his concentration. His stiff arms loosened. His shoulders began to quake as his mind fought for control. Fighting the panic, Zon wrenched his neck as far back as he could, forcing his forehead and nose to break the water's surface. His knees, lower legs, and hands remained sunk in the muck. As refreshing air filled his lungs, his thoughts steadied, as did his arms. He felt awkward lying there, but kept his thoughts on his shoulders.

Over the months of preparation, he'd learned to focus his thoughts. He envisioned them as very narrow and intense beams of laser light emanating from his mind. This helped him to better focus and aim. Once his body was erect in the pool, Zon took his first step as a paralyzed man--his first step on jungle soil, his first step as a new man, built from nothing and held up only by raw human will. For countless months he'd lain on his back, mastering his mind for this moment, and it had finally arrived. He, who'd had no reason to live and every reason to die, had turned failure into triumph. Emotions filled his heart. Standing on the bank, he smiled, laughed aloud, then dropped, face first, to the grassy carpet like a sack of wet cement, having lost complete concentration. Zon spit grass and rich brown Mother Earth while continuing to laugh and preach to himself the importance of continuous concentration. He had to stay focused. Raising his head, he locked his eyes on the hilltop and peeled the smile from his face. The sun peaked over the horizon behind him. Sending forth his beams of thought, he slowly lifted himself again, the effort taking over fifteen minutes. Just as slowly, he took his next step, one of many, toward the hilltop.

Now he stood, enraged and triumphant, on the hill. The view was spectacular. The arena, people, and dazzling colors almost overwhelmed him. But just as his limbs started going limp again, he caught sight of the old man on the field. Instantly, his mind steadied as his eyes narrowed in on him. Zon felt the rage toward the elderly native build within. He knew it would scatter his thoughts and leave him a humiliated heap, tumbling down the hillside into the midst of his captors. These people had taken so much joy in his rotting for all these months above that pool. He knew they'd rock the earth with thunderous laughter if he fell helpless before them.

"I won't let that happen," he said, and fought his growing rage. Still, it grew. For months he had watched this cannibal coming and going, fully capable of talking, sharing, or helping him. Yet, out of pure meanness, he had chosen not to. Rage was not only justified, it was demanded. Internally, he felt his beams of thought shifting, being pulled away from his muscles, joints, and bones, to fall upon that solid white ball of rage that quaked deep in his gut. Like steel spears, his thought beams pierced the ball at every angle, trying to destroy it--to contain it. Through his mind's eye, he saw small hairline fractures form on its surface, like an egg cracking open, as his will to stop it stole more of his thoughts. His body shook madly as he stood, slowly losing control.

Below, the old man raised his head and fixed his stare upon Zon. He then extended his left arm and pointed his index finger to the hilltop. As he did, each person seated about him locked their eyes on the old man and started to sing. The old man stared and pointed at Zon. The crowd stared at the old man and sang. Rare silence of this seventh morning was split by the sound, like a dried oak log, hit dead center with a sharp five-pound wedge. The music started in one octave, then quickly spread to four, the strong bass note dominating.

Inexplicably, Zon's great ball of rage instantly disappeared. Thought beams collided in the center, melded, then burst forward in all directions, engulfing his inner-self, mind, then body. His body quaked as waves of raw energy soaked his being.

Surprised, Zon opened his eyes and looked down onto his glowing form. The old man continued to point. The crowd continued to sing. As Zon watched, the frail muscles in his thighs and legs quaked violently, then swelled, regaining the appearance they had the day he'd graduated from college. One by one, his bones, muscles, tendons, and sinew bloomed, recapturing all of the strength, poise, and youth that he'd known before. Within, his heart leaped as the feeling of crisp grass pricked at the bottom of his feet. Sunbeams warmed the front side of his body as dormant nerve endings sprang to life. Body and mind tingled as Zon witnessed the miracle before his eyes. His backbone flexed, then straightened; his arms trembled, then tightened. He rolled his hands into fists. Shiny knuckles popped as long dormant bones glided gleefully over one another.

His body regained all that it had lost. But once completed, neither the music nor his reevolution stopped. His skin darkened and began to glow. Every muscle in his body kept growing, inside and out, and felt as strong as steel. Never before had he felt this strong, this invincible. His eyes fell closed as he sensed his own blood pulsing through his heart and vessels. The feeling of blood flowing was exuberant, and it, too, bloomed into a still greater feeling, one of flowing raw energy.

Zon opened his eyes and looked down on the old man. He stared hard, and thought it odd that he could count the old man's hair follicles on his balding head from such a distance. Abruptly in unison, the crowd stopped singing and the man in center field snatched his arm down to his side. Then, like a giant black eagle crouching to launch from its perch, Zon bent his knees till his bulging thighs touched his enormous calves. In one smooth motion, he launched skyward, as if following the path of the sun. He rose twenty, forty, sixty feet into the air, arcing gently over the center of the arena, then fell earthward. Landing, he planted his feet solidly back to the ground, standing not two feet from the old man. Zon towered over the man who knelt down before him, head bowed, eyes closed. Slowly, the old man raised his head, and looked into Zon's eyes.

"Welcome to Beinin," he said with a gentle smile.

* * *

Like a programmed robot, Zon reached down and cupped the old man's head in his mighty hands. Lifting him from the ground, he held him to his face.

"I am Idrisi," the African said calmly. Zon was surprised by his words. He expected a plea for mercy. For months, every spare thought had been spent on dreams of getting even with this man. Now was that time. He'd read fear in the old man's eyes after the birds had eaten the grain about his head. That fear had to have been magnified after seeing him standing on the hill, a paralyzed and helpless creature, so blatantly abused. This aged and frail bag of bones knew of his own guilt, and now experienced the sheer power of an enraged man who had every right to seek revenge. Guilt should have silenced him. Fear should have melted his spine. Having his head lodged in this huge pair of bone-crushing hands should have had him pleading for his life. But the old man calmly smiled in his lotus sitting position, though he dangled from his neck in midair.

Instinct guided Zon's actions. The multiple miracles that he'd just received confused him. But the sight of the old man, now in his grasp, allowed his earlier plans of revenge to proceed without thinking. With no emotion, he squeezed the frail head and cast a puzzled stare into his eyes. Suddenly realizing what he was doing, Zon quickly set him back on the ground. Feelings of rage also returned as he stood there, towering over the seated figure before him.

"Why?" Zon yelled down at Idrisi. The crowd remained silent and watched Idrisi and the naked he-man standing before them.

"We did what we must," the old man replied.

"And what was that? Punish me? Torture me? Destroy me? You don't even know me! What did I do to you to deserve this?" Zon's enraged voice boomed in his own ears like it never had before. Idrisi replied slowly and calmly.

"Is that all you see, punishment and pain? Look closer." He paused. Zon looked down on his body. "Are you as you were?" the old man continued. "Feel your strength. Count the hair upon your head, the blades of grass beneath your feet." Zon shot a maddened glance back into Idrisi's eyes. Though he counted the hair and grass subconsciously, his mind still struggled to understand his treatment.

"I laid out there on that cross alone, helpless," Zon continued madly. "You could have talked to me, or helped me, or anything. But you did nothing . . . nothing but keep me alive--to suffer!"

"Did you suffer? Was your body in pain?"

"No!" Zon shouted. "You know full well that you heaped the worst kind of suffering on me. No, you erased my body and attacked my mind."

"Yes, that is so. Your suffering was all in your mind." Idrisi smiled at his own words.

"Stop playing with me!" Zon shot back. "I didn't imagine that cross or the months I spent on my back, living on bread and water. No one should have experienced the loneliness and solitude that I was forced to." Idrisi looked up into Zon's eyes before speaking.

"And--is that all? Suffering, and suffering only? Was there not more?" Zon's stark gaze softened a bit as he considered the question and thought of the eternity he'd spent on the cross.

"Oh, the birds. Yeah, they were there, unlike you. Yeah, the birds were there, but they aren't people. And that still doesn't excuse your devilish behavior."

"So, in the birds, you found friends of a thousand. And yet, you were--alone?" Idrisi looked deeper into Zon's eyes. Zon's squint softened. His thoughts followed Idrisi's circle of questions like a dog on a leash.

"No, I mean, yes. No! I'm not a bird. I couldn't talk to . . . well . . . I did talk to them, but they couldn't . . . I mean I didn't . . ." Zon stopped babbling and tried to think. For years he had prided himself on being able to talk anyone into circles of confusion, yet never falling in himself. But Idrisi had confused him with just a few simple questions. Not only was he in confusion, he couldn't find a way out. Idrisi spoke again as Zon stood puzzled.

"You suffered from loneliness, surrounded daily by a thousand friends. And from that friendship, what did you gain?" Zon, still mildly confused, answered slowly.

"Huh? Oh, the birds. Yes, we talked to each other. I could make them . . . no . . . coerce them to do things." Zon's fists loosened. His bulging arms fell limply at his side. Wrinkles in his forehead relaxed to an even brown smoothness. His mind plunged deeper as he considered his re-evolution. "Their song, their language, rhythm was the key."

"The key? To what?" Idrisi whispered. Zon's head twisted slightly to the left and his eyes rolled skyward, focusing into thin air.

"I studied those birds to avoid suffering."

"*Why* is not important. *What* is."

Zon started to answer, but didn't. Taking a step back, he rubbed his woolly head and tried to understand what was happening. Inside, he held contempt for the old man and his people. But it was hard to harbor these feelings and deal with the old man's logic at the same time.

"So," Zon finally responded, "your torture was designed that I might learn."

"That is so," Idrisi answered with a broad smile. "We placed you to learn. We gave to you the birds to teach you."

"You did what?"

"We gave to you food, that you may starve yourself."

"Wait a minute!"

"And we gave you solitude so that your anger would grow. You are a strange one." Idrisi paused, but for a second. "Anger, curiosity, purpose, ambition. These are your drivers. They fuel you from within. Through the birds, you had to learn. We gave you reason."

"All of that, just to teach me rhythm?"

"No, my friend. Can you not see?" Zon looked again at his enormous body. A deep breath sent a gust of thunder through his veins. The old man was right. Though the suffering was long, he'd acquired far more than just rhythm. Staring at his flexing hands, he asked, "What is this?"

"The birds, as do all animals, they know," Idrisi answered. "Through them you, too, began to know . . . yourself." He chopped his sentences, as if searching for the right words. "What you found in the birds, you also found within yourself. You gained this, not by knowing where to look, but how to look. Your search has shown you what all have in common. At the heart of life, you found . . . "

"Rhythm," Zon whispered.

"That is so. But that is only the key. It is there that song, thought, and matter unite. There, they are all the same."

Zon struggled to understand. "Sound, light, all energy exists as waves," he said, thinking back to the many physics and chemistry classes he'd taken. "All have their own distinct frequency or rhythm. Even matter itself, when you get right down to it, all of it is made up of a few basic components, arranged, rearranged, and dancing about each other to make up all the different . . . everything."

"Yes," Idrisi replied. "Yes, now you start to see."

"It's not what they are made of," Zon said. Wide-eyed and feeling again on the brink of a fresh discovery, he rolled on. "It's the pattern and repetition that make each unique. Waves, patterns, repetitions, all are rhythmic. Mastering the rhythm and being able to distinguish it in anything else allows you to harmonize with it. And in that harmony, you can then influence it." Zon pulled his eyes from the horizon and stared at Idrisi, anxious to receive the African's agreement.

"We call it 'Bolo'," Idrisi said reverently.

"Have you got it?" Zon asked.

"Enough questions for now."

"But . . . "

"Enough for now. This time is not ours. We must yield."

"No. I need . . . " Zon started, but Idrisi cut him off by raising his right hand and pointing toward a single sitting space on the lowest bench in the arena, among the children.

"There," he said. Zon turned to look at the space, then back at Idrisi.

"Thanks for the invite, but I've never felt so alive and free in my entire life. I want to run until I can't run anymore. I want to see this place, everything, for the first time. I want to soar again . . . "

"Enough!" Idrisi demanded. "There will be time for that later. For now, I yield. Sit." Zon started again to argue, but felt strangely compelled to take his seat. Without another word, he turned and walked over to sit. Oddly, his nudity hadn't bothered the children, nor the caring adults that sat about. Two men stood as he approached the bench, holding a finely arrayed garment which they wrapped about him as he turned.

As he sat thinking and looking about the crowd, a strange melody came to him. He began to hum it--simultaneously with every man in the arena. The songs of the day had begun.

"A story! A story! A story!" Idrisi sang from the midst of the crowd. The music remained low and steady, yielding the perfect backdrop to the old man's solo.

As they sang, Zon heard the most incredible account of the history of Beinin, the history of man, he had ever heard. From the beginning of man, Idrisi sang forth the events of the past. Zon sat spellbound, like the children, until sunset. As the sun disappeared below the horizon, all music ceased. Everyone rose, then slowly shuffled out of the arena. Many greeted Zon with broad smiles and engulfing hugs. The show of joy and affection was good medicine for him, restoring his faith in the goodness of man.

As the last of the Beininians passed through the exit, Idrisi approached him.

"I know of your many questions," he said, "but now is the time for rest. Go. Take your rest. I will see you at the waterfront, tomorrow." Without waiting for a response, Idrisi turned, as he had done so many times before, and briskly walked away.

"The lessons continue," Zon huffed, noting the return of Idrisi's loathsome behavior. But his heart was exuberant, his loins overflowing in energy. Zon removed his robe and looked again at his body. He still could not believe how he felt nor what he felt he could do. Instead of using the exit, he turned, then bolted back up the hill. The same hill that had taken him over an hour to climb that morning passed instantly beneath his galloping feet. In just seconds, he found himself standing at the pool front by his wooden bed. Taking a deep breath, he dove headlong into the pool and swam its length like a torpedo, finally surfacing in the waterfall. Moonlight shimmered off the fall. Zon looked through it, then fell back into the water. Holding his breath, he lay on the bottom a full ten minutes before rising again. The water was dark, yet he looked about the depths with ease. Then, without taking a breath, he bolted back across the pool, using a picture-perfect butterfly stroke. Coming to its bank, he stood up and looked into the trees. In spite of the darkness, he was able to spot each of the birds that had so reverently stood by him. They were all nested and asleep and Zon felt deeply compelled to join them. Climbing effortlessly onto his bed, he stretched his arms and legs onto the cross, laid back his head, and fell asleep.

* * *

Zon was awakened the next morning, as always, by the falling dew upon his face. He looked about and saw the scurrying birds. Using his thoughts alone, he greeted them, each of whom responded as it went about its daily routine.

"Greetings!" With a start, Zon turned and saw Idrisi standing as he had been the day of his arrival, on one foot with the other foot lodged solidly against the inner knee of the other leg. Zon sat up and answered.

"Good morning." The motion of sitting up felt foreign, yet so pleasurable. Zon wiped his woolly head with his hands and smiled at the thoughtless commands and absolute obedience of his limbs. "Who would have thought that making a fist could feel so good," he said, more so to himself, than Idrisi. Talking to himself no longer bothered him. "To feel my hands rubbing against one another, to have them feel so normal, so normal . . . " Zon's eyes bulged in panic as he threw his feet down into the water, stood up, and looked down his body. "What happened? I'm . . . I'm normal." All of his body parts had returned to their original size and shape as when he had first entered Africa.

"This is so," Idrisi said with a smile.

"But where's the Bolo?"

"It is as it should be. Please sit down." Idrisi motioned Zon to sit on the bank beside him. Shaken by the loss of superhumanness, Zon unsteadily moved to the bank and sat.

"Long ago," the old man began, "we of Beinin learned that, *I* am within. But *we* are without."

"What?" Zon answered, not understanding the words and visibly shaken by his loss of superstrength. "You're not making sense. Yesterday, I was superhuman. Now I am just human. You . . . " Idrisi cut him off.

"Yesterday, we restored you. We reunited your body and mind. We made your muscles sound. We made your organs and bodily functions as they were. We went no further." Zon recalled that the Beininians were singing steadily and directing their song at Idrisi, who directed it at him. He responded indecisively.

"You . . . made me into what I was . . . "

"No." Again, Idrisi cut him off before he could finish. "We returned you to what you were. We went no further."

"But I was superhuman. I became more than I was."

"But that was not *we*, that was *I*."

"I? You did it?"

"No. It was not I." An utterly confused Zon looked into Idrisi's face.

"Look, either you did or you didn't. Which?"

"I did not."

"Then who?"

"I."

"I? Who is I?" Zon asked. Idrisi cocked his head toward Zon, stared for an instant, then answered through a broad grin.

"You."

"Me?"

"Yes."

"I made me--super?"

"Yes. As was said, I am from within." Still grinning, Idrisi asked, "Who cast your limp body into the water?"

Zon answered, "I did, through Bolo."

"Yes. And who walked you to the hilltop?"

"I did, also through the Bolo."

"So. Who made you what you were?"

"I did?" Zon answered, more in question than answer. Idrisi spoke calmly to him, as a teacher to a child.

"Yes, also through the Bolo. It was you who took what was and made more. Your Bolo, great enough to make the paralyzed walk, was being stolen by the thief of your enormous rage. We took that rage, freeing your power from its burden. Where did it go?"

"What? My power? That's what I've been trying to figure out. Where did it go?"

"Where did you tell it to go?"

"Tell it to go? I didn't even know then that had it!"

"Ah, but it did exist, and you sent it. It followed your thoughts. Think. Aside from the rage, where were your thoughts?" Zon paused a second.

"They were on my body. I wasn't going to let it collapse and be laughed . . . " He caught himself in midthought. "Yes, I see now. With my rage gone, by mind, and therefore the Bolo, was absorbed into my body, straining to make it work. But you'd already healed my body. I was ecstatic over being able to feel again, at feeling strength in my flesh. It felt so . . . " Zon became caught up again in the jubilant passion as he spoke, but Idrisi interrupted.

"As I am, so too, Bolo."

"Yes. Bolo followed my joy into my body. The power that made me walk, also made my body huge and powerful?"

"Yes."

"So, why am I not super, now?"

"Where is your mind?"

"Right here with me, I . . . I guess."

"Is it as it was yesterday, as you climbed the hill?"

Zon didn't answer. Yesterday, his mind had been acutely focused and single of purpose. Today, it was aglow with feelings, anxieties, inquisitions, and the like. He turned again to Idrisi.

"You telling me I can turn it on and off, make myself super?"

"Yes, if you so choose."

"I can turn the force that is within me on and off as I please?"

"That which you call a force within you is always within. It respects the boundaries of your mind."

Zon felt his thought moving along with Idrisi's.

"Yes. As my mind expanded, so, too, did that power. Bolo. I feel as though my thoughts are a thousand times what they were. If that's so, then, so, too, must be the Bolo. And if it is always there, then it must be a matter of focus and direction, not on or off."

"Precisely." Idrisi's answer slid easily through his grinning lips, like the proudest of fathers.

Although he stared back into Idrisi's face, Zon's eyes glassed over with fantasies of his newly found powers. He smiled slightly as he pictured himself atop skyscrapers, his body bursting forth with bulging muscles atop muscles. Idrisi suddenly lost his smile. He spoke firmly.

"The mind must be clear and focused. The spirit must be clear and focused. Do you understand?" Zon, seated and starry-eyed from coddling his dreams, didn't respond. Idrisi put his foot down, stepped over to Zon, and whacked him on the side of his head.

"Hey! What'd you do that for?" Zon smothered the stinging spot with his hand and looked up into Idrisi's taunting smile. Without a word, Idrisi drew his hand back and smacked the other side of Zon's head. With both sides of his head stinging, Zon jumped to his feet and grabbed Idrisi's wrists. Idrisi, while still smiling, jerked his right hand free, smacked Zon in the face, then returned his hand to Zon's clutch. Zon fumed. Idrisi snatched both hands free, and with a sweeping backhand, slapped Zon across his face, launching him into the air to land several feet away, on his back. Sitting up groggily, he watched the ancient man approach. Backpedaling on all fours, he tried to escape the onslaught, but couldn't. Idrisi quickly caught him, reached down with his left hand and grabbed a huge chunk of Zon's hair. Using it as a handle, he threw him through the air like a rag doll, to the middle of the pool. The water stung his sinuses as it rushed up his nose.

Idrisi had powerful Bolo and was using it extremely well, Zon realized. To stop him, he had to use his own. Thinking of the old man's last few words, Zon attempted to focus his thoughts as he swam toward the surface. But as his head popped up, a steel-like hand latched onto his hair again and began dragging him back toward shore, leaving the wake of a speeding boat behind. Once on shore, Idrisi slammed Zon onto the grassy bank. Zon picked his head up, shook it, spun around onto his butt, then quickly stood up. Breathing heavily, he looked down onto Idrisi, who stood not a foot away, smiling broadly. Zon's body ached from the beating. Angrily, he balled his left fist and swung it at Idrisi's head. Idrisi ducked and countered with a stinging punch to Zon's rib cage. Zon grimaced, then pulled his hands up and grabbed at Idrisi's arm. Idrisi blocked his reach, then with a pointed finger, struck him in the joints of his shoulders. Zon's arms froze in place. His muscles strained as he tried to free them. With motion as smooth as silk, Idrisi quickly struck Zon in his knees, buckling them and slamming him back hard to the ground. Idrisi moved over his badly beaten protege, staring gleefully. Zon looked into his eyes. He was helpless--again.

Idrisi spoke as if nothing had happened. "Where was I? Ah, yes. The mind must be focused and clear. So, too, the spirit. Together, there is the Bolo. And with the Bolo, I am within." Zon's chest heaved as he drew a deep breath into his exhausted lungs and allowed some of the rage to exit as he exhaled. He quit wrestling with his locked joints. Completely outdone, he snapped his eyes shut and began centering his thoughts. Concentrating had been easier when he couldn't feel anything. Now he had competing thoughts as every nerve ending in his body delivered its own message of feeling, pain, and urgency. He thought back to the day before, as he had fallen from the cross and into the water for the first time. He imagined himself there again, falling and focusing, ready to face the drowning depths. As he focused his thoughts, he envisioned them as tight beams of laser light once more. Following each, he saw them spanning out in all directions, some to aching muscles, some to his locked and disabled shoulder and knee joints. But the great majority fueled two great balls of light, one of his rage that had grown from the attack, the other, his humiliation from the beating. Patiently, he gathered each beam, one by one from his pain, then from the nerves, and directed them toward the smaller ball of humiliation. The effort made him dismiss his ego, at which point, the ball of humility shrunk, then eventually, disappeared. The beams of thought converged in the middle, united into one large beam, which Zon then aimed at the ball of rage. It, too, had become smaller. As soon as the great beam of thought hit it, it subsided, then vanished and the converging beams united, shining upward.

Zon directed his thoughts toward his shoulder joints, which instantly slid free, as did his knees. One by one, his thoughts subdued the points of pain throughout his body, then returned their gaze upward. Then, instead of directing his transformation, Zon held his beam, his Bolo, erect and ready, and opened his eyes. Idrisi stood above him still, and spoke in the same even tone.

"Rage is a thief," the wise man said. "It misdirects your focus. So too, envy, jealousy, lust, hate. All rob you of what is within. What has your mind, has your spirit." Idrisi stepped back from Zon.

"'As a man thinketh, so is he,'" Zon whispered, repeating a phrase so often quoted by old folks during his youth. Idrisi laced his fingers together before his chest. He spoke reverently.

"I am not, without the mind. I am not, without the spirit." Zon nodded his head once as a sign of his understanding, but didn't speak. "Master you them, then I am within." The riddling sound of Idrisi's speech ceased. Zon felt he understood him, even before he spoke.

* * *

The two sat casually on the bank for hours, Zon asking questions,

Idrisi answering. Idrisi allowed him to fashion a loin strap from the robe he'd worn the day before. A woman silently delivered grain and water just before the sun reached its zenith. Birds sang overhead as the two crunched their lunch.

"You've got it," Zon said, referring to the Bolo. "Do all of you have it?" Idrisi didn't answer right away, but stared intently into Zon's eyes.

"Yes. All God's children's got rhythm," he joked.

"You know what I mean. Not just rhythm, but the Bolo." Zon marveled at Idrisi's excellent English. Idrisi answered jovially.

"It took us generations, from the beginning of time, to understand. At first, it was just a feeling. Then some found that song altered life, health, events. Always, one among us used rhythmic rituals to fight sickness, evil, despair."

"Witch doctors," Zon said. Again, Idrisi paused, but for a second. He had done so after every question put to him, though most times, unnoticeably. This time however, as Idrisi paused to think, Zon, with his own mind completely focused, did notice it, as well as something else far more haunting. "Your answers," Zon said, "There's something wrong."

"I speak the truth," Idrisi responded.

"No. Not lies, but those are my answers," he said. "They're your thoughts, but that's how I would have said them. That's what's wrong with them." Zon studied Idrisi's smiling but silent face. "You're reading my mind. You are reading my mind," Zon gasped. Idrisi, already aware of his thought, responded calmly.

"Yes, I know your thoughts. Look about inside. There I, too, can be found." In his mind, Zon felt about until he defined Idrisi's presence, then felt suddenly violated. Idrisi appeared as a narrow concentrated beam of thought, but colored oddly from any of his own. With more curiosity than malice, Zon aimed his own thoughts at Idrisi's. Instantly, the foreign image disappeared. Zon smiled. It reassured him to know that he could still maintain his privacy.

He looked at Idrisi, expecting him to comment, but he didn't respond. He just sat, pleasantly smiling.

"Can you enter my mind as you please?" Zon asked. Idrisi didn't answer. *Something is still wrong,* Zon thought. *The old man had no reason to stay silent. Indeed, he had every reason to respond, but he didn't. Maybe he couldn't.* Zon redirected his thoughts upward and felt Idrisi's presence reenter his mind. The old man smiled broadly and spoke.

"With the Bolo, you may choose to let another enter, or prevent that entrance." Zon cocked his head in curiosity. Every passing moment brought him greater amazement at the power of the Bolo.

"You can't speak English, can you?" he asked the old man, like some TV supersleuth who'd just solved a mystery.

"No, at least not on my own," answered Idrisi. "The words and language that you hear from my lips all belong to you." Zon shook his head in disbelief. Idrisi continued. "The mannerisms, actions, and reactions are all yours, at least, my interpretation of them."

"So we can talk, mind to mind?" A resounding 'yes' acquiesced across Zon's mind before he finished his question. He could hear Idrisi speak, but not from his mouth. And the language he heard wasn't English nor anything that could be spoken. "Now," Idrisi said, "you shall enter my mind, but be warned. One's mind is like the universe, vast and endless. You have thought of the infinity of the universe before. Think of it again. No bounds, no end. The thought of traveling on without end has been for you, incomprehensible, yet you handle the thought by simply choosing not to think too deeply of it. So, too, is the mind. It is just as vast and endless. Your own mind does not appear so, because it is your reference. It is from where you look."

People can't smell their own breath, Zon thought, drawing it as comparison to what Idrisi was saying.

"Yes, as your own breath, you cannot fathom the endlessness of your own mind. But as you enter another's, it will be shockingly clear. Exposure could be confounding. It could drive you to insanity. Therefore, I caution you. Accept what you see. Do not compare mind to mind. Do not judge."

Zon and Idrisi gazed onto the small glowing orbs of fear and anxiety that had materialized before them in Zon's mind. Zon quickly directed them gone. He asked, "How do I do it?" Within his head, Idrisi directed him.

Guide your thoughts into mine. You must reach out and see my thoughts, then guide yours into them. With some reservation, Zon directed his mind into Idrisi's. His body shuddered as he entered, and Zon fought an intense urge to scream from the initial reality of being inside another's mind. The feeling was similar to jumping headlong into an ice cold pool. But what he saw was unimaginable. Quickly joined by Idrisi, Zon was taken on a guided tour of his thoughts, his feelings, and then most incredible of all, his experiences and past. It was like having the imagination plugged into a movie screen, where every thought conjures up picture-perfect imagery.

In a matter of hours, Zon experienced what would have taken months to tell. No detail was omitted.

* * *

Their joint mind sessions, guided tours of Beinin, exercises of body alterations, and Bolo use continued daily for seven months. Zon soon came to realize and accept what he had once known to be impossible. Beinin was like no other place on earth. Its inhabitants were human, yet much more. Their minds expanded beyond imagination, giving them the ultimate power of Bolo. Yet each remained individually human. Idrisi had called Zon's Bolo *Zonbolo*, because it belonged to no one else. It could not be manifested nor removed by anyone other than Zon. Bolo was also unique to Beinin, and for very good reason.

"The evolution of Bolo took generations upon generations," Idrisi had shown him. All man possessed the seed of Bolo, rhythm, and many had developed it to various degrees. However, only Beininians had developed it to Bolo. This was so, as Zon discovered, because of two oddities which separated them from the rest of mankind. First, Beininians had no vice, which also meant, no ambition. They lived wonderfully simple lives, but in a manner that any modern man would call the ultimate in primitive. Nakedness hadn't bothered them because in a real sense, they couldn't see it. Theirs was to live and let live.

"Man has dominion over the earth," Idrisi had said, "God, over man. Those outside destroy the earth to dominate one another. When there is an encounter, both seek to alter one another." There couldn't have been a better definition of the blind ambition under way that was slowly destroying mankind. Yet Beinin was not under that threat of destruction. The power that is Bolo evolved in Beinin only and was deliberate. "Beinin is the center," Idrisi had put it, as he showed Zon the beginning of Bolo. That distinction had given the Beininians enough time to evolve, first to hear rhythms, then to sing, dance, to follow rhythms of the eyes in painting, sculptures, and the like. Early attempts at manipulating life's natural rhythms resulted in medicine men, witch doctors, faith healers, and other forms of the *black arts*.

But, unlike the rest of the world, with no vice, practices with the rhythms turned inward, to encompass the universe from the mind within, rather than from the body without. The strength of Bolo grew with each passing generation. Other peoples, living about Beinin, visited, but found their ways backward and boring. Each of the Beininians spent their days fasting and singing. And since everything of value within Beinin was also in abundance about Beinin, most visitors simply left, taking the taste of Bolo, and anything else they desired, with them. Ritual dancing and witch doctors abounded throughout the surrounding regions, but Bolo did not evolve there, since ambition aimed it all outward.

Yet another factor prevented Bolo outside of Beinin. Colonization. "Arrested development," Idrisi had termed it. Each of the surrounding nations experienced arrested development due to the ambition of outsiders. Wars and colonization froze cultural development all over the world, each at various levels of growth toward Bolo. For Beininians, age gave them a head start. Location, in the center of Africa, gave them greater time to develop. And with only one common goal, Bolo was inevitable. For them, as the onslaught of deadly, religious and ambitious missionaries reached their borders, they achieved Bolo. Realizing the danger from the outside, the Beininians united to cut away from the world.

Zon found the idea of cutting away fascinating. "And what does 'cut away from the world' mean?" he asked. Idrisi searched Zon's mind, but found no reference to explain. He then picked up a pebble. Placing it on a large rock, he said, "Beinin exists within. The outside stops on one side and begins on another."

Begins on one side and stops on another, Zon thought, but still didn't understand. Idrisi continued.

"If you stand here," he said, placing his finger on the boulder, to the left of the stone, "and look into the stone . . . " He then placed the index finger of his other hand onto the opposite side of the boulder. ". . . then you see not the stone, but the other finger." He paused while Zon thought. "And if you step toward the stone . . . " Idrisi moved his finger toward the stone, and as it approached, miraculously, his finger disappeared into its side, emerging instantly on the opposite side, as if the stone wasn't there. He moved his finger back and forth several times to show the effect. Zon sat dumbfounded. He'd read countless theories of co-existing dimensions and teleportation, but all had flaws. Now he sat witnessing the miracle of discontinuous time, matter, and energy, shown to him by what the world would have described as the most primitive of people. In awe, he asked, "Are we in a place like that stone, another dimension?"

"Yes. So, we stay as we are. Here, there is no outside. Our air, water, earth, all life, all is separate from beyond." Zon looked about, into the sky. He tried to imagine what a rift in the planet's spherical surface would look like. Idrisi spoke. "There are many eyes above, that stare, trying to see, but they see not. For the outside, we do not exist."

"Eyes?" Zon was thinking of aliens, but Idrisi found the correct word.

"Satellites, the eyes of man. They pass overhead, staring down, trying to see what they cannot."

"How?" Zon asked, still stunned over the revelation.

"To do such," Idrisi explained, "all of Beinin must unite. Thoughts become thought. Souls become soul. Then, through one, Bolo is directed to do what must be."

"Like the day when I was healed," Zon said. "Everyone sang and pointed at you."

"And I at you," Idrisi finished. "Only when all within are united, can the rhythms outside the within be altered." To Zon, this meant that no one person could alter the state of another, nor his own surroundings. One could only alter one's self.

"So, it was you on that old tanker," Zon quizzed his teacher. "I've suspected that for a while, but couldn't understand how you could possibly have been there--until now." Idrisi smiled at Zon's sound reasoning and accurate deduction.

Beinin, home of an ancient civilization, existed in its own dimension. Like a giant quilt, Zon wove Idrisi's chronicles together, understanding and believing more of the impossible with each new stitch. He had to believe it. He was a part of it. He was living it.

5
A VIRGIN'S QUEST

Zon stood silently looking northeastward. Idrisi stood a foot behind, off to his left. Both stared into the new morning's horizon. Zon spoke matter-of-factly, his gaze fixed, his eyes like onyx stones, set deep in his finely chiseled face.

"I owe you much," he said.

"You owe me nothing," Idrisi responded with equal detachment. "I have given you nothing. Through me, it has been given to you." Zon turned and faced his mentor, looking down into his up cast grey eyes.

"Three years ago, I had no face, no body, no life. Yet, here I stand." He lightly caressed his perfectly sculpted lower jaw. "My face, though not as it was, is whole again. I can feel, not only from head to toe, but to the very tips of the hair on my head." Idrisi stared intensely into Zon's eyes. Zon turned back to look into the distant horizon. "My hands— there are no bullet holes, not even scars from the attack of those mercenaries." Slowly, he rung his hands, then gripped his lower back with his palms. "My back is renewed, my hands renewed, my life renewed. Here I stand, yet, do I? In a real sense, that young college graduate, eager to take on the world, died the day I fell from that plane. My life, goals, aspirations, relations, all ceased. Yet, here I stand with a face that no one outside has ever seen. I am someone who has never existed."

"And yet," Idrisi broke in with his usual antagonistic style, "you now are a part of something that has always existed. You have not your old face and body, yet, do not those that you have suffice?

What you were before physically cannot compare to what you are now. Are you not stronger, faster, more agile, and quicker than ever before?"

"All this I am. But why? Though I'm stronger and faster, you, my father, are far stronger and quicker. If speed and quickness are needed, then why not you?"

"You are right," Idrisi answered and stole a quick smack from Zon's unsuspecting head. "You are good, but I am better . . . physically. But the greater part of you, no gunman can harm, no poisonous animal can take away, nor any force of this world replace. That which is your soul is greatest. Your heart is pure, your spirit unbridled, your very soul alive, burning with passion that I can know . . . only through you. With these traits you were born. I, like all of Beinin, possess but a taste of these.

None of us carry your knowledge of the outside world," the ancient African continued. "And most importantly, none of us are driven. We are as we are and that is good. We need and desire nothing else, as it has been from the beginning of time. We have no battle to fight, no diseases to overcome. We seek only the harmony as one . . . the Bolo. So have we remained for so many generations. Drive is not needed. It no longer exists for us."

Idrisi's eyes softened. A small smile curled his lips. "Not so with you, young one. The passion that you so fondly display is a must to survive in the outside world. On the outside, you struggle to live. We have no such struggle here, and have lost that drive to excel, to conquer.

"What is life without a goal, without ambition?" Zon asked.

"Would you not pay the price of ambition," the old man sighed, "to live in the Garden of Eden . . . forever?"

So that's paradise, Zon thought, *everything needed to do everything, but no need or desire to do anything.*

As he thought, his mind wandered back to one of the many tales Idrisi had told over the past three years.

"Curiosity drives desire," Zon countered. "Desire yields ambition. So what of the Kaldaca Stone?" he asked, challenging the old man's philosophy.

"Ah, yes," Idrisi responded. "Kaldaca." Gazing skyward, Idrisi launched again in telling the ancient tale from a time before Beinin fell within. "Kaldaca often explored places . . . " he began as his eyes froze in a blank, wide-eyed stare. He spoke slowly and deliberately, as though dictating for print. " . . . A place where mother Earth's trembling blossomed forth formations of stone."

"You mean an earthquake," Zon interrupted.

"Yes, an earthquake. It unearthed stone from far beneath the earth. Kaldaca was so curious. Always, he sought all things new and spent not a moment to complete that which he began. His work, he left undone. That which he built, he never finished. Strange habits from visitors he readily adopted, like smoking. His pipe spewed disgusting smells as he trounced about.

Once, while exploring a newly uncovered mound, Kaldaca discovered a large crystalline, pale yellow stone. It was solid, perfectly round, seven feet across and like diamond, hard and crystal clear. This was a wonderful find and Kaldaca was beside himself with delight. Quickly, he retrieved his family, and together they lifted the huge sphere and carried it back to his dwelling.

News of the orb traveled fast and many came to see the amazing find. Kaldaca would lean lazily against it, as if it were some giant pillow and blow blue-grey smoke rings all day. Such a sight. Such a spectacle. And there he sat daily, content with the admiration of those who passed.

All was well in Kaldaca's world," Idrisi continued, "until the morning the rainy season began. Kaldaca approached his orb as always, but stopped short as he looked upon it. Raindrops vaporized the instant they struck the orb. But there was no mist. Kaldaca reached cautiously and touched the orb. It felt cool and dry, yet hissed ever louder as rain fell upon it. He ran to his dwelling and returned with a large bucket of water. Many would have gasped at the sight of him running, since he rarely hustled for any reason. Proceeding to the orb, he splashed water over it. The water instantly sizzled away as it struck the surface, then bubbled through the trailing liquid, like boiling water. But the orb and water remained cool to the touch. Kaldaca was amazed. His orb could boil water, cold water, without heat. Dreams of bigger spectacles clouded his mind as he stood dripping in the rain. Then the idea came upon him as if someone had dropped the orb upon his head. Without a word, Kaldaca rushed off to wait out the storm.

After the rain, he approached the orb with chisel and hammer. Though hard to break, he hammered for days on the seven-foot orb, until he had cut a flat bottom and hollowed out its middle. The structure resembled a tall, round, clear and completely smooth tub. Gathering all the scraps, he fashioned a base on which to stand his tub. Many had gathered to watch him work.

After he finished, he generously stuffed his pipe full of coconut husk. Then, striding proudly to his spa, Kaldaca climbed in and sat down. Once there, he clapped his hands slowly. One by one, his family emerged from his dwelling, each armed with a large bucket full of water. The ten of them proudly wobbled to the tub, surrounded it, and fixed their load on their heads, ready to empty on Kaldaca's command. After looking about to be sure of everyone's fixed attention, Kaldaca laid back in the tub and motioned his family to pour in the water.

Bubbling and boiling started immediately as the water touched the tub surface, creating the perfect spa. Kaldaca looked about proudly as onlookers gazed through the crystalline walls at the spa-like action. He felt slightly light-headed, no doubt from his euphoria of being so amazing to the people. He reached up and again clapped his hands. His younger son ran up and handed him a flint rock. Kaldaca then motioned both his family and onlookers away so that all could see his glory. As the people respectfully eased away from the spa, Kaldaca struck his flint rock to his pipe.

Such thunderous noise was never heard before in Beinin. Even the invader's cannon fire did not compare to the sound produced from Kaldaca lighting his pipe. The blast leveled the crowd and threw onlookers flat to the ground. The grove of coconut palms that surrounded Kaldaca's spa shred into splinters. The spa sat empty and stable just as it had been. But neither Kaldaca nor the water were in sight. As the crowd sat up, recovering from the blast, droplets of rain started hitting the ground about them. Suddenly, a flood of water came tumbling from the sky, followed by a howling Kaldaca."

Idrisi always paused here to chuckle at his own tale. "Today, Kaldaca's spa sits there," he continued, pointing at the crystalline yellow monument by the arena's entrance, "as it did centuries ago, as a reminder of what was. No one has smoked in Beinin since. And no one else has ever used the spa."

When he had first heard the story, Zon rushed over to the spa-tub. Idrisi followed. "It's crystalline," Zon said, tapping the tub. "And you say that it was perfectly round when Kaldaca discovered it. So, it must have melted to get that shape. Something in great abundance, that melts . . . yellow crystals," he pondered. He thought hard as his eyes roamed the ground. And it was there that he saw his answer. On the ground, laid a large gold nugget. He picked it up and examined it. *Gold*, he thought, *as common here as quartz is in the U.S., covered over with soil and rock, forced down to the depths of the earth for thousands, perhaps millions of years, slowly melting from the heat, then crystallizing to form crystalline gold. But this crystal, though similar to diamond in character, behaved more like platinum in its ability to catalyze reactions.* "It breaks the water down into its elements," Zon explained to Idrisi, as if the wiseman had the need to understand. Holding the gold nugget in one hand, a piece of the Kaldaca stone in the other, he added, "Oxygen and hydrogen. That was the bubbling Kaldaca experienced and the light head." Laughing, he added, "And that's why he was blown to Smithereens. When he struck that flint, he ignited the gases, creating the explosion. He literally blew himself away."

"For whatever the reason," Idrisi replied, breaking into Zon's scientific analysis, "the spa remains there, as it was.

* * *

The sun rose toward noon as the two men stood like granite, solemnly talking. "Truly," Idrisi said, "In that time, there was passion among us. But that was before. Inside, we lost the need for passion. But such passion," he said with a smiling glance toward Zon, "is needed by the one chosen to return to the world. Such passion can only exist in one born of that world. Such a one is you." Zon smiled faintly to ease the intensity of Idrisi's words. He turned again to the eastern horizon and slapped his rippling thighs.

"It's a James Bond thing, I suppose," he said. "A new face, new unregistered finger prints, fallen from the face of the earth for over three years. I guess I could go about anywhere, and do about anything. Problem is, what in the world am I supposed to do?" Zon turned again to face his friend. "You have taught me well," he said. "I now know how to do . . . anything. But it's not the *how.* It's the *what* that bothers me. What am I supposed to do?" Zon searched Idrisi's eyes for an answer.

"I will tell you the truth," Idrisi responded. A somber look invaded his smile. But, just before speaking, he burst into a radiant grin, answering, "I have not the slightest idea." Idrisi chuckled as he stared into Zon's confused face. "I was to heal you," he said. "I did. I was to train you. I did. I was supposed to answer all of your questions that I could. I did. And now, I am supposed to send you on your way. I'm doing that now." Idrisi's smile broadened. "You must admit. I am very good at doing what I do. Ha Ha!" Zon watched those deep-set African eyes dance with glee at the cleverness of his own words. It was this unquenchable joyous spirit that had allowed him to trust, respect, and love such an unorthodox, but learned, character. "But I do know," Idrisi continued, "that you know."

"I know what?" Zon responded.

"I don't know."

"You don't know that I know, or you don't know what I am supposed to know?"

"What."

"So you do know that I know, right?"

"Yes."

"Therefore, I know what I am supposed to know, I just don't know that I know it."

"Yes."

"Well, how am I supposed to find out what I already know?"

"Good question," Idrisi replied, now sobering back to his original stoned-faced composure. "You tell me what you know."

Zon smiled unbelievingly at Idrisi, then, realizing his sincerity, responded, "Tell you. Tell you what? I just told you that I don't know what to do. Yet you say that I do. Out there, I'm nobody, unknown and unmarked. And I've been chosen. Why? Because of my heart and soul. Now, I don't know about you, but to me, it makes no sense.

"Continue," Idrisi countered.

With a look of disgust, Zon proceeded. "I've been given the strength and ability to do most anything." He paused and stepped away from the old man. The strong African sun baked down on the two, enriching their bronze bodies to an ever darkening hue. Zon pinched at his clean-shaven chin and peered deeper into his own thoughts before continuing.

"The part of me which is being sent back into this world, through me, that which is me, and has always been me, is my heart and soul, born into and of the outer world. If this has been retained, then is it to guide me?" Idrisi didn't respond. "I know this world from what I have seen as an orphaned child and as a second-class citizen because of the color of my skin. I have experienced racism and hatred from many different angles. Yet, I also know of the gift given to those who are being walked upon. Rhythm makes us as one with God's universe, and therefore, one with God. That rhythm can be faint, yet, with proper guidance, can move mountains. My brothers, here in Beinin, have achieved oneness with this earth. You have obtained that mustard seed of faith, that ability to move mountains. Through this, all have everything. Yet, no one desires anything. Outside, just the opposite is true."

Looking down into Idrisi's eyes, he asked, "Is it that oneness that I am to bring to the outside?" Still, there came no reply, just a reflective stare. Turning back to the horizon, Zon continued. "Unity must be obtained with the earth and universe, as here in Beinin. Yet this can only be obtained as you have done. Here in Beinin, you were free of the world. This was the only place untouched by the world long enough for you to become one."

Zon stopped talking, but his thoughts continued. He opened his mind for Idrisi. Idrisi squatted fully to his haunches in the full sunshine. *Please continue,* he relayed to Zon, assuring him of his presence and full attention. Zon proceeded without words, his thoughts splashing across the cinema screen of his mind in full color as he and Idrisi looked on. Visions, as fast as thoughts, paced fervently across their minds. And each man studied them and their individual meaning, trying to derive a purpose for it all.

You said that outside, Zon began, *man alters the physical, which then distorts the natural rhythm.*

That is correct, Idrisi responded.

That distortion, it could destroy the world.

That is possible.

Could it destroy Beinin as well? This time, Idrisi did not answer, nor allow Zon to retrieve the answer for himself. Frustrated by the old man's silence, Zon asked aloud, "Then, am I to save the world?"

"Again I tell you that I do not know," Idrisi chimed onto Zon's disappointed ears. "I am listening." Zon's mind again engaged to replace the speech between the two.

"So, I'm supposed to save the world," he said sarcastically. "Guess I'm supposed to do it by using the ole rhythm method, huh?" he laughed.

"And what of rhythm?" Idrisi asked, ignoring the crack. "African man has the rhythm, not because of the color of his skin, but because of whom he is, inside. He is eldest and the least corrupt. He's sought it as the ultimate route to joy. Outside, power is sought and belongs to those who alter the physical and distort the rhythm."

Zon's thoughts began swirling about like earthworms in a can. Seeking to end the befuddling conversation, he cleared his mind. Unsatisfied with the lack of an answer, he took consolation in having all of the pieces of his quest on the table, though scrambled as they were. He and Idrisi stood and stared into the midday sky for several minutes.

"I can't do this alone," he said finally to Idrisi.

"True," Idrisi offered. "But in the world, there are many people. Yours is not to do it alone. Yours is simply to start it. Others will finish."

"I'm glad you said that," Zon replied. Images of flying around the world, strapping naked people to wooden crosses, danced across his mind. "But how . . . "

"The time for questions is enough," Idrisi interrupted. "I have told you all that I know." Zon breathed deeply as he turned to his mentor. "Idrisi, I know what I've got to do, but I don't know how I am going to do it, yet. I'm leaving this place, maybe to start a revolution. And I know that it's got to begin in the United States.

"Are you sure?" Idrisi asked.

"Nope. But there's no place like home," Zon answered. He sucked in a deep breath that would start his journey. As he exhaled, familiar drums and singing filled the air to open the portal to the outside. As the harmonious voices grew, he peered sadly into Idrisi's eyes. This was good-bye to his father. Idrisi, saddened also, spoke, not of their parting, but of Zon's quest.

"Look upon the statue." Idrisi motioned toward the large, black, shiny, glass-smooth onyx statue that stood on the far side of the arena.

Zon turned and stared as he'd done so often over the past two years. "It's beautiful," he replied.

"Yes, but it is more. It is also you."

"How so?" Zon asked.

"Ahhh. That is for you to determine," the wiseman philosphied. "We all determine ourselves. Some look on the statue and see strength, others majesty and art. Some see heart-felt love and warmth. It is neither man nor woman, warrior, god, nor beast. It is for you to determine. It is designed to be so."

"Just what I need," Zon said, gazing onto the crystalline figure, "more riddles."

"God be you," Idrisi said lovingly to his son. The music, from the people gathered in the arena, grew steadily louder. "Remember all that I have taught you," Idrisi bellowed over the music. "Especially remember this. Your healing belongs to Beinin. All that you have become belongs to Beinin." Zon felt a sudden twitch between his legs. "You came to us not knowing of the world."

"You mean, a virgin," Zon corrected.

"Yes, to be blunt. Now you leave, still a virgin. That is how you must remain. What has been given you is of Beinin. Only through Beinin can that be changed."

"You mean I can't . . . make love outside?" Zon asked in disbelief.

"Not can't," Idrisi countered, "but won't. You abstain. Through Beinin, a gift was given to you. In return, this is your gift to Beinin, and only Beinin can receive it." Zon looked pitifully at the old man.

"I'm twenty-four years old!" he pleaded. Idrisi placed a solid hand upon his left shoulder and pushed him toward the arena. "So let me stay here a couple more years. I'll gladly shower my gift upon deserving Beininian womankind," he said in a mixture of laughter and terror. Though amused, he envisioned the lustful dreams and thoughts awaiting him in his future, in the world outside.

"No. You must leave now," Idrisi countered. "But stay as you are. As you lose what is Beinin's, so too do you loose Beinin, and the Bolo."

"Oh! Such wonderful news for my departure. Any other joyous tidbits you'd like to share before I go?"

"Just this," Idrisi added calmly, "You have become my son. I will miss you."

By this time, the music had risen to a near deafening volume. Idrisi and Zon embraced as the veil of Beinin was lifted. Slowly, Idrisi stepped away from Zon while waves of music poured over them like a mighty rushing wind. A tear ran down Zon's cheek.

"We will meet again, my son. If not here, then . . . somewhere else." Idrisi grinned as Zon stepped back and slung over his shoulder a small sack carrying a chunk of the Kaldaca stone.

With his head held high, Zon's massive chest heaved to hold back the tears. "Good bye, my father," he whispered as Idrisi, along with the sweet melodies of Beinin, faded to nothingness.

* * *

"Idrisi!" Zon yelled at the top of his lungs. "Idrisi!" There was no answer. He turned slowly to face west, then northwest. Before him, on all sides, were wide grassy fields of ripened yellow grain waving with the breeze. Zon closed his eyes then lifted his head slowly to get his bearings. "Now home, the great United States of America, is that way," he said, pointing northwest. "But the road home is not often straight, nor a direct one." He turned directly north, then without hesitation, sped off into the tall African grass. Naked and running, he looked perfect-picture, the perfect African heathen that the world had come to expect, to ignore.

Three years had passed since he'd entered Beinin to heal his wounds and master Zonbolo. Though he'd used his newly developed skills routinely there, this was his first opportunity outside. Everyone within Beinin had obtained some level of Zonbolo. Idrisi was a master. In Beinin, talking or doing anything with anybody included not only speech and the physical, but the mind as well.

As Zon ran, his mind fell to his feet and paced them briskly. He could set any pace and sustain it for as long as he desired. Soon he entered dense jungle and became aware of hundreds of animals about him. But a small cry from a grass thicket stopped him dead in his tracks. Zon approached slowly. As he got there, he saw a dead black panther lying beside a small cub. A pack of jackals had gotten the best of the creature as she protected her lair. Zon's approach had frightened them off. The cub lay crying beside its mother. Cupping the cub in his palm, he stroked it between the ears. The stroking soothed the cub, though he knew the tears had not stopped within.

"There, there, now. Poor little fellow," Zon said with the gentleness of a grandmother comforting a hurt child. "Why don't you come along with me? I'm going to save the world. You can watch. It'll be fun." He laughed as he realized the irony of his comforting words. "Well, maybe not the world, but I can save you, little fellow." Kneeling down onto the jungle carpet, he quickly fashioned a lash to carry his new found friend safely about his shoulders. But as he completed the sling, he felt four creatures approaching. The jackals, that had momentarily retreated, were returning for their prize . . . plus.

"Fight or flight?" Zon debated. Grabbing the little cub, he stuffed it butt-first into the lashed pouch, threw it over his head and about his shoulders, then blasted off just as the jackals broke from the jungle. Zon stared into the jungle before him as it rushed by in a blur. The laughing howls of the hyenas were close behind. Two of the ravenous animals clung to the panther carcass while the other two pursued the new prey. Zon listened to the yapping dogs' steps fall away as he sped through the dense flora. He then slowed to allow the animals to catch up. His slower speed and the smell of his fresh manly sweat urged the animals forward to collect their rare chocolaty prize. Each animal lunged forward with each step, snapping and swinging their front paws at Zon's heels. However, with each forward thrust, Zon too thrust forward. He was matching the animals, stride for stride and lunge for lunge. The closeness of the prey, coupled with the greed of the dogs, allowed this cat-and-mouse chase to continue for a mile through patches of jungle and grassland. By the end of the chase, fatigue slowed the animal's pace to nearly half of what it originally was.

Then, one jackal stopped and panted to catch its breath. The other pursued, but too stopped after twenty-odd paces further. Zon stopped as well, turned and faced his would-be consumers. The animals were winded, their furry underbellies wet with sweat and the occasional water puddle they crossed during their pursuit. Zon glistened in the evening sun with the invigorating sweat that covered his body. The innocent kitten sat bright-eyed in her pouch, aware for the first time of the sound of forty mile-an-hour winds rushing by her ears and streaky-green colors rushing past her eyes. The leaping and panting jackals had amused her during the chase.

Zon smiled at the on-looking and outdone assailants as he stood not more than five feet from the closer one. Wiping the sweat from his brow, he flipped it across the closer animal's dripping tongue. The jackal, tasting the sweat, lunged again at Zon, who turned, and with a blast of speed, disappeared into the jungle.

* * *

Zon thought deeply as he sped along. He'd pulled a kitten from the jaws of ravenous beasts. To set it free now, on its own, would simply mean mere postponement of its premature death. Much had to be done before this creature could be set free to seek and fulfill its own destiny. Idrisi had often referred to a similar lesson from the Bible, the one of Moses and the Iseralites. They too had been pulled from the jaws of destruction, and could have been set free immediately. But instead, they were lead about, cared for and trained for forty years. Then they were set free in their own land, to make their own destiny. The cub had time to wait.

6
OUT OF AFRICA

The northern coast of Africa is claimed by four countries: Egypt, Libya, Algeria, and Morocco. Zon had entered Africa at Morocco, which until then had been some mysterious country that had no location. It was just a name, a backdrop of mystery and espionage for an old cartoon series. Casablanca, in Morocco, belonged to Humphrey Bogart. It had no origin, no time, people, nor space, nothing of its own. Yet, here it was, distinctly African, distinctly Moroccan, full of its own mystery and fairy tale. So, too, Tripoli, Libya, a name honored in the U.S. Marine's theme song, yet a place unknown to millions of Americans. It carried its own flavor and mystique, oblivious to the Euro-paint applied to it before reaching the young minds of America. The same held true for Memphis and Cairo, both of African Egypt, as well as Ethiopia, Sudan, and the small country of Somalia, with its crystal blue waters and white sandy beaches.

Zon traveled on foot through these countries, as well as Nigeria, Chad, and Zaire. It had taken him six months to explore them. And he left wanting to know far more than he'd discovered in his ancestral birthplace. But his mission drove him forward, and it had to begin in the United States. It was late October when he finally arrived in Tripoli, where he secured a flight with no identification nor passport.

It was on this, the last of three days in Tripoli, as he headed for the airport, that a wind of intrigue caught his attention. The city was afire with rumors of a coup attempt. Government leaders were dashing back and forth between buildings, heavily guarded by armed soldiers. Rebels had acquired backing from some unnamed source. But it wasn't the politics or internal affairs that had drawn Zon's interest, though he had major questions concerning the affairs of the world. For instance, in a world dominated by European descendants, why were all of the major villains such as Gadhafi, Hussein, Castro, and Aidid distinctly African? Beyond that, however, there was something else, something familiar in the air that heightened his interest far beyond curiosity.

Downtown, in the midst of the street vending, Zon approached a merchant who talked feverishly as shoppers paused. With every customer, he'd burst into an agitated, yet whispered monologue. Zon had dressed to fit in with the common Libyan. But as he drew near, the merchant fell silent. *"He's only talking to people he knows,"* Zon thought.

The merchant fixed a stare into Zon's eyes as he approached. Zon saw an opportunity to get the information. As the merchant stared, Zon intruded into his thoughts. Immediately, the merchant grew blurry-eyed and began to weave back and forth as he stood behind his stand of leather wares. This was the first time that Zon attempted to join his mind with another outside of Beinin. There, everyone could allow or refuse such an intrusion. But his encroachment had been too direct and strong for the unsuspecting commoner, who now staggered drunkenly about from the intrusion. Realizing this, Zon stopped his efforts. The merchant fell backward onto a slate wall behind him, then fell to the concrete. People about him quickly rushed to his aid, Zon being one of them. Muscling his way to his downed victim, he and several others helped the street vendor to his feet. The merchant steadied himself and began shaking his head clear.

As the merchant rested on his human supporters, Zon again fixed upon the man's thoughts and suggested that he had a message to deliver. The merchant, still groggy, turned his head left, and with eyes closed, whispered into Zon's ear, "Tonight, in the warehouse at Elcabar and Tusanc . . . we arm . . . we begin." The merchant shook his head once more, opened his eyes, then looked up to see to whom he had delivered the message. Zon, sensing his rising eyes, stepped beyond his sight, melted into the crowd and walked off.

* * *

"We are enough! We can return our beloved country to our forefathers!" The shouts were loud and echoed between the tall barren walls of the warehouse. An assembly of nearly 300 men huddled, surrounded by large wooden crates. Most were dressed for work, in khaki shorts, light gauzy shirts, and sandals. Each also wore a wrap about the head and face, concealing their identity. One plump man stood before this congregation atop a large crate. He was dressed differently from the rest, in a finely tailored European suit, with a long flowing royal blue robe draped across his shoulders and a checked orange and white wrapping about his head. His face wasn't covered. His brown skin gleamed a pale blue in the florescent warehouse light.

"We have waited long enough!" he shouted. The crowd answered during each break with a loud roar and knifed fists swinging in the air. "The madman has ruled this country for thirty years, and where are we today? Our children are not learning our ways, but theirs. The money that we pump from the ground now infests us like plague; we pursue it instead of Allah! Are we to stand idly by and watch our family, our children, our homes, or our country rot away like a diseased dog?"

"No!" resounded the incensed mob.

"Come, my friends!" the speaker continued. "Let us unite! Tonight, we march into that palace in the name of all the Sansui, of all that's holy, led by The Almighty Allah! Tonight we march to take the head of Gadhafi! There are few of us now, but I promise, when we take his head, many of our brothers who are too frightened to stand will join us! Tonight, we will taste victory!" With this, the crowd ignited into continuous chants of "Allah be praised" and "Down with Gadhafi." The men turned about, marching in circles as they chanted. The fat man stepped from his podium crate and made his way through the crowd to the back of the warehouse. There, he approached two white men.

Zon sat overhead, hidden in the shadows of the large center rafter, high above the brewing mob below. After slipping through an unlit alley and working his way around a pack of large, hungry, wild cats, he had found an unlocked window, high in the warehouse roof. He'd shed all but a tight fitting black loincloth. His naturally black skin suitably hid him in the darkness of the night. Curiosity had happened him upon an evolving revolution. This mob below was scheming to overthrow Mu'ammar Gadhafi and his regime.

Here again, Zon felt the sting of his true ignorance of the world. His only education of Libya came through a few newsreels, all showing Gadhafi to be an insane madman, a butcher who should be eliminated at any cost. But Zon's recent education made him at least question his adopted source of information. Was this not a leader of one of the most powerful nations of the world? Maybe he was mad, as was Hitler, but both men were backed by a nation. Yet, both could be evil. And what of the news source itself? Was it not controlled by politicians? Was it not in their best interest to maintain instability in all of the non-Euro-dominated countries of the world? These thoughts sparked a painful memory, a memory of the words of his assailant aboard the plane, who had so mercilessly slaughtered him and his fellow passengers. Zon thought of the mercenary's words, his pulse quickening with the resulting anger.

"Who wins is not important," the mercenary had said, "as long as they keep fightin' and killin' each other, then none of 'em will rise to threaten us. Our job is to keep them destabilized." Zon's eyes tightened to a squint as he relived the speaking of those words, the beating, shooting, fall, and death that followed. He wondered where these revolutionaries below him stood in the overall picture. Were they, too, just pawns being used to destroy themselves? Or did Gadhafi truly deserve annihilation? He looked down at the fat Arab approaching the heavy crates.

The two soldiers faced away from him. The fat Libyan approached with a broad smile on his face.

"Ya done good," the tanned blond spoke jovially, yet in a low voice. "Looks like the coup's about to stew."

"Idiots," the Libyan said as he wiped a bead of perspiration from the bridge of his nose. "They are sheep. They believe . . . anything. Tonight, many of them will die, as so it should be. It is good for them to die, and for what better cause . . . than mine." He disgustingly slid his eyes away from the would-be soldiers to the true ones who stood before him, then continued his soliloquy in an even more pompous tone. "But the throne of Libya will be returned to its rightful place. My family is heir to Libya, from the days of El Seba. The throne belongs to me." Though the speech was passionate, the fat man's heart was full of hunger and greed for the power and riches of this wealthy African country.

Prince Tasman turned and pointed into the crowd with a fat, ringed index finger that resembled a plump shrimp as it uncurled.

"Their lives are nothing," he said, then looked skyward, raising his fist high into the air as he spoke to the rafters. "I tell them to fight, and they will do so. Tonight, we will succeed where others have failed . . . " Suddenly, as if struck by a lightning bolt, Prince Tasman dropped his triple-chinned face, cast his eyes upon the ground, then turned and bowed toward the two white soldiers seated next to him. ". . . with your generous help . . . of course," he humbly added.

"Prince Tasman," the taller of the two soldiers began, "Your men are ready. So are our arms." The soldier stood, turned, then opened the box upon which he sat. Reaching in, he retrieved an automatic rifle. "Here are the M-16s, as we promised. We've also got small grenade launchers over there. There is more than enough weaponry to blow your Kadaffy-duck to kingdom come." The prince winced at the demeaning name used for Gadhafi. Even though he hated this man, it remained difficult to hear outsiders speak so of his countryman.

"As I have told you," continued the prince, "what happens to Gadhafi is of no concern to me. I will dethrone him. If that means killing him, then so be it." The soldier replied calmly, as he placed a heavy hand on Prince Tasman's shoulder.

"I understand your cause and your mission, Prince. But please understand ours. Gadhafi is our enemy, and we want him dead, understand? D-E-A-D. You want the throne, we want Gadhafi eliminated. You've got the men and the opportunity. We have the weapons and the funds. Together, we both can win."

The prince looked indignant and began to speak, but the soldier gestured him to silence by raising his extended palm. "Remember Prince," the soldier warned, "there are a lot of would-be rulers of this land, many with far more clout than you. You'll need our continued support to rule. And we can guarantee our support in keeping you in power." Prince Tasman bit his tongue. He was planting a hook deep in his own hide for these mercenaries, and they could care less about him or any one else. Yet, this was the only way for him to regain control of Libya's vast riches, the only way he could restore himself and his family as heirs to this land in his lifetime. He needed them and they knew it.

"You are right my friends," The prince replied politely and stately. "Come. The time for talk is over. My men await your gifts."

Turning pompously, he addressed his army. "Men, as I have promised, here are your weapons." The crowd burst forward at this announcement, eager to handle the guns. The two mercenaries stationed themselves, each by a stack of boxes. As the rebels approached, the soldiers passed out rifles. A handful of men toward the rear of the crowd received hand-held grenade launchers. The soldiers worked their way through the bunch, showing each revolutionary how to use the weapons.

Zon sat high above in silence. He was witnessing the beginning of a coup that could change the world. Should he intervene? Was this his fight? He knew little of the politics of this land. Gadhafi was a name that he'd been taught to hate by America's media. But if nothing else, he'd learned during his stay in Beinin that the media was the most effective weapon to vanquish one's enemy. With it, a multitude of minds could be manipulated without a shot being fired.

"*As a man thinketh . . .*" Zon thought as he watched. Was Prince Tasman the rightful heir? Was Gadhafi as evil as the media painted him to be? Zon pondered these questions as he leaned effortlessly against a dusty inclined girder.

Then, he saw something that lay all questions aside. Inside him, the quiet cool of curiosity was quickly scorched by a fit of uncontrollable rage. His body shook with anger as he finally caught sight of one mercenary's face. There, clear as day, was the scar cut across the left eye, the short blond crew cut, and haunting blue eyes of the man who had so savagely beaten him and the seven other passengers aboard that old transport plane. Beads of sweat formed on his forehead and nose. His body rippled as opposing muscles strained against each other. He had not been prepared for this, though he'd learned so much in the three years since that horrid day. As he stared down into that wretched face, he could feel all of it . . . his consciousness, his control, slipping . . . oozing out of his skull, being replaced by an avalanche of revenge.

Suddenly, he was confused, his mind in battle with itself. To spring forward for the sake of vengeance was against all that Idrisi had taught him. Yet, that was all he could think of. He now possessed the power to avenge himself against these demons. This fact alone edged him forward, tempting him to jump right in the midst of the crowd and rip the living flesh from their bones. His body glistened with sweat as his powerful legs prepared to launch him into space and toward the floor. He was going to maim, kill, and destroy those who had done the same to him. As he crouched down, each of his old wounds, the bullet holes, torn flesh, broken back, and broken bones, united in a cry of pain, a cry for revenge. Zon sank his fingers into the girder as he launched himself over its edge.

But his anger caused him to jump with far greater force than needed. And that split second of physical exertion also gave his conscience just enough time to sneak in a rational thought. "Revenge is its own worst enemy," Idrisi had quoted each and every time Zon thought of his would-be murderers. "It has no friends. If you have it, then it has you . . . and you are lost. Your mind," he said, tapping his stiffened index finger into Zon's temple, "it is clear. It is pure. Zonbolo can exist. Revenge will invade . . . take your thoughts, your purity. Zonbolo will be captive."

Zon's mind redigested Idrisi's words as he rose vertically over the girder. The thought locked his hand solidly to it as his body stretched fully in a handstand. His momentum, however, carried him to his zenith, then pushed him over the side and downward, where only the cold concrete warehouse floor awaited, forty feet below. His thoughts were mixed. Vengeance pulled him to the floor, but Idrisi's words locked his hands to the girder. The results were as mixed up as his thoughts. The girder groaned as it twisted against the adjoining beam.

Zon hung from the girder as it slowly bent, yielding to his massive 200-plus-pound frame and downward thrust. As it bent, he peered below. The crowd of revolutionaries had all received their weapons and proceeded outside of the building while he had been deep in his thoughts. Only he, the mercenaries, and Prince Tasman remained, the three on the floor now peering up into the rafters, where he dangled like a bunch of grapes. As they looked on, the girder gave way, dropping Zon to the floor. The three onlookers watched the nude black body fall behind a stack of boxes. There was no noise to mark the landing.

"The fool must have hit something soft," the startled soldier suggested as he smiled to his partner.

"What was he doing up there?" Prince Tasman asked. "Could Gadhafi have spies?"

"I doubt it," came the nonchalant response from the shorter, more solemn soldier. "Probably just a vagrant, aroused from his nest."

"Couldn't be," answered the other soldier. "We both checked and secured this place just before Tasman's terrorists showed up. That nigg . . . " the scarred soldier caught the word in his teeth before it escaped. With a quick glance into Prince Tasman's insulted face, he continued with his corrected speech, " . . . n . . . numbskull got in and up there while we were here." Prince Tasman, eager to go outside to instruct his troops before they scattered, dismissed Zon's untimely intrusion.

"Forget him. We have a mission, and it has already begun. I go. We will meet here again, in the morning . . . if we are successful. If not, I will meet you in Debarga so that we can begin again. Agreed?" Prince Tasman looked into the lead soldier's eyes, who returned the stare blankly. The scarred soldier continued to watch the stack of boxes hiding Zon from sight.

"Sounds like a plan, Chief!" the lead soldier exclaimed as he whipped his arm over the prince's shoulder. "We've done our part." Then, while pushing Prince Tasman toward the door, he added, "Now you go do yours." Prince Tasman resented being touched, pushed, laughed at, and patronized. He rolled his eyes at the soldiers, but did not pursue the matter further. Instead, he snatched his head around, causing his head wrap to whip about behind him as he walked briskly through the door. His men were waiting for him outside, gathered about a box on which he quickly mounted to give instructions . . .

and from which to wave them onward as they departed.

* * *

"Now," the lead soldier said as he closed the warehouse door behind the prince, "let's find our nosey nigger."

"Now that's a plan!" came the overly enthusiastic response from his partner. He reached in the box nearest him and retrieved his Uzi, pulled the cartridge, convinced himself that it was full, and snapped it back into the weapon.

"You circle to his left. I'll go to his right. The nude dude is probably harmless, but he got his black ass in here without us knowin' it. Could be more than meets the eye."

Zon had landed lightly on his feet behind the boxes. The brief fall had stolen his thoughts away from his passion for vengeance, allowing him to make a soft landing. As he touched down, he instinctively darted to his left, silently, out of sight, moving round until he was fully behind the soldiers. Once there, he felt secure enough to relax . . . permitting the thoughts of vengeance to resurface and dominate once again.

But he didn't fight them this time. Instead, he submerged in them. He watched, crouched behind the gun crates, as the soldiers circled behind the stack of boxes where he had fallen. The lead soldier drew a foot-long hunting knife as he rounded the corner of boxes. The other soldier emerged around the adjacent corner simultaneously. Professional training synchronized their movement without speaking.

"Where the hell did he go?" fired the lead soldier as he kicked at a small pile of trash lying near where he expected to find Zon. The floor was clear, except for the trash.

"Nothing back here that would have broken that fall," the lead soldier whispered to his partner. "We've got a bogey here."

"Bogey smogey!" sneered his partner, nearly loud enough for the revolutionaries outside to hear. "Whoever he is and whatever he got while he was up there, is going no further. Let's find his black ass." The soldiers each spun around. Crouching, they proceeded around the corners from which they had emerged. Again, they rounded the front corners together, each rising to full stance as they gazed upon the sight awaiting them. There, standing twenty feet in front of them by the opened weapons boxes, was a tall, muscular, black, glistening, body--holding a loaded grenade launcher aimed directly at them.

"Think he knows how to use it?" the scarred man asked in a jovial, rather condescending manner.

"Sure, he knows how to use it, but he hasn't. That means he wants something. And that something is going to give us just enough edge to kill his ass." Both men spoke out loud, wanting Zon to hear. Though they talked to each other, the words were meant for Zon, to confuse him, raise question, doubt, disbelief, amazement, anything that might reduce his concentration.

"You think we can jump away from that grenade in time if he launched it?" the lead soldier asked, staring hard at the grenade launcher.

"Nah," answered his partner, continuing the mind game, "we'd probably be blown to smithereens. He's got us and he knows it. All he has to do is pull that trigger." The scarred soldier's eyes begin to dance as he cut a smile toward his partner in anticipation of a fight. He then smiled back at Zon and began stepping slowly toward him, his own finger fixed gingerly against the trigger of his down-pointed Uzi. As he took his first step, he taunted Zon.

"Come on, nigger, pull the trigger." He stopped, dropped his head, and began laughing at his own witty and poetic line. Again raising his head and stepping forward, he repeated it over his own chuckle. "Come on nigger, pull the trigger!"

Zon watched as the soldiers slowly eased toward him and away from each other. He wanted so badly for them to recognize him, but they didn't. Beinin had done too good a job in altering his features. Still, he wanted the hands of time to turn back, to put him back on that plane so he could refight the battle, possibly save some, if not all of his fellow passengers, and then throw these jackals from the plane. He wanted to go back to that time which now bred such rage inside him. He wanted to go back . . .

But as this thought kept replaying in his head, he suddenly realized that he could never go back.

"The past cannot be changed, only learned from." Words of wisdom again sprang to his mind from the mouth of Idrisi. "A fool tries to forget the past and is doomed to relive it again. An even greater fool tries to change it. Now, tell me," Idrisi had once said to him when he had attempted to justify his need for vengeance on the soldiers, "which kind of fool are you, hmmm?" Zon didn't have an answer then, but now, it suddenly dawned on him.

He stood coolly as the soldiers approached him, aiming his grenade launcher at the stack of boxes between them. Prince Tasman and his men had departed and all was silent outside. During their first encounter, Zon and his fellow passengers had suffered badly because of their naivety. None of them had anticipated such an attack. None of them were skilled in fighting and each relied on their fear and emotions to muster their defense. Meanwhile, their assassins relied on skill, planning, training, and practiced execution. All odds had been stacked against the passengers.

And the same was happening again. Zon had had a clear advantage over the soldiers when they didn't know who he was nor where he was, but his rage had given both away. Arrogantly, he had stepped forward in a show of power. But they, being trained, quickly took advantage of his misplaced heroics and were now gaining the upper hand. His own rage had placed him in a position that could cost him his life. Loss of control had made him easy prey.

These sobering thoughts happened quickly as the scarred soldier began stepping and repeating his lyrical line. Zon's anger dissipated. Quickly shifting his eyes from left to right, he took aim at the boxes in the middle of the soldiers and fired the grenade. The soldiers instinctively dove outward from the boxes the instant Zon pulled the trigger. The scarred soldier hit the hard cement floor shoulder first, then tucked and rolled up to his feet. As he came upright, he fired his Uzi toward Zon. The bullets found only boxes. Zon, too, had leaped away as he fired. He knew they'd expect him to stand there and count the bodies, since they'd just told him that they couldn't escape. He dove to the right, rolled into the shadows, then moved low and swiftly toward the lead soldier, who was just rolling up to his feet from behind another pile of boxes.

Standing firm, the soldier searched the lighted floor for Zon. As he watched the bullets from the Uzi rip into the boxes, he felt a tap on his back. The combat-hardened soldier pivoted to his right, coiled his right elbow, and shot it viciously toward his surprise attacker's ribs. His long knife was clenched hard in his right fist, ready to cut into the attacker as his arm unfolded from the blow. Zon stood poised behind the soldier, awaiting the attack. As the bone-crushing elbow approached him, he skillfully blocked it with his right forearm. But before the arm could uncoil to engage the knife, Zon struck the soldier like a viper, in the back of his right shoulder joint, freezing the rotating socket bone in place. The soldier's pivoting momentum threw his body toward Zon. He thought he'd been shot, but ignoring the pain, clenched his teeth to counterattack. Leaning forward, he brought his right leg up for a roundhouse to Zon's midsection. Zon, anticipating the move, struck the soldier at the base of his spine as he leaned forward, freezing his legs and hips in position. The soldier, now bent and locked at the waist, seething with pain but dripping no blood, had no other choice but to fall headlong into the empty cardboard boxes before him. His free left hand broke his fall, but he found himself sprawled out among the empty boxes, knife in hand, his legs and right arm immobilized.

The commotion of the fall drew the scarred soldier's attention. He hadn't noticed his partner's ensuing battle until he'd fallen helpless from the shadows. Behind his twitching commanding officer, he saw a shadow melt into the surrounding darkness. He raised his gun, but held his fire.

"Like greased fuckin' lightin'," Scarface murmured, trying to anticipate Zon's next move. Twice now, the bogey had moved silently behind them to attack. Realizing this, he pivoted quickly about to secure his rear. His anticipation was correct, and almost on time. As his machine gun completed the 180, Zon was in the air, feet first, hurling toward him. Aiming for the gun, he struck it with the heel of his foot, dislodging it from the solider's grip before he could fire. The scarred blond stumbled back into the open, but did not fall. The gun slid helplessly toward the crate of other weapons. The soldier drew down into an oriental fighting stance and pointed his flexed hands and fingers at Zon.

"Look like we gonna have some fun," he hissed, continuing with his twisted sense of humor. His partner lay twitching behind him on the floor, trying desperately to flex his frozen joints free. Zon stood silent, staring at the joker. A light perspiration made his body glisten.

"Thas' right," the blond said, "you and me. Let's get it on." He stepped his left leg high over his right in a long arching fashion as he peeled his contorted right hand gracefully down the length of his left arm, to assume the same, but reversed, position. His dance continued through a routine of slow, graceful, and deliberate moves in the open area, first circling clockwise, then counterclockwise about Zon. Zon turned his head to follow, but not his body.

"Ya know somethin', boy?" the soldier taunted, easing ever closer to Zon with each word, "you're 'bout to get the ass-whippin' of your life. Ya know, I would have been top graduate in my martial arts class," he bragged, stepping in a foot closer, "but someone dared me to jump the instructor." The soldier slithered about as slyly as the words from his lips. "Put him in the hospital for two weeks, broken bones, few missing teeth, severely crushed nuts. Got suspended for a month while he was recuperatin'. I believe he hit me once, no, twice." The soldier smiled dryly, though Zon could feel him concentrating harder than ever.

Finally getting to the ideal striking point, Scarface jerked about several times till he was convinced that Zon wasn't going to move. He then eased as far right as he could, forcing Zon to crane his neck to its limit, severely cutting his field of view. The soldier lifted his leg again as if he were going to circle once more, back to the left. He'd managed to get within three feet of his prey. But instead of stepping over his leg, he lunged forward, planted his left foot on the floor, and swung a powerful roundhouse right kick toward Zon's head.

Zon watched the maneuvering calmly. His own self-control was what he needed. He fought back bitter memories of the scene onboard the plane, but just for a split second. Survival and victory rested on him internally.

The soldier's foot approached his head, but Zon didn't flinch. As it neared, he clinched his right fist and struck the oncoming leg bone, stopping the kick and badly bruising the soldier's shin. Instinctively, the soldier coiled his right leg, holding his knee chest high in perfect form, then threw the same foot toward Zon's stomach in a side kick. Again Zon countered with a crushing punch to the soldier's exposed shin. The soldier, now almost touching Zon's right shoulder to his chest, pulled his leg down and threw a series of punches with both hands. Zon countered, stopping each blow before it made contact by smacking the oncoming wrist with the side of his own, all with his right hand.

The soldier abandoned his first attack strategy and launched instantly into close-quarter fighting, throwing hard jabs and rakes with his elbows, head, and knees and seizing every opportunity to grab Zon by the head, side or neck. Zon blocked every lightning fast blow with a matching move. The soldier had thrown over thirty blows in ten seconds, none of which had landed. Tightening his neck, he snapped his eyes shut and lunged his flat forehead toward the bridge of Zon's nose. Zon coiled his left arm and planted his large rock hard elbow in the soldier's oncoming head. Teeth, cushioned by thin, bursting lips, cracked as bones collided.

The soldier recoiled, staggered back a couple of steps, then shook his head. He heaved his breath. Sweat soaked his camouflaged shirt. He stared intensely into Zon's calm eyes. His right leg ached from the punches to the shin. Bending over, he planted his hands on his knees to rest. He started to speak, but instead, spit blood and a broken front tooth from his mouth. The spittle struck the floor in a glob of streaky red and clear ooze. A small bead of red saliva clung to his lower lip. He didn't bother wiping it off.

Zon stood calmly as the soldier gathered his thoughts and recomposed his strategy of attack. He wasn't going to quit and Zon knew it.

"I tell ya, dark meat." The soldier had rediscovered his mouth. "You hit like a mule. I ain't never fucked wit' a brown mule before." The soldier pulled himself upright, and leaned slightly to his left to reduce the weight on his bruised right leg. Return of the smart mouth told Zon that the soldier's new strategy was complete and already into play. Still, he decided to wait, to watch, to learn.

The soldier shuffled to the middle of the open floor, between Zon and the crate of weapons, away from his disabled partner. Instead of going back into his fighting stance, he stood upright. His left hand massaged his bruised right wrist as he spoke.

"Let's see what round two's gonna look like," he said as he managed a smile with his mangled lips. Stepping right foot in front of left, the soldier drew in his fists into a left-handed boxing stance, and half-stepped his way toward Zon.

"Ya good in math, huh, boy?" Scarface taunted. Zon didn't respond. "Got a little test for ya. I'm about to put my left foot clear up yur ass." The scarred face twitched as the soldier made an unexpected wide-eye smile. "And I want you to count my toes as they slide 'tween yur cheeks." Hopping into the air, the would-be boxer did a quick foot shuffle as he returned to the floor, bobbed, wove his head and stepped in to deliver a left jab to Zon's chin. Zon blocked the shot, as well as the next three, as he had done before. The soldier persisted, throwing useless punch after useless punch. He threw yet another right, leaned back as if to throw a roundhouse, but instead drew up his right foot and slammed it hard into Zon's chest. Zon saw it coming, but let it land squarely, where it hardly phased him. Instead, the force of the kick launched the soldier backward into a rolling heap. And he rolled head over heel--right into the crate of weapons. He'd planned this all along, to seek a weapon, his weapon. Rolling to his feet, he grabbed his Uzi from the floor, locked it in his grip, and aimed it at Zon, who once again, was nowhere in sight.

"Shit!" the soldier screeched, his T-shirt dripping with sweat. He clinched the weapon hard in his hands, wrapped its leather strap twice about his arm, and assured himself that it would never again be kicked free. He swung wildly about, looking for Zon, pointing his gun in every direction, ready to fire instantly. A grin occupied his face, though this one was more of madness than humor.

"I'm gonna kill you! You black bastard!" the soldier screamed madly as he spun about, fearing an attack from any direction. "Disappearin' like a black ghost. Guess that makes you a spook, huh?" He laughed, hoping his taunts would force Zon to reveal himself. Only silence answered.

Zon had taken back to the rafters, and watched from above. He'd grabbed a handful of small screws from an open box as he leaped from the floor. He considered tossing them about to draw off the soldier's fire, but decided against it. This soldier was all too seasoned to fall for such an elementary stunt. Instead, Zon slung the screws directly at the gunman, hitting him in the arms and shoulders. The soldier reeled from the attack. Projectiles sliced through his skin like buckshot. Zon, quickly following the last of the shrapnel, landed on top of the soldier and knocked him to the floor. The soldier managed to hold on to his gun and aimed it skyward as he fell, pulling the trigger and riddling the roof with holes. Zon ducked the fire and kicked the gun. Scarface scrunched his face and yelled through clenched teeth as he tried to shoot Zon. Grabbing the hot end, Zon held it away until the gun clicked empty of ammunition. Zon snatched the gun away, threw it into the darkness, and stood over the soldier. The soldier, however, did not attack. Instead, he dropped his head to the floor and began laughing hysterically. Zon, tiring of the games, kneeled down and punched the soldier in the side of his head, which instantly knocked the laughter and consciousness out.

* * *

Zon stood up immediately after delivering the blow. Though he'd dreamed so long of this moment, he found it hollow. The pleasure of avenging himself against this assassin had been no pleasure at all. In fact, as much as he'd grown to hate this man, he could hardly generate the will to strike out and hurt him. Defense and stopping his assailant had been easy, but to willfully hurt or kill was another story, even if well deserved. Zon's thoughts surged as he walked back toward the disabled but conscious lead soldier. All his life, he'd been taught to never willfully hurt or kill, and had never before gotten the chance to do either until now. Could he do it? Would he have to do it? The answer had to be yes, but was it going to be? Did not his dislike for harm or death cause him to continually wait, to continually allow time for his enemy to regroup, readjust, only to attack again and again? If allowed, would this never have ended, his enemy attacking with ever renewed, more desperate and deadlier attacks? What would be accomplished? Never-ending circles with the attacker in complete control, able to fight or laugh, or join forces, or whatever, at his leisure? Nothing would ever change until someone got lucky, or made a mistake.

But nothing would get done. No progress would be made. Zon thought of his days back in college, on the basketball court. It had always seemed odd that he played his best basketball when outmanned. If the teams were even, his shot would be off. Worse still, if the man covering him was pitifully outmatched, and his team didn't need him, then his contribution would be nonexistent, no matter how hard he tried. It was always the same. Once even, in an intramural play-off, he'd been matched up one-on-one against a short blond fellow with a broken arm. Zon lost the game eleven to seven.

Now it all made sense. In his own little world, he wanted no one to lose. At most, he'd play for the draw. But what if the world were counting on him playing for the draw, like these soldiers. Was he doomed to wait until he eventually lost?

"Nonsense," Idrisi had explained. "In a game, winning and losing are the same. Therefore, play for the game itself. But understand, life is not a game. It must be lived. If it is to be made better, then make it so."

Zon pondered as he approached the soldier, still struggling on the floor to free his joints. His game with the scarred soldier brought him dangerously close to death. He had played it too long, but it had taught him a valuable lesson. For the first time that night, Zon spoke.

"How's it feel?" he solemnly asked the soldier.

"Just who the hell are you anyway?" the soldier replied.

"I'm the man who's put an end to you and your partner over there." He nodded his head in the direction of the other soldier. "Beyond that, I'm not quite sure myself."

"I'm not quite sure myself," the soldier mocked. "You haven't stopped anything. Who sent you? Gadhafi? KGB?"

"You wouldn't believe me if I told you. At times, I don't believe it."

"It don't matter. You didn't stop the revolt," the soldier said, finally giving up trying to free himself. "They're probably blowin' a hole in your fearless leader's head right now." Zon held his head up and listened to the silence as the soldier finished his words. He could hear in the far off distance approaching cars or trucks, rushing toward them.

"My guess is," Zon replied, "your soldier friend's wild gunfire may have alerted this whole city to your mischief. If my guess is right, you'll be finding out here in a few minutes."

"Is my friend dead?"

"No."

"You gonna kill us?" the soldier asked. Zon hesitated before answering.

"Would you kill innocently?" he asked the soldier. "Would you rape innocently?"

"Listen, you jungle bunny, in case you haven't figured it out by now, nobody's innocent. All of us, in one form or another, are as guilty as sin! I've killed and I've raped, and would do it again for the right cause."

Zon stared down into the villain's wild eyes, then remembered his gyrating hips as he raped the dead body on the plane.

"How can you attach guilt to a dead body?" Zon asked passionately.

"What dead body? What are you talking about?"

"I was on that plane. Remember? Three years ago . . . it was bound for Zaire. You and your partner hijacked it." The soldier stopped struggling and pondered.

"Oh yeah . . . ," he sneered, "We iced several nobodies, and . . . that girl. My buddy over there shot her before I got a chance to . . . " The soldier paused, noticing a change in Zon's demeanor. "Yeah," he said slyly, "She was about the nicest piece of dead meat I ever sunk my prick into." He laughed. Once again, the game had begun. If his partner wasn't dead, and if Zon was right about approaching vehicles, then there was a chance for him to escape. Zon had proven more than a worthy opponent in battle. He'd witnessed that. But he obviously had no experience in it because he talked too much.

The seasoned soldier opened his mouth, seeking to keep his captor yakking, but realized a sudden touch of wooziness, which passed as quickly as it had come.

"She wasn't your sister, was she?" he continued. "No, she was too pretty. And you . . . too dark." The soldier laughed again. "But where were you? We killed everyone onboard."

"I was the one that shoved you as I jumped from the plane," Zon answered, speaking stiffly, noticing the anger that had built in his voice.

"What? That was you? No shit! Boy, you knocked that girl clean out of my hand . . . and . . . and I caught my tool in my zipper! You know, I was so mad after that, that as soon as me an' my buddy landed, I grabbed the first jungle girl I could get my hands on and finished my business. Don't believe I missed a stroke either." The soldier watched Zon's eyes for reaction, hoping to strike a nerve. He had gotten to Zon again, but not quite enough. "Oh yeah," he continued, "I blew her brains out first with my pistol. I find dead meat so much more satisfying." The soldier added a smile. He wanted his partner to awaken or the doors to bust open, but detected no activity from either.

He opened his mouth again, convinced that Zon wasn't going to kill him. But as he started to speak, Zon cast his eyes away and scanned the warehouse. He then walked off toward a stand of small boxes.

"Hey! Where ya goin'?" the soldier yelled. Zon paid him no mind. He tried to read the markings on the box, but all print was in Arabic. Zon thrust his fist through the box, shattering the wooden crate top into splinters. Reaching in, he retrieved a can of olives. Quickly throwing those aside, he walked over to the next stack and did the same. Canned jelly. In the third stack, he found canned tuna. Zon grabbed a can and returned to the cadaver-loving soldier.

"Hey, where'd you g . . ." The soldier hadn't finished his sentence when Zon marched up to him, reached down, grabbed the knife from his right hand, and in a single swing, split the soldier's trousers from waist to cuff.

"Hey! What're you doin'?" The soldier wailed, peering down at his exposed leopard-spotted bikini briefs. Reaching in with the knife, Zon cleanly cut those away with a single stroke. "What are you? Fag?" The startled soldier exclaimed as Zon dropped the knife, just out of his reach.

"No," Zon answered calmly, "I was just wondering if you were as good with living meat as you were with the dead."

"Huh?" The puzzled soldier exclaimed as he watched Zon, not knowing what to expect next. Zon jabbed his stiffened forefinger into the can of tuna, then emptied its oils and juices onto the soldier's genitals.

"Hey! Hey!" the soldier yelled ever so loudly, hoping to arouse his partner, "that ain't alive . . . and it's cold as hell." Zon shook chunks of the canned fish onto the soldier's legs, then began walking for the rear exit. As he strolled, he could hear the sound of approaching sirens, though they were still some distance away.

"What are you going to do?" the soldier yelled as Zon stepped out of his sight, leaving a trail of tuna as he stepped away. Zon spoke with an air of detachment.

"I'd say your gun-running days are up. Judging from the sound of those sirens, the Libyan authorities are about to invade your little arsenal here and they probably won't like what they find. I'd bet, too, that they probably have been trying to get their hands on you two for some time. I'm going to leave you to them. As for you and your sexual perversion," he said, stepping halfway through the small exit at the back of the warehouse, "I met a few wild numbers on my way in here that would just love to get a hold of you."

"What?" exclaimed the soldier. Zon knelt down in the doorway and whispered tenderly,

"Here, kitty, kitty, kitty!" Seven of the large, hungry wild alley cats, the size of small dogs, charged him. As they caught scent of the can in his hand, Zon tossed it across the warehouse and into the disabled soldier's lap, then shut the door behind him.

* * *

Troop carriers pulled up outside the warehouse entrance as two others sped around the sides toward the back. Zon scaled the alley wall and headed for the harbor. He'd decided to take a boat, rather than a plane, back to the United States. It would take longer, but he was in no hurry.

Soldiers with automatic weapons jumped from the trucks, ran to the closed front door, then froze.

"Listen," called the platoon leader, as they pressed their ears to the door. Through the heavy wood floated frenzied screams of carnal pain . . . and carnivorous delight.

7
BACK TO THE USA

Billy Davis sat on a high stool, shivering with anxiety. The small, white plastic cup in hand, which had been nearly full with sixty dollars in quarters, now felt light in his grasp. Coins barely covered the bottom.

"Come on, now!" he shouted silently under his breath, as he reached his right hand into the cup, retrieved a quarter, and dropped it into the slot machine. His eyes were red from lack of sleep. They strained, trying to follow and coax the spinning pictures to match up.

"Come on, baby, we five hundud behind. Cain't go home broke. This is you . . . this is you . . . be there fo' me . . . come on, sweet Jesus!"

The night before, Billy's coaxing of the gambling machines had been calm, almost sensuous. Now however, it was frantic. The night of gambling had left stubble on his aging face. His clothes, like his mind, were in utter disarray.

It was 4:00 A.M. on a Saturday. Billy had arrived in Atlantic City that Friday evening. He'd taken only a brief moment when he arrived to check into his room, shower, and eat a quick burger out on the boardwalk. The rest of the time had been spent at the slot machines. His trembling hand steadied as he pulled down on the machine's arm.

"Come on, baby. Ya just don't know! It's got to be. It's just got to be." Billy's face crinkled as he spoke the last words before releasing the arm. He watched with crying eyes as the multicolored fruit spun to a stop.

"That's it, baby. Got an o'ange, need another . . . need another

. . . yeah . . . yeah . . . got two . . . got two . . . one mo' . . . one mo', baby . . . roll on . . . roll o . . . " The third spinner stopped on a bunch of purple grapes and Billy's quarter fell into the return pan, cranking out its metallic laughter as it spun to a halt. "Shit . . . shit . . . shi . . . i . . . t !" Billy's slobber dripped into his cup as he punched away at the machine. "Ya piece a shit, ya rotten piece a shit." He pressed his broad nose against the faceplate of the machine as he spoke. His jaunts and taunts, though subdued, were still audible to passersby.

"Piece a sh . . . " Billy caught himself in midword, pulled his face away from the machine, and cut his eyes around. A small crowd had gathered. Some were snickering, others stood with their mouths drawn up in disgust. A security guard, who stood in front of the group, stepped forward and addressed him calmly.

"Sir, you are disturbing our other guests," he said. "If you can't control yourself better, we'll have to ask you to leave."

"Oh . . . ah . . . sorry 'bout dat," Billy whimpered and flashed a sheepish grin at the guard, who along with the onlookers, turned and moved on. He dropped his head, turned back to the machine, and reached down to retrieve his returned quarter.

"I know it's gotta be this machine . . . this machine . . . number one-thirty-two. That's ma lucky numba. Come on, neah. Baby, do me right." Again, Billy guided his quarter back to the hungry mouth of the slot machine. "Once a year, once a long-assed, sorry-tailed year," he muttered as he inserted his remaining coins. "Just one time da whole fuckin' year, I come here. I put down my job, take care home business, leave the wife and kids, get a deacon at church to stand in fo' me, and come play deese sorry-ass machines." Melon slices, cherries and oranges came up on the machine. "Fixin' dem ol wone-out cars . . . folks nowadays 'spect ya patch the patches on dem old wrecks for nothin'. But I do it. I do it better'n most. Make a damn good livin' of it, too . . . for me and that fat white tight ass I work fo'. Shit, aughta start my own shop. Make my own damn money. Put *his* fat ass to work."

Billy paused, then smiled at his words. "Seems like I say dat eva year when I come here, den go right back home and keep doin' what I always done. Always the same ol' song."

Billy peered down into his cup. There were four quarters left.

"A dolla, the story of my life. Down to my last damn dolla. Came here with five hundud." He grabbed a quarter and placed it to drop, begging and pleading the machine as he stared on. Just as he went to release the coin, he froze. An eerie feeling came over him, as if someone were staring a hole right through him. He snatched the coin down from the machine and turned. Behind him stood a . . . a bum, wearing checkered double knit polyester bell-bottomed pants, a tattered cotton shirt, raggedy blue flip-flops, and a heavy dog-eared cap pulled well down over his head, causing his ears to stick out. His back and shoulders curved forward and his mouth hung slightly open. Oddly enough, his teeth glistened and he had no unpleasant odor about him.

"Who let choo in heeya?" Billy scoffed at the bum, but got no reply. "Thought they stop y'all at the doe . . . Wha' chu waunt?" He stood squinting at the bum, who stood speechless. "Ain't gonna speak?" Billy asked. "Suit yaself, then." Cautiously, he returned the coin to the slot, but kept half an eye on the stranger. Though he appeared harmless and simple minded, the bum was larger than Billy, and that was enough to warrant caution.

As the coin neared the slot, the bum started shaking his head slowly back and forth, first left, then right, then left, the motion catching Billy's eye. Billy stopped again.

"Wha' da hell do you waunt?" Billy demanded. Again, no reply. "Look . . . move on! Go fin' some otha loosa." Billy turned back to the machine, dismissing the bum, dropped the coin, pulled the handle, and listened as the slot machine spun to another disappointing halt.

"Shit! No fuckin' luck! No fuckin' luck!" He turned his attention completely to the machine again as he grabbed another coin. "Look, it's now . . . or neva," he pleaded. "Come on sweetness, bring ah leetle back fo' me." Billy went to kiss the coin before he fed it to the machine, but stopped as he realized the bum was still watching. Lips puckered and sweat forming on his brow, he faced the bum again, who, after shaking his head "no" twice more, turned his eyes toward a machine two down from Billy's and nodded toward it.

"Wha?" Billy said with a chuckle. "You wan' me to listen ta you? Oh, you gonna share some of your luck with me, huh? Well no the-hell-thank ya." Billy's coin ricocheted off the internal machine parts after he dropped it. The wheels spun and stopped, with no sweet sound of falling coins.

"Load Jesus!" Billy grimaced, then fell against the slot machine as he whispered his screaming cry of mercy. Visibly shaken, he stuck his trembling fingers into the cup for his last quarter. Grabbing hold, he clinched it in his fist and squeezed as if trying to burst it open to reveal a new hoard of coins. Opening his eyes, he pushed away from the machine and raised his hand to drop his last coin. Stopping at its zenith, however, he turned slowly to the bum, expecting to see more head shaking. To his surprise, the bum wasn't shaking his head, but nodding "yes." Billy's knees started knocking.

"Oh, shit," he groaned. "Now a bum agrees wid me. I'm doomed, sho as hell, I'm doomed." Billy chuckled hysterically at himself, smiled, dropped the coin in the slot, and pulled the handle.

"Please, please, please, please . . . , " he chanted. The first wheel rested with cherries up, then the second, then finally . . . the third. The red light atop machine 132 shone and spun wildly as twenty-five dollars in coins splashed into the tray.

"Oh baby, my sweet baby," Billy sang aloud. He grinned from ear to ear as he shoveled the small fortune into his cup. "Fill my cup. Let it overflow! Hey, mo' money, mo' money, mo' money . . . " No sooner had he grabbed the last coin from the tray that he raised it again to feed the machine. But, before he dropped it, he peered over at the bum, who was again subtly shaking his head no.

"Oh, shit. Not again." Billy searched for a positive sign in the bums eyes, but found none. Instead the bum motioned to another slot machine two down from him, where a middle-aged white woman was pulling the handle. Billy watched as three gold bars popped up to her window, followed by bells, sirens, and thirty-five dollars in coins falling into her possession. His eyes bulged, then dove back deep into their sockets. His eyelids wrenched closed behind them. He then turned, expecting to see a look of "I told you so" on the bum's face. Instead, he saw the same dumbfounded face nodding at another machine four over to his right.

Nearly tumbling over backward, Billy leaped from his stool, then ran to the machine and played a quarter. The sound of bells, whistles, and falling coins hardly covered his shouts of ecstasy. Twenty-three dollars fell into his possession. He turned back toward the bum, who was limping stiffly away, his arms hanging rigidly down by his side. At first, Billy leaped after him, but realizing how his conspicuous winning and joyous shouts could alert others to the charm of the bum, he quickly collected himself. He straightened his collar, brushed off his coat sleeves, sniffed twice to clear his head, and looked around to be sure no one was watching. Then, he nonchalantly paced after the bum, who had rounded the end of the bank of one-armed-bandits and stood still. Billy did not approach him, but, watching his eyes, followed him to machine ninety-four, to which he stepped up to and dropped in his quarter, pulled the handle, and received another twenty-five dollars. Scooping up each one slowly and as inconspicuously as possible, he collected his winnings and followed the bum around the casino floor, winning every time. The bum's pace slowed after ten wins. The sound of other machines paying off their players sounded in between, confusing Billy's wins in a sea of scrambled bells and falling coins.

"Hey, hold up a minute," Billy whispered loudly toward the bum as he struggled to his side. He had long since discarded his white cup and was carrying his 2,000-plus dollars' worth of coins wrapped in his jacket. The load was heavy, but he managed. He continued to talk to the bum.

"Hold up heeya minute, so I can go turn this silva ta cash." The bum froze. Smiling, Billy backed away slowly toward the cashier's window, but kept his eyes firmly fixed on his lucky charm. He was afraid that the bum would disappear or take up with someone else while he was away. Still, he had no choice because of the weight of the coins. Once satisfied that the bum wasn't going to move, Billy turned and hustled away.

"I'll be right back, neah. Doncha go nowhere!" Billy shouted back as he darted through the thinning crowd toward the cashier's window.

* * *

Back in Morocco, Zon knew that whatever it was he was going to do in the United States, he wasn't going to do alone. There would be many people, well versed in their art, to complement his effort.

After a visit to the newsstand and bookshop in Morocco, he collected his bag (with Boo-Boo and the Kaldaca Stone) and stowed away on an empty Greek-registered oil tanker headed for the shipyard in Chester, Pennsylvania, just outside of Philadelphia. This ship would enter at the Delaware River and sail upstream, passing within a few miles of Atlantic City.

The journey took two weeks, which gave Zon plenty of time to study his literary treasures of Washington, DuBois, X, Thomas, Fuller, Brown, Diop, Kejufu, Jones, and others. It also lent him time to meditate as he searched for the purpose of his quest.

In the evenings, he jumped ship to fish beneath the waves for food for Boo-Boo. He ate nothing during the journey.

"Hungry stomach makes a hungry mind . . . and willing hands," Idrisi had quoted, too often. Zon spoke calmly to Boo-Boo as he stared into her eyes. He sat easily in the hook of the large anchor which hung from the front left side of the ship. Boo-Boo sat contentedly upon his lap. Her tail swayed lazily in the misty sea air. She had grown quite a bit during his journey out of Africa and was now the size of a large dog. Yet, she purred contentedly as Zon massaged her between the ears with his forefinger.

"Everyone I know back home would laugh if I told them what I was going to do," he confided to his feline friend as the vessel made its way into the mouth of the Delaware River. The huge ship crashed against the waves as it moved along the water, but Zon and the cat could hear the hunting seagulls and crashing surf in the far distance. They had been at sea for thirteen days. Zon had grown lean from fasting, Boo-Boo fat from lack of exercise. "We'll be leaving tonight," he said to the cat. "Welcome home." He let forth a small sigh. Boo-Boo purred gently as the ship headed inland.

The beaches of gray sand, combined with the broken skyline of concrete and glass, signaled their arrival in Atlantic City. Zon had jumped ship during the night while still several miles out. He had tucked Boo-Boo and the Kaldaca Stone snugly inside a waterproof sack. The cat was not used to the cold and could have easily drowned. The Kaldaca Stone would have begun immediately to spew bubbling gases toward the heavens if it came in contact with the water. Zon held the dark sack high above the icy water as he swam to shore, the sight resembling the traveling periscope of a submarine. Swimming for such a distance in bone-chilling waters was no great feat for him, though it would have been impossible just a few short years before. Boo-Boo held no fear as she crouched inside the pouch. Zon talked to her calmly as he swam. Tremendous effort had gone into securing his anonymity, and it was an absolute must for him now. This unannounced entry into the United States maintained it.

Standing on his native soil gave him a serene sense of comfort. He stood naked but for his loincloth, on sandy Atlantic City Beach, his lean body glistening with icy droplets from the Atlantic. The feeling of the sand, the twinkling city lights, and smells of the frosty boardwalk filled his mind with long-forgotten thoughts of home, his friends, his life, and past dreams of his future. A small spark of sadness lit in his chest. He would never realize the dreams that had been so solidly planted in his mind by the loving and caring people who surrounded him as a child. Cars, women, good times, beach trips, weekends, all were now only dreams of a young boy's past that would never be fulfilled. And what of his past friends, were they in the midst of all of this predestined pleasure? Were they married, working, rich, alive? For the first time, Zon felt the emotional loss of his life, his past, his present, his dreams. But, he was now far more than he ever could have been before. Yet it did not ease the sadness that accompanied the memories of his past.

Zon stood quietly in the cold as two lovers, strolling the deserted beach, passed by him and laughed.

"Get some clothes on, fool!" shouted the larger black silhouette, without turning his head or missing a stride. The words didn't faze him, but did retrieve him from his past and might-have-been future. He stood naked on a cold Atlantic City Beach. Casinos, the boardwalk, gamblers, and people lay before him.

* * *

Clothing had been so unnecessary in Beinin and most of Africa for the last four years, not because of heathenism, as most of American history had taught, but purely out of necessity. Clothing protects from heat and sun, or the lack thereof. One equipped with dark skin and generations of exposure had no need for protection. Therefore, clothing, instead of protection, was necessary only for humility (or to reduce bouncing during times of extreme exertion). Although the temperature was near freezing, Zon felt neither cold nor humiliation as he stood on Atlantic City Beach in the pale moonlight. He stood quietly, taking in the industrialized scene. The sand, though gray, appeared as blue as the moonlight. His skin took on a blue hue as well. The Bolo established his bodily comfort from within, making him all but oblivious to the chilly climate.

Still, it was more important for him to fit in here. This was home, his home, and he needed to fit in. Clothes were the first order of business. Zon found a line of clothing hanging across an alleyway in the lower part of Atlantic City. The old tattered clothes barely fit, but were a perfect disguise. He retrieved a dog-eared hat from a trash can in that same alley, as well as a pair of leather boots with holes in the soles. But before he could put them on, a shivering bum lying next to the can clawed them away from him. Zon, seeing the greater need, let the boots go. The bum cast aside a raggedy pair of flip-flops as he pulled on the old boots. Zon serenely grabbed them, slipped them over his feet, and walked away.

"Clothing down," he said contentedly. "Next, I need some wheels, my own special kind." Satisfied with his progress, he walked toward the Golden Palace Casino.

No man was an island, and Zon wasn't about to be the exception. He needed people, not necessarily rich or black or young, but those with a gift--and who could be trusted.

People walked widely around him as he stood at the Golden Palace entrance, some holding their noses, others tossing a quarter of their winnings to him and several other street people who stood near by. Zon watched each, listening to their conversation as they passed. None of them fit the mold he'd formed in his mind of his first recruit. He stepped to the doorway, but was quickly confronted by three large men, two European and one Hispanic. All were large and muscular. Zon curled his shoulders over and dropped his mouth open, then stepped back out of the door. The bouncers turned and moved back inside. He stopped at the bottom of the stairs, rubbed his chin, and looked about as he pondered a means to inconspicuously get inside. Well-financed and formerly-financed patrons walked freely back and forth through the giant doors. Just then, a tall old man dressed in jeans and boots came waltzing out of the casino wearing a grin that stretched from ear to ear.

"Out of my way, boys!" he yelled at the bouncers as he careened through the doors. He was nearly drunk. His wallet bulged with the night's winnings. "I'm fifty thousand dollars richer!" he yelled. A young blond hung on to his arm, pulling him through the exit. She spoke, coaxing the old man.

"Come on, baby. Now you don't want all of these people to know our business, do ya, honey?"

"What do you mean, our business?" the old man replied. "I won this money. It's mine. If ya good, then I might give some of it to you. But doncha get uppity now, young filly." The old man reached around and slapped the girl on the buttocks. "This is my money," he said again as he reached to retrieve his wallet. Pulling out twenties, he began waving the greenbacks back and forth as he and the lady descended the stairs. "I'll do with it as I damn well please."

"Okay, baby, whatever you say. Come on, let's get away from here." The young girl spoke apologetically, eyeing the money in the old man's hands while pulling at his left arm.

A long black limousine sat on the curb, waiting for the approaching couple. The old man started to put his money back, then turned, his eyes widened with a thrilling revelation. He yelled toward Zon.

"Hey, you! Come get this!" Zon walked slowly up to the man, held out his hand and received three crisp twenty-dollar bills. The girl grabbed at the money, but missed as Zon crushed the bills in his fist, turned, and walked away.

"What in the hell ya do that for?" she screamed at the old man.

"How the hell do I know?" he yelled back. "Besides, it's my money, ain't it? I can do whatever I please. Get in the cab and shut up!"

Zon climbed the stairs slowly as the cab drove away. He'd had plenty of opportunity to practice his mind linking during his voyage across the Atlantic. Many of the tanker crew members had thought, said, and done deeds not completely of their own free will. Zon also had learned he could, at best, only suggest and influence his thoughts upon others. But he couldn't make them do anything they didn't want to do. Oftentimes, he couldn't read their thoughts either, but felt this skill would grow stronger with time. He'd suggested to the old man that he give his money away to show the lady who was in charge. Since this was in line with what the old fellow was thinking anyway, he readily obliged.

As Zon stepped through the door, the first of the hulking men approached him. Zon folded one of the twenties between his fingers, then laid it into the man's chest. The bouncer, surprised by this gesture, grasped the note and stepped back. The second was there waiting, but received a twenty, as did the third. Each stood holding the money and looking puzzled as the ill-clad bum walked past them and down the corridor to the casino floor.

* * *

It hadn't taken Zon long to spot Billy Davis. He'd told his life story to the slot machine as he sat playing his money away. From this overheard conversation, Zon knew Billy would be his first recruit. He watched him lose most of his money, and decided the best way for them to become acquainted was for him to win the money back.

Studying the slot machine, Zon quickly defined the sounds of the spinning wheels that carried the pictures about. Proper alignment of the three or four wheels as they spun to a halt meant an instant payoff of various sizes. Four-wheeled machines carried ten possible slots of alignment, which meant a nearly infinite number of possible combinations. However, their alignment was the key, of which there were relatively few. Wheels, stopping in proper alignment to pay off, sounded different. Zon listened until he became attuned to those sounds. The wheels, though randomly showing their colorful pictures, exhibited a pattern of sounds in which a payoff was deeply buried. Using his keen sense of hearing, Zon studied the patterns until he had deciphered their rhythms. Having done this, it was simply a matter of listening and playing in the right sequence to always hit the payoff.

Billy had returned from the cashier's window. He'd exchanged all but twenty dollars of his quarters into greenbacks. Zon knew he had to be convinced to cooperate. What better way to do this than win his money back.

"Where now, buddy?" Billy smiled broadly as he spoke to Zon. Though much friendlier than before, he maintained a respectable distance. Winning back his money had not overcome his distaste for a bum. Zon, instead of moving on to the next win, stood still.

"Now what, buddy?" Billy asked politely again. Zon gave Billy a quick glance, then walked off across the colorful gambling floor. Billy craned his neck to and fro as he followed at a respectable distance, trying to keep up with Zon yet trying not to appear too conspicuous nor in too big of a hurry to follow. Zon zigzagged his way away from the slot machines through the thick corridor of blackjack tables, then, between the roulette wheels, past the large seated poker tables, and into a darkened corner near the back of the casino. Long, sheer white drapery hung from the ceiling, just in front of the corner. Zon walked behind the curtain.

Billy's hopes rose and fell as Zon walked toward, then by each of the gambling stops. He moaned aloud as Zon walked off the gambling floor.

"Oh Load, boy! Wha's wroung?" Wha's wroung now? Ya lose your touch?" Billy stood outside the curtains, his back turned to Zon. He spoke calmly, trying not to move his lips. Reaching behind the curtains, he grabbed Zon by the arm and tried to pull him out. Zon didn't move.

"Hey. Wha's up? Man, you cain't quit on me now. You and me, we can . . . "

"You said you'd build a garage," Zon broke in. Billy whipped his head around to stare into Zon's eyes. Zon's speech, voice, and solid response caught him completely off guard.

"Wha'd ya say?" Billy asked as he stared.

"Turn back around. Don't look at me." Zon waited as Billy, confused now more than ever, turned back to the casino. "You said you'd build a garage if you ever got the money."

"Yeah, I said it. But wha's that got ta do wit' you, and why didn't ya speak up earlier . . . and how come ya can talk so good . . . and where did . . . "

"Listen," Zon interrupted again. "How much would it take?"

"Take? To do what?"

"Build your garage." Billy was confused. This sudden shift,

coupled with the fatigue from the long night of gambling, blurred his thinking. He couldn't figure out what to do. He decided to answer the bum's questions until he could decide his next move.

"Oh . . . ya mean some place fo' me to tinker on my caw, or a nice big place a business?"

"The nice business place."

"Where I could fix a broke caw, or build a caw from scratch?"

"From scratch."

"Ya mean scrap metal to road?"

"Yes." Billy paused. He was still confused. The bum wasn't who he appeared to be, and that meant maybe he couldn't be trusted. But he had helped him to win back his money . . . but was that a con? And why was he so interested in the business? What was his plan? Billy had to know more, but he didn't open his mouth to ask more questions. Instead, he thought of the money he carried in his pocket. The bum had been good for that money, and was now asking if he needed more. Was he teasing, or could he really help him acquire his dream? And what harm would it be in humoring the bum? He was even. At worst, he could return with just a bit more money than he'd left with. How much would such a shop cost anyway? The welding stall and all of its equipment, the engine diagnostics, body shop, storage, air compressors, lifts . . . the list was long.

"'Bout $300,000." Billy let the words slip easily from his lips and chuckled lightly as he once again realized he was talking to a bum. "Why you ask? Ya gonna help me with the cash?" he snickered.

"Yes." Zon answered in the same serious, yet pleasant tone.

"Yeah, right," Billy said with a huff. "Look. If ya say ya will, then ya will, only let's get back to the slots, okay?" Billy's lust for gambling filled his voice with a pitiful plea. Zon continued.

"It must be a large place. You must own it, alone."

"Ya serious 'bout this shit, ain't ya?" Billy asked as he turned and stepped away. "Okay, okay. I seen what you can do with the machines," he said, speaking his thoughts. "If someone a told me that ya coulda done it, no way in hell I wouda believed 'em. But I seen it wit' my own two eyes. Now, ya wanna gi' me mo' money. Somethin' 'round $300,000. Ya jus' wanna gi' me dat money ta build my own place, right?"

"Yes," answered Zon.

"Well, wha's da catch?"

"There are several," Zon replied with a faint smile. "First, you'll gamble no more. Next, you'll maintain complete ownership of your shop, regardless of your income or success. Finally, you will tell no one of me, how we met, or of our business together."

"Business together?" Billy replied. "What business together?"

"I'll bring to you drawings and plans for a car. You will build it." Billy stared back at Zon without speaking. Finally, a chance had come for him to change his life, as he so often had spoken and dreamed of. Even if it never materialized, or he failed in the trying, it wasn't going to cost him anything.

"It sho' would feel good ta tell that slave-drivin' boss of mine off." Billy smiled broadly at Zon. "Listen, I'll do it. All ya got ta do is get that sweet cash ta flowin'. But I guess we'd betta get started if we goin' ta clear that kinda money with the slots."

"Just one more slot," Zon said, watching Billy's head pop up like a deer caught in approaching headlights.

"Ya mean I'm gonna hit the big one tonight? Load Jesus, man! That machine ain't paid off in two years. It's got over seven hundut thousand dollars in instant payoff, plus a hundut grand a year fo' da next twenty years. If I, ah, we hit dat, we'll have all da money we could ever wan'." Billy started shuffling his weight from foot to foot. Zon smiled.

"You will hit on that machine tonight. You take all of the money. You're going to give some of it away, build the shop and my machines, and run your business." Zon walked away as he spoke. When he got within sight of the Big Jackpot slot machine, he stopped.

"There will be cameras. I don't want to be associated with the winnings. You go on from here. Once you get the money, go home and begin what we have planned. Don't worry about me. I'll contact you." Zon paused for a second and held his index finger up toward Billy's face as if to silence him. An elderly white man stepped up to the Big Jackpot slot machine to play his dollar coin. Zon listened.

"Oh, no!" Billy screamed under his breath. "Somebody gonna beat us to our money!"

"Quiet!" Zon hushed Billy, and listened. The old man dropped five coins, pulling the arm down five times. The large machine spun and clicked loudly, drawing little attention from other gamblers nearby. The machine spun each time to match no more than three of the five "jackpot" markings necessary to win. After the five spins, the man turned slowly and walked toward the casino exit.

"Go back to the cashier," Zon said, turning back to face Billy, "and retrieve one-thousand, two-hundred and eighty-two dollars in silver dollars. It will take that many to win."

"Wha'?" Billy responded. "Ya neva said a thang 'bout me riskin' my own money. Man, I just won it."

"You'll win on the one-thousand, two-hundred and eighty-second pull," Zon responded assuredly.

"Ya sure 'bout this?" Billy looked long into Zon's confident eyes. Reaching into his pocket, he retrieved his wallet, took out the cash, turned and shuffled toward the cashier, talking aloud as he went.

"I must be the bigges' fool this side of heaven. Riskin' my own money on a bum . . . on a *bum*!" Even worse, promisin' ta quit gamblin'. My mama always said a bird in the hand's worth two in the bush. I should jus' keep on walkin'. But seven hundred thousan' dollas. Can't just walk away. Just can't. I done lost my mind . . . been 'wake too long, tha's it. My brain's fried . . . Southern fried wit' a side orda biscuits and redeye gravy. Shoot," he added as he smacked his jowls, "must be hungry, too." Billy walked up to the cashier and retrieved the silver-colored coins, then returned to the jackpot machine, mumbling all the way.

"Well, here goes nothin'," he said as he perused the open floor about the machine. He saw no bum, just other gamblers carrying the same hope as he, that of instant fortune. Reaching into his large bucket full of silver dollars, he began singing and dropping the coins in rhythm:

"This ain't no damn fun . . . I'm droppin' ma money for a bum."

8
RAPE OF AURORA

Zon sat quietly upon the cool wet concrete at the street corner, his legs extended and crossed, his eyes fixed forward in a penetrating stare. A warm July mist hung in the air. Across the street stood the county jail of Aurora, Mississippi, a small town that time had passed by. The eighties and nineties had graced it with ample luxuries of modern man, but had stopped far short of gracing the minds of its citizens.

Neighborhoods were racially divided, black people to the west, whites to the east. Air-conditioning resided on the east side, along with most of the indoor plumbing. The population was forty percent black, yet all of the town officials were white, from the mayor right down to the town drunk. Black vagrants were jailed or run out of town. Voting district maps resembled tracks left by a herd of lovesick snails, cutting back and forth in no set pattern, intentionally drawn to empower the white vote. And it did the job well, a living model for the new South Africa's apartheid-free society.

In spite of air-conditioning, fuel-injected four-wheel-drive monster trucks, and computer-designed auto stereo systems, life floated along as if it were the 1930s, rather than 1990s, in Aurora, Mississippi.

Zon pondered Aurora's time warp as he stared through the mist. The thoughts were not at all upsetting, just puzzling. Time stood still, not in the place, but in the people, in whites and blacks alike. Since his return from Africa, he often listened to black leaders, preachers, and politicians. He'd listened before his journey to Beinin as well.

Now, though the words were the same, he heard a different message. Over and over, Idrisi's wisdom rung true about every speech.

"God teaches us all," Idrisi had taught, "where blame lies, there lies also power." He had to look up as he talked to Zon and often shook his head in disgust as he lectured. "Blacks in America . . . you are blameless." Opening his hand wide, he'd smack Zon firmly on his shaven head, sometimes delivering one smack per word for emphasis. People from the outside always kept three or more thoughts going at once, even in their sleep. Zon was no different. The slaps allowed only the present, that which he now saw and heard, to occupy his mind.

"I listen to your leaders and laugh . . . ha!" Idrisi had continued. "Their words are filled with 'they', never 'I'. They brought us over here . . . they won't give us a chance . . . they hate us . . . somebody ought to do something," he'd whine babyishly. "In everyone, it is always the same." He then stared hard into Zon's eyes. "You know," he'd snap. "You think, by magic . . . if the fault is not yours, then you are not responsible and you have nothing to do. Only people with something to do, do something. Therefore, you do nothing. You have nothing to do. The world becomes worse, but you are free to do as you please. You have accepted no blame. You have accepted no power. Yet you cry because you are powerless." The words sunk deep into Zon's mind, as did respect for this wise Beininian man.

Most people in Aurora, black and white, blamed everyone else. Still, that left all the more power to the few, the proud, and in this case, the evil. Aurora needed cleansing, a push in the right direction . . . and they were about to get it.

Zon's clothing was soaked, though his skin remained dry from body-fueled evaporation. He wore worn-out jeans that stretched tightly across his thick bulging thighs and a brown *pleather* (fake plastic leather) coat that hung to his knees when he stood. The coat collar stood up straight, silhouetting his face in the misty streetlight. It was a simple, effective disguise. The locals, black and white, were all too eager to judge a man by his look.

The streets were silent but for the fluorescent lights buzzing overhead, and the occasional candle fly crashing into the bulb. Rain droplets, formed by the light mist falling on this hazy night, dripped steadily from the inclined, gutterless building roofs.

Inside the jailhouse, Sheriff Don Baker and two deputies bantered nervously with one another.

"If you're not in this with us, then get the hell outta here!" Sheriff Baker screeched. His neck bulged with swollen veins. His cherry red face looked more like that of a heart attack victim rather than sheriff. Brad Duncan, the younger deputy, had cold feet. He wanted to leave and have no part of the night's events. Yet, he was afraid to leave, afraid of his family, his lost friends, and his own conscience if he walked out the door. He turned, faced the sheriff sheepishly, and spoke through his constricted throat, trying to sound as arrogant and outraged as his superior officer.

"I'm in this, too. That nigger has to die tonight, but we ain't gonna kill him . . . l-l-least not here, are we?" Sheriff Baker looked at Brad.

"You chickenshit," he said. "Don't you worry 'bout who, when, or where. All you need do is stick around, turn your back, and wake up in the morning as innocent as you were the night before. Things have changed. I don't know which is worse, niggers or nigger lovers. Them damn Feds will be crawlin' up our asses. They care less 'bout that boy back there than we do. But now days, moral decency and racial pride takes a hairy-assed backseat to politicin' and money makin'. There'll be nigger lovers, long's it keeps the money flowin' into their greedy pockets. Ain't no damn difference 'tween right and wrong no more."

Don's gaze dropped to the floor as his voice trailed away. In his mind, he visualized the scene of tomorrow morning: the TV cameras, the federal and state police, all the outraged and self-righteous gathered into his tiny jailhouse. He jerked his head around to face Brad and Jason Attux, the other deputy, who looked on with startled expressions. "There'll be an investigation," the sheriff said solemnly. "We're on our own. Them fed'ral boys'll offer us sympathy, but that's 'bout all we can count on." Don paused thoughtfully. "But, them boys love themselves a victim, so that's what we gonna be." He grinned as he thought through the cunning of their plan. "The boys'll come in here, bang us all on the head, take old Johnny back there, and carry out justice. We'll be bruised up a little, but it's a small price to pay to put things right again. Yeah," he sighed. "We'll be just innocent victims, overpowered by an unknown mob and left here unconscious in ole Johnny's cell."

The aspect of innocence and justice went over well with the two young deputies. Both breathed a sigh of relief, until they realized that they'd just traded their unbreached skulls for contusions and possible concussions, all in the name of justice.

Zon sat like melting ice upon the sidewalk. Misty rain dripped off his crumpled wide-brimmed hat. It was 11:30. He peered over and beyond the jail, then fixed his focus on the small knoll several hundred feet beyond. There, he spied twelve men stealing their way through the muddy thicket. Sounds of snapping branches, sucking noises from boots breaking free of the mud and an occasional "yelp" from one of the men being raked across the face by briars easily found their way to Zon's enhanced ears.

He followed their movement down the knoll until they disappeared behind the jail. His muscles tighten with anticipation. It had been a while since he last confronted an adversary, physically, and he welcomed the opportunity. Mental conquests had their place, but a man's body was built to fight. Zonbolo exploded from within, transforming his body, awakening his senses. This was The Bolo, older than the pharaohs, refined during a time when only savagery existed north of the Mediterranean. Energy engulfed his body as his muscles flexed, bulged, and hardened. He sat motionless, but his clothing seemed alive, struggling to contain his pulsing flesh.

Though he sat as motionless as the sidewalk, he caught the eye of a couple of locals exiting a bar at the street's end. He felt their gaze as they stepped through the pub's exit. Neither was drunk, but both had had enough and needed to massage their egos. An unsuspecting victim on a quiet street corner was more than adequate to inspire them into a little razzing and black ass-kicking to top off the night. Zon remained statuesque, seated on the corner, in the misty rain.

"Would'cha lookie there. Now there's a darky needin' a ass-whoopin' if'n I ever saw one." Cal, the larger of the two, spoke in a low, drunken manner, hoping not to alert the bum on the corner.

"Damn it, Cal," Peck, the smaller man snapped as he careened an ounce of tobacco juice across the bar's picture window, "can't you find somethin' more worth our while to fool with? That old nigger over there ain't gonna fight back. He'll just stand there, doin' and sayin' whatever he has to save his ass. Hell, we oughta be lynchin' that ole coon in the jail, 'stead a sweepin' the sidewalk with Uncle Tom over there." Peck was a little more drunk than Cal, but had a bit more common sense.

Cal was known as the town bully and rarely passed up the chance to further his name. He towered over most people in Aurora and had been the local high school's Mr. Everything in sports. But he'd missed any hopes of college or a sports career because of a bum knee, a lazy streak as wide as the Mississippi River, and grits for brains. Laziness and lack of brains would not have kept him out of college, but nobody bets on a lame horse. For the last three years, he'd hung around the town doing odd jobs while carrying a huge envy-green chip on his shoulder, constantly reminded him of his miserable life. Self-worth came only by making other people's lives as miserable as his own. And in this, he didn't discriminate. Pain and anguish in his victim's eyes were his reward. But he was careful not to step on the wrong people's toes. His father, Sheriff Baker, couldn't get him out of everything.

"Shut up and come on," Cal barked. "We'll take along a coupla' these two-by-fours . . . brighten his shit-eatin' smile with a few wood chips. Maybe that'll put some fight in 'im." The two retrieved wooden studs from a small pile in the bar's alley. They eased up behind the old bum, hoping to cut off any exit before he got a chance to run.

Zon stared at the jail, but listened to their steps, studying each as they approached. He *saw* them through his hearing. The lead man was six-foot-seven, weighed 277 pounds, was right-handed, and had a slightly lame left leg. His stride was uneven, not just from the bad leg, but also because of the three feet of two-by-four that he carried in his right hand. His beer gut pulled him over slightly so that each step fell heavily upon the balls of his feet. Though bulky, this man was strong and fit--and was to be dealt with first.

The smaller man's strides were more even and balanced, though far less rhythmic due to the alcohol he'd consumed. He carried his two-by-four in both hands, used it to steady his balance and stood six-foot two at 170 pounds. The burn of their alcoholic stare on his back intensified as they drew nearer. Zon allowed them to approach to within striking distance.

Cal leaned over and whispered to Peck. "Is he deaf or just stupid?" Peck squeezed out a snicker, caught himself laughing, and froze, knowing for sure that their victim heard him. Zon did not move. "Well, hell," Cal wheezed, his voice low, but intentionally audible. Still, Zon didn't stir.

"I'll wake him up with this board," Peck threatened, raising the two-by-four. But Cal caught it in his powerful hand as it swung overhead.

"Now, Peck," Cal teased, "what fun is he dead?" He stepped out from the shadows, dropping the two-by-four to his side like a baseball bat. Neither of the two had taken notice of a difference. They thought they'd walked up on a sleeping boar hog, ripe for slaughter, but had unknowingly encountered a coiled serpent, ready to strike.

"Hey, boy!" Cal shouted. "Stand up, boy! I'm talkin' to ya!" He wanted to taunt this defenseless rodent before squashing him beneath his feet. Zon didn't answer, but rose silently and turned to face him, looking first to his feet, then scanning his entire body until he stared upward, into Cal's dull eyes. "Why ain't ya runnin'! Answer me!" Cal yelled, looking down at Zon, who was silhouetted by the town hall lights. He stood, hands by his side, like a misty black shadow.

Quickly growing impatient with the vagrant's silence, Cal staggered to Zon's right. Stale beer-breath quickly fouled the moist night air. This fight could have been avoided, but Zon needed these two to exercise his physique for the night. More important, he needed to deliver his business card, after the fact, to this sleepy town. Cal raised the two-by-four, yelled, then lunged at Zon. Peck stood watching. Zon locked his eyes onto the board, then struck it hard with his right hand as it neared his head, snapping it cleanly on contact. Catching the broken end in his left hand, he hurled it into Peck's forehead, hitting him squarely between the eyes and knocking him cold. Cal charged by from the momentum of his first attack, broken board still in hand. Zon punched Cal in the back of his head as he passed, knocking him flat on his face, groggy, though conscious. He then jumped down onto the fallen giant, lifted him like a side of beef, and threw him fifteen feet over into the building's shadows. Grabbing Peck by the collar, he dragged him effortlessly over to join his partner.

Cal pushed up from the pavement as Zon approached, but a punishing knee to the chest forced him back to the ground. Instinctively, Cal grabbed for Zon's throat. But before he could deliver the ominous grip, Zon struck him in his right shoulder joint with a stiffened finger. Cal grimaced in pain. Using the same finger, Zon struck him again in the throat, numbing his larynx. Turning, he struck him in the sides of his hip joints, locking his leg stiffly in place, then peered down as he rose. Cal lay on the pavement, helpless, unable to move or make a sound, though he struggled to strike at Zon, who stood within inches of his head.

Zon stared at Cal as Peck snored soundly by his side. "Zim bala lek mo nuevoe unendrisa. Tol mallak un Zon!" He spoke in the ancient Beininian dialect, saying, "Tell them all that the change has begun. If not by them, then by Zon." He knew the brawny youth had no hope of understanding him, but it really didn't matter. He wanted Cal to hear and remember. The bully would carry the secret of this shameful beating for a long time, while wandering the Auroran streets, looking for an old black kung-fu-kicker who spoke Greek. Wasting no further time, Zon reached down with the second knuckle of his middle left finger and struck Cal above the temple to unite him with Peck in a drunken slumber. The two men lay unconscious, concealed neatly in the shadows of the ally.

* * *

Zon turned and walked hypnotically back to the street corner. He did not sit, but stood away from the streetlight, casting a long shadow down the wet pavement. The group of men had entered jail from the rear while he was tucking Cal and Peck in for the night. Each of the vigilantes wore old, dark long-sleeve shirts and work pants now heavily soiled from their slippery trek down the hill. Their muddy hunting boots tracked the clean tiled jailhouse floor.

Marvin Burns, the self-appointed leader of the pack, grabbed his son's shoulder, crossed his left leg up and over his right knee, and began wiping the mud off his shoes. He'd forgotten his hunting boots. Instead, he wore the shoes he'd worn to court that day, his best pair of tan wing tips.

"Damn!" he exclaimed. "These shoes gonna be ruined! My wife'll have a hissy!" His son, Jake, stood steady under his father's weight and laughed along with a couple of the other men. Marvin's concern over his shoes and his wife's reaction seemed ironically funny, considering the reason for them all being there.

Jake was nineteen. This was his first *Justice Run* and he felt proud to be with his father. They'd often hunted game together, and Jake had many kills to his credit. But this would be the first human soul that he would help liberate. The thought caused butterflies in his stomach, though he had longed for this day. He'd sat many times before and listened as his father and friends drank and told of their many Runs of the past. They spoke fondly of the lynchings, car-draggings, bull-whippings, and other such punishments used to return uppity niggers and errant whites to their place. It drew them closer together, bonded them in their common beliefs. For most of his life, Jake longed to be a part of that circle, to stand in his father's shadow, but was always too young, that is, until now. Tonight, he would join his father and comrades in maintaining life as God willed it to be. Though a bit apprehensive over taking a human life, the exuberance of just being with his clan far and away overcame any other feelings.

"Well, what's it gonna be?" Marvin grunted as his massive foot fell back to the floor. Sheriff Baker stepped into the middle of the lynch mob.

"My boys and I cain't have no connection," the sheriff said. "You know there'll be an investigation. We got no friends in the state office." He paused, looking around the room of friends and neighbors. "Me and my boys all agree. You just conk us on the head, and put us in ole Johnny's cell. We get rescued in the mornin' . . . with witnesses. We'll only see the ski masks. No robes, hoods, or faces. Ole Johnny'll be a swingin' and we cain't identify no body . . . ceptin' his." Sheriff Baker and Marvin stood grinning into each other's face.

"Well, boys," Marvin chimed, "it's hangin' time." He stepped around Sheriff Baker to Johnny's cell.

"Hey, boy," he squawked as he pulled his ski mask back over his head, "stand up. We're going to pass sentence on you." John Jackson cowered deeper into the cell corner.

"Please, Judge Burns, sir . . . You'se a law man. You ain't suppose ta' do this."

"Well, now," Marvin grinned back, his mask propped atop his long pale forehead. "Hey boys, guess what? Righteous Johnny here's going to tell us all how things are supposed to be." Approaching the cell, he hiked up his trouser leg and parked his muddy shoe on the lower crossbar. Leaning forward, he pressed his face through the bars. "I suppose," he started, "you think its okay for you to violate our women? Did you think we were just going let you have your way with one of our own? You've done wrong, boy," he said, as if talking to an errant toddler. "You were tried, convicted, and now you're going to die."

John's gut wrenched as Marvin spit out that last word. Sweat streamed miserably down his face as the key clanged into the cell door. Masked white men crowded into the small cell. John's heartbeat thundered in his ears. Time lost direction.

A mistake had placed him here, a misjudgment that was going to cost him his life. The vigilantes all grabbed him at once, some holding him while others took the opportunity to punch him in the kidneys, groin, and stomach. John escaped into unconsciousness as Marvin duct-taped his mouth closed, slipped a dusty burlap sack over his head, then secured it with yellow nylon rope. He paused in the cell as his men carried John's limp body through the rear door. "Like I said, justice always prevails," he announced.

Over the last three days, Zon had sat unnoticed in the back of the courtroom as the Honorable Judge Marvin Burns presided over John's trial. Marvin sat soberly upon the bench, totally confident of the outcome. He smiled, having greeted the all-white, all-male jurors by first names when he entered. The prosecutor, Lloyd Clark, also showed this cockiness during his opening statement.

The unsure faces in the court were all seated near the defendant's table. John had been appointed a young black lawyer who had built a solid defense. But the faces and general demeanor of the jury during and after the prosecution's opening statement quickly turned his confidence into doubt. John's wife, Paula, and his two older kids sat behind him. Sarah, his older daughter, wept steadily throughout the trial. Zeb, his oldest son at sixteen, sat quietly behind his father. He'd known for some time about his father's womanizing, yet had accepted it as one of the necessary evil's of life. His mother often talked of leaving him because of it. Zeb's heart crept to his throat every time he thought of his folks splitting. He loved his mother deeply, as well as his father. In spite of his womanizing, John was a good father and had developed deep ties with his children, especially Zeb.

Zeb sat solemnly staring into the judge's bench. Memories of fishing, hunting, first driving lessons, and ball game trips all passed before his eyes during the trial. But these visions had been rudely paralleled by those of his father sitting dead in an electric chair, or gasping for air in a gas chamber, or dangling limp from a rope. His mind raced from one scene to another, his gut wrenching into knots from his thoughts. He was losing his father forever, right before his eyes, and all he could do was sit and watch.

One other distorted face resided in the courtroom, that of Annie Hudson, the prosecutor's chief witness. Rising slowly, she took the stand, where she sat as if in a trance. Her face was mauled, strained. She constantly looked down, her eyes staring into her wringing hands. Though pale, she was somewhat attractive with a small narrow nose, extremely thin lips, and small crows' feet at the corners of her mouth and eyes. Her hair was tied in a bun. She'd retained her small girlish figure despite her mid-fortyish age.

John had been charged with her rape, and had been jailed since the event. Annie hadn't been so lucky. Instead of sympathy, she received ostracism from her fellow white Aurorans. All of her tea-friends stopped visiting and inviting her to parties. Local grocers sent their colored help to fill her orders, no longer bothering to visit as they had done so often in the past. Hell had only begun the day that they were caught in bed together.

She and John had been lovers for well over three months. He had been hired by her husband, Talbot, over ten years earlier, to keep the grounds of their estate. Talbot died five years later, leaving Annie alone in a town too small and uppity to provide her with more than female companionship. Talbot had married Annie for her beauty and had kept her as naive and ignorant as she was the day they married, locking her into this small town, under his dominion. While incapable of handling business or other worldly matters, Annie had remained a vibrant and passionate woman as the years passed. Eventually, after Talbot's death, this same passion led her to seek out John, a willing and most able partner.

At first, fear made them both very discreet. Annie feared loss of reputation, John, loss of life. But, as time passed, John's confidence and ego grew. He divulged their secret during a drinking binge. Word soon traveled from his friends to their women, across the color line to the white women, then finally to the white men.

Not long after, Judge Burns, along with eleven of *the boys*, gathered outside the Talbot estate during what would be the last rendezvous between John and Annie.

"Listen, boys," Marvin said as he eyed the Talbot home, "we'll go right up there and catch them in the act so there'll be no denying. Grab that nigger and beat the shit out of him, then take him down to the jail. I'll have a talk with little Miss Annie." The twelve crept up to the house, and once inside, quietly sent the maids home. Passionate moaning and groaning filled the air as the mob climbed the stairs. Each step delivered louder moans and greater disgust.

Tom Jefferies kicked the door in, exposing Annie, naked, sweaty, and straddled over her terrified lover. Marvin stomped over to the love nest and slapped Annie across the face, knocking her onto the floor at the far side of the bed. John bolted for the window, but was cut off by two of the mobsters, one of whom punched him in the gut, then kneed him in the face. He landed, naked, across the bed. Four men grabbed the bed sheets and bound him within like so much dirty laundry. Using the knotted sheet, they dragged him out into the hall, where they paused to punch and kick the human bundle until it lost consciousness. Large bloody red blotches spotted the white sheet. Once the mob's blows no longer resulted in grunts and recoils, they rolled the limp mass, head over heel, down the staircase.

Annie sat on the floor beside the bed, crying. She had wrapped herself in the flowery bed comforter. Her hair hung long and stringy about her face. Judge Burns stood over her as he watched his cohort chase the rolling body down the stairs.

"I think your darky lover boy is dead," he said in a pious tone. "Know what you're going to do now?" Annie shook her head as she stared upward through teary eyes. Marvin stepped over and sat on the bed. "First of all," he sighed, "if old lover boy survives his journey to jail, then you're going to file rape charges. Do you understand?" Annie closed her eyes, trying to get a grip on the situation. She was going to be thrown out of Aurora with nothing, onto the streets like a common beggar. Judge Burns and his friends could destroy her--or save her.

"Please Marvin," she begged between pitiful sobs, "have mercy. I was so lonely . . . please have mercy . . . please!"

"Save your begging, bitch!" Marvin answered. "You'll find no sympathy here. Now shut up and listen." He stared down at her, then caught sight of her left breast she'd unknowingly exposed. "Now listen to me," he snapped. "You're going to file rape charges, do you hear me?" Annie bowed her head in agreement. "You'll have a disgraced life in this town, but it's better than no life at all. Why, had this been a few years ago, we'd have dragged you out along with that nigger and lynched you, too."

Annie's eyes bulged. She never thought that the sexual ecstasy that she and John had enjoyed would threaten her life. Maybe his, but definitely not her own. She stopped crying and looked up at Marvin and noticed his face growing flush as he spoke.

"What you've done is bad," he preached, "not just for us, but for our coloreds as well. The respectable people of this town must live with your disgrace, and the coloreds are going to have to be taught a lesson so they don't forget their place. You've messed up everybody's life, Annie." Marvin placed his hand on her shoulder. "Now, I'm going to put things right again for you," he said, softening his voice to a more fatherly tone. "But you're going to have to help. You've got to file charges against the nigger. Do you understand?" Again, she nodded.

"Good. Now, at his trial, you'll testify that he forced himself upon you. He snuck up here after your maids had gone. You resisted, but he was too strong. He raped you and left you here, tied up."

Marvin stood as he talked, walked over to the window, and watched as his men drove off to the jail with John. "Do you understand Annie?" he asked, stepping slowly back toward her, fondling the nylon rope in his pocket. Stepping between her and the bed, he held out his right hand and reassuringly called her name. "Annie?" She looked up at him. Her face was streaked with heavy tear-washed makeup that had been so carefully applied, not an hour before, to impress John. The bruise on her lip had puffed and reddened from Marvin's strike across her face. Marvin peered mysteriously into her eyes. She looked into his, and saw hope in his strong extended hand.

"He's like John," she thought staring into his face, "not just in their size and age, but like John, and Talbot before, offering salvation, a strong hand, and gentle smile that could make everything all right again." A forced smile slowly spread across her face as she lifted her left hand to place in his. Marvin gently took her hand and smiled back. Annie tightened her grip on the bed comforter to rise from the floor without exposing herself. She drew in her long shapely legs to stand, but suddenly stopped. Her tense smile turned quickly into a winching grimace as Marvin's hand engulfed hers, crushing it, as he would have a wad of paper.

"Marvin, you're hurting me!" she cried out as she grabbed at his fingers with her right hand. Marvin grinned madly at her effort, squeezing her hand all the harder. "Marvin! Please!"

"Oh, ah aims ta, Miss Annie! Ah aims ta!" he bellowed, mocking her color-filled lover. She gasped, struggled, and pleaded. Marvin drew back his left hand and again struck her across the face. In one motion, he slung her hard, facedown upon the bed. The impact knocked the breath from her, leaving her dazed and gagging. He tied one end of his rope to her left wrist, the other to the lower right end of the headboard.

"Marvin," she moaned, forcing his name through puffed and bleeding lips. Shamelessly, he grabbed the bed comforter, which she clutched unconsciously to her breast, and jerked it away, leaving her naked and dazed. Stepping around the bed, he secured her left hand to yet another rope, then leaned over and jerked it, drawing her face down to the mattress. Holding the rope tight, Marvin secured it to the lower right end of the bed post.

Annie recovered from Marvin's blow as he secured her arms to the bed, and began struggling desperately to free herself. She was pinned to the bed, her shoulders and breasts burrowed deep into the mattress. She could lift her head, but barely enough to pivot it from side to side, allowing a glimpse of Marvin from the corner of her eye. Marvin stood at the foot of the bed, eyeing his handiwork.

"Now, don't that look nice," he teased as he gazed at Annie's nakedness. She drew her legs up, trying to hide her shame. "Now, Annie, this is no time to be shy," he mocked. He reached over and grabbed her right ankle and tied it with a rope.

"Marvin," Annie begged, "for God's sake. Don't do this." But he paid her no attention and secured the rope's free end to the bed's tall footboard, then did likewise with her left foot.

When finished, he again stood at the end of the bed, gazing at Annie. He had tied her legs apart. She lay fully exposed, her upper torso glued to the mattress, her legs and hips, spread, suspended and helpless. Annie's frantic wrenching at the ropes caused her hips to gyrate, exciting Marvin even more. She was scared, injured, helpless, humiliated, and now, completely at Marvin's mercy.

"Oh, Annie!" Marvin shouted, "This is going to be so good to you!" Like a circus announcer, he stepped back and forth around the bed, shouting and undressing. Stripping to his shorts, he grabbed his belt, then walked to the head of the bed. Annie held her head up and rolled her eyes pitifully up to meet his. But as she opened her mouth to beg, Marvin whipped the belt across her face. She squealed in pain, then began sobbing loudly. Marvin jumped on the bed and stood on his knees between her legs.

"Well, nigger lover," he laughed, "and I do mean, nigger lover, let's see how good you can be with a real man." Snatching down his shorts, he leaned in against her, gripped her thigh with his left hand, then struck her repeatedly across her back with his belt.

"Marvin! No, Marvin! God, please stop!" she cried in agony. Marvin swung madly till he was out of breath.

"Ya know," he huffed jokingly, finally stopping and gasping for air, "I never followed a nigger anywhere." Long red whelps swelled and burst forth with blood on Annie's back as he spoke. "And even though I'm tempted," he said, rubbing himself against her, "I'm not about to start now. So Annie, you're in for a special treat."

Annie's bloody back and loud sobbing drove Marvin into a frenzy of ecstasy. He struck her several times again across her back with his long, thick leather belt. Annie answered each lash with louder and louder screams.

"Oh, God! . . . Oh, God! . . . Oh, God! . . . Oh . . . " she sobbed, her cries for mercy reverberating throughout her house. Marvin, unable to withstand the excitement any longer, threw his belt across the room and grabbed Annie's thigh tightly.

"Oh Annie," he gasped, "Annie . . . Annie . . . baby . . ." Madly, he placed himself to sodomize her.

"No, Marvin . . . please . . . No, Marvin, no . . . ahhhh!" Reaching up, Marvin grabbed a handful of her long brown hair. Her neck cracked as he wrenched her head backward while thrusting himself forward, forcing himself where no man belonged. Annie screamed hysterically. Marvin ripped at her flesh.

This was rape, at its ugliest. Marvin's actions had nothing to do with love. He lusted after domination and control, derived pleasure from hurt and humiliation. Every action sought to maim and degrade Annie. The lower she became, the greater his satisfaction.

Mercifully, Annie eased into unconsciousness as he continued his abuse. Her body became a dangling piece of meat, dripping blood from open wounds, passing along sweat from a sadistic rapist. Marvin never noticed her sleep.

* * *

Annie relived Marvin's attack as she sat on the witness stand. Her soul ached for vengeance; her stomach churned as she considered declaring the truth to this so-called court of justice. But these thoughts quickly passed, along with her last ounce of self-respect. What was her word against the mighty Judge Marvin Burns? He and his army of jackals were in control and she knew it. Her one and only hope lay in her obedience to him, in living his lies, accepting his justice.

Annie rolled her eyes high to steal a look at John, though her face hung down toward her folded hands. John sat quietly at the defense table. This was the first they'd seen of each other since they were snatched away from their love nest. She gasped lightly, managing a glimpse of him. His strong face was badly bruised, his full lips puffed and stitched, his eyebrows taped with pink, flesh-colored Band-Aids that stood out against his coffee-colored flesh. Although his face was badly beaten, his large brown eyes still sparkled as they gazed toward her. Sensing his stare, she quickly snatched her eyes away. Yet, that brief instant in which their eyes again met was enough to jettison her deep into her thoughts.

She sat staring blankly into her hands as the district attorney lectured and paced the floor. He painted Marvin's version deep into the jury's and cameras' minds with his words. But Annie's thoughts wandered into the past, back to the moments of sensuous joy that she and John had shared. Slowly, and ever so unnoticeable, a faint smile danced across her face. This was the first time since Marvin's brutal assault that she had managed to sustain a pleasant thought long enough to derive joy from it.

At first, she had been ashamed of her lust for John. But the shame quickly passed as she accepted the fact that she was still a vibrant, youthful woman, with all of the feelings and desires that she possessed when her husband, Talbot, was alive. His death was sudden, unexpected, and devastating, yet she couldn't accept a social and emotional death for the rest of her life because of it. It took five years of loneliness, self-denial, and internal strife between her moral fiber and desiring flesh before she finally chose her path.

Then came John. Annie knew she could never love another man, especially a black one. Her Southern upbringing had well established their inferiority in her mind. John just happened along at the wrong time.

She had routinely sat alone in front of her sitting room window in the late afternoon, peering out over her well-manicured garden. This was her private place, where she sat, sometimes for hours, wondering, thinking, sometimes sleeping, but always dreaming of her fantasy life. In her thoughts, Talbot was warm and alive. His hands softly caressed her heaving breasts, his arms encircled her small waist, drew her hard against his hot, sweaty chest. His tongue teasingly licked her open lips ever so gently, begging to be allowed inside. These well-rehearsed thoughts were vivid and often left her slumped in her heavily cushioned chair, lustfully entwined within her own arms. The cold reality that awaited her after such episodes fanned her lustful flames. Over time, her sensuous fantasies grew longer, more frequent, and less private.

John worked daily out in Annie's flower garden, but kept mostly in the shade during the hot summer afternoons. It was from there, unseen, that he first spied her in the window of her large air-conditioned sitting room. He watched with curiosity as she nestled her face and body into that fluffy lounger, her eyes closed and mouth open, lost in her fantasy lover's arms. Watching her soon became a part of his daily routine.

As the days passed, her actions on the couch became more brazen. He soon found himself aroused as he watched her wriggle and gyrate, madly embracing herself. It was then that he decided to invite himself into her life. He was a well-skilled and well-experienced lady's man, having often used his well-equipped body and fine features to arouse a lady's interest, and just as often, her sensuality. He wooed them, in spite of his twenty years of marriage, used his bulging biceps, irresistible smile, and smothering embrace to lure and conquer. His words, whether spoken while embracing on the dance floor or in bed, were smooth and sweet, dripping with honey.

Yet, this affair would be special and dangerous for him. He often cheated on his wife with both married and unmarried women who longed for guaranteed lengthy episodes of lustful pleasure. But he had never dared to approach a white woman, though he'd often teased and flirted with them. Hiding from an enraged husband was one thing, but hiding from a lynch mob was another. Still, Annie was alone and in desperate need of company, and he couldn't pass this chance to add another feather to his cap.

The challenge of a forbidden love, coupled with the daily arousal that each was experiencing, led to them finally coupling. And they delivered to each other. Annie lived out her lustful fantasy while John massaged his ego with a white woman, adding yet another notch to his belt.

* * *

On the witness stand, Annie's head rolled back. The smile upon her face was broad and glowing, as she sat on the stand. She had unknowingly escaped back into her fantasies. An erotic moan broke free from deep within her throat.

" . . . then, ladies and gentlemen of the jury," Prosecutor Clark continued, unaware of Annie's drift, "this poor, innocent, defenseless child," he preached, pointing back at the witness stand, "was mercilessly and brutally raped by this serpent . . . this animal . . . slug upon the earth!" Lloyd reached the climax of his heart-wrenching soliloquy and shot an accusing finger at John Jackson as Annie's moan blurted forth.

"Mrs. Hudson! Please!" Lloyd yelled. Racing quickly to her side, he whispered, "Get a hold of yourself for God's sake. You're making me look bad." Turning to the bailiff, he said, "Somebody get some water." Annie jerked erect as Lloyd's voice broke her trance. Immediately, she began to cry, realizing what had happened.

The tears were her sorrow. She was on trial with John, and would receive similar justice from this kangaroo court. After being violated, raped, and beaten, she was going to be convicted and then sentenced to spend the rest of her life alone, with empty dreams and cruel memories. Alone, imprisoned in a town of do-good hypocrites who would punish her for the rest of her life.

Water from the bailiff cleared her mind. She stood, prepared to perjure herself. In a few words, she destroyed her former lover's life. John's wife stared hard at Annie's mangled face.

"Serve the bitch right," Paula thought, then returned her gaze to John. "The nigga's finally eatin' some of the shit he's been feedin' me all these years," she thought, a slight grin dimpling her cheeks. She wanted John to suffer for what he'd done, but she didn't want him to die. She knew he didn't rape Annie. She turned and gazed around the courtroom. "Shit," she mumbled under her breath, "haf da women in here knows firsthand how my man treats a woman. Rape and beatin' just ain't his style." Inside, her love and disgust for John struggled to see which would wrench her heart from her chest first.

"Ma, you okay?" Sarah, John's oldest, had noticed her mother talking to herself. Paula hugged Sarah tightly.

"Yes, honey," she answered softly. "As usual, yo daddy's got me goin' crazy."

Annie's testimony was totally unconvincing, yet sustained a

forgone conclusion to the jurors whose minds were made up long before the trial started. John's lawyer presented an excellent case. Witnesses attested to the three-month long love affair. Annie's maids witnessed the "mob" entry into the house on the day of the alleged crime. And John's badly bruised body couldn't be denied while much of the prosecution's case offered conflicting testimony.

The jury returned the guilty verdict on the third day of trial, after ten minutes of deliberation. Zeb clutched his father and cried. Paula and Sarah tightened their embrace.

"It's okay, son," John said, trying to console Zeb. "This ain't over, not by a long shot. You see them cameras?" He motioned toward the row of television cameras filming the trial. "The world knows this won't no fair trial. My lawya's gonna appeal this to folks outside Aurora. I'll be free." Zeb looked into his father's eyes, then rested his head on his chest as they embraced.

"Let's go, boy," Sheriff Baker mumbled as he grabbed John from behind by the handcuffs and began pulling him backward, out of the courtroom. Zeb's hands broke free from clutching his father's shirt.

"'Bye, Daddy," he said as tears streamed down his face. "I know ya gonna be okay."

9
AURORA'S JUDGEMENT

Zon watched through the small jail house window as several of the masked men carried John out the back door. Sheriff Baker and his deputies walked into John's cell and dropped to their knees, facing the wall. Three of the hooded men stood behind the officers and on Marvin's signal, struck them simultaneously on the head with night sticks. Blood gushed as the men fell over.

"You hit them too hard!" Marvin yelled. "You were supposed to knock them out, not kill 'em! Doc, get over there and make sure they're okay." Doctor Roger Craig shuffled quickly to the policemen's side. He examined Sheriff Baker carefully, handling the old man's bloody head as he would a small overripe melon.

"They're all alive," he said. "But Don here has a concussion for sure. We'd better get him to the hospital."

"No time," Marvin said. Turning toward the door, he ushered out those who remained. "They'll be all right."

"This ain't right, Marvin!" Doc Craig yelled. "Come here! Look at Don!" Marvin stepped over and looked into the sheriff's paling face. Blood oozing from his head wound formed a small puddle on the floor.

"Oh, he'll be all right, Rog," Marvin replied. "Can't you give him something?"

"Like what? How 'bout I just write him out a prescription for a new skull. Will that do it?" Doc Craig strangled his words and eased toward Marvin as he spoke. "I tell you. We better get him to a hospital. Now!" Marvin returned Doc Craig's stare with a cold piercing look. He then pressed nose to nose with the doctor.

"I *said* they'll be all right. Now get your ass through that door!" He shot his extended index finger toward the door, and with his eyes, dared the concerned physician to defy him. Doc Craig didn't speak, but dropped his gaze, took a last look at his wounded friend on the floor, then walked sheepishly out into the darkness. Marvin closed the door as he followed. He didn't bother looking back.

Zon stepped through the narrow window onto the cold jailhouse floor as the back door closed. He had shunned his ragged disguise and dawned a jet black tank-top, knee-length biker shorts, socks, and sneakers. The tight fitting black suit bulged from the rippling muscle underneath. Quickly, he moved to the cell where the sheriff and his deputies lay unconscious, grabbing the key from the desk as he passed. From outside, faint sounds crept in from the mob moving up the hill toward their trucks parked just beyond.

Zon stooped down to examine the officers. Satisfied that the two deputies were not seriously hurt, he stuffed one under each arm, then trotted to the officer's lounge. Quickly, he stripped the two, then placed the larger one facedown on the night watchman's cot. Grabbing the smaller one by the waist, he piled him on top of the larger one, facedown as well. As he stacked the officers, he spotted a canister of super glue on a work table, then smiled. Dropping the limp body, he retrieved the glue, emptied it into the smaller policeman's pubic area, then dropped him back on the other officer, forming a human sandwich. Neatly folding their clothes, he placed them at the foot of the bed, covered them to the waist with a bed sheet, then sponged off the crowns of their heads. Their hair covered the scars and knots left by the bludgeoning. As he flipped off the light and set the door lock, he looked back at the two men. "Good night, girls," he whispered, then shut the door and trotted back to the jail cell.

Sheriff Baker had a severe concussion that, combined with his bad heart and high blood pressure, would kill him by morning. Doc Craig had covered the sheriff's skull and clothing with bloody fingerprints during his examination. Careful not to disturb the fingerprints, Zon scooped the dying man up in his arms and tossed him lightly upon his shoulder. He wiped the blood stains from the cell with a towel, then ran out of the rear jailhouse door. Cranking trucks sounded from the distant hilltop as Zon hurried down the alley toward his car. Once there, he laid Sheriff Baker gently in the backseat, jumped behind the steering wheel, and raced off to the hospital.

* * *

Aurora General Hospital sat on the far east end of town. Zon killed his headlights and motor as he approached and rolled to a stop on the street, away from the lighted emergency entrance. Hurrying around the car, he slid Sheriff Baker onto his shoulder once more and eased up to the emergency exit, hidden in the old building's shadows. A folded wheelchair stood a few feet shy of the attendant who sat on a stool reading just inside the automatic sliding glass doors. Zon stood erect and fixed a cold stare upon the attendant's eyes. The attendant looked up from the comic book, slid off his stool, and walked to the doors, causing them to swoosh open. But a brief survey of the shadowy darkness satisfied his sudden curiosity. He turned away and stepped back toward his stool. The doors slid shut behind him. Just as he focused away, Zon struck from the shadows to the door, being careful not to activate the motion detector, and noiselessly snapped the folded wheelchair open, not two feet from the attendant. He sat the sheriff gently in the chair and returned to the shadows as quickly as he had come. Racing back to his car, he eased the driver's door open, slipped the transmission into neutral, pushed the car around then down the empty street, and jumped inside as it rolled. After a quick start, he sped off into the night.

Meanwhile, the attendant finally reached his seat and spun around to remount the stool. As he turned, he spotted the limp body in the wheelchair outside the glass door.

"How the hell?" the young man exclaimed, dashing through the doors in time to see a set of tail lights disappearing in the distance. Rushing around the wheelchair, he pushed Sheriff Baker's limp body into the sleepy emergency ward.

"Emergency! Emergency!" In a mad and uncontrolled dash, the excited attendant trucked past two nurses' stations. While yelling at the top of his lungs, he closed in fast on Doctor Gentry, who stood talking at the end of the long corridor. Immediately, three porky, middle-aged nurses dressed in white from head to toe, fell in line behind him, screaming desperately in an attempt to stop him. Approaching the doctor, the attendant dug his feet into the floor, but his momentum dragged the two right into the doctor's legs, the chair's footrests striking his left shin bone.

"Damn it, Buford!" Doctor Gentry screeched, wrenching his left leg up over his right knee and grabbing hold of the fresh wound. The confused attendant regained his footing, then stood reddened from the run and collision.

"Oh ah, sorry, Doc."

"Buford!" the out-of-breath nurses screeched as they arrived, one by one, and pulled the slow-minded but swift-footed attendant out of their way.

"My God! It's Sheriff Baker!" the lead nurse exclaimed, cupping the sheriff's chin. "Someone's cracked his skull! Get him up on the gurney." Together, the five wrestled the overweight sheriff onto the wheeled cot.

"Prep him for X rays," Doctor Gentry ordered. "How'd he get here?" He worked over the sheriff while directing questions at Buford.

"Don't know. I turned 'round and he's just . . . there. But I did see the tail end of a car ridin' off, though."

"You mean somebody just dumped him?"

"Yeah, I guess." Buford looked down at the sheriff's clothes as the doctor studied his wound. Suddenly, he spoke out of revelation. "I bet whoever owns them bloody fingerprints can tell us what happened." Doctor Gentry glared at the naive attendant, but didn't reply. "I'm gonna go call the sheriff," Buford continued.

"Hey, moron, this *is* the sheriff," the doctor replied.

"I know that," Buford defended, "I meant I was gon' call his office. See if his deputy's there." The mocking stares from the doctor and nurses burned a hole in the back of Buford's head as he ran off to find a phone. After a few minutes, he came trotting back, nearly out of breath.

"Ain't no answer at the sheriff's office." A cold lump formed in the pit of Doctor Gentry's stomach.

"This whole thing is starting to smell," he said. "Call the State

Police."

"Sure thing!" Buford yelled, then ran back down the hall.

"Hey," Buford squawked into the phone, "is this the State Police?"

"How can we help you, sir?" a starchy Southern female answered.

"This is Buford Simmons at the hospital in Aurora. Our sheriff's been beat up and dumped here at the hospital and none of his deputies are answering the phone at the jail. We think somethin's wrong." After a lengthy exchange of questions and answers, Buford hung up, then picked up the receiver and dialed again.

"Hey, Harl? This is Buford Simmons at the hospital. You wake?"

"You idiot," Harold Mangum, the news anchor of the only television station in town, answered. "It's one in the morning. What in the hell do you want?"

"Somethin's goin' on," Buford grinned. "Sheriff's down here and hurt real bad. Ain't no answer at the jail and I done called the State Police. They supposed to be here in about an hour." Harold Mangum grinned through his grogginess, thoughts of instant stardom, his name and perfect face on every television, and getting out of this small rat hole of a town raced through his head.

"Thanks for the tip, Buford. Now, ahhh, don't you call nobody else, okay?"

"You gonna put me on T.V.?"

"Oh . . . of course, Buford. I'll let you tell the whole story. Just don't tell anyone else."

"Sure thing, Harl." Buford hung the phone up with a smile, then started leafing through the thin phone book, looking for the number for Jackson City's TV station.

* * *

The trucks motored eastward, single file out of town. Marvin's truck led the pack, followed by Jim Tate with John's bound body sprawled across his truck bed. Behind them followed two other trucks. Jake rode with his father in the lead truck. He sat quietly on the passenger's side, bouncing back and forth as the red 1994 Ford Bronco bounded over roots, rocks, and mud holes toward the hanging tree.

"Ain't been up here in while," Marvin spoke as he negotiated the narrow path. The four overhead lamps on his roll bar burned brightly, yet even combined with his headlights, barely cut through the overgrowth. Marvin glanced toward his son. "You scared, boy?"

"No," Jake answered, "this is just . . . kinda new to me, that's all."

"Don't let it bother you, son. I've been up here at least twenty times for hanging, though the last one, as I recall, was some twelve odd years ago. I tell you, it feels good to be back. People stay away from this place. Most of the good folk are too damned timid and pretend that it doesn't exist. And the niggers," he snorted, "are too scared to tread near here." Reaching over, Marvin slapped his son reassuringly on the back. "Don't worry. You've got a few butterflies now, but that'll pass soon. Things will be right again. If we nip this thing in the bud, we'll save everybody a lot of trouble. The state won't have to pay for more trials. Aurora will stay a safe place for decent folk. More coloreds won't have to die or be beaten because they'll stay in their place. Think of it this way. We're doing everybody a favor." Jake heard his father's words, but the message never reached his mind. He couldn't stop thinking of John's lifeless body swinging back and forth from a tree, his neck broken from being hanged.

"Don't worry about me, Dad. Like you said, it's just butterflies. Besides," he said, forcing a tight grin to his face, trying to impress his father, "be a shame to waste such a perfect night for a hanging." Father and son smiled at one another.

The four trucks rolled deeper into the wood. Two men, their masks removed, rode on the back of the second truck with John, two others in the cab, two more on the back of Marvin's truck, and four each in the trailing trucks. Marvin's truck bumped and jolted as he maneuvered through a wide but shallow creek. On the other side, the bank rose nearly vertical, twenty-five feet to meet dense blue-gray forest, split cleanly in the middle by a tall narrow black hole. Marvin steered his truck up the steep bank and directly into the entrance. Beyond the black hole stood a clearing fifty feet wide, surrounded by thick hardwood forest.

A large oak tree stood solitary in the middle. One of its lower branches had been distorted, growing perpendicular to the trunk, twelve feet above the ground. The thick branch reached out ten feet, turned, then grew skyward. In a park, it would have made the perfect anchor for a bench or tire swing. Instead, for the last fifty years, it had been used for righteous murder of black men. Yet, this monolith had stood unused for more than twelve years, as witnessed by the height of undergrowth surrounding the clearing. Marvin slowed, then steered to the right as he entered and continued to circle until he reached the opposite side. Then he maneuvered his truck to face inward. His lights bore down on the center of the clearing. The two trucks at the rear of the convoy took similar positions about the circle, bathing it in an eerie glow. Jim Tate's truck, with John in the back, pulled into the center. The truck bed came to rest directly underneath the crooked branch. The warm drizzle had now turned to a misty fog, which scattered the headlight beams, encapsulating the scene in soft hazy light.

John had regained consciousness as the trucks crossed the creek. He tried to sit up, but his assailants stomped him back to the truck bed. Though partially blinded by the sack over his head, he could see through the loose weave of the burlap. His eyes stung from the dust in the old bag. His hands were tied behind him, his mouth, taped shut, though his legs remained free.

Jumping from the trucks, the lynch mob began yelling and hooting at the top of their lungs, secure in the distant isolation of their private place of justice. Jim retrieved a bottle of bourbon from his truck, opened it, took a large drink, then passed it around. Another bottle had been passed back and forth from truck to truck during the journey from the jail.

It was 1:15 on a Thursday morning. Doctor Craig, anxious to get back to his warm dry bed, spoke first. "How we gonna do this?" he shouted over the rabble-rousing. Jim Tate jumped on the back of his truck and retrieved a thick rope.

"Seems pretty simple to me," he said and flung the heavy rope into the air toward the crooked branch above. "Stand him up, rope him down, and I just drive off. Then we can all go home and get some sleep." He smiled as he searched the misty branches for the returning noose, which suddenly barreled down from its journey around the limb, and struck him in the face. The clearing filled with laughter as the mob watched Jim stumble about on the truck. Steadying himself from the blow and the laughter, he grabbed hold of the dangling noose, turned and gave John a punishing kick in his gut. The laughter grew. Jim flung the loose end into Bob Dancing's chest. "Ah, shut the fuck up an' go tie that end off," he yelled. Still chuckling, Bob passed the liquor bottle to Jake, then walked over and secured the rope around the oak tree. He then strolled back to the group, still laughing, and took his place in the pass-around line.

"Stand him up!" Marvin yelled. Tom Jeffries and Herman Bowls jumped into the truck bed to help Jim wrestle John up to the noose. All of them had drunk enough to raise their spirits and body temperature. John, who lay tightly bound in the truck bed, panicked as the men grabbed him, and began kicking at everything within reach. His worn heavy boots caught Jim Tate in the knee and sent him somersaulting over the truck bed. The remaining three lynch men began kicking John in the gut and privates to calm him, while those on the ground rekindled their laughter toward Jim.

"Jake, grab his feet!" Doctor Craig yelled as he stood on the ground. Jake stood silently by the rear right corner of Jim's truck as he had since they'd arrived. He took swigs from the bottle as it passed but was unconscious to all other rebel-rousing about him. His eyes stared into the darkness, but his mind rested on the man in the back of the truck, who'd be dead within the hour. Jake stole occasional glances at the wriggling body on the truck bed floor, vividly picturing himself on the back of that truck, trussed up and struggling with all of his might. The more he tried to cast this vision from his mind, the stronger it became, as though he were being possessed.

"Jake!" Marvin yelled from the driver's door where he stood, "grab the nigger's feet!" Jake broke free of his guilt-ridden conscious, snapped his head up, then stared at his father. "Grab the boy's feet!" Marvin repeated, stressing each word and pointing at John's worn, black leather boots. "It's okay son, it's okay."

Jake looked down, into the dimly lit truck bed, onto the raging battle. Jim was back on the truck, kicking John with a vengeance. Jake grabbed John's right leg. He jerked it, then reached out to secure a better grip. But just as his hands closed over John's exposed ankle, Joe Dancing yelled, let go of John's neck, and slapped himself on the shoulder.

"Shit!" he yelled and clutched his throbbing shoulder. Surprised by the scream, Jake let go of John's ankle. John, with his feet and neck free, dove back to the truck bed, spun onto his back, then kicked wildly. One of his boots caught Jim squarely in the groin. Jim rolled up, like a salted snail, grasped his privates with both hands and once again fell over the side of the truck. Halfway to the ground, he, too, yelped like Joe then hit the ground, with one hand on his privates and the other planted solidly on his left buttock. He rolled over onto his back and opened his mouth to swear, but swallowed his mouthful of chewing tobacco and spittle. Doctor Craig had started around the truck for Joe, but turned to inspect Jim, who was grasping, choking, and gagging.

"What the hell's wrong with yoo . . . ahhh!" yelled Doc Craig, slapping his forehead, then right leg.

"What is it? What is it?!" Jake yelled as he watched the melee.

"Bees!" screamed Joe, popping onto his feet. As he spoke, the two remaining men in the truck, along with Marvin and Jake, received bee strikes almost simultaneously.

"This is impossible!" Marvin protested as he sustained yet another strike on the back of his head. "Bees don't fly at night!" Each man, four standing on the truck, and twelve on the ground, swung madly in the air with their arms and outstretched hands, trying to fend off the invisible attackers.

"Tell 'at to the ga'dam bees!" Doctor Craig screeched, taking yet another hit. "One of you idiots must have run over a hornet's nest! Head for the creek. Forget the damn trucks, the windows'r down!" Yelling his instructions as he ran, Doctor Craig led the group around the front of the hanging truck through the clearing and down the steep bank to the creek. Everyone rushed after him except Marvin, Jim, and John. Jim slowly rose to his feet and hobbled painfully toward the clearing. Two bee strikes hit him in his left hand and right cheek as he reached the edge. Stumbling madly, he tumbled down the steep grade.

Marvin stood at the rear of Jim's truck. He listened to the distant splashing, but stared defiantly at John, who lay calmly on the truck bed. "I don't see any damned bees," he said in spite of his two throbbing head strikes. Scanning the clearing, he realized the attack had ceased. He stopped swatting the air and thought back curiously on the attack. Although many of the strikes had been a split second apart, no two people were ever stung simultaneously. And through all of the commotion, John had continued to fight and kick, but he never jerked in pain from an apparent bee sting.

"Don't bees like dark meat?" he said aloud.

"He wasn't stung," came a voice from directly behind him. Marvin's eyes flashed wide, then quickly narrowed into slits as he spun around to see Zon, standing not two feet behind him. "Isn't technology amazing?" Zon spoke in a low deep voice as he stared Marvin in the eye. Raising his right hand, he allowed a small object that resembled brass knuckles with a tail to dangle from his middle finger.

"What the hell is that . . . and who the hell are you?"

"These are your bees," Zon said, referring to the little marvel in his hand. It was actually a modified version of a Zimbali blowgun, small, yet effective when provided with the right darts and venom. Marvin didn't wait for any more answers. Despite his throbbing stings, he lunged and wrapped both of his powerful hands around Zon's throat.

"You're not going to use that blowgun on me again, jungle bunny!" Marvin grimaced through tightly clinched teeth as he tried to press the ends of his thumbs deep into Zon's esophagus. Zon stared into Marvin's eyes as he stuck his blowgun into his pocket. Marvin was strong, his powerful hands having choked many people in his lifetime, yet they were having no effect on the massive rippling black neck. Zon stood rock-solid as Marvin drew himself in face to face.

"Judge Burns," he said in a steady, unrestrained voice, "you are the guilty one. Your justice has finally come full circle."

"Go to hell," Marvin growled, "you greasy . . . black . . . watermelon-eating . . . coon!" Zon stared coldly into Marvin's enraged eyes, but didn't respond. "You musty son of a bitch!" Finding his choke hold ineffective, Marvin maneuvered to deliver a hard knee to Zon's abdomen. But as his knee rose, Zon embedded his elbow into it. Marvin scowled with pain, recoiled, then dangled his leg limply toward the ground. Aching now from the stings and crushed muscle and cartilage, Marvin pressed still harder to choke his opponent. Sweat popped from his forehead and upper lip. His mind started to reel from the pain and predicament.

Just then, he thought of his compatriots at the foot of the hill, swimming in the stream. "A simple diversion," he thought, "followed by a quick call for help, and we'll have two for lynching." His pain eased as he visualized himself clear of this situation. Drawing in a quick deep breath, he flexed his jowls and hocked up several ounces of spittle to launch into Zon's face. His mouth filled, but as he pursed his thin lips, Zon quickly reached around to the small of his back and struck him on the base of his spine with a stiffened right index finger. Marvin's body wrenched from the small blow, the choking spittle slipped down his throat and into his lungs. His good leg, that supported all of his body weight, instantly gave way. He fell backward, choking, coughing, and gripping his sides as he hit the ground. His legs and hips quivered in spasms. His hands now gripped his own throat as he struggled desperately to clear his lungs. With choke-induced tears blurring his eyes, he watched Zon's watery image move over him.

* * *

"Shut up! Listen, d'ya hear that?" Doctor Craig spoke as he sat up in the chest-high creek water. In the distance, he heard two blaring sirens. "Someone's set off the fire alarm. Somethin' must have gone wrong."

"I'll say it has," Jim replied. A twinge of fear peppered his voice. "First, we nearly kill our entire police department . . . Say, you don't suppose someone's found them already, do ya?"

"No, no, of course not," Doc Craig replied. "Probably just a housefire or somethin'."

"Beat-up police," Jim complained, "now bees that sting at night . . . and where in the hell is our fearless leader. Pardon me, boy," he said throwing a spiteful look at Jake, "but your daddy's a might pigheaded. Always gotta be in charge, tellin' ev'rybody else what to do, never listenin' to nobody. Why, I bet he's up there right now tryin' a' tell 'em bees where to go. Either that or he just ran off in the opposite direction 'cause ole Doc over there thought of hittin' the creek first."

Laughter bubbled forth. Every one of the drunken and soaked mob, except Jake and Doctor Craig, laughed at Jim. Rising slowly to their feet in the calm stream, the laughing mob began wringing their clothes free of the warm, but sobering water. As the splashing calmed, Doctor Craig angled his face to Aurora.

"Listen, you idiots!" he yelled. "This ain't no time to joke. That siren means that someone'll be looking for us, especially Fred!" He turned to point at the startled, dripping fire chief among the crowd. "Hell, we all make up most of the fire department! We've been in this water for a couple of minutes now and we're all still smartin' from them bee stings. But we got to get back up there fast, get that nigger hung, and get our asses back to town in a damn hurry, or we all could end up on trial for murder!" The harsh reality of Doctor Craig's words landed a jolt to each of the men. Their faces paled as they looked on.

"Well, hell," said Fred, falling in the line of men that formed to reclimb the hill. "This ain't near the fun it use ta be." The reluctant group shuffled out of the water and began climbing the hill, back toward the clearing. Three minutes had passed since they'd been chased off by the bees.

* * *

"Who are you?" Marvin managed to ask through his agony. Zon stared down at him. Thoughts of the innocent men, women, and children who had suffered because of him urged Zon toward vengeance. Without a word, he stiffened his finger to deliver his final blow to Marvin's temple. But as he bent over the helpless man, sloppy mud-laden footsteps sounded from the creek below.

"Marvin!" Doc Craig yelled as he entered the clearing, quickly glancing around the trucks and shadows. Jim and the rest of the lynch mob stopped at the clearing entrance and waited to see if the good doctor sustained any further stings. Aurora's sirens grew louder by the second in each man's ears. Each repetition seemed to repeat Doc Craig's words of "trial for murder."

"Get in here!" Doc Craig yelled. Panic was slowly settling in on them. "Now get up there and get that rope on that nigger!"

"We've got to find my father," Jake said as four of the men jumped into the back of the hanging truck.

"We can't wait on your daddy, boy. He ran out from the bees like we all did. He oughta be walkin' up any minute. But, we ain't got time to wait. We gotta get this done and get back to town to cover our own asses."

Jake gazed around, bewildered and scared. He shuddered as he took in the damp, ill-lit scene, the men struggling in the back of the truck to leash their victim, Jim sitting behind the wheel of his truck, revving the engine, the other trucks cranking up, preparing to race back to town, and no sign of his father. Doc Craig stood peering at the group in the back of the truck. Three of the men struggled with their victim, who continued to wrench and kick while mumbling loudly underneath the canvas. Fred looped the noose over his head and tightened it.

"Got 'im!" he yelled. The three released the hooded man, who bounded to the side only to be caught by the taunt noose. The four hangmen then jumped clear of the truck.

"Finally!" Doc Craig yelled. "All right. Let's get the hell out of here! Jim, you first." Jim smiled as he shoved his truck into gear, gunned the motor, released the clutch, then looked up into his rearview mirror to watch. All four wheels dug into the soft turf, spewing the pungent mulch into the black forest. Then they gripped and the pickup lurched forward. The truck bed slid from under the dangling man's feet. The tailgate struck and broke his knees as it passed.

"Yeah! All right!" the lynch mob whooped as the sickening crack of a breaking neck echoed around the clearing. Jake stood shaking at the edge of the clearing, staring out into the darkness, trying not to witness the event behind him. But the revving engine startled him and he spun around in time to see the body careening off the truck tailgate. Nausea churned in his stomach, then crawled up his throat, as he watched the swinging body convulse and shake. He bent over to heave, but in doing so, his eyes caught sight of the muddy two-tone shoes on the hung man. The rising puke froze in his throat as he bolted toward the body. Each step closer brought a clearer view of the wing-tip shoes and the paling white skin showing from underneath the dead man's loose shirttail.

"Daddy! Daddy!" Jake ran to the body, grabbed hold, and screamed at the top of his lungs. The lead truck, halfway through the clearing exit, screeched to a halt, as did the other two while the boy's screams rang out. "You hung my daddy!" Jake yelled as he struggled to free his father.

"Oh, my God!" Doc Craig yelled, running toward the reunited father and son. There, he lifted the body up as Jim's truck backed up. Fred, on the back of the truck, reached over and sawed the rope in half with his knife. Three of the men lowered Marvin's body to the ground, none of them accepting what their eyes were seeing. Jake clung to the body, crying and puking. Jim and Fred wrestled him clear as Doc Craig rushed in to look. Cutting the hood from over his head, Doc Craig glared into Marvin's bulging eyes and pale contorted face. Jim, Joey, Fred, and Bob turned their heads and gagged.

"Oh, my God," Doc Craig repeated. Jake broke loose and dove back onto his father.

"You hung him! You hung my daddy!" Doc Craig rose slowly to his feet and peered helplessly into the dark, damp forest, trying not to see the dead friend and newly orphaned son before him. His mind clouded over and he grew nauseous.

"We done hung Judge Burns," he said dismally. Jim and the other men panicked, loaded themselves into their trucks, and sped off toward Aurora. The bee stings on each man had stopped throbbing, but the swollen knots, instead of shrinking, had turned an odd green color, marking each man as members of the lynch party.

"We killed the judge," Doc Craig recited deliriously. "And maybe the sheriff . . . and where is John . . . and how the hell did all this happen? This wasn't suppose to happen." Bewilderment and nausea filled his gut while his ears rang with the ever-present sirens that prepared the town for the arrival of the green-stained lynch mob.

* * *

Zon leaned back and submerged his bronze body into the cool fountain water that fed the pool behind his cabin. Boo-Boo stretched lazily on the grass, just beyond. The Friday evening sun painted the sky golden red. Reaching to the edge, he pressed the buttons of the remote control, switching on the TV mounted under the distant canopy. The six o'clock news had just begun. Slowly, he scanned the channels, searching for reports from Aurora.

"Steve, it all happened on a hot, misty Thursday night here, in Aurora, Mississippi." Harold Mangum gave a quick mysterious stare into the camera as he took in his next breath. The scene then switched to the Aurora city jail, where suited men scurried slowly about. "This morning, at 3:00 A.M., Mississippi state investigators arrested two deputies, Brad Duncan and Jason Attux, for attempted murder. Channel Twelve Action News was there." The screen changed again and showed the jailhouse front of the night before. The deputies, handcuffed and partially nude, were being escorted to the rear door of a waiting police car.

"Chief Investigator Shorty Peters," Harold continued, "pieced the story together, and had these comments." Investigator Peters' broad face filled the screen, silhouetted by an early morning sun.

"We b'lieve," Peters spoke slowly with a deep Southern drawl, "that Shr'ff Baka' spected these two dep'ties of bein' . . . gaey." He gagged on that last word, his face puckered with disgust. "We foun' in thar, in bed . . . naekid . . . strugglin' ta git apaut. Them kind git hung eva naeh an' den, ya know."

"Chief," interrupted Harold, "did they confess or acknowledge their crime or hidden lifestyle?"

"No . . . thay jus' tried ta co'vrit up. The little un jus' sobbed, while Attux, the big'un, raved on, sump'in bout hooded nigra's and a jail break."

"Well, what about John Jackson, the convicted rapist, he's no longer in the jail, is he?" Harold strained to impress the audience as he raised an inquisitive, heavily made-up eyebrow.

"Oh . . ." he groaned." Ah . . . Near's we kin tell, Shr'ff Baka, feared fo' the boy's safety, so he up an' hauled'm and his fam'ly over ta the jail in the next county. Thas whar they's at naea."

"Amazing."

"Yeah, ain't it?" Peters remarked. "Anaway, whan'e got back, he must ta foun' dem boys . . . like we did." Chief Peters pursed his lips and rolled his eyes wide like an old gossip in the midst of her glory. "Ratha'n let'n out their secrit, the two musta' attacked'm. I hear theya kind can be rufless . . . when id comes ta theya privcy."

"Chief, Sheriff Baker now lies in a coma at Aurora Hospital," Harold added. "We've learned from a reliable source that there were bloody fingerprints all over his head. Have you been able to identify them, or been able to talk to the sheriff?"

"No, we ain't, yet. Shr'ff's in purdy baed shape, but we 'spect him ta come 'round soon. Then he'll . . . "

Zon punched the channel button slowly. He noted the slow whine of small motors that aimed the satellite dish on the distant hill. Another channel soon locked onto the screen.

"In an even more bizarre, yet unrelated, story," started the Channel Five news anchorwoman in Jackson City, "Judge Marvin Burns, the sitting judge who convicted Jackson earlier that day of first-degree rape charges, died last night, apparently from a freak hunting accident. Witnesses say that Burns and a small group of men were out coon hunting when they were attacked by a swarm of African killer bees. Each man, in a panic, ran blindly through dense forest to escape. Judge Burns apparently ran into an old barbed-wire fence, which became entangled around his neck, snapping it as he ran past. Judge Burns, who was declared dead on arrival at Aurora General Hospital, was reported to be a kindhearted and righteous member of this small town, who now mourn his untimely passing."

Zon tapped the power button and turned the TV off. He eased his head back into the waterfall. A subtle smile spread across his face.

"Information . . . disinformation . . . both are power," he thought. "Add another to the list. Columbus discovered America. Malcolm X hindered the civil rights movement. In the struggle for freedom, Black South Africans destroy each other. A starving Somalia has to be bombed so it can be fed. And now, a town full of lynchers is pitied, praised, and immortalized." He sighed as the falling water began its soothing effect. "Talk is cheap . . . and so is the media."

10
RUN ON THE MARKET

Crawford Carrington walked slowly down the hall, paying little attention to the droves of dark-suited, printed-tie wearing brokers that scurried past him. The starting bell of the Exchange wouldn't sound for another thirty minutes. Each hurried broker knew that the saying "the early bird gets the worm" was not only true here, but absolute. One had to be ready to strike fast and furiously to make it on Wall Street. Facts had to be checked, inside information, verified, considered, and then either incorporated or discarded. Phone calls had to be made. Investing strategies and sell points had to be defined, tested, and retested, all before the starting bell. Sharp brokers, with a little luck, could profit substantially during a heavy day of trading. And this was going to be a heavy day. It was a Monday morning after heavy trading in the German and Japanese markets and a groundswell of sell-offs by the end of trading on Friday. Today, any good broker could practice the "buy low, sell high" strategy and show ten to fifteen-percent profit on his investment. Of course, for every good investor on the floor, there were at least three poor ones with bad information, second-guessed moves, and poor buy-sell strategies that provided better investors plenty of opportunity for profit-taking.

General excitement of the anticipated heavy trading day filled the back halls and main trading floor with brokers eager for the starting bell. Each belonged to some brokerage that had bought their way onto the floor to trade. Most, if not all, were equipped with portable phones and computer access. The ticker tape, the liquid-crystal two-foot high running board that encircled the large trading floor and flashed the trading stock's name and current price, blandly blinked on and off, warming up for the start.

Glassed-in booths, fifteen feet wide and ten feet deep, with tiered floors, formed the upper rim of the trading arena. These were the special offices reserved for the largest brokerages. Above them was the balcony, where tourists and would-be brokers stood to watch the process.

Crawford Carrington stepped nonchalantly through the crowd, to his booth, located at the center line of the trading floor. Five men inside stood anxiously as he entered the room.

"Good morning, sir."

"Good morning, sir."

"Sir."

"Mr. Carrington, sir."

"C. C." Each of the white men stood and all but bowed as Crawford cast an acknowledging glance around the room. He didn't speak. The room was fashioned into a control center, like that of a cruiser. In the center, at the rear, on the highest tier, stood a captain's chair. Computer terminals were mounted to the far left and right of the room. On the lower front deck, just right and left of center, stood two additional terminals, each connected to large forty-five-inch display screens that could be seen only from the inside. In the back left corner sat an observer's chair, reserved for Mr. Crawford Carrington, sole owner of Carr-i-Dodge Investments. Warren Hayes sat in the captain's chair. He was the lead broker for the firm and had been so for the past five years. Through his market savvy, the firm had maintained twenty-two percent profit for four of the last five years.

Five years before, this room would have been filled with twenty to thirty brokers with their ears pinned to telephones, each scrabbling and yelling, trying to direct the next move. However, each successive year, more computers were added and upgraded to the point where two brokers could now do the job of thirty. Those two, David Muster, and Michael Hasteen, sat at opposite ends of the room on the second tier. At the two center stations, Steve Michaels and Jack Freeman sat before their terminals. Unlike the two on the sides, the center terminals were used to visually track trading progress instantaneously. On the right screen, Carr-i-Dodge's profit index was plotted by the minute, with room enough to show the full eight-hour trading period. With a touch of a button, Jack could change the graph to display other information, such as the Exchange index movement over the past hour or index comparisons between today and yesterday, last week, or last year. Warren used this information to pace and confirm his investment moves.

Steve Michaels, on the left screen, had the same equipment, but instead of following Carr-i-Dodge, his job was to follow the competition. The firm had managed, through some very illegal means, to obtain a direct link into the Stock Exchange's computer system. This system was designed to be a one-way information link that allowed firms to automate their trading. Carr-i-Dodge had managed to go one step further. Besides receiving their own information, they also could receive anyone else's who traded on the exchange. This allowed them to monitor the success and moves of their competition. Warren knew that all of the other large firms had made the same under-the-counter deal with the Exchange.

Both front terminals were hooked into a mainframe, which received market information by the second from hundreds of market analysts around the world. Together, this trading system rivaled the NASA network in sophistication and technology. Today, however, it was going to surpass it.

All five men moved to take their seats as Crawford headed for his chair.

"Muster. Hasteen. You may go." Warren Hayes spoke to the men without looking at them.

"Sir?" Jack Hasteen replied, frozen, as he thought of his three small children.

"Report to the personnel office at once. You've been . . . reassigned." Warren continued to stare straight ahead into the large screens, as did Michaels and Freeman. Crawford proceeded to the observer's chair, poured himself a drink from the freshly stocked bar, and sat down. Without another word, Muster and Hasteen removed their headsets and walked toward the door. They knew that they'd both just lost their jobs. Both had performed well for the firm for over ten years. Both knew, too, as did all of the men in the room, that in business, there is no future, no guarantee, only the present. With faces stunned and reddened, both men shuffled out of the booth.

"They were contract?" Crawford asked casually as he sipped and stared into his drink.

"Yes sir, C. C." Warren answered back.

"Good." Ever the profit taker, Crawford smiled as he thought of the money just saved by the firing. Contracted personnel were paid no benefits. This included severance pay. Hayes and Michaels cut nervous eyes at each other, then looked back at the screens. They, too, were under contract.

"Michaels," Warren ordered, "reboot the system and yield to my terminal." He swung his mobile keyboard from its storage cabinet in the arm of his chair to its working position before him. Michaels didn't reply, but began immediately punching keys. The two screens went blank, relit in static snow, then to standby brilliant blue. Warren punched his secret access code into the keyboard, retrieved four three-and-a-half inch disks from his shirt pocket, and proceeded to reprogram the computer using the disks. The entire process took less than five minutes. Freeman and Michaels turned to watch. Crawford sat nursing his Bloody Mary. As he finished, the screens returned, and showed the same index profiles they'd shown before the reprogramming.

"What's changed?" asked Freeman.

"We've integrated a complete loop in the programmed trading system. Now, all trading will be done by computer. We need only monitor." Warren spoke with jubilant pride as he watched the new programming scan on the big screens.

"Didn't we try that several months ago?" Jack Freeman asked. "As I recall, it worked, but not as well as the system we were using at the time." Warren recalled the pride he'd felt three months before when a similar, fully computerized system, had failed. He, along with the four terminal technicians, outperformed the system by eight index points. The programming worked, but it was slow. It took time for the system to digest, test, and verify each move. Although it made far fewer mistakes, it couldn't act on hunches or predict nonlinear trends as well as the man-machine combination. Warren, surprised by the new system then, was ecstatic when his team outperformed it. But the experience had also taught him. He knew that he had been lucky that day, but luck happens. He also knew that, sooner or later, a better system would be devised, and rather than being replaced by it, he was going to be a part of it. He became part of the new system's development team, and was instrumental in its development without informing his own trading team. Together with the original programmers, they'd devised a smart system that could take hunches through logical analyses as well as transform nonlinear trends to linear. The programming had been tested secretly and repeatedly against Warren and his trading team's performance for weeks and had managed to outperform them consistently by three points.

"This one's better, far better," Warren said as he cut a conceited grin toward Crawford, who had been invited to witness the new program's performance. The two computers standing at the far ends of the booth, like the two technicians that had operated them, were obsolete and would be removed as soon as possible.

"What's payout on the new programming?" Crawford asked.

"Including the two techs' salaries, three months," Warren answered.

"Making profit, and the Exchange hasn't opened yet," Crawford beamed under his breath.

Although the booth was soundproof, floor monitors were turned on at low volume, filling the room with a familiar white noise hum. As the clock started ticking off the last minute, Crawford rose from his chair and strolled to the glass front. Across the floor in the opposing booth stood a similar figure with drink in hand. He could have been Crawford's exact double but for the bald head and golfer's tie. It was Sam Drayson, managing director for McAfee-Smith, the leading trader on Wall Street.

"Good news must travel fast," Crawford said.

"What?" Warren replied.

"Sam's here. He must have heard of our new programming and is here to view its performance firsthand."

Crawford picked up the binoculars and focused on Drayson who stood, along with several other executives in his booth, spying back at him. Crawford lowered his binoculars and held up his glass, gesturing a toast to his audience.

"That son of a bitch," Sam Drayson sang aloud with a smile. "That SOB thinks he's got us by the short hairs. Redfern!" Drayson snapped at his lead broker sitting in the captain seat, as he turned away from the glass. "What's been our margin over Carr-i-Dodge?"

"About seven tenths of a point daily average, sir," Redfern answered sheepishly. Drayson turned back to face the glass as he received Redfern's answer.

"And whose ass is on the line?" he continued, raising his binoculars.

"Mine . . . sir," Redfern replied.

"Just wanted to be sure we understood each other."

"Yes, sir." A nervous Redfern pulled himself to the edge of his seat. They, too, used the man-machine combination for trading, which had been the lead system in the industry. But Redfern was a better broker than Warren. Combined with the same hardware, software, information, and technical support, he had shown his superiority consistently in the profit-taking margins for the past five months. Indeed, his becoming trade team leader five months ago had prompted Carr-i-Dodge to look for a better system.

Crawford stepped lively as he moved back behind the display.

"Michaels, I want you to follow McAfee-Smith all day. That Irish asshole Drayson beat me by nine strokes in a golf match last week. I want to know the minute you get a tally . . . so I can laugh in his face."

"Yes, sir," Michaels replied as he accessed the Exchange's index. After several keystrokes, "McAfee-Smith" leaped across the vertical axis of the response screen. At that moment, the starting bell sounded on the main floor. Warren cut the floor audio monitors and started the auto trading program. Crawford leaped back to his seat, refreshed his drink, and lit a cigar.

"Well boys, it ain't good money . . . until it's our money," he said as he watched trading begin on the screens.

The automated ticker tape started overhead. Brokers rushed to and fro, yelling, trading, selling, and buying. Keyboards chattered while tickets ripped and fluttered to the ground like snow. The viewing galleries above the melee quickly filled.

"Mr. Carrington, sir," Freeman said.

"What?" Carrington growled.

"I've changed the index output so that the number shown will read as an end-of-the-day figure."

"What?"

"The current index will be projected forward as if it were the end of the day," Warren attempted to explain. "This way, we'll know at all times what our end-of-the-day performance would be, if we had maintained current performance to the end of the day." Crawford grabbed his cigar from his mouth and held it in the same hand as his drink.

"All the fuck I want to know," he scowled, "is how far am I ahead of fuck-face over there." Crawford understood their point, but the thought of avenging himself with Drayson consumed him. He had made his desire for information perfectly clear.

"You'll know, sir, every second," Warren replied, as he stepped down next to Freeman and leaned down to his ear.

"Try that brown-nosing trick again, you ass-wipe," Warren whispered, "and you'll be standing in the unemployment line with Muster and Hasteen. You'll address me only. Got it?" Warren gestured at the screen as if he were talking technically.

"Yeah . . . yes, sir," a humiliated Freeman replied.

"Sir," Michaels said, his eyes scanning the screen of marching numbers and charts, "total volume numbers are in. We're ahead of the market by fourteen points." Freeman struck several keys and his display showed three concurrent graphs, adding a new point every minute. The bottom graph was the overall Exchange profit index, running at 7.8. Far above that was the McAfee-Smith Index, standing at eighteen, then the Carr-i-Dodge at twenty-two.

"Yes!" Crawford yelled. Warren smiled at his success and cuddled back into his chair. He folded his keyboard back into storage.

"Leave it there, Freeman. There's nothing else to do but sit back and enjoy," Warren grinned.

Every minute, a new point was added to each of the three trend graphs. The Exchange graph varied sporadically, moving down to 6.7. McAfee-Smith fluttered somewhat, but held at eighteen. The Carr-i-Dodge had grown to twenty-four. Crawford sat back in his chair, chuckling.

"This is great!" he said to Warren. "Where do you think we'll finish?"

"At this pace, it'll probably be at twenty-nine for the day," Warren answered. Crawford smiled.

"Ahhhh," he sighed. "Let me go over here and gloat a bit." Crawford popped out of his seat. He'd gained a slight buzz from the Bloody Marys. As he waltzed down the tiers to the glass front, the phone rang. Warren answered.

"Yeah . . . oh." Warren handed the phone down to Crawford.

"Hello."

"C. C., old buddy. How's business?" Sam Drayson tried to hide the concern in his voice and spoke jovially from the other end.

"Sam! How they hanging, guy?"

"Oh, not bad. Listen, what's going on?" Crawford bit his lip, trying not to giggle out loud. He pulled the phone away from his head and covered the mouthpiece with his hand.

"It's Sam," he said, gesturing the phone toward the glass and laughing out loud at Warren. "He's shitface with envy. Wants to know what's going on." He put the phone back to his ear and played along.

"Sam . . . yeah, same old shit, how about you?" Crawford's fifty-five year old face reddened as he choked back his glee.

"I've been watching the activity. You're doin' pretty good but . . . " Concern was trickling through Sam's voice, but Crawford hadn't sensed it. He cut Sam off in midsentence.

"Why thanks, Sam old buddy. We've been working at it. Sorry I can't talk about it right just yet."

"Uh, yeah, that's okay, Crawford. Look. I've known for some time that you were working on a new system. Hell . . . I've even got one myself. I've just been waiting to see what yours could do. But . . . who's got this other system?"

"Other system? What other system?"

"You know darn well what other system. Don't play coy with me. We both know about the tie-in to the Exchange monitor. This guy's blowing us both off the map."

Crawford pulled the phone from his ear again and stepped in front of the screens. Freeman's screen showed the same three plots. Warren was using Michaels's console to follow along and second-guess the computer's buying and selling moves.

"Warren," Crawford said, holding his hand over the receiver and staring hard into the consoles, "pop up the top performers on one of these screens."

"Easy enough, C. C. They're already there," Warren responded with a smug, cheesy smile and pointed at Freeman's screen.

"Quit fuckin' around you conceited ass and pull up the top performers." Crawford's eyes bulged and blinked as he tried to clear the alcohol from his head. Realizing Crawford's seriousness and tipsy state, Warren stepped over to Freeman's console and obeyed the order. The screen blinked, then displayed index graphs for the top ten traders on the day, followed by labels flashing beside each.

"Damn! Damn it!" Crawford screamed at the screen. The Carr-i-Dodge index stood at 24.5, and showed a small upward incline from the start. The McAfee-Smith index still held at eighteen. Seven other plots fell below McAfee-Smith. But one plot stood out from the pack of nine like a sore thumb, showing a growth from 16.6 at the start to over thirty-seven points in less than three market hours.

"Who the fuck is that?" Crawford's strangled voice cut into Warren's ears.

"I don't know. Michaels . . . punch him up . . . what's the label . . . T. Simmons. Get it up, Michaels!"

"Yes, sir." Michaels's screen went blank momentarily as he performed the file search.

"That kind of performance is impossible," Warren said as he examined the graph. "Whoever it is must have one helluva system." Crawford had forgotten about the phone in his hand. Realizing that Sam was still on the other end, he placed it back to his head.

"Uh, Sam . . . listen . . . ah . . . I didn't think you'd see that one. Yeah . . . it's mine, too."

"You saying you've got two systems?" Sam replied in disbelief.

"Uh, yeah, but I can't talk now. I'll get back to you." Crawford pulled the phone away from his head, rushed over, and hung it up.

"That's got to be one huge mother," Warren said as he waited for Michaels to finish.

"Warren!" Crawford bellowed, "what is this? I thought you said that there was nothing else out there like our system. It was supposed to run fucking circles around every damn system on Wall Street. You said . . . " Crawford was ranting when Michaels broke in.

"Sir, I've got him. It's T. Simmons and Associates."

"T. Simmons. Who the hell is that?" Crawford asked.

"I've never heard of him, either," Warren responded. "What booth is he in?"

"He doesn't have a booth, sir. It's a trader on the floor."

"What? Where?"

Michaels punched several more keys, then responded.

"He's got block two-thirty-eight."

"You mean that some schmuck on the floor is kicking our ass?" Crawford raved.

"Look," Warren said, "it's just another program. We can . . . " Crawford cut Warren off in midsentence.

"Just another program! Just another program! Listen to me, fuck-face." Crawford stepped over to Warren and spun him around from the console. "Whatever it is, it's more than just another program. That's our reputation. Carr-i-Dodge lives on investors who expect us to be on top. They give us their money because they know that they can do no fucking better. If word of a better . . . and I do mean . . . better system gets out, the pack of scum-sucking wolves'll drop us so fast it'd make your head spin."

Warren had been thinking of the programming and not the business end of things. Crawford was right. Carr-i-Dodge couldn't afford to be beaten by such a superior system. Their new, fully automated programming was supposed to put them back on top again, over McAfee-Smith. Maintaining the number one performance slot could net them billions of dollars of business in a year's time.

Crawford stepped away from Warren and down to the glass. Grabbing the binoculars, he scanned the floor for block markers.

"What was that number again?" he asked.

"Two-thirty-eight, sir." Crawford slowly scanned the marker poles on the floor.

"Two-fifty . . two-forty seven . . . two-forty . . . two-thirty eight." Brokers and runners rushed back and forth by the desk below the marker. Crawford focused and waited for an opening.

"There . . . I got him. I'll be damned . . . "

"What is it?" Warren asked. Crawford paused.

"The NAACP must be working overtime. The firm's got a nig broker on the floor."

"Sir," Michaels interrupted, not taking his gaze from his screen. "T. Simmons is a small, minority-owned firm. They list only three employees, including a secretary."

"What?" Crawford screeched. "How could some piss-ant firm like that afford this kind of system?"

"They can't, sir," Michaels answered. "Our sources indicate that they don't posses the assets."

"What? You telling me they're ripping our asses without a system?" Crawford asked as he stared at the black broker.

"Wait a minute," Warren said. "Is he wearing a headset?"

"Yeah," Crawford replied.

"Where is he?" Warren stepped over to the window and grabbed a second pair of binoculars. Crawford pointed him out.

"Uh huh. Just as I thought. C. C., watch his mouth. He's not talking into his phone set. He's just making orders with his terminal, and listening to whomever is on the other end."

"So?" responded Crawford.

"So, whoever's on the other end of the phone has the system. That's how he's doing it." The room hung silently for a second before Warren continued. "He's not analyzing. No one could at that rate. He's just trading. Whoever is on the other end of that headset has the system. That guy's just a mouthpiece, or in this case, simply a pair of hands."

"What are our options?" asked Crawford.

"Sir?" Warren responded.

"The way I see it," Crawford said as he lowered his glasses, "either we've got to improve our performance, or stop his."

"We're doing all that we can do," Warren said.

"Even if you plug in and aid the programming?"

"C. C., I'm already in the programming. That machine has done everything that I would have done, plus. At this point, there is no way we can do better."

"Then we're going to have to pull Mr. Simmons's plug."

"We can't do that." Warren spoke cautiously to Crawford, who stared madly back into his eyes.

"Michaels!" Crawford growled.

"Sir?" Michaels squeaked.

"Can we scramble or disconnect that terminal from here?"

"No, sir."

"Can we cut his phone line, stop him from talking to whomever it is on the other end?"

"No, sir."

"You telling me that there is no way we can stop him from trading?" Crawford spoke as his stare kept Warren silent. Freeman found his voice.

"Sir, Warren is right. There's no way we can stop that guy from trading, short of dragging him off the floor."

Crawford dropped his eyes and bit into the cigar between his teeth.

"Then we'll just have to drag the black scumbag off the floor." Crawford slammed the binoculars down on the table by the glass front and climbed the tiers to his chair. Flopping down in it, he grabbed the portable phone from the end table next to him and began dialing.

"Hello, New York Police Department. Captain Princeton's office." Crawford spoke harshly.

"Yes, this is Captain Princeton's office," a polite woman's voice replied. "I'm sorry, but the Captain is tied up at the moment. May I take a message?"

"He'll want to talk to me. Tell him it's Crawford Carrington."

"One moment, please." Crawford chewed his cigar as he waited.

"C. C., what can I do for you?" Crawford smiled when he heard the suck-up tone in the captain's voice. It had been quite a while since he had last called on him.

"Princeton, I've got a situation. Get two of your uniformed men down to the Exchange floor. There's a black man, middle-aged, wearing an olive green suit, in block two-thirty eight. I want him arrested and held."

"Yes . . . sure, C. C., but on what charge?"

"How the hell should I know? Make one up. Just get him off the floor and put him somewhere where no one can get to him. I want my boys to talk to him first. Do you understand?"

"Yes. I'll have a couple of men on the floor in minutes."

"Good." Crawford didn't smile as he hung up the phone. It was good to have favors owed to you, especially in situations like this. And half the city officials in New York owed him favors.

The black broker on the floor scared Crawford. He had made it his business to know the market, old and new. Hundreds of people were on his payroll to make sure that Carr-i-Dodge got the latest and best equipment, programming, and personnel. And in that pursuit, there was no right or wrong, no legal or illegal, only win or lose. Carr-i-Dodge rarely lost. Only once over the last five years had the firm lost a battle, and that was when Drayson had hired Joshua Redfern right from under his nose. Redfern would have replaced Warren.

But the new programming was going to make up for the last few months of trailing McAfee-Smith. Carr-i-Dodge would no longer have to bargain away the profits in kickbacks to keep its clients from jumping ship to Drayson.

T. Simmons and company had changed all that. There was a better system, and all of the larger firms knew it. But Crawford would soon have the only known link to that system, the trader on the floor. If he knew anything, then his programmers, along with some arm-twisting from the police force, would get it out of him. For now, it would be enough to just stop him from trading.

"How the hell is he doing it?" Crawford asked Warren, who sat deep within his own thoughts.

"I haven't the foggiest. If I wasn't watching it with my own eyes, I would've believed it."

"Could it be some scam?"

"I'd doubt it. We've tried all the angles to rig and fix trading and came up with nothing. No, this guy's trading." Warren had moved back to Freeman's screen. Freeman had plugged directly into T. Simmons's computer trading line. Each sell, volume, and rate from the mystery broker flashed up on the screen.

"This guy's trading is phenomenal. Look." Warren pointed to the screen. "See this one? At purchase, this was just a mediocre buy. But watch its totals." New purchases flashed up, then scrolled down the screen. As they progressed downward, the totals column values changed with the price. As the purchase that Warren pointed out scrolled down, its value increased, which drove up the total value.

"You see? This guy's system made these buys here, here, and here," he said, pointing the screen. "That made the price of this one fall," moving his finger up the screen to the newly purchased stock. "Then it made these buys, which made the purchased stock's price go sky-high."

"That doesn't seem so amazing to me," chimed in Crawford, drinking his Bloody Mary--without the tomato juice.

"If that were it, then it wouldn't be. But watch the prices on all of the purchases," Warren said in amazement.

Freeman leaned in to view the screen.

"All of their totals are going up," Crawford said.

"Exactly," Warren replied. "The stocks that this system uses to push other stocks up or down are being pushed themselves. Each purchase is forward and backwardly integrated. That way, all of them profit, almost exponentially."

"Well, can't we do that?" Crawford asked.

"At our rate of development, it'd take us another five to ten years to develop that kind of system. And then only if we had the base programming," Warren said as he watched the screen. "Besides, by then, the government would probably be forced to ban the system, once everybody got it."

"Why?" Crawford asked.

"Ten or fifteen of these systems, operating simultaneously, could bankrupt this country in a day. Just one system, today, stands to make a fortune."

Crawford's eyes glared as he imagined the billions he'd be making if he had this mystery system.

"Maybe we can get at this system through the guy in two-thirty-eight." He pushed himself from his chair as he spoke, and walked over to the glass. "What'd this guy start with, Michaels?" Crawford asked as he scanned the floor exits for police.

Reading down the screen, Michaels answered, "He bought in at

$10,000 at the opening bell."

"That's not much," Crawford replied.

"No, sir, but at his current rate of earnings, he'll have turned that into nearly . . . seven hundred and fifty million dollars by market close."

"Holy shit!" Crawford careened. "We've got to get that guy off the floor. He'll destroy business for us all. Where are those damned policeme . . ." Crawford swallowed his last words as he watched two policemen step onto the trading floor from the main north entrance. The two slowly pushed their way through the ravenous crowd of traders.

"Come on . . . come on! Get him out of there." Crawford said under his breath. "Freeman, what's his index?" Again, Freeman struck his keyboard and read aloud from his screen.

"T. Simmons has risen to forty-four, we're standing at twenty-four, McAfee-Smith at eighteen. Totals for the day so far . . .
T. Simmons is up . . . one-hundred and thirteen million dollars."

Crawford stood stone-faced as he watched the policemen finally reach the black man. Once there, each grabbed an arm. The man looked up from his terminal in complete surprise. After a brief exchange, he sat back down, keyed in several strokes on his keyboard, reached around the terminal and turned it off. Upon removing his headset, he threw on his jacket, picked up a brief case, then reached his hands behind his back to be handcuffed. After cuffing, the three pressed their way through the crowd toward the north exit. Scurrying brokers, around the scene, stole split-second stares at the arrest, but none missed a stroke on their terminals as the black broker was hustled off the floor.

"T. Simmons's rate's dropping, sir," Freeman sang out.

"Let me know the minute it stabilizes," Crawford said. He walked back to Warren, who sat in his captain's chair.

"Warren. You go down there and find out about that system from the trader. Take anybody with you that you'll need. I'll arrange to have some persuaders there ahead of you, so he'll be sure to cooperate."

"But, what about our system?" Warren whined. "It's not even lunchtime yet."

"You said that there's nothing to be done except monitor. These gentlemen can do that," Crawford said, motioning his head toward Michaels and Freeman.

"But what if something goes wrong?" Warren's voice reeked of desperation. He didn't want to leave the system . . . his system. After working feverishly day and night, the programming had become a part of him, as if it were his own child. "But, if something should happen," he continued, "I'm the only one who knows how . . . "

"It will run without you," Crawford said, crushing every word between his teeth. Just then, Warren realized his job, too, was going to be cut as soon as the new system was proven out.

"You've spent the better part of the last three months assuring us that nothing can possibly happen to it." Crawford's speech showed no sign of emotion or tact. "Consider the T. Simmons incident your next assignment." Crawford's words left Warren speechless. "I'd say your best move would be to get enough from old jungle boy from block two-thirty-eight to make you valuable to us again." Crawford turned his back on Warren as he finished and sat on the edge of Freeman's desk.

Warren stood with his mouth open, as thoughts of his own stupidity ground his consciousness to powder. How could he have been so blind? All of his painstaking effort to put his own trading savvy on computer had cost him his own job. He'd held nothing back, wanting the system to be the best. It should have brought him reward, but . . .

"Come on, C. C. You can't be serious about this. I built this system. I've made billions for the corporation over the past years. You can't just dump me out . . . "

"Mr. Carrington!" Freeman's shout silenced Warren's pitiful pleas. "The T. Simmons index has stabilized at 2.5 . . . but . . ."

"But? But what?" Crawford shot back.

"But Carr-i-Dodge is down to 19.2 . . . and dropping."

"What?"a surprised Crawford responded as he dashed to look at the screen. Warren joined him. "What's happening?" Crawford asked. Michaels punched up Carr-i-Dodge's activity on his screen.

"The system is still operating, sir," he replied, "but it's making bad moves." Warren, grinned over the sudden occurrence, then winced at Michaels's insult to his system. Though glad about the fall in performance, his ego couldn't let the insult pass.

"It's not making the wrong moves," he said indignantly. Crawford turned instinctively to Warren. "Then, what the hell's going on?" he asked. Warren kept his indignant smirk on his face and looked the heartless businessman in the eye.

"I can't say. You just fired me!" he said, like a hurt schoolgirl. Crawford stiffened as he cut his piercing eyes to Warren. Never had any subordinate talked to him that way, before or after being fired. But he realized that Warren had him over a barrel. Something was wrong, and Warren was the only one who could fix it. Revenge on him would be sweet, but it would have to wait.

"Look, Warren," he said, "I didn't just fire you. I was merely trying to persuade you to go interrogate that broker. You're our best man, and I know it. No one else understands the market, nor these infernal machines, as well as you. I picked the best man to do the job that needed doing and if given the chance, would do it again." Crawford's speech, unlike any of his other comments of the morning, was full of passion and flattery. Warren fell for it hook, line, and sinker. With chest swollen and face red, Warren turned with a big "I told you so" look at Michaels and hustled him out of his chair in front of the left terminal.

"You're saying that I am still trader team leader?" Warren spoke toward the screen before him as he sat and began punching the keyboard, but his question was clearly aimed at Crawford.

"Absolutely," responded Crawford, his voice dripping with sincerity.

"Carr-i-Dodge is down to fourteen and falling," Freeman piped in. Crawford grimaced.

"I'll need that in writing," Warren said as he typed.

"Fine."

"Now."

"I'm right on it," Crawford replied, all but bowing as he stole a panicked glance at the index screen, then dashed back to his chair. Warren continued to punch away at his terminal.

"For five years," he added, then paused typing. Freeman and

Michaels glared at Warren. Crawford gasped in a deep breath. His eyes bulged, then closed to a fine squint.

"All right," he said, then went on with his writing. Warren smiled, then started typing again. Michaels, standing behind Freeman, who was seated at the totals terminal, leaned in and whispered,

"Oh yeah. He's a dead man." Freeman smiled as he nodded. With a grin, he added, "I'm next in line for his seat."

Warren panned through Carr-i-Dodge's activity.

"Just as I thought. The program is working properly. It's making the same calls as I would make, but . . . " He paused as he set the screen to automatically scroll up.

"Index down to 5.7," Freeman announced. Crawford jumped from his seat.

"We're lower than the fucking Exchange average," he growled. "That means we're giving our fucking money away." He crumpled the makeshift contract in his fist and pounced down the tiers to Warren.

"Warren, you fix this thing, or else."

"Where's my contract?" Warren said nervously. Crawford finished balling up the paper and threw it in Warren's face.

"Fix this damned thing, or you'll never work in the market again," Crawford growled like a wounded bear. Warren cowered like a lamb. Without a word, he turned back to the screen and watched the scrolling numbers.

"If the selection is right," he started, "maybe the purchases are not going through." Warren's fingers danced over the keyboard. Two additional columns were added to the scrolling screen. Warren watched for a few moments.

"We're holding at 4.2," Freeman beamed jubilantly. Warren paid him no attention, but stared hard at the two new columns of numbers.

Crawford paced the floor like an expectant father as he waited on the computer jockeys.

"This can't be," Warren said aloud as he sat stunned after watching the screen for ten minutes. "This is impossible."

"What? What?" Crawford yelped, as he tried to follow Warren's eye movement to decipher what he was seeing.

"Some . . . thing, some program is shadowing our own."

"So? We've shadowed other programs before. It never caused another system to crash," Freeman said.

"No, no, you don't understand. Another program is shadowing our own, but the shadow is moving in front of ours, not behind it."

"So . . . we're shadowing it?" Crawford asked.

"Yes . . . and no," a confused Warren replied. "Our program is calculating its own moves, and they're the right moves, but it then plays right into the shadow's last move." He stared silently into the screen after he spoke.

"You're making no sense," Crawford shouted, slamming a frustrated fist down on the terminal top.

"To put it simply," Warren said, "someone is playing the market, not to win, but to make Carr-i-Dodge lose."

"What?" Crawford replied skeptically.

"That's got to be it," Warren continued. "Some system out there has deciphered our program, but they've gone it one step better. They're calculating our next move, then calculating an opposing move, like a giant chess game, all before we make a purchase in the market from our first calculation." Warren paused as he watched the puzzled looks on the three men's faces slowly fade. "Then, the opposing order is placed a split second before ours, which changes the pricing and positioning on which ours was calculated."

"So when our order goes in," Freeman said, as he picked up on Warren's theory, "the purchase is wrong . . . for the new conditions."

"Exactly," said Warren, and turned back to the screen. "So, instead of profit taking, we keep catching the price change as it moves in the wrong direction."

"But prices can't change that much so quickly, can they?" asked Michaels.

"Ah . . . that's the beauty of computer trading. We're working in a world of split seconds, not minutes. The moves are small, but fast." Crawford ran his right hand fitfully through his closely cropped hair.

"And we can't do a damned thing about it," Warren added. "I've already tried altering our programming, slowing and speeding up our activity. The shadow compensated for each change within two trading moves."

Gray roots eased out of Crawford's scalp, as he unconsciously pulled at a handful of hair. As his clenched fist slid down his head, he froze. Spinning about, he said, "Warren, what kind of system would it take to do all of this?" Warren continued to stare innocently at the scrolling numbers.

"I'd say a computer system roughly the size of the Twin Towers."

"And the programming, is it possible?"

"I don't know of any system that could do that."

"And this system would have to somehow have tied into ours, at least so that it could stay just one step ahead, right?"

"That'd make sense," Warren answered. Freeman and Michaels stared at Crawford, who stared down at the back of Warren's head.

"Turn the system off," Crawford whispered as he turned to Freeman.

"Sir?" Freeman whispered back.

"Turn the damned thing off," Crawford repeated slowly and deliberately. Without responding, Freeman typed in the shut-down sequence. Both screens immediately went blank. The dark screen broke Warren's trance on the scrolling numbers.

"What happened?" Warren asked as he spun around in his chair. Crawford stepped to Warren, grabbed him from the chair, and slung him toward the door. Warren did a wild square dance up the tiers and landed awkwardly in a heap on the upper tier floor.

"You rotten son of a bitch!" Crawford yelled, as he recoiled from throwing Warren to the door. "What kind of fool do you take me for?" Warren remained on the floor, but lifted his head dizzily to look at Crawford.

"Was it Drayson? He paid you to do this, didn't he? That's why he called over here, setting this whole thing up." Crawford paused to get his breath.

"What are you saying?" Warren managed to say as he climbed to his feet.

"Only one person could have made these screens read as they did," Crawford surmised. "Only one has had access to the programming from day one. And that same one has managed to conveniently be here to explain the impossible to us poor fools." Crawford had caught his breath. His building rage turned his aging face beet red. Michaels and Freeman backed away from him.

"All of you . . . get the hell out of my booth . . . Now!" he shouted.

"But Mr. Carrington," Freeman said, "we had nothing to do with this."

"That asshole on the floor couldn't have the brains to pull off something like this alone," he growled at Warren. "You were helping him, tracking our stock's downfall with such glee. And you," he said pointing at Michaels, "you're supposed to know computers. Why is it that I was the first to realize that impossible computers and impossible programs are impossible. You played along with your buddies, didn't you, you spineless scumbag?"

"No, no sir," responded Michaels. "Please sir, I need my job. I . . . "

"I said, get . . . the . . . hell . . . out! The lot of you! You're fired! Get out!" Crawford reached around, grabbed the keyboard from Michaels's desk, and flung it at the three traders. The attached cord stretched taunt, then recoiled, snapping the board back toward Crawford. Seeing it coming he ducked, but not quickly enough to dodge it. The blow knocked him backward. His head banged into the glass wall. Crack marks irradiated from the point where his head struck. Small splatters of blood trickled down the glass as Crawford sank unconscious to the floor. Freeman flung open the door and ran out. Michaels stepped over to the phone and dialed 911. Warren crawled down the tiers toward Crawford. He grabbed the limp man, rolled him over, scooped up the crumpled contract beneath him, turned, then walked out of the door.

* * *

Downtown, across from Captain Princeton's office, several officers were questioning Tim Simmons, the owner of T. Simmons Brokerage.

"Tell us again, how did you end up doing the trading?" A mild and exhausted voice floated from the far corner of the room. There, a young policewoman sat, drained after questioning the broker for over an hour. Two other men were in the room. One sat at the desk with Simmons, resting his chin in his hand. The other sat on a bench by the door.

"The story's the same, no matter how many times I tell it." Tim Simmons stated. "Three weeks ago, I get a phone call. This guy on the other end says he wants to trade some stock. Since that is my business, naturally, I encouraged him."

"Who was this guy?" asked the policeman seated closest to him.

"I never found out," Simmons answered. "He asked me to explain how he could go about trading. I explained that, for a small fee, I would buy for him any stock on the market that he wanted, or, for an additional fee, I'd invest his money for him and build him a portfolio." No one asked any questions. Simmons continued. "So then, he asked me how he would know which stock to choose, or that I was making the right buys. I told him his best bet was to read as much current information on stock market trading, or any events that might affect the market, and follow the activity of other markets around the world. Then I told him that that was what I did for a living, and it would be best if he let me invest for him. He then took my address and said he'd get back to me."

"Why did he pick you?" asked the lady cop.

"He said he picked my name out of the black pages."

"The what?" asked the cop seated on the bench.

"The black pages," Simmons responded, "It's like the yellow pages of black businesses. People use it to find minority owned companies when they want to do business."

"So this guy was black?" asked the lady cop.

"I couldn't say." Simmons said, "I never saw him."

"So then what?" asked the cop at the table.

"Last week, I get this package in the mail." Simmons reached down and retrieved a wide, bubble-lined white envelop, which he pushed toward the policeman on the other side of the table. "Inside, I find this piece of paper, a portable phone and headset, and $20,000 cash." Again Simmons paused as all of the cops shook their head in frustration from hearing the same story over and over. They were looking for flaws, but none surfaced. "I'll read the note again." Simmons picked up the paper without waiting for a response and read it in an obsessively bored voice. "It says, 'Mr. Simmons. Half of the $20,000 enclosed is yours as payment for your services. The other half I want you to invest. Place the $10,000 in your account for trading on this coming Monday. Please trade for no one else. Go to your station on the trading floor, put on the head phone, and wait. I'll call one minute before the market opens. Please expect to trade all day, with no lunch break." Simmons paused to clear his throat, then continued. "Please route all proceeds from your transactions to the account listed below." The cop at the table broke in. "We've checked that account number at Crown City Bank. It was registered to a John Doe."

"Was?" quizzed the lady cop.

"Was," he answered back. "It was set up so that the funds were transferred instantly to another account."

"And whose was that?"

"Another broker on the trading floor."

"Same M.O. as Mr. Simmons here, I presume?" she asked nonchalantly.

"Yep, exact same, except his letter instructed him to trade directly with the money received in the account, and he got his phone call at 11:15."

"The exact time we arrested Mr. Simmons," she said.

"Whoever set this up knew we were going to take Simmons off the floor. He had a backup already in place." The cops stared at one another, each waiting for some brilliant revelation to solve this mystery. None came.

"Anyway," the plump cop at the table continued, "this other trader claims the caller rattled off the orders fast and furious, but showed no profit for about an hour. Then, his profits suddenly took off like a skyrocket."

"That's the way mine were all morning long," Simmons chimed in. "I remember wishing I hadn't squirreled back that money he paid me, like I did. I would have been a multimillionaire if I'd've invested mine with his. But I figured that anybody crazy enough to bulk mail that much cash was going to lose his shirt in a hurry."

"Anyway," the cop interrupted again, "the other broker claims that he traded that way until the end of the day."

"Where'd the money go this time?" asked the lady cop.

"Back to Crown City Bank, into another John Doe account. But this time, the account was set up to transfer instantly to an account in

Barbados."

"How much was the total?" she asked.

"The bank records show a total of seven-hundred and eighty-five million, five-hundred ninety-seven thousand, eight-hundred and seventy five dollars and eleven cents--all untraceably stowed away in the Tropics."

"Have I done anything illegal?" Tim Simmons asked out of frustration. He had been held and questioned at the police precinct for over eight hours, had nothing to eat all day, and was two hours overdue at home. The police hadn't allowed him any phone calls. Just then, the phone rang. The lady cop picked up, but didn't speak.

"You can go," she said as she hung up the phone.

"Thank you," Simmons said as he popped up, grabbed his jacket, and walked out of the door.

"Sweetest scam I've ever seen," said the cop at the table. "Perfectly legal, untraceable, and anonymous. It's like it never happened."

"It never happened," said a loud voice over the intercom. Captain Princeton spoke through the microphone from where he sat behind the two-way mirror of the interrogation room. Crawford Carrington sat beside him. He wore a heavy gauze bandage on the back of his head. "Did you hear me? No report, no comment, no nothing. It never happened."

"Fine by me," said the lady cop as she rose from her chair. "Let's go home. Doing nothing all day can really wear you down."

11
BODIES OF GOLD

Zon sat submerged in thought, sipping peacefully on freshly squeezed mango juice. The taste was sweet, but not nearly as pleasing as it had been in Beinin. He drank it slowly, calmly. The thick juice returned his mouth, his taste buds, his thoughts to Beinin, where he had eaten nothing but fresh vegetables, fruits, and juices. Everything was juiced, sweet, tree-ripened, and fresh, much like the place itself. Yesterdays were treasured memories of days gone, and tomorrow, the hope for the same yet to come. But today, the present, was forever fresh. Never was there confusion of memory nor expectations present reality. Each joyfully occupied its own place, in time, in Beinin.

Mango juice at the Body O'Gold Fitness Center was as different from Beinin's as the people. People here, like time, had somehow lost their freshness. They plowed into every moment, anxious over the future, while longingly, regretfully staring back into the past. In America, joy had become a verb instead of a noun. Very few sought it, yet everyone wanted to experience it through achievement, acquisition and competition. America . . . the land of competition, winning at all cost, taking no prisoners, stepping in or on anything, not to win, but to stay in the lead. Here and now, there is no winner, only one . . . winning.

The juice, like soothing tonic, slid easily down Zon's throat. Playfully he chased the liquid around his mouth as he chased thoughts around his mind. He was hopelessly lost in his thoughts, oblivious to his surroundings, and that was just where he wanted to be. He'd found the Body O'Gold Fitness Center just west of the center of Charlotte, North Carolina. It was the only place in town that served exotic fresh fruits and juices. The place was upscale and offered the best in fitness equipment and facilities. It also sported a juice bar that was well lit, with plenty of tables and chairs. The clientele was the professional, after-work crowd seeking a good workout and conversation before they crawled home or back to work.

Zon sat quietly at a table in the back corner of the room. He'd never tried any of the fitness equipment during the three months that he'd been coming there. Normally, he just sat in his corner, faced the wall and sipped juice. Tight biker shorts, tank top, baggy cut-off sweat shirt, and beach-comber shoes were the closest he could get to comfortable, yet inconspicuous nudity.

The tables were naturally finished, with beautiful wood grain shimmering though hefty protective polyurethane coats. Each had six matching chairs about them. Zon sat on the edge of his seat, his long legs extended outward and crossed at the ankles. And he always sat alone. No one ever joined him or attempted to talk to him, except the waitresses, who politely brought him juices and immediately left. His posture and seating choice clearly sent a message of "Do Not Disturb."

But that wasn't true.

He wanted friends, but was afraid. Deep down inside, he was lonely, but scared to face the cost of ridding himself of that loneliness. Idrisi had made his *quest* sound so serious, so vital. He couldn't let anything deter him from it, though he still wasn't sure what it actually was. Friends would mean attachments and curiosities, and he couldn't be completely honest about either. Friendship would also mean women, and Idrisi had made that issue painfully clear.

"Your virginity belongs to Beinin," Idrisi had said, which meant it wasn't his to give away. To any of his would-be women friends, he knew he'd be a potential and most eligible mate. Before Beinin, there had been many women friends, but his demented mind had always kept his interactions in check. Could he now, being older and far lonelier than ever, control those urges and still be friends? And if those urges were controllable and he became friends, dare he chance hurting a woman who became attracted? Would the women of today accept a healthy, straight man who didn't want to get physically involved? Would men friends accept him as being straight once they realized that he didn't chase the ladies? For Zon, there were no easy answers to these questions. Until now, it had been easier to avoid them by remaining alone. Sooner or later, he'd have to face them.

In Beinin, there had been many friends, men and women alike. And the astounding beauty the women possessed had put his inner control to the ultimate test. But he had learned to control his desires, though it had taken multiple failures and extreme effort. He'd learned as he prepared to leave, that Beininians rarely wore clothing, but had worn modest coverage--explicitly for his sake. Zon chuckled as he sat remembering the earlier days of countless slaps upon his cleanly shaven head. The glistening orb made the perfect target whenever Idrisi wanted to make a point.

"Don't see the pain," Idrisi had recited continuously, while he stung the skin on Zon's skull with repeated smacks. "Don't see the pain."

"Well stop hittin' me up side my head then," Zon would respond in frustration.

"Focus your mind. Decide what will get in and what will not, what will dictate and what will not. You must learn to focus your mind, with or without physical stimulus . . . dismiss the pain . . . focus your thoughts." Zon's head would go numb and Idrisi would switch to the other side as they trained. In time, Zon learned to focus through the pain and all other outside influences. And he had shaken his head in painful disgust when he finally rediscovered something that he'd known from the start. His mind, his thoughts, his perception of the internal and external, were all based on rhythm. To get to that control, he had to define a rhythm, then get all that he perceived to that one rhythm. "Set the rhythm . . . get the rhythm . . . get control," he'd repeat. The same magic of music, whether in jazz or the latest top-of-the-charts, was now the avenue to his power.

Once he'd perfected control, the head slaps ceased. Zon soon became able to set it and get it instantaneously. That was, until the new stimulus came. One fine morning, instead of their normal routine of running about the countryside exploring, training, and learning,

Zon was stood atop a large rock, with eyes wide and mind focused. Suddenly, a parade of Beininian women emerged from behind the rock. Not one wore a stitch of clothing.

As he caught sight of the first beautiful form, Zon lost concentration. A beam of lust began bouncing about in his head. The more women he saw, the greater his lust grew. He began squirming as his physical body also began to react.

"Stand still," Idrisi insisted. "Focus your thoughts. Open your eyes," Zon darted his eyes back and forth, from body to body, body to sky, sky to cloud. "Focus, and watch," Idrisi demanded. Reaching up, he effortlessly lifted Zon from the rock and placed him in the midst of the parade, which didn't help him at all. Idrisi started slapping him on the head again. Zon struggled to focus. Just as the fiftieth (he was counting) gorgeously earthen body rounded the rock, a line of nude men followed. Zon turned his head away.

"Look!" Idrisi shouted. Zon turned back. Immediately, a beam of humiliation burst onto his conscience. The one of lust substantially subsided. The various sizes of the men embarrassed him. The fact that he was looking shamed him. Then to look upon the women excited him. Fifty nude males joined the females, then they all sat about Zon and Idrisi. For the full day, and for weeks afterward, the naked hoard conferenced on the nature and beauty of the human body. Through this, Zonbolo grew ever stronger.

Controlling his lust was one thing. But could he accept the presumptions and potential heartbreak of would-be friends?

"Maybe a few good friends," he said softly, "and I've got a couple already." He smiled and thought of Billy Davis and Boo-Boo, his panther-friend and faithful companion. The young cat had grown to full size over the eight months that he'd been back home. With a very small portion of the money from the stock market, he'd bought a 100-acre farm thirty miles outside of Charlotte. The land had been owned by a hunt club and was kept naturally wild. The club had stocked it yearly with quail and deer, or whatever its members wanted to hunt.

Zon had learned of the place as he stood on the spectator's gallery, above booth fourteen at the New York Stock Exchange. There, two middle-aged white men had talked of it as they surveyed the room.

Zon had caught only pieces of their conversation from the back of the gallery where he stood dressed in dull grey coveralls and a matching cap. He purposefully resembled janitors who cleaned after the high rolling traders. His phone headset resembled a radio. To the average passerby, he looked to be a loitering janitor, listening to the latest hits. Dark glasses had hidden the crazed movement of his eyes as he cut them back and forth, following the electronic ticker tape. All day, he'd stood in the nook just behind one of the large round support columns, reading numbers, analyzing, computing, and executing his moves over the phone.

He'd expected Carr-i-Dodge to interfere with his trading and was prepared to react while staying well within the letter of the law. There was no insider information used, just a greater-than-normal understanding of the rhythmic dynamics of the stock market. High dollar traders used computers to their advantage. Some, like Crawford Carrington, acted as if they owned the Exchange.

Zon hadn't known what to expect from him, but had prepared for the worst. Standing just above them, he'd honed in on Warren Wilson after he'd heard Crawford Carrington arrange Tim Simmons's arrest. Though reading minds outside Beinin had been nearly impossible, Warren's thoughts had turned out to be quite simple to read. Unlike most outsiders, Warren was concentrating hard on the computer programming. Like a hypnotist's swinging jewel, his concentration had keenly focused his thoughts, which allowed Zon access to the Carr-i-Dodge programming. Once he had it, it was simple to play the market against it. The changes that Warren attempted were just as easily undone.

Zon had opened bank accounts in cities, all under aliases. He pulled money from the Barbados account into each, and invested a great portion back into the stock market, assuring a high and sustained income. He also had anonymously rehired Tim Simmons, the floor trader, to manage portions of his portfolio. A real estate broker purchased the 100-acre farm for him. He needed a place, well marked and fenced, for Boo-Boo, as well as his own seclusion. A hired ground's keeper kept the place looking as if it were still in full use.

"Another juice?" a young waitress's voice interrupted.

"Ahhh . . . yes . . . thank you," Zon replied with a smile. The waitress, assuming that he'd want another, lifted the large filled glass from her tray, placed it in front of him, took the empty, then walked away. Zon stared into the table as she left.

"Time to go see Billy," he said as he sipped at the new glass. After leaving Billy in the casino, Zon took several months to draw up plans for a special car, and had delivered them to Billy three months earlier. Billy had purchased a shop, instead of building one.

"No use in reinventin' da wheel'," he told Zon apologetically, feeling that he may have welshed on his original promise.

"Man after my own heart," Zon had responded, much to Billy's relief. Billy promised the car would be ready in three months, in spite of its unusual features. He didn't like the plans he'd been given, nor could he see the sense in building a car, from scratch, that would never run.

"Whas dis?" he'd asked, after scanning the drawings.

"It's a car," Zon said with tongue in cheek.

"A caw? Dis ain't no caw. Dis a piece a shit."

"Can you build it?" Zon asked, ignoring the laughter.

"I," Billy responded egotistically as he rolled his eyes at Zon, "can buil' anythan', includin' dis piece a shit." He gazed back at the drawings. "Ya see, son, some thangs you jus' gotta' take on fait', like I tell my wiaf," he smiled. "Course wit' you, dat fait's a sho bet." He nudged Zon in the side with his elbow. "By the way," he continued,"you neva' said yo' name."

"Zon."

"Zon? Zon who?"

"Zon. That's all."

"Ooookay," Billy sang back, "whatevah' ya say, boss man." Warm laughter filled Zon's heart as he'd left that day.

"Guess I'll go see my . . . friend," he said aloud as he rolled the near empty juice glass under his nose. It felt good to call someone that. "Yeah, I guess Billy is my friend," he sighed aloud.

"Maybe you could use a few more," came a soft voice from behind. Zon had been so entrenched in his own thoughts that he hadn't noticed the noisy and giggly approach of five young women.

Four of them had walked flirtatiously across the room, dragging the fifth along.

"Ah . . . mind if we sit down?" A surprised Zon nodded yes. The five encircled the table. Each looked anxiously back and forth at one another, then at Zon. One of them, who looked to be mid-twentyish and wore a designer sweat-suit over her tights, held several single dollars spread out like playing cards in her hand.

"My name's Nikki," said the one who had spoken first. Zon looked into her beautiful cat's eyes, at first. But he couldn't keep his eyes from dancing away from them and hungrily down her body. He followed her broad sensuous smile down to the smooth round mounds of her overexposed breasts, then on to take in the gorgeous curves of her hips and thighs, all of this as she made her way to the chair nearest him and sat down. She was gorgeous and Zon was staring down into her chocolatey cleavage, now just inches away from the tip of his nose.

With great effort, he broke his stare and looked around the table. A nervous grin split his face. He had been so wrong . . . so wrong. Beinin didn't have a lock on the feminine beauty of the earth. Maybe it was simply the first time in his life that he was able to see a woman's beauty as it truly was, not through his oversized eye of lust. He'd worked long and hard to gain control, and felt that he had mastered it. But he'd been surprised and was unprepared for this onslaught of women, of beauty, of skin . . . luscious caramel, butterscotch, coffee, and chocolate, covering swerving hips, taunt thighs, full lips, round calves, teasing . . . teasing . . . torturing . . .

Zon dropped his head and closed his eyes.

"You all right?" Xia, the one in the warm-up suit, asked. Zon wanted control. He delved deeply into himself, grappling for the errant band of lust that had escaped. Finally corralling it, he raised his head and answered calmly,

"Yeah, I'm okay. I'm Zon." The women giggled loudly.

"Zon?" quipped Tanika, the tall and slender one who sat directly opposite him, with her arms folded across her chest. Her permed hair was pulled up, adding greater height to her frame. "What kind of name is that? Is it short for something?"

"No. That's my name . . . Zon."

"Everything about you that short . . . sugar?" Jasmine, seated on his right, asked suggestively. She was the lightest toned of the group, or "high yella" as Tanika called her, and wore heavy, shiny lipstick over her large, voluptuous lips. Zon smiled down at her, but didn't respond.

"We've been sitting over there talking, . . ." Nikki said. She was the most facially beautiful of the group, short and buxom, and wore her long auburn hair pulled back, then twirled to fall over her right shoulder. Her leotard was the lowest cut, exposing the most breast. The bottom of her outfit slimmed to less than a shoestring as it submerged into the cleavage produced by the top of her firm round hips. She was in every sense of the word, a model of sensual beauty, and she knew it. She nodded toward the table they'd just left. Looking coyly at Zon, she continued, "when one of us just happened to notice you . . . again." She paused with a smile. "You've been coming here quite often." Still, Zon didn't respond.

"Would you quit flirting?" Tanika quietly shouted at Nikki. "Ah . . . ah . . . you've been coming here quite often," she mocked. Her words roll off her lips with overexaggerated sweetness. Again, they all giggled. They had been having a great time all evening before they rushed Zon's table. And if they had there way, those good times were going to continue. "And you better cover up those breasts," Tanika added, "before you catch a chest cold yo' mama won't be able to cure." The giggles turned to laughter. Zon, along with the rest of the table, stared into Nikki's caramel cleavage.

"Hush, girl," Nikki shot back. "Don't hate me 'cause I'm beautiful." She pursed her glossy lips in mock indignation before uncontrollable laughter parted them, revealing perfect teeth.

"Anyway," broke in Arlisa, "we've seen you here a lot at the Body of Gold, always alone, always in this corner, always facing the wall. We were wondering . . . " She cast a wry smile as her sentence trailed off without a finish. She appeared the perfect blend of Nikki, Tanika, and Jasmine: tall, medium-sized chest, and very pretty. She wore a modest red leotard and tights, with red and white striped ankle warmers. Her hair appeared naturally curly and she wore it loose, behind a headband.

"Wondering? Wondering what?" Zon asked. In frozen silence, the women looked at each other, none appearing to know what to say next.

"You see, we meet here twice a week," Nikki said, rolling her eyes innocently toward the ceiling, yet flexing her torso enough to make the top of her exposed breasts quiver. Such a move took practice, and she appeared well rehearsed. In a girlish, sing-songy fashion, she continued. "We come here to get away. You know, work out, relax, talk, have fun . . . "

". . . pick up guys," Tanika injected to finish Nikki's sentence, causing a blush to darken her face. The others didn't laugh this time. Most looked away, trying unsuccessfully to say "Not me" with their body language. Zon looked at Tanika. "You see," Tanika continued, "Between us all, we've gotten to know every man in here." With a look of disgust, she added, "Some, we've gotten to know real well, I mean, real well." She drew out the word "real" for emphasis and rolled accusing eyes away from Zon and onto Jasmine. The others followed her stare.

"Don't you even try that with me, girl," Jasmine popped back. "Just because you've got Doppie sitting at home waiting on you doesn't mean you can just . . . "

"His name is Dabney, Dab-ney," Tanika shot back, knitting her brow and leaning in to challenge Jasmine.

"Dabney, Doppie . . . " Jasmine quipped girlishly as she looked around the table, "I didn't notice the difference when I met him. Did you, ladies?" The remaining three held comment.

"Anyway," Xia interrupted, "let's get back to the game." Xia, the fifth of the group, was pretty as well, but held her head down, making it hard to see. Her hair was long and jet black, setting off her even butterscotch skin tone. She was of medium build, but her designer sweat suit, which she wore over her workout tights, hid all of her physical attributes. She shook the money in her hand lightly, breaking the tension. Nikki, taking the cue from Xia, touched Zon lightly on the hand.

"Yeah, we play this game. You see, when a new guy joins the club," she said as she smiled at him and pulled her hand away, "we try to guess his gam . . . ah . . . story."

"His story," Zon repeated.

"You see," continued Arlisa, "we all guess something major about him."

"Then," Nikki exclaimed, "after one or more of us," she paused to smile at Arlisa, who instantly smiled back, suggesting a past episode of fantasy involving the two, "gets to know him, we see who's guessed best."

"What kind of guesses?" Zon asked as an ancient thought of his virginity surfaced.

"You know," Nikki said, "how old you are, what's your profession, where are you from . . . "

"How big is your . . . " Jasmine strung out the last word as the women's mouths fell open, ". . . bank account," she finished with a smile. Xia dropped her head; a bright blush covered her face.

"Yeah." Nikki disrupted Jasmine's attempt to make a suggestive connection with Zon. "We've become pretty good at it."

"In here, it's pretty easy," Tanika added, taking a quick survey of the room. "The men are all the same." Arlisa turned to Tanika.

"Now, homegirl," she said, trying to mimic Tanika, "was it not you who, just a few before-Dabney months ago, said, 'Go to a health club, get a healthy man. Go to a nightclub, get a night crawler.'" Arlisa had placed her right hand saucily on her hip as she mocked Tanika.

"She met Dabney in a nightclub," Jasmine slid in, then glared at Tanika.

"We didn't meet in a nightclub, Miss Butt-Loose-as-a-Boot." Now, Tanika's hands were on her hips and her neck was flexing violently, trying to keep her head from flying off. "And even if I did find him in a nightclub," she voiced saucily, rolling her eyes, "at least I've never made love in one, or in a men's room, or on a pool table, or . . . "

"Okay, okay," Arlisa, who sat between the two, said, trying to restore order. "Tanika's right. All the guys in here have a lot in common. For instance, you can't work out here regularly unless you are a member."

"And to have a membership requires a steady income," Nikki chimed in.

"And steady income means the 'W' word to the fellas," Arlisa continued.

"Whore?" Tanika jabbed, rolling her eyes at Jasmine.

"Work," Arlisa corrected, casting a look of intolerance at Tanika, who sat laughing. "All of these guys have jobs. You know the saying: got to have a J.O.B., if you want to be with me. The club prescreens them for us." Arlisa caught herself smiling at the commonly discussed situation, but realized that, unlike before, the topic of discussion was present. She coolly bit her lip and slid back in her seat. Zon sat quietly, though attentive, as the preliminaries continued.

"Yeah," Nikki said. "And workout time is also family hour. The place is well lit," she added while gesturing toward the ceiling lights. "So the married ones are easy to pick out."

"Since this is a health club," Jasmine began, "you have to at least dress the part, even if you don't participate. You'd be surprised what a tank top and a tight fitting pair of biker shorts reveal about a man." She glared at Zon as she spoke. Assured that he was staring back, she slowly panned down his body, then tried to stare a hole right through the table and into his lap. Slowly rolling her eyes back to his, she added, "We get to take inventory before we pursue." She suggestively spread her lips and slid a finger into the corner of her mouth. Zon continued to stare, but didn't speak. Nikki, Arlisa, and Tanika watched Jasmine's sensual advance. Each then stared at Zon for reaction. Zon looked around the table, then quaintly smiled at Jasmine.

"Married?" Tanika snapped at Zon, trying to catch him off guard.

"No," Zon responded. Nikki reached across the table and pulled a dollar from Xia's hand. Zon watched her take the money, then nodded his head in understanding.

"Right answer gets the money," he said.

"Yeah," Nikki giggled. Following Jasmine's lead, she leaned in closer to Zon. Her right breast bulged further out of her low-cut leotard as she coyly pressed it into the side of his upper right arm. He felt the soft sensual flesh caress his shoulder.

"They're teasing me," he thought, "trying to get me hot and bothered." He felt Nikki slowly and ever so slightly roll her breast against him. That's why Tanika had not taken Jasmine's latest opening to jab back at her. The game was far more than a few inquisitive questions. Arlisa, Jasmine, Nikki, and Tanika were getting their jollies by trying to get him as hot and bothered as they could. And Xia, was she going to get off just by watching? He looked suspiciously around the table. Nikki rubbing, Jasmine sucking her finger, Tanika and Arlisa smiling, waiting for their chance. And Xia, so innocently looking on.

"What if nobody's right?" he asked.

"Then Xia gets to keep the money," Arlisa answered. "She doesn't bet, so we let her hold the pot."

"She doesn't do much of anything, right, Xia?" Tanika momentarily stepped away from the planned attack. Remaining true to her own character, she couldn't pass up the chance to razz someone. "You see, Zon, honey, her name is spelled with a 'X', not a 'Z.'" Tanika smiled wryly at Xia, who looked back innocently with a deerlike gaze. "The 'X' stands for 'not'," she blurted out with a laugh. "That child loves not, dates not, tries not." Tanika laughed aloud. The rest, including Xia, giggled lightly.

"Are you gay?" Arlisa asked quickly of Zon.

"No," he said with a dismissing chuckle. Tanika, Nikki, and Arlisa reached in and each took a dollar. Zon laughed, realizing Jasmine had bet that he was.

"You never made a play," Jasmine said, sour from making the wrong guess. "Why haven't you tried to make a play?"

"Is this one of the game questions?" Zon asked.

"No," Tanika responded, "but it should be."

"Well, if I answer it, who'll get the money?"

"No one," Nikki said.

"Then why should I answer?"

"Because," Nikki responded.

"Because, it's only a game," Jasmine finished.

"Are you afraid to answer?" Tanika asked accusingly. Zon thought briefly before answering. "No," he said with finality, "it's your game. Let's play." He looked coolly about the table. Jasmine, sitting to his right, eased closer and slid her hand onto his thigh. He let it stay there.

"Okay," Nikki said. "What do you do?"

"Yes or no questions only," Zon replied.

"Whose game is this?" Tanika argued. Zon thought up a great comeback to her question, but chose to hold it.

"I studied engineering, but lately I've dabbled in the stock market." No money exchanged hands.

"Unemployed, huh?" Tanika asked.

"I don't have a job, if that's what you mean. But I prefer to think of myself as being . . . independently wealthy." He smiled wryly. The cat-and-mouse game went on. Jasmine and Nikki each pulled a dollar from Xia's hand.

"So why haven't you tried anything with us?" Jasmine insisted.

"Let's just say," Zon replied, "that I've committed to something that won't let me come on to anyone."

"Engaged?" Nikki asked as she straightened up from her caressing slump.

"In a manner of speaking," Zon said unapologetically. As he spoke, the three inquisitors eased back in their chairs. He was amazed at their apparent respect for another woman's property. *Get whatever you came for, unconditionally* seemed the theme for men, Zon thought. But with women, maybe it was different. Until now, he had been fair game for these women, something worth toying with before hunting down. No longer was that the case.

"Well, committed is not married," said Jasmine as she continued to stroke his right leg.

"Independently wealthy, huh," Tanika muttered unbelievingly. "Just how big is your bank account?"

"Now, you're getting personal," Zon answered. "Let's just say that I have what I need."

"Do you have, or are you expecting, any kids?" Nikki asked with much of the schoolgirl excitement gone from her voice.

"No," Zon replied.

"This isn't so much fun anymore," Tanika declared, sensing the group's disappointment. "You ladies ready to go work out? It's 8:05. The last aerobics session just started." Dance music resounded from the distance. The health club pumped the aerobics class music all over to remind some and entice others in. All of them rose from their seats.

"It's not over," Zon said, looking about the table.

"Oh yes it is, sweet cheeks," Jasmine replied. "And you'll never know what you missed." She swished her butt in Zon's face as she dismounted her chair.

"I played your game," he insisted, "now, you have to play mine."

"Game?" Arlisa said, as she eased back in her chair.

"You said that you were engaged," Nikki added.

"No," Zon countered, "you said that. I said that I had made a commitment. That doesn't necessarily mean one of marriage."

"Sounds like a line to me," Tanika interjected. "Well, are you engaged or not?"

"Your game is over," Zon replied. "Are you going to play mine or not?"

"Not," Tanika blurted back. Arlisa and Jasmine, both seated, looked up at their would-be leader.

"Are you afraid?" Zon asked Tanika. She stood silently with her arms crossed, giving him the first full view of her slim, yet lovely frame. Without a word, she moved back to the table and sat down. Nikki followed suit.

"Well?" Tanika addressed Xia, who was the only one left standing. Xia looked around the table for a sympathetic face, but found none.

"I'm . . . I'm not staying," she said, then quickly walked away.

"Like I said," Tanika offered, "the girl don't . . . period."

"That's okay," Jasmine said as she squeezed next to Zon. "More for me."

Wanting to retake control, Tanika said to Zon, "Your game packing enough for all of us, big man?" The women laughed lightly, and moved in tightly about him. Arlisa gripped his right leg, Jasmine, on his left, reached her right hand around the small of his back, then shot her left hand toward his crotch. Zon caught her hand before she reached it.

"Wait a minute," he said, peering at Jasmine, "let me tell you how my game is played." Grabbing both their hands, he eased their arms onto the table.

"I want to give each of you . . . something," he said with a hint of suggestiveness.

"You have got to be out of your lying, unemployed, engaged-but-not mind," Tanika countered. "I think you've gotten the wrong idea about us." She looked sincerely into Zon's eyes. "I know that we've been flirting with you all night. Hell, we're still flirting with you. But we don't know you. Our flirtations were all in fun, nothing serious."

"So I figured," Zon said, "but that doesn't change a thing. Let's play my game. I'm sure you'll find it . . . revealing." The women looked at each other in disbelief.

"If any of us reveals anything," Tanika declared, "it's going to be you."

"You're going to strip for us?" laughed Nikki.

"Not likely," Zon answered. "All I need are your hands."

"You're gonna have to do your own hand-jive, honey." Arlisa joked.

"Speak for yourself, girlfriend," Jasmine responded, then jerked her hand free and dove it again for a handful of Zon's lap. Quickly, he caught her hand and returned it to the table. While doing so, he started tapping his foot on the table leg.

"Give me your hands," he said to all of them.

"A man's favorite line: gi'me," Tanika said as she cautiously slid her hands across the table. Nikki did likewise. Taking their hands, Zon piled them together in the middle of the table, then put his own across the top.

"Now, close your eyes," he sang slowly.

"Kiss my ass," Tanika sang back, in the same voice, then jerked her hands away. The women laughed. Zon looked at her, but didn't speak. Still laughing, she slid her hands back into the pile and closed her eyes. "All right. Let's get this over with," she said. Zon continued to tap on the table leg, but now a bit harder than before.

"Listen to the rhythm and hum along with me," he said as he closed his eyes and began humming. Nikki giggled, Arlisa hummed, Tanika huffed, and Jasmine started moaning.

"He said hum, Jasmine," Arlisa said, holding back a giggle. "H . . . h . . . hum, with a 'H', not a 'C.'" Opening her eyes, Jasmine stared incredulously at her friend, who sat cracking up.

Ignoring them, Zon continued to hum a strong melody in a deep, penetrating baritone voice.

"Oooh, that's all right," Arlisa commented as she finally caught the melody. Nikki had her eyes closed and was humming along. As Arlisa joined in, Zon moved up a third, harmonizing with the two who sang.

"Oh yeah. We're gonna have church!" Jasmine added with a laugh. She closed her eyes and started humming, a third higher than Zon, making three-part harmony. Her church choir upbringing rang out as clear as a bell. Tanika, though still apprehensive, couldn't help but feel the draw of the music and the moment. She watched as the four of them swayed and hummed softly in perfect harmony, a melody which they all seemed to know. Strangely enough, she knew it as well. She closed her eyes and tried to recall it. Humming along on Zon's note, she searched her mind for the memory.

Gently, the group swayed back and forth, humming and ad-libbing the melody whenever it seemed to fit. Zon dropped down a full octave and added a mysterious syncopated bass line to the melody. Each sank deeper into the music. As they sank, sounds of the fitness center in the background faded slowly away. Sensing their preoccupation with the music, Zon gently removed his hands from the top of the pile, lifted himself silently from the chair, and strolled away.

Realizing the change, Tanika popped her eyes open. Across the room, by the entrance, she spotted Dabney looking over at her. She jumped up from the table and hustled across the room where he stood.

"Dabney!" she yelled as she approached. "Who told you to come here?" The short round man's knees knocked involuntarily as she approached.

"I, I missed you, baby-girl," he said lovingly, hoping to see similar affection in her eyes. Tanika walked right up to him and slapped him across his head. He ducked and partially blocked the blow with his covering forearms.

"Don't you call me baby-girl in public!" she screamed as she wailed away at his head. Dabney flinched from the blows, but didn't step away.

"I . . . I just wanted to see you," he said again, his voice pleading for sympathy.

"Tanika!" Tanika's eyes bulged from the voice in her ears.

"Tanika!" Slowly, she turned around.

"Yes, Mama."

"Girl, how long you been standin' there doin' nothin'," her mother yelled as she stomped across the room. "Didn't I tell you to clean this room?"

"I am cleaning the room, Mama," Tanika respectfully answered.

"Well, ya doin' it too slow. How the hell do ya expect to make somethin' of yaself, goofin' off like that all the time." Tanika stood in disbelief as her mother strolled up to her with open hands held high. Tanika drew her arms up to cover her head.

"Mama, I . . . I only been in here a few minutes. Give me time. I can finish . . . "

"Hush yo mouf! Hush yo mouf!" her mother yelled as she wailed away at Tanika's head. "How many times do I have to tell ya? Nobody gonna give you nothin', ya hear me? Nothin'!" She continued beating Tanika, who sank helplessly to the floor. "Ya work is too slow. Ya' homework, it ain't right. It ain't enough." She quit beating the little girl, but continued to preach. "Oh, I know . . . expectin' some *man* to come into ya' life, givin' you this and givin' you that. Well it ain't gonna happen, ya hear me!" She slapped the little girl across her back. "You gotta do it fo' yaself. Make ya own money, make ya own way. Don't let nobody in close. They get in. They take it all. They take ya money. They take ya ass. Take ya mind . . . leave you with nothin' but a bunch of hardheaded, no-good chil'rens ya gotta take care of."

Tanika's mother started wailing away at her again as her own words brought bad memories: flowing tears, more pain that made her swing away at her own child, her own cowering child who just wanted to . . . "

"Please, Tanika," pleaded Dabney, "I'll go. I was just worried about you." Tanika watched her own hands come down hard on Dabney's bruised bald head. She froze. Seizing the moment to escape, Dabney reached down, picked up his glasses, and hurried through the door. Tanika sank into a ball in the middle of the floor.

"Oh, God!" she sobbed aloud as gushing tears fell into her hands. "All I ever wanted was to please you, Mama," she cried. The light twinkled as it passed through the tears in her eyes. "But I never could. I never could," she blurted, then broke down completely. Her face fell into wet hands that rested on her folded legs, on the cold, shiny floor.

After what seemed an eternity of tears, Tanika wiped her eyes. "Dabney. Oh, Dabney. I've done you so wrong and you've done nothing but try to please me." She paused, lifted her head slightly, and wiped away more tears. "I loved my mother, God rest her soul, but I've punished myself and everyone else around me for her long enough."

Tanika wiped at her eyes, trying to drive away the tears, but found she couldn't open them. Straining to do so, her eyes suddenly popped open. Before her sat Nikki, Arlisa, and Jasmine, all of them holding her hands and swaying. But none of them were humming and they all seemed to be in a trance. Slowly, she eased her hands away from the pile, got up, and walked toward the changing room.

"Poor Dabney," she said and slipped through the spring-loaded door.

Nikki opened her eyes. From the aerobics room, instead of the normal loud exercise music, she could hear a cheering crowd. Jumping from her seat, she ran over to peer inside. As she got closer, she could hear the crowd chanting over and over, "Nik-ki! Nik-ki!" Not since Grady High School had she heard such a sound. As she reached the door, a man wearing a top hat and tails stepped out to meet her.

"They're waiting for you," he said with a broad smile. Nikki stepped through the door, beyond which was a long runway, rimmed with dazzling lights. A long, full-length mirror sat at the far end. The crowd sat about the runway and up the walls. The light hid all but their silhouettes as they cheered.

Stepping inside, she peered down the runway into the mirror at herself, young and beautiful, in her cheerleader's outfit. With pom-poms in hand, she rushed out onto the runway. The crowd went wild. She kicked high, twirled about and she flawlessly performed her routine. Onlookers cheered with her every move. But as she repeated her steps, the cheers died.

"More! More!" the crowd started yelling. She spun over to the mirror and peered in. She saw herself, beautiful, with the full figure of a woman. Reaching down, she ripped the skirt from around her waist, revealing skimpy tights that showed off her vivacious hips. As the skirt ripped free, the crowd went wild, and again started shouting, "Nik-ki! Nik-ki!" She danced back down the runway to the crowd's cheers. They loved her, and she, their cheers. But as she made her second round, the cheers once again turned to calls for more. The sound hurt her ears. Wanting the crowd's cheers, Nikki froze in front of the mirror and stared at her profile. As they watched, she reached up to her low-cut leotard and pulled at the neck until her breasts popped free. Immediately, the crowd went ecstatic. She stared at her own breasts, noticing how perfectly sensuous they were. Cheers of her own name dazed her mind and she again danced across the runway. But, as she turned at the end and shook her bountiful bosom at the crowd, the cheers turned again from "Nik-ki! Nik-ki!" to "More! More!" Not bothering to return to the mirror, Nikki slid out of the rest of her outfit, revealing her bodacious hips and perfectly trimmed pubic mound. Again, the opiate of cheers filled her ears, but for only a moment. As she stood there, nude and perfectly beautiful, the crowd's cheers turned again to "More! More!"

Nikki was dumbfounded. She was giving all that she had, yet they wanted more. Running to the mirror, she looked in and saw herself, perfectly beautiful, perfectly sensuous. She smiled into it and whispered her own name. Thinking it a mistake, she ran again to the center of the runway. The wrong chant continued, then faded to silence. She stood there, fully exposed, perfectly beautiful. Yet the crowd still wanted something more. Nikki backed off to the mirror again.

"Why can't they see me?" she asked.

"Can you see you?" the tall man in the top hat, standing behind her, said.

"Yes," she answered, staring into the mirror.

"What do you see?"

"I see me."

"Look out there," he said, pointing to the crowd about the runway, "Now, what do you see?" Nikki stared out into the crowd, but the glare from the stage lights prevented her from viewing her audience.

"I see shadows," she said. "Shadows of my fans. They love me," she added with a smile.

"Are you sure?" he asked, then stepped aside. From behind him, emerged another teenaged cheerleader similar to Nikki, but different. She paused to check herself in the mirror, then ran out onto the runway. Immediately, the crowd exploded into cheers.

"Why are they cheering?" Nikki asked. "She's just a cheerleader!"

"And so were you," the tall man said. Nikki thought hard, trying to understand. She gazed again at herself in the mirror. Her legs were long, full and sensuous, her hips, round and firm, as luscious as two caramel apples, her breasts, large glistening dewdrops crowned by chocolate-mint discs. And her face, glowing with the beauty of the angels.

"It doesn't matter what they see," she said, "I know what I see." She smiled then glanced out on the runway at the cheerleader, who now faced the shouts for more. Looking back into the mirror, she repeated, "I know what I see." A warm feeling engulfed her as she, for the first time, felt her self-worth emanating from within. Closing her eyes, she danced back down the stage, smiling broadly. The young cheerleader gloomily walked off. Starting with her skimpy panties, she redressed before the crowd which cheered louder as she drew on each garment. There, fully clothed, she stood, eyes closed, smiling. The crowd's cheer grew. The crowd saw . . . her. The crowd was . . . her. The crowd was the mirror, reflecting what it saw.

Feeling greater joy than she had ever felt, Nikki, wanting to stare into the mirror, into herself, opened her eyes. Before her sat Arlisa and Jasmine, swaying and holding her hands. Startled, she snatched her hands away. Rising from the chair, she looked about for Zon and Tanika, who were nowhere in sight. She felt wonderful and wanted to just float around the room. Turning, she spied herself and her skimpy outfit in one of the many mirrors in the bar.

"I think I'll go change into something a bit more comfortable." With a gentle smile, she walked whimsically through the quiet room toward the dressing room.

Jasmine felt warm and snuggled as she sat with her eyes closed, her mind drifting in no particular direction. The music in her ears soothed her. The melody was slow and alluring. She felt a growl ease to her throat as the music conjured up deep sensual feelings inside her. Voices from behind caught her attention. She turned to see. Before her was a large parlor; in the middle was a sunken dance floor. All about, people stood in formal dress, talking, eating, socializing, some even dancing. She watched from where she stood outside the great hall.

The evening air seemed chilly, but she felt toasty in her long, furry coat. As she stepped up to the door, she got a closer look at the people. She knew most of them, especially the men.

"There's Rasheen," she said as she stepped through the door. Like the Cinderella story, all music stopped and every head turned as she appeared in the room. As she watched, all of the men slid a hand into their trouser pocket, fumbled their fingers about, smiled confidently, returned them to their side, then went back to chatting and dancing, as if she had just turned and left.

Rasheen had been Jasmine's latest lover. They had met in the health club a week before, and had made passionate love in the rear seat of his Volvo that same night. He stood talking to a short blond woman as they sipped champagne. Jasmine swished her hips wildly as she walked up behind the blond. She smiled as she came, eager to rekindle the flame with Rasheen. He saw her coming, slipped his hand back into his pants pocket, but continued talking with the girl.

"I admit it," Rasheen said to the blond as Jasmine came to an anonymous halt behind her, "the Bandits are good. They gave us quite a run the last time they were in town. But that was then. This is now." He shot a cunning look at the girl.

"They beat the Jays then, and they'll beat them again tomorrow night as well," the blond said, throwing a challenging laugh at Rasheen.

"Wanna bet?" he asked.

"No," she replied. "Frankly, I'm tired of taking your money." They laughed.

"Look. We'll go to the game tomorrow night," Rasheen replied. "I've got the tickets. If the Bandits win, you pay me back for the tickets. If they lose, I'll buy dinner this time, too." He cast an eye at the blond, who stood considering the challenge. Jasmine stood silently behind them.

"That bet is no different from the last eight you've made with me. And I'm getting fat from all the free meals that you've had to buy." She contemplated his offer. "Okay," she said, smiling sweetly into Rasheen's eyes, then added confidently, "I suppose you might as well drive again, too." Both laughed and embraced slightly to acknowledge their date.

"Uh hum," Jasmine cleared her throat, trying to draw Rasheen's attention. The blond paid her no mind. Jasmine tantalizingly slid her tongue between her lips and stared longingly into Rasheen's eyes.

"Ahh, would you excuse me for a moment?" he said to the blond.

"Sure," she answered politely. Without another word, Rasheen stepped around the blond, grabbed Jasmine's right hand with his free left one, then, using it like a leash, pulled her toward the exit, all while keeping his right hand buried deep in his pocket. As they neared the exit, Rasheen turned, opened the large closet, then pulled Jasmine in behind him and closed the door.

"Oh, I see you've got that same feeling," Jasmine squealed in an excited and seductive tone. Apparently not hearing her, Rasheen whistled softly as he quickly dropped his trousers to his knees, reached down, then retrieved the condom from his right pant's pocket.

"Uh, you are glad to see me," Jasmine said as she watched him slip the rubber on. "Did you miss me?" Without a word, Rasheen slipped around behind her and pressed down on her shoulders with both hands. "Ohhh," she sighed with an approving smile. Realizing his desires, she dropped to her knees.

Moments later, an unchanged Rasheen emerged from the closet, checked himself, then proceeded back to the blond. As he stepped away, the closet door reopened and Jasmine stuck her head out. Her hair was slightly mussed, but all else was intact, and she felt good. Like the last time, Rasheen had proven more than capable of satisfying her. Looking back into the large hall, she saw him standing again, nonchalantly talking to the blond. She walked toward him, but he didn't look up as she approached. Her anger grew as she neared him. He was intentionally ignoring her.

"Hmmh, his loss," she huffed. As she stepped by them,
Rasheen said to the blond, "Win or lose, we always have a good

time." The blond eased into his arms as they lightly kissed.

Jasmine paced away. Then she saw Cole, a man from her office that she'd had a one-nighter with. He was sitting in a window seat, beside a thin, attractive woman. He, too, brought back lusty lovemaking memories as she stared at him. Wasting no time, she slinked over. Seeing her approach, Cole slid his hand into his pocket while he conversed.

"Are you sure?" The faceless woman asked Cole, as Jasmine stepped up behind her.

"Sure I'm sure," he replied with a huge grin.

"Well, if you're sure, then I accept." The woman leaped into Cole's lap, wrapped her arms around him, and they kissed. Cole, fighting hard to maintain his balance, pulled his right hand from his pocket, and reached into his left, retrieving a small ring box. Jasmine didn't speak, but stared suggestively at the heavyset man as she stood listening.

"Pardon me for a minute, baby?" he politely asked the young lady on his lap.

"Sure," she replied, "but hurry back." The woman stood up, then sat on the other end of the window seat. Cole smiled apologetically at her, stood, thrust his hand back into left pocket where he left the ring box, then stuck his hand deep into his right pocket while grabbing Jasmine by the hand. As he dragged her toward the exit, he pulled a condom from his pocket and held it high. Jasmine stared at the wrapper as she trotted along behind him--to the closet.

Moments later, Cole emerged from the closet, flung the spent jimmy-hat back across Jasmine's spread fingers on the floor, then closed the door. Returning the smile to his face, he rushed back to his bride-to-be's side. Jasmine looked across the room as she stepped from her love nest. Cole was on one knee, looking up into the thin woman's eyes. The woman quickly blushed, then gasped as Cole handed her the diamond he had carried in the ring box.

"Nigga' didn't even talk to me, the old dawg," she sighed remorsefully. Not wanting to ruin the glow from the physical ecstasy that Cole had just given her, she dismissed him, and again looked about the room. She spotted Lamont, a tall, very young, and very talented man she'd let pick her up one night at a bar. He stood talking to another man, who was just as tall, and just as fine. Thinking it a bit safer approaching two men instead of one, she pressed her hair smooth, then walked over.

"Me and my boys, riet," Lamont spoke, more so with his hands, than with his mouth. "See, day di'n know mi' action see," he said, as the other man laughed. "We took 'em down, downtown. Shot the pill. Brown streak in homey's draws was stainin' the flo'." Both laughed loudly, then slapped mock high-fives. Lamont spotted Jasmine walking over, then nodded to his partner. The other man looked, then both slid hands into their pockets. Jasmine walked up wearing a broad smile.

"Hi, fellas," she said. Without a word, each grabbed her by a hand and pulled her back to the closet.

"Wait a minute!" she shouted, as the two walked with giant basketball-player steps, dragging her reluctantly behind. "Weren't you two just talking basketball?" she winced while trying to wrestle her hands free. "Let's talk basketball. Boy," she exclaimed. "Did you see Chicago last night?" They neared the closet door. "I . . . just wanted to talk," she screeched as Lamont opened the door and stepped in. The other man dropped Jasmine's hand.

"Gedit on . . . gedit stron', but doughn' be too long, my brother," he said to Lamont. Jasmine heard the condom foil rip open as Lamont pulled the door to. Moments later, he emerged.

"The bitch can go . . . do wha'cha know," he sang to his partner. Laughing, Lamont tagged hands with the other ball player as if in a professional wrestling bout, then ushered him into the closet.

"I don't even know you," Jasmine said, but didn't get a response. After a few minutes wait, Lamont stepped away from the front of the door, allowing his friend to step out.

"Yo, yo, yo, yo," Lamont said as the other emerged, "so ma boys jetted down da cout . . . an' . . . an' . . . homeboy . . . he be tryin' ta front . . . " The two talked and laughed, engulfed in a world of pick-up basketball as they walked away.

Jasmine crawled slowly from the closet, staring solemnly at the floor. She stood up, then looked slowly around the room. Each man, upon noticing her, slid a reassuring hand into his pocket. With her head hanging, and in complete bewilderment, she walked unsteadily toward the bar. A wave of hands pulled up, dove deep into pockets, retreated, then returned to their owners' sides as she passed through the room.

Not looking up, she slid onto the last open stool at the bar. Confused, she sat staring into the bar surface, trying desperately to understand Rasheen's, Cole's, and the ball players' peculiar reaction to her.

"Dawgs," she growled aloud in disgust. "Dawgs!" she repeated as she stared into the bar. Drops of saliva spewed as she barked the word over and over. "They don't care," she continued. "They'll leave wife, girlfriend, child, or Mama just to get a little ass." Her voice whispered, but her anger screamed. "Get it, give nothing for it, then ignore your ass when they're through." She raised her gaze to rest on the dark long-neck bottles stacked behind the bar. "All they want is that short moment of ecstasy. Don't care where, don't care with whom. They'll use anybody . . . anywhere . . . anytime." Anger constricted her breath. Opening her mouth, she began panting, and found it soothing.

"Still," she said with a devilish grin, "dog or not, they got this girl off. First time," she chuckled, "every time." Physical satisfaction from each man was slowly overtaking her emotional thrashing from being used.

Feeling much better, she decided to order a drink. Raising her head, she looked down the bar for the bartender, who was nowhere in sight. Reflections from the one-handed men bounced tauntingly off the mirrored wall behind the bar. Jasmine ran her eyes down the long glass, searching for the bar man, but her gaze froze suddenly in horror as she met her own reflection. There, sitting between the two men to her right and her left, sat a panting, long-tailed, floppy-eared short-haired yellow dog, staring back at her.

Shuddering in horror, Jasmine opened her eyes. The table was empty except for Arlisa, who sat holding her hands. Jasmine ripped her hands away from the table and stared at them. They appeared normal. Rising quickly, she ran to the mirror at the juice bar and peered in. Lusciously tanned skin dominated her sweetly familiar reflection. Wiping small beads of perspiration from her forehead, she collected her thoughts. It was near closing time and the bar was nearly empty. Jasmine steadied herself on a bar stool for a moment. Taking in a fresh breath, she walked toward the exit.

Arlisa lay trembling upon the delivery table.

"Push! Push!" the doctor yelled at her. With eyes squinted closed and with all of her might, Arlisa pressed down, trying to turn herself inside out. A nurse stood by her left side, squeezing her hand, comforting and encouraging her. Tears poured down her cheek as she strained.

"Mama!" she screamed. "Mama!"

"Hush, child, and push," a forceful yet reassuring voice said from the left of her bed. Arlisa turned and looked into her mother's face.

"It's coming!" the doctor shouted. Arlisa pushed hard, but didn't break her gaze into her mother's eyes.

"I wanted you there," she said calmly to her mother.

"I know, child, and you know I would have been there if I could."

"I know," Arlisa replied, "Oh, Mama." With tears of joy, Arlisa reached up and embraced her mother as the doctor wrapped the newborn and placed him on her stomach.

"He's beautiful," her mother said as she looked into the gently wrapped bundle. Reluctantly pulling her arms free, Arlisa scooped the baby up and held him to her mother.

"Nobody told me," Arlisa said apologetically. "All they ever said was, 'don't.' I had to figure the 'do' out on my own. Guess I didn't figure very well, huh?"

"It's all right, child," her mother said. She smiled broadly as a round tear streaked down her face. "He's beautiful, and I love him almost as much as I love you." She took the baby into her arms and cuddled him. Stepping over to a chair, she sat down gently and toyed with the baby's fingers.

"My, my," her mother said, looking up at Arlisa. "Is that a Ph.D.?" she asked. Arlisa stood before her in black graduation cap and gown.

"Yes," Arlisa said, smiling proudly into her mother's face. "And I graduated with honors, too, Mama."

"You were always so smart," her mother replied, "Even as a little thing . . . the way you'd sit at that piano and pluck out tunes. No one would have guessed that you were only five." Arlisa blushed, but smiled deeply at the bountiful affection pouring from her mother's lips. "And I'm so proud of you," she added.

Standing, she slid her free arm around Arlisa's waist while holding the baby securely in the other. An overjoyed Arlisa threw both arms around her neck. Her broad gown sleeves draped over her mother and the baby's face.

"Oh, Mama," she said, "I wanted you here so much. I needed you here so badly." She sobbed into her mother's ears. "Too many times, I had to face these times alone, by myself."

"I know, baby," her mother said comfortingly, "but you had friends." Arlisa pulled her arms from around her mother's neck and joined hands with her sorority sisters as they danced around her little baby in the middle of the human circle.

"There were friends," Arlisa said as she stepped along in the human chain. "Family too, at times. But they weren't you. I needed you." Arlisa choked up as she spoke.

"That's all right, child," her mother said as she pressed the girl's face to her shoulder. "Go 'head and cry." She stroked Alisa lovingly across her shoulders as she held her. "Shhh," she whispered. "Mama's here now." Arlisa cried with joy, with sorrow. It felt so warm, so wonderful to be held, to be engulfed by someone who loved you more than they loved anyone else.

"You don't know how long it's been," Arlisa said between sobs. "I can't remember the last time that someone just held me . . . just . . . held . . . me."

"That's all right, child," her mother reassured her, "I'm here, for as long as you like. I'd like nothing better than to hold you . . . forever." The thought thrilled Arlisa.

Feeling better, she eased her arms from around her neck, grabbed her mother's hand, and pulled her over to the sliding board in the park. Taking her son, she held the little one-year-old high on the board and let him slide clumsily down to her mother's waiting arms.

"So many times, I'd bring him here," Arlisa said. "We'd play for hours, between classes, whenever we could." Grabbing the toddler, she lifted him back on the board, then released him. "I'd talk to him, but I'd dream of you." Arlisa grinned with joy as she watched her mother and son glide into one another's arms at the end of the sliding board.

"Some dreams do come true," her mother said.

"Come on." Arlisa slipped her fingers between her mother's and pulled her proudly, lovingly along. The three strolled through the small park, talking, laughing, and crying for hours.

"Well, I guess I've got to get on back now," her mother said regretfully.

"No!" Arlisa shouted.

"Don't worry," her mother said. She leaned in and kissed the little boy. "I'll be back, whenever you like."

"No!" Arlisa screamed again. "Mama!" She stared down at her shiny patent leather shoes as she kicked and screamed. She didn't know why she was crying . . . why her uncle was trying to hold her. She didn't want to be held. "Mama!" she screamed over and over. Freeing herself from her uncle's grasp, she ran up to the casket and caught the lid as they lowered it over her mother. But she, a small, frail, five-year-old, was no match for its great weight. "Mama!" she screamed through her avalanche of tears.

"Baby," her mother's voice sounded faintly. "Mama will never leave her baby."

Arlisa popped her eyes open, expecting to see her mother's beaming face once more. But instead, she saw a table and five empty chairs and the back of the juice bar. Tears ran down her face. Slowly, she sniffed, then smiled, in no hurry to go. It had been a dream, but a dream had never felt like this before. Easing back in her seat, she let the tears trickle down. Then, with a start, she sat straight up. "My baby," she whispered. "My baby."

12
WATER WINGS

"Mango juice to go, please." The observant bartender reached underneath the counter to retrieve a large paper cup of mango as Zon approached. After pressing a top on, he slid it to Zon, who smiled then slid him a twenty to cover the night's drinks. Zon then removed the top and poured a third of the refreshing drink down his throat. Motioning the barkeep to keep the change, he turned as he pressed the lid back on the cup and looked at the four women who sat quietly, their hands joined in the center of the table. Their eyes raced around under their lids. Each swayed gently in their seats.

"That's the quietest that I've ever seen that bunch," the bartender remarked, motioning toward the ladies' table.

"Yeah," Zon replied, "I bet." Easing away from the bar, he walked toward the hall that lead to the aerobics room and exit. "I wonder where they went?" he thought. Their smiling faces reminded him of his first entry into his own dreams. The effect was similar to hypnosis, but could reach much deeper into the mind. Proper entry allowed you to see to the roots of your own feelings. Whatever was there, was revealed. Zon wondered if any of them might see something which they shouldn't. After all, he was playing amateur psychiatrist. Then he remembered Idrisi's words:

"Nothing is better than the truth. Nothing. An untruth is sweet, only for the present. For the past, it did not exist, therefore it has no foundation. The future, built on the untruth, has no foundation. It will last for a season, but will inevitably fall."

"They'll be okay," he reassured himself as he paced toward the door. As he approached the exit, he heard loud upbeat music and hand claps in semi-unison emanating from the aerobics class. Since it was on his way, he decided to look inside for Xia. As odd as it was, she intrigued him. "Nobody's that innocent," he thought skeptically as he peered into the large room. The people in the class were all shapes and sizes. The fat ones hung to the middle and toward the back wall. They wore loose-fitting clothes, trying to hide the fat. Women with the model figures always stayed up front and on the outside. Their outfits, like those of the women who attacked his table, were tight, skimpy, and showed off whatever assets they had. In the middle were the faithful few, generally interested in getting into shape, but not wanting to be seen. And in the back were the sexually deviant men, craning their necks for a free shot.

Zon figured Xia for one of those faithful few and looked for her toward the middle.

"Looking for me?" Surprised, Zon turned to see Xia standing behind him, smiling. Her sweat suit looked fresh and every hair was in place.

"Oh, yeah," he said. "I thought you were going to work out with this class."

"I was, but then I figured it would be no fun without my friends, so I decided to run a few miles instead."

"A few miles?" Zon asked, doubt permeating his voice. "Must have been an awfully fast run. And you didn't even break a sweat." He brushed her forehead lightly with his fingers, then rubbed them together.

"Oh. There was no one else on the track, so I took my time. I must've lost track of my progress. Anyway, I feel much better." Xia stepped away from him as she spoke and looked around the corner.

"Where are the girls?" she asked.

"Oh . . . ah . . . they're still at the table," he answered. Xia stepped up the hall, then stared across the large room at the four silent, swaying figures.

"What did you do to them?"

"Oh, I just gave them something to think about."

"You've hypnotized them."

"How did you know that?" he asked, surprised by her quick and correct analysis.

"It's my profession. I'm a psychologist."

"Huh oh," he responded, feeling like a cat with caged bird's feathers caught in its whiskers, "I haven't exactly hypnotized them. I just suggested they . . . hold hands . . . and sing."

"You did that with hand holding and a song?"

"Well, all I did was make the suggestion. They've done the rest." Xia didn't approach her friends, but stood in the hallway and observed. Zon watched her as she watched them.

"You're very observant," he said.

"That's what psychologists do, observe," she replied, not breaking her stare at her friends. "So tell me, where did you learn the technique?"

"Technique? That wasn't a technique. An old man showed me how to relax once. You know, relieve stress. I just shared it with them." He paused a moment. Xia continued to stare at the group. "So," he continued, "you've been observing . . . all evening?"

"What?" Xia responded softly.

"Were you observing earlier, when we were playing the game?" Xia dropped her eyes to the floor, then folded her left arm up to wrap a hand about her neck. Sliding it slowly back to her side, she answered without looking at him.

"Yes. I was observing."

"How long have you been observing these women?"

"Three weeks."

"You writing a book?"

"No."

"Why then, if I may ask?" Zon craned his neck downward, trying to look into her eyes, but did not move closer.
Sensing his stare, she slowly pulled her eyes up to meet his.

"I'm just . . . curious," she said shyly.

"Curious?"

"Yes," she replied as their eyes met. Zon couldn't help but smile as he drank in the loveliness of the large brown orbs, clear as dual moons floating on still water. With the sincerity of an angel, she said, "I want to know how they feel, how women this age think and feel. I've never lied to them, nor tricked them. I just wanted to know . . . how it is to be them." She returned a small smile.

"But you're one of them," Zon replied softly. "How do you feel?"

"Are you trying to help me now?" she asked wryly.

"Yeah," he said after a second of reflection, "I guess I am."

"Why?"

"Why? I don't really know." Casting a mysterious glare at her, he said, "You're the shrink. Could it be that I'm getting a kick out of it?" They both laughed.

"Well if you are, then you're in need of some serious help," she said, laughing a bit louder and staring deeper into his eyes, as if searching for something.

Feeling very relaxed with her, he playfully remarked, "That sounds like an invitation." Xia choked on her chuckle.

"A what?"

"Are you asking me out Ms. Psychologist?" Zon repeated, playing out the charade by stepping closer and staring hard into her beautiful brown eyes.

"No . . . no . . . I have to go." Without another word, Xia cut her head away and started walking to the change room.

"Wait!" Zon shouted gently. He hadn't expected this reaction. "I was just kidding. Please don't be offended." Xia stopped in her tracks, then turned back toward him.

"You're for real, aren't you?" he said, making more of a statement than a question. Xia didn't respond. "Listen," he continued, "I didn't mean to offend you. We both seemed to be playing with each other. Maybe I went a little too far."

"No. You weren't offensive," Xia said. "I was just surprised. That's all." They smiled cautiously at each other.

"I've got to go," Zon said, "but it was nice talking to you."

"And it was nice talking to you, too." Waving his hand, Zon backed away.

"'Bye."

"Good-bye," she said, watching him go. Zon turned toward the door.

"Hey," Xia called as he grabbed the door handle. Stepping up to him, she said, "You're for real, too." With a big smile, she added, "Maybe I'll see you next time you're here. We'll share a juice." Zon smiled back.

"You're not looking for a new subject to study, are you?"

"No," she laughed, "I can talk to you. As a matter of fact, I've talked more to you tonight than I have to anyone this week."

"Not all of your observing is by choice, is it?"

"There you go again," she quipped. "Now let's not forget who the analyst is between us, okay?" Her smile was mirrored on Zon's face.

"Whatever you say, Doc."

Zon turned and leaned his back against the door. Normally, this would have been a good time for a boy and a girl to politely kiss one another on the cheek, but this wasn't normal. Zon felt good as he talked to Xia, not lustful, just . . . good. Sure, she was pretty, but more like sister pretty. The loveliness of her eyes was more than matched by their complete innocence.

"Maybe I've just found another friend," he said to her in a low, gentle voice.

"I know that I have," she responded, and placed her hand gently upon his forearm. "I'll see ya." Without another word, she turned and walked down the hall. Zon stood and watched her until she reached the aerobics room, then he turned and slid through the exit.

* * *

"How bad is it?" Emory Jackson leaned delicately over the fender of his vintage Mercedes, trying not to let his 100 percent wool, European cut, full length overcoat touch the car. He'd bought the car over a year before, and had brought it to Billy Davis regularly for maintenance.

"Oh git back 'fo you git a smudge," Billy said, shooing the brilliant lawyer away from the car. "Ah'll tell ya in a minute." The lawyer backed up as Billy moved from the front of the car to the left side, then leaned in deep under the hood. Lifting his left leg, he hoisted himself onto the covered fender. His body weight caused the front of the car to dip. Emory, feeling helpless in the huge garage, looked around. He spotted four chairs by the wall directly in front of his car. With briefcase in hand, he walked over, quickly inspected the chairs for dirt, then sat down. Billy continued working under the hood with a light and screwdriver.

"Hey, Rasta Boy!" Billy yelled.

"Yeah . . . wha' choo wan'," came a young, but heavily masculine voice from the other side of the garage.

"You come an' see whad' I want!" Billy yelled back, "you sorra 'scuse of a trainee." Emory laughed at the exchange.

"You've got some new help?" Emory jabbed at Billy.

"He's new, bud he ain't no hep a' tall." After waiting a full minute, Billy grew impatient. "Rasta Boy!" he yelled again, louder than before.

"I'm comin'," the teenager answered indignantly as he rounded the back bumper of the car. "Wha' choo wan'?" Billy, crawling down off the car, walked over and stared down at the floor over which the young man had just passed. "Wha' choo lookin' fo'?" the boy asked angrily.

"Da slimy snail track yo' slow ass musta lef' gettin' over here," Billy replied. A disgusted smirk covered his face. Emory nearly burst his gut trying to hold back his laughter. The boy stood enraged as he stared at Billy.

"Git in de car an' ton id ova, when I say," Billy instructed the boy, then climbed back under the hood. The boy shuffled over to the car door, opened it, turned on the ignition, rolled down the electric window of the driver's door, closed it back, then stood waiting for Billy's orders.

"Ton id ova!" Billy yelled. The boy hit the switch. The starter engaged, but the car didn't crank. "Okay! Okay!" Billy yelled. The boy backed away from the car and stood for a few minutes. Billy continued to work. Growing tired of standing, the boy finally shuffled over beside Emory and sat down.

"Why does he call you Rasta Boy?" Emory asked.

"I'on know," the youth replied.

"Cause 'e don' work, das why," Billy interjected without looking up. "Ya see, Rastas, day keep plen'y jobs. Da' boy needs a job . . . needs ta be mo' like dem Rastas." Billy's voiced strained a bit as he stretched to test an oxygenator sensor located deep on the back side of the motor. "He's ma sista's boy," he continued, pulling himself from under the hood. "His daddy figu'd I could teach 'im somthin'. Ain't dat right, Rasta Boy?" Climbing from under the hood, he looked at the fifteen-year-old as he wiped his hands. "His daddy should'a tanned his hide mo' when he was young. Waited too long fo' he stawted ta raise 'im. Now e's got a head like a rock . . . and a mouth like a old woman. Ain't dat right, Rasta Boy."

"Ma name's Tevin," the teen scowled.

"Don't choo huff up at me, boy," Billy replied sternly. "I'll tan ya a bran' new shade a black and tell ya daddy I did." The boy bit his lip and looked down at the floor.

"So," interrupted Emory, "what's the verdict?" He nodded at the car.

"Ya gonna hafta leave it ova night," Billy said. "I'll pick up a sensa at the Merc place damarraw. Be no chauge to puddin' id on." He stuffed the grease rag in his pocket, removed the fender covers, then pulled down the hood.

"You mind if I ask you something?" Emory said.

"Naw, go 'head," Billy replied, as he folded the fender covers.

"You know all there is to know about every car that I've seen you work on," Emory said. Billy shrugged. "You must have spent years in school."

"Yeah," Billy replied, "I got ma four year degree in Industrial Arts from A & T State University, in '51, and gone back fum time ta time, maybe fo eight mo'. Why you ask?"

"They never made you take any English courses while you were there?" Emory said with a laugh. "I mean, if poor pronunciation was a crime, they'd have thrown you under the jail by now." Rasta Boy joined in the laughter. Billy peered at them both, but didn't respond. "What are you laughing at?" Emory, still laughing, said to the teen. "You talk just like him. This must be a family thing." Tevin's laughter abruptly stopped and Billy's began. Looking at Emory, Billy replied in exaggerated articulation, "I may choose to speak," he said while mockingly bowing like an English butler, "in any manner that so pleases me." Emory's laughter choked in his throat. "I've learned the King's English," Billy continued, "mastered it, to tell the truth. But to socialize or caaasually communicate with such ahhhhrticulation, frankly, makes me sick." He smiled as he plopped down beside his nephew. "Look at id dis way," he said. "Kang's Anglish is just anatha language." I can use either whenever I need or want to. As long as you get the message . . . ain' nuthin' bu' da thang, chicken wang." Emory reached over and slapped Billy five, both laughing approval at his wit.

"Dat ain't no language," the teen retorted.

"Who says it ain't?" Billy replied with a grin.

"Said id on TV."

"Do I speak it?" Billy asked.

"Yeah."

"Do you understand it?"

"Yeah."

"Do you speak it?"

"Yeah."

"Do I understand it?"

"Yeah."

"So wha's da definition ova language?" Tevin wrinkled his brow in thought, but didn't respond.

"Well?" Billy insisted.

"It's da way people speak ta each udda," he finally replied.

"We speakin'," Billy said, holding his hand out again for Emory to slap home payment. "Sounds like language ta me." Impudent disgust covered the young man covered face.

"You can't believe everything you see on television. Right, Billy?" Emory said.

"Das right," Billy replied.

"You know, Billy," Emory said as he cast his eyes to the garage ceiling, "I'm a little ashamed to admit it, but I use to believe that boob tube a little too much. I'm thirty-eight years old and for most of my life, that thing had me convinced that white women were more beautiful than black women."

"Day au," Rasta Boy chimed in. Emory and Billy's mouths fell open.

"Who says?" Billy asked.

"I do," replied Tevin.

"Who told you?" Emory asked.

"Nobody hada tell me. Ah seen it fo' maself."

"Where?" Emory asked again.

"All ova, ever'where." Emory and Billy looked into one another's eyes, then simultaneously said,

"Television."

"Let me tell you something," Emory started preaching. "Boy, don't you believe that mess for a minute. Your mother is a beautiful woman. Your sister is beautiful."

"An dem knucky-headed kids ya gonna have someday," Billy added, "day gonna be preddy, too." Though he laughed, he shook his head in disgust. He eyed his nephew who sat there so convinced, so sure of himself, never bothering to make sure for himself. Watching his cockiness, Billy decided that now was a good time for a lesson in humility and plain common sense.

Sniffing once, he leaned into the young man, but as he opened his mouth to speak, the door in the distant wall of the large multibay garage squeaked open. The conversation paused as the three turned simultaneously to watch a tall young black man step quietly into the room. The man carried a large leather-covered brown box in his left hand. He wore dark pleated pants, black loafers, and a heavy coat with the collar turned up against the blustery wind blowing outside. Large dark glasses covered his eyes and a large wide brim hat sat tilted upon his head.

"You know this guy?" Emory asked Billy as the stranger approached.

"Ah . . . yeah. Ah know em." Billy was hesitant of the stranger until he recognized the straight perfect teeth and broad shoulders of the bum who had helped him win in Atlantic City.

"Hey," Billy said as he stood and stretched a hefty mechanic's hand at the stranger, "ah . . . Zoom . . . ah . . . Zon. Is zat right?"

"Yes, that's right," Zon said with a big smile. Emory eased back into his chair and took his hand from his coat pocket.

"Here, ah . . . let me intraduce ya." Billy backed from between Zon and Emory.

"Dis is Em'ry Jackson. He and I go way back. Grew up in the same neigba'hood. He's a big-shot lawya now, bud he still comes aroun'." Emory stood and extended his right hand to Zon, who grabbed it tightly. The two stood eye to eye as they shook hands.

"Em'ry," Billy continued, "Zon."

"Mr. Zon," Emory said apprehensively.

"No. Just Zon," Zon added with a smile.

"You legit?" Emory asked as their hands snapped apart.

"Legit?"

"Yeah, the box, hat, and coat make you look . . . like a crook." He searched Zon's face for a reaction. Zon calmly dropped his smile and waited for the inquisitive lawyer to continue. "And it takes a real crook to wear dark glasses at night."

"I'm legit," Zon replied calmly. "For my own reasons, I prefer to remain . . . covered."

"Yeah," Billy chimed in, "lee da man alone. He's ah 'ight." Billy stared at his distorted reflection in Zon's glasses as he stepped back between the two men.

"Aren't you going to introduce the young man?" Zon asked.

"Huh? Oh," Billy said gruffly, "ah didn't plan to. Stand up, boy!" Billy raised his voice and motioned the boy to his feet.

"Dis ma nephew, Rasta, ah mean, Tevin Cummins." Zon stepped around Billy and offered Tevin his hand. Tevin stared into the large hand, but didn't offer his own.

"Shake da man's han', boy." Billy growled as he twisted his face into a knot.

"I don' know 'im," Tevin retorted, still withholding his hand.

"You don't know me," Zon said, "but you know your uncle. Trust him, not me." Tevin stared at Zon's open hand, then at his uncle's eyes. Billy motioned him to shake. Reluctantly, the boy took Zon's hand.

"You tawk funny," Tevin said to Zon.

"Rasta!" Billy yelled at the mouthy youth. "Boy," he started, then bit his lip to hold back his cussing. "Go . . . go wait fo me in da truck." Tevin pulled his hand away, shoved it in his pocket, then dragged his feet as he walked toward the door.

"Pawdin him," Billy apologized for Tevin, "he need mo raisin' and 'bout a pound bead off his hide." Emory shook his head in agreement. Zon didn't respond.

"Em'ry," Billy spoke to his longtime friend, "you gonna hafta 'scuse us." Billy started walking to the door, inviting Emory to join him. Emory followed along. "Caw me damarraw, 'bout fo'. Ah'll have ya caw reddy by den." He opened the metal door and swung it wide for Emory to exit.

"You sure everything is all right?" Emory asked as he peered over Billy's shoulder at Zon.

"Everything's fine," Billy said clearly and calmly. "Trust me. Ah been workin' on a caw fo' him, too. He jus' came ta pick id up."

"I'll see you later, then," Emory said, then turned and walked down the street toward the rental car that awaited him. He turned the collar of his overcoat up as he walked, trying to stop the chilly air. Tevin sat lazily in his uncle's new Ford pickup with the windows rolled up, his eyes closed, and the music blasting inside. He didn't see Emory as he passed.

"Closed eyes . . . just like his mind," Emory said, as he walked by the truck.

* * *

"Nice place," Zon said as Billy walked back to join him.

"Id'll do," Billy replied modestly. "Didn' see the sense in buildin' a brand new 'un, so I bought dis un." Billy smiled proudly as he looked about the huge garage. It had four forty-foot bays; each one was fifteen feet wide, fifteen feet high, and with its own roll-up door. The building was practically new. Billy's old truck production and repair company had just built it two years before, but had placed it on the market due to hard economic times.

"Ah'll neva foget dem faces," he said, staring wide-eyed through Zon. "They'd aw seen on TV when ah won the big money. Most of 'im shook ma hand in congrat'lations . . . 'cept fo' ol' fat Robbut . . . ma boss.

"Don' think dis changes nuthin'," he said ta me, scoatchin' me wit' dem hateful eyes, like I was some turd he was tryin' not to step in." Billy's breath quickened as he thought back to the senseless pain his racist boss had subjected him to over the past fifteen years. With a huff, he shook his head as if coming out of a dream, and looked at Zon. "Ah started work here in fiddy-two," Billy said with a laugh, sliding his hands into his back pockets. "Day use ta send me out thru da snow, down da bloc, to da back ah da cafe 'cross da street ta get dem coffee. Took me a extra ten minutes ta wawk da block, when day could da jus' crossed da street." A look of pain covered his brow as he spoke. "Bud I did it doe, ev'ry day." A small sigh escaped his lips.

"Bud thangs could da been worse. Like when ol' fat Robbut stawted work here, coupla years ago. Boy was determined ta gi' me a haud time." Billy shook his head lightly while Zon listened patiently. "One time, he was tryin' ta show off in front a his buddies. Told me if I didn't hurry up, he was gonna put his foot up ma ass." Billy laughed, then turned to look Zon directly in the eye. "Ah told him, 'Ah'll go get off the clock an' we can go out back, 'cause I wanted ta see 'im do it. I told 'im I didn't b'lieve he could get dat big fat-ass foot a his dat high." The two laughed knowingly. "Ah tell ya," Billy continued, still chuckling, "ya neva seen such a red face b'fo in ya life. Ya boy stormed in ta the stow manager's office and tried ta get me fired. Course, day couldn't do dat. Couldn't replace me. And day knew it. Ol' Fat Boy, he didn't know dat I knew." Billy puffed his chest. "Boy's had it in fo me eva since, though."

"So, where is he now?" Zon asked.

"Huh? Ah, when I came back from 'Lantic City, I went righ' inta the managa's office, afta Fat Boy faced me up. Made a deal righ dere on da spot and bought dis place." Billy started laughing again. "Den ah walked out past ol' fat Robbut and foun' da janita. Hired him as my new managa. Fat Boy'd been givin' 'im a hard time, too. He walked ova and axed Fat Boy ta step inta his office." Pearly white teeth shone from between Billy's lips as his laughter grew. "Po boy quit on da spot. Da whole shop laughed him out da doe."

"Self-righteousness can be a terrible thing," Zon added. Billy looked around as he drew deep breaths to rinse away the laughter.

"At boy knew me long fo' he met me," Billy reflected. "His daddy knew me, too, long fo' I was born. Told Fat Boy all 'bout me. All fat Robbut had ta do was squint hard 'nough, till it got dark 'nough fo him ta see dat his daddy was right."

"The only way to be right, by definition, is to have the luxury of seeing only what you want to see," Zon reaffirmed, then looked about the garage.

Billy, sensing Zon's curiosity, stepped around him and walked toward the far end of the garage.

"I put in da wall, like ya said," he explained, pointing at the barrier at the far end of the garage and motioning Zon to follow. As he approached a small door in the massive wall, he dug his right hand deep into his pocket. "Na, 'uh . . . which one is it?" he asked aloud while fishing out a single key from the midst of the massive bunch on his ring. "Nobody's been in heah, 'cept me," he continued as he stuck a key into one of two large padlocks on the door. "De walls a' solid on awl sides. The front doe's awl metal, and locked from da inside." Both locks fell from the door. Zon stood patiently behind the master mechanic, holding the large brown leather box in front of him. He removed the glasses, hat, and overcoat and discarded them. Billy pressed the latch handle and pulled the door open. Stepping in, he felt along the wall in the dark room and fished out the light switch on the wall.

"Dis is awl I been workin' on since ya brought me da drawin's. Made a couple a ma regulas mad. But day'll savive." Billy stepped into the room and looked around, then turned back to Zon.

"Come on in," he said, swinging his open hand slowly toward the car that sat in the middle of the floor. A flare of anticipation gripped Zon's stomach as he made his way through the door.

"Hea's ma baby," Billy said, with an air of fatherly pride.

"It's beautiful," Zon exclaimed as he walked to the front bumper and set his box on the floor. Before him sat a car that was low, flat, and matte jet black. The front end flattened to a solid sharp edge with no open grill or light sockets. A large spoiler rimmed the bottom of the bumper. A low profile, oval, bug-eyed glass bubble stretched across the car where the front seat would have been. The glass was tinted and mirrored, preventing him from seeing inside. The opening appeared wide enough for only a front seat. The tires were wide and low profile, with smooth flat rims that matched the black matte finish of the car. Except for the break at the wheel wells, the car looked to be made of a single piece of metal.

Zon walked admiringly around the car. The rear was wider than the front, and flat on the end. The very end was made of wide grill work. Looking into the grill, he saw two large cones extending just behind it. A low one-foot wide round mound protruded from the car. It started at the back of the glass bubble then ran down the middle of the body to the tail. It grew wider to the sides as it approached. A large spoiler protruded out of the trunk top. The support legs were nearly two feet wide, the crosspiece, two and a half.

Peering underneath, Zon saw a finish just as smooth as the top, with no exposed piping, axles, or supports. Except for the wheel wells and bubbled passenger area, the car would have appeared the same, upside down.

"A work of art," Zon sighed as he walked back to the front of the car where Billy awaited him.

"Yes, Lowd," Billy replied. "Too bad id don't work." Without reacting, Zon replied, "Show it to me."

"Wif pleasure." Billy said, and moved in close. "I stawted wif a Stef' . . . ya know . . . dat Chrysla car, wide wheel base, flat profile." Billy swept his hand along the sleek line of the car as he talked, caressing it as one would a beautiful woman. "Couse," he started, then paused. Emory's comments about his speech came to mind. "I gutted it and replaced all the plastic and polymer with chrome-nickel steel alloy . . . per yo' instructions." He peered expectantly at Zon, who didn't seem to notice the language change. "That alone cost a fortune." Billy moved down the right side of the car. "Made two bodies, welded them together, and cut out the wheels. Took out all that complicated suspension, replaced them with individual units, fully retractable. And ah added these retractable spoilers here on top and on the front and back." He pointed at the large air foils, then reached down and hit a concealed button. The back of the low bubble popped loose.

"Come here," he said. "Climb in." Zon stepped into the car on the driver's side and scooted into the seat, which delicately contoured to his backside from head to toe.

"You can adjust all of the contact points," Billy said, pointing out the adjustments. Zon pressed a couple of the adjustment buttons on the side of the seat, but nothing happened.

"Oh . . . " said Billy, "I forgot." Turning from the car, he stepped across the garage bay, retrieved an air hose, walked back to the bubble, and connected it to a quick-release fitting behind the passenger's seat.

Continuing as if he never left, Billy said, "The whole car is pneumatic, works off air pressure. Air rams are mounted on each side of the car body and routed into tanks, to build the pressure necessary to operate the car. The system has two backup units and piping. It's the most reliable, and since I didn't have to worry about an engine, suspension, or power train mechanics, I had plenty of room to add backup systems. The electronics are also powered by the engine exhaust, ya see--no batteries."

Point after point of detail floated from Billy's mouth as he described his handiwork. Zon stared down into the console. There was no steering wheel. An array of gadgets, meters, and displays stared back at him. Billy pointed at his armrests.

"You steer the car from here." He placed his hands on wide grips located at the end of each armrest. To this were attached an array of levers, buttons, and switches. "Either side will control the wheels. The pedal on your left is the brake. Press lightly," he emphasized, "the disc pads on all four wheels and wide tires were designed for stopping this thing. And believe me, they'll get the job done." Billy choked a little, then cleared his throat.

"Something the matter?" Zon asked.

"Ahh, no man," Billy answered, slipping back into his more comfortable vernacular. "Dis is yo car, built just like you wanted it, right?"

"Yes," Zon replied, "but you've also made some major design changes and additions." Beaming a smile, he added, "And I like them all. You were definitely the right man for this job."

"Well, thank ya," Billy said again, then pointed back into the console. "See those gauges?" he said, pointing at the dash between the seats.

"Which ones?"

"Wait a minute," Billy said, then hustled around to the other side of the car and climbed into the passenger seat.

The ease at which he climbed inside the car told Zon that the master mechanic must have sat in these seats many times before.

"These gauges," Billy said. "This one is your speedometer, measured by the wheels. This one measures your speed, by anemometer. Here is your general direction compass, and over here . . . " Billy continued pointing and describing gadgets to Zon until he had covered all on the middle and far passenger console.

"And what's this?" Zon pointed high on the dash, over the

middle console.

"Oh, that's a bank of fuzz busters, you know, radar detectors," Billy bragged. "I put in four, case one or two failed." Laughing, he added, "I figure a vehicle like this is going to be breakin' some speed limits." Billy's small snips of laughter suddenly erupted into guttural guffaws.

"What's so funny?" Zon asked innocently. Chuckling, Billy replied, "Come on, man. Let's cut the bullshit." He emptied his face of the laughter. "I know ya put a lotta money in dis caw, 'bout four-hundat thousand dollas or mo'."

"Not to mention the garage," Zon interjected.

"Yeah, das righ'," Billy continued, "but you and I both know dat, as preddy as it is, it won't work." With a sense of hopelessness, Billy looked over into Zon's eyes. Zon smiled back. "Look, son," Billy continued, "this musta been some fanasy fo you, righ'? Ta buil' some supa car. Well, it's sho been one fo' me." He eased back into his seat, and looked up through the glass hood, into the garage ceiling. "I neva had da opatunidy to buil' anythang from scratch, from da groun' up. I've put ma hot in dis o' girl." He reached out and rubbed the leather-covered dash. "Bud' as fine as id is, it don't work."

"And what's wrong with it?" Zon asked, breaking his polite silence. A disgusted Billy loudly exhaled.

"Ah'm damn sho glad you fin'lly axed." Fixing his hands high on the dash and seat, Billy pried himself out of the car.

"Get out," he said flatly. Without a word, Zon popped easily out onto the floor, on the opposite side of the car.

"Pull the lever on the back side of that seat, then raise it up."

"Have you ever heard the word, 'schizophrenia'?" Zon teased, alluding to Billy's flip-flopping dialect.

"Just raise the seat," Billy retorted. Reaching in, Zon raised the driver's seat. Billy did the same on the passenger side. "The seats ride on geared pivots," he said. "That's the reason for the gears under here. But, ya see back there?" He pointed deep into the dark cavity of the car. Looking in himself, he could barely see. "Wait a minute." Turning about, he retrieved a flashlight from the tool chest along the garage wall. Returning, he rested the light beam on two identical objects sitting side by side, located at the very end of the car, where the trunk would normally end. A large metal, funnel-shaped cone protruded out of the back of each shiny cylindrical vessel. There were no mechanical devices or piping connected to them, but they were securely welded to the heavy steel chassis. Thermocouples were welded onto each cone and cylinder.

"Ya see those?" he said again to Zon.

"Rocket engines," Zon said with a smile.

"Right."

"Don't they meet design specifications?"

"Yep," Billy replied, "but, we ain't got to the problem yet."

"How much thrust?" Zon asked. Billy started to chuckle again.

"Depends on whatcha burnin'. Wit jet fuel, 'bout 10,000 pounds of thrust each. Wit' acetylene or hydrogen, around 30,000 pounds total."

"How much does the car weigh?" Zon asked as he examined the engines.

"Little ova a ton," Billy answered, then added through his chuckles, "fifteen tons a thrust pushin' one? Be like firin' a bullet out'a coat forday-five . . . if they ever got fired," he added with a heavy dose of sarcasm. "Which brings us to this thing here." Billy moved the light beam forward to rest upon a large metal sphere, located low and just behind the contoured seats. On the back of the sphere, a small thick pipe protruded, split, then led into each of the engines. Small pot-shaped mounds were mounted on the large cylinders, where the pipes were welded in. Dual ignition wires ran into the top of the mounds.

Billy pressed a button on the inside car wall. A small rush of air whisked out, then the orb split perfectly down the middle and the front side slid forward, exposing the inner sphere. The wall of the three-foot wide orb was four inches thick and comprising several layers of steel. The inner wall was lined with a shiny blue alloy. A harness hung from a thin rod that was fixed in the bottom of the front hemi-globe. Mounted on the back of the front orb was a small cylinder, which had pipes welded into its side that led off into either side of the car walls.

"This is . . . what did ya call it?" Billy asked, with a hint of disgust.

"Converter," Zon answered, unshaken.

"Yeah, converter. Anyway, it'll feed the fuel through this tube, then through these tubes to feed the engines." Billy worked the light along the fuel's path as he spoke. "The fuel burns in the engines and the temperature from that will force the hot stream of gases out of that small hole in the back of the engine cylinders, into the nozzles. The pressure differential created there, between the gas at the nozzle exit and the air behind, generates the thrust."

"It all sounds good to me," Zon said jovially.

"Good?" Billy bellowed back. "Good? What kind of fuel do ya expect ta work in this contraption?" Zon started to answer, but Billy cut him off. "Can't be solid, nor gaseous fuels. You've set up piping and containment for liquid. Even if it were, you've got no means to control a solid burn. This thing would fire and wouldn't stop until you exhausted the fuel, which'd put you on the moon." Billy worked his hands on and off his waist as he ranted. "And it can't be jet fuel, diesel, or gasoline either. Dere ain't no pumping system on dis green earth, nor in dis kit caw a yours, that could force the fuel into the engines, through those orifices, once they started firing. That's why jets use *turbines*, today."

"Turbines aren't nearly as efficient as rocket engines," Zon said calmly. "They're heavy, have tons of metal and moving parts, and couldn't handle start and stop driving." Billy's eyes bulged incredulously.

"Didn't ya just hea' me?" he asked, straining to contain his frustration. "You got no fuel!" Billy thrust his arms out to his sides, then slapped his hands to his legs, adding an audible exclamation mark to his statement.

Sensing his frustration, Zon, who had been leaning over the car, straightened up.

"Oh, we've got fuel. Where are the tanks?" With a loud huff, Billy rolled his lips tight to keep from cussing, then pointed at the tank ports to the top and inside of the car's walls. Zon twisted the cap off the tank on the driver's side.

"You got a water hose?" he asked calmly.

"Don't need no wata'," Billy shot back, as he plowed his hand over his forehead and through his closely cut hair. "This thing's completely air cooled. You need fuel, f-u-e-l, fuel! Fool!" he screeched.

"Where's the hose?" Zon insisted as he fidgeted with the tank cap.

"Shit!" Pent-up frustration broke from Billy's lips as he stomped over to the wall, turned on the water valve, and stretched the long green hose over to Zon. Then, while casually looking into the completely outdone mechanic's eyes, Zon thrust the water nozzle into the fuel tank opening and squeezed the nozzle release.

"No! You moron!" Billy yelled, but it was too late. Water gushed forth, contaminating the fuel system with city water, as Zon stood by calmly humming. Billy grasped his face with both hands. Then, while peering madly through his fingers, he backpedaled until he fell against the cold brick garage wall.

"Why de Lowd give all the money to the morons?" he asked himself aloud.

"You want to go on a test ride with me?" Zon asked as nonchalantly as ever. Locking the nozzle open, he lodged the hose in the opening and walked to the front of the car.

"Naw," Billy replied, whimpering and completely outdone. "You go 'head wit' yo' crazy sef. I godda take ma nephew home." He turned and walked toward the door. "An' don' worry," he added, "if the boys from de looney bin ask . . . I ain't seen ya."

"What?" Zon replied. Billy didn't respond, but kept walking toward the large door.

"Ah, dis latch heea will open the big doe," he said, deciding to humor the young fool. "Ah'm goin' ta take ma nephew home." Billy shuffled to the small door and pushed it open. Looking back, he shook his head in an emotional mix of pity, for Zon's lunacy and bitter disappointment over his expensive and chance-of-a-lifetime project ending so miserably. Deep inside, he'd hoped that Zon had just one more miracle up his sleeve, to allow the car to operate. After all, he'd worked the slots in Atlantic City, and had come up with the drawings--and the money--for the car. Why not a miracle fuel as well?

The closing door pushed coldly on Billy's back as he stepped out into the chilly night air.

* * *

Zon retrieved the leather box he'd set on the floor by the front of the car. As he walked back to the filling tank, the nozzle clicked off, signaling full. He inserted the water nozzle into the right tank, then reset the latch. Out of the box, he retreived the crystalline gold rock that he had brought from Beinin, the Kaldaca stone. It had been chiseled into the shape of a star burst, with multiple arms of crystal emanating from the center. Carefully, he lowered the stone into the converter, secured it in the harness, then hit a button. Again came the sound of rushing air, then the two half moons slid together, sealing the stone inside the converter.

For several weeks, Zon had experimented with the stone. To his delight, he'd found that it could instantly convert water to its basic elements of hydrogen and oxygen, even at pressures well above fifty tons. The small valve on the front of the converter fed water into the valve reservoir under low pressure. Then it rotated to seal away from the tank and opened into the converter. In this manner, the fuel tank and converter always remained sealed and separate. The valve was a tiny rotating door, with its speed of rotation determining how much water was fed to the converter. Once in the converter, the water would instantly convert to the two gases, which would build up pressure to feed the powerful engines. There, the gases would burn, providing thrust, then escape harmlessly into the atmosphere as water vapor.

Zon eased the two contoured chairs back into place. The water nozzle clicked full again as he finished with the passenger's chair. Removing it, he secured the tank caps, walked to the driver's side, then hopped back into the car. Leaning back comfortably, he adjusted the chair to gently cup his legs, buttocks, back, shoulders, neck, and head.

"Feels a little better than that cross," he thought as he clicked the seat belts into place. "Well," he said aloud, "here we go." Placing his right foot firmly on the brake, Zon eased the other one lightly onto the accelerator. He listened as the valve slowly spun, the water disintegrated, and the pressure built in the converter. He felt a light click of the accelerator as it made the electronic connection to set off the igniter. Suddenly, as the igniter glowed red, an outraged Billy burst back through the small door.

"That sorry-ass, no-count, good-for-nuthin', lazy-boned, ghetto-blastin' . . . " Billy's words froze in his mouth as he heard the mild roar of the engines igniting. With eyes bulging and a wide grin splitting his face, he rushed up to the car.

"Wha'd jew do?" he screeched at a smiling Zon. With his foot set firmly on the brake, Zon pushed lightly on the accelerator until he heard the wide tires screeching as they struggled to hold the car in place.

"Ya done good," he said to an ecstatic Billy. Billy wrenched his head back and forth, gazing at the car. Stunned, he struggled to believe what his eyes and ears were telling him. Finally finding his voice, he said, "Wha . . . What's it burnin'?" Zon opened his mouth to explain the water in the tank, but Billy cut him off. "Nawww . . . I don't wanna know." Still grinning and barely able to contain himself, he asked, "Hey . . . hey . . . does dat test ride offa still stand?" Like a kid with a new bike, Billy tried to look at Zon as he spoke, but pranced about the car, his hands never losing contact, poking, examining, wanting to experience every single working piece of the machinery he had so masterfully built.

"I'll wait on you," Zon said.

"Huh?" Billy replied, then slapped himself in the forehead with his right palm. "Oh!" he yelled. "Dat boy! Ran my battry down blastin' my radio all dis time, loud 'nough for da dead to hear." His anger momentarily robbed him of his excitement. "Yeah, I came back for the cables. Yeah . . . you . . . you wait. I'll be back in twen'y . . . ten minutes." Billy ripped the cables from the wall and backed blindly out of the door, never taking his eyes off the car.

Moments later, Zon heard screeching wheels outside as Billy pulled his truck to a hurried stop. Almost ripping the door off the hinges, he burst into the garage and slid to a stop beside the car. Zon stood outside, examining the engine.

"Wow!" Zon said jokingly, "You said ten minutes, but you've only been gone five."

"I didn't stop," Billy said, out of breath and eyes glued to the car, "not even to let Rasta Boy out." Catching his breath, and the absurdity of his own words, Billy eased out of his trance and began to laugh. Zon joined him.

"You didn't show me the conversion," Zon said.

"I think you'll like it." Billy responded, then stepped over to the console. Looking in, he reassured himself that the pneumatic system was at full pressure.

"Watch," he said, beaming a wide smile. Pressing a button on the driver's console, Billy then stepped away from the car. Instantly, the left end of the oval glass bubble rotated toward the middle of the car hood. The seats continued to face forward, and the console to the rear, but the driver's seat and console moved to the front and the passenger seat slid to the rear, up and over, behind the driver. The entire cockpit tilted downward as it slid down the nose of the car. Meantime, the front fenders slid back, leaving a sharp rounded nose. At the rear, the fenders and bumpers collapsed, then mechanically spread out to the side. The grill, covering the engines, slid up, then disappeared into the car body. The rest remained intact, with the rear and horizontal flappers spread wider, the horizontal legs now attached to the solid top of the wings. Flappers eased out of what were the fenders to complete the triangular wings. Before their eyes, Zon and Billy watched the flat and wide car transform into an aircraft.

Billy hopped into the cockpit.

"Watch." Working the same levers at the ends of the armrest, Billy fanned the rudder on the back of the air foil. Motioning toward the left wing's edge, he worked the turning rudders on the back of the wings.

"What about the variable wing pitch?" Zon asked excitedly. With a flick of his fingers, Billy caused the wide flat wings to move in and out from the body.

"Billy, you're a genius." Zon said appreciatively.

"I jus' followed the recipe . . . like any good cook," Billy said modestly, but his glowing face expressed his true feelings.

"Look here," he said to Zon while flicking a switch, low on the end of the armrest. Instantly, the shells covering the nozzle exits split and cupped behind the engines. "Das yo' reverse . . . and yo' brake," Billy said. "I'd advise you go easy with both at first."

"Let's go for that test drive," Zon said as he checked his watch. It was well after midnight. "We should be able to run about without much trouble."

"Now you said, no lights," Billy cautioned Zon, referring to the lack of head, tail, and clearance lights on the car.

"That's right," Zon replied. "We won't need any." With a big smile, Billy lifted himself out of the cockpit and onto the floor.

"Whateva you say, boss man. I've learned . . . I've learned." He sang jubilantly, then rushed to open the large garage door. Zon set the conversion switch back to "car." As the vehicle reconverted itself, Billy hustled back. Climbing nimbly inside, Zon ignited the engines, threw them in reverse, and eased the car out of the garage. Billy closed the large door, secured the garage, then jumped in beside Zon, and secured the bubble.

"Let her rip," he exclaimed as his seat belt harness snapped into place. With a wild look in his eye, Zon pressed down on the accelerator. Feeling the powerful thrust from the engines, he released the brakes.

"Whooweee!" Billy yelled as the G-forces pinned his head and body to the seat. With tremendous effort, he peered out through the glass canopy. "It's dawk! I can't see a thang! Can you see? I hope you can see!" Buildings and lights rushed by his eyes in one continuous blur. Zon sat calmly in his seat and maneuvered the car through the turns and toward the highway. The speedometer eased passed 300 miles an hour as they sped onto I-95, heading toward Washington, D.C.

* * *

The large overhanging street lights raced by in a blur as Zon and Billy cruised down the five-lane, well-lit highway. Zon stared straight ahead, concentrating on the controls and teaching himself to handle the vehicle completely by feel. The car bounced and swayed occasionally as he experimented. Ever so often, it actually lifted from the road's surface, floated about the marked lanes, then returned to the ground, the free-wheeling tires marking each touch back with a rubber-burning screech. After a bit of practice, the tires eventually stopped turning as the car cruised a hair's width above the pavement. With a flick of a switch, Zon retracted the wheels into the enclosed wheel wells.

"Boy," Billy exclaimed. He watched the blur of lights and trees go by, unaware that they were no longer on the ground. "That's a smooth ride." Zon didn't comment, but continued concentrating on learning the car. Occasionally, they'd zoom by a car on the nearly deserted highway, but Zon was always on the opposite side of the road by the time he approached, then passed the unsuspecting motorist. Little noise came from the jet-car, particularly when cruising, so other drivers on the road were hardly aware of it until they saw the blurry dark shadow pass by.

As they sped along, the radar detectors occasionally beeped in succession, then stopped. Billy, thinking they had malfunctioned, began tapping on each as they beeped.

"Wha's wrong wit' dese thangs?" he said under his breath.

"They're picking up radar," Zon added calmly.

"How fast we goin'?" Billy asked. He craned his neck to see the speedometers. Without glancing down, Zon said, "Three-fifty five. The air foils won't keep us down if we go any faster."

"Three-fidy-five!" Billy shouted. "Ya mean the cops are clockin' us at three-fidy-five? Man, if day ever catch us, day gonna lock us up and thro' way da key."

"They've clocked us," Zon responded, "but they can't catch us."

"Wif radios, day don't need ta catch us."

"You mean they'll use roadblocks, like the one up ahead?" Zon said callously.

"Where? Where?" Billy shrieked as he craned his neck and squinted into the fast-approaching distance. At first he saw nothing, but within seconds he saw faint blue lights glowing. They quickly grew into large, blue flashing lights, then almost instantly turned into four marked police cars that blocked all five of the northbound lanes of the highway. Just as suddenly, Billy and Zon zoomed past. Zon had effortlessly maneuvered around the roadblock into the median between the north- and southbound lanes, then back onto the highway, varying the front and rear air foils' pitch for guidance. He had lowered the motionless wheels momentarily before they passed the roadblock, so any officer who might have caught a glimpse would have only seen the speeding blur of a car. The policemen, gallantly standing behind their cars, watched helplessly as their hats blew off and their pants legs flapped from the breeze created by the black shadow.

"Sheeeiiiit!" Billy squeaked, suddenly realizing what they'd just done. "You can bet yo' ass they gonna have the whole road blocked--wif tanks, up ahead." The familiar signs marking the district limits zoomed by as Billy checked his watch.

"Man! We made dat run from Richmun ta D.C. in twen'y minutes! Whoa! My baby'll flat . . . out . . . fly." He blew a kiss at the console.

"Fly," Zon said, staring straight ahead. "That's a good idea. Will she convert while we ride, on the fly?" he asked the master mechanic.

"Who da fuck knows?" Billy responded with a gawky look on his face. "I didn't even think this sucker would run." Shaking his head, he said, "Awl I know is, it's suppose ta."

"Watch your legs." Zon hit the button to activate the conversion. Billy shot a bewildered look at the driver, then pulled his legs high into his chest as his seat rose then swung high and backward to the middle of the passenger cabin. Zon's seat pivoted as the entire cockpit, glass bubble and all, slid forward and down the nose of the vehicle. Billy found himself looking directly over the back of the driver's seat. From his higher perch, he watched the fenders quickly melt into wings. Craning his neck, he saw two long tongues of flame reach out behind the jet-car. Zon gunned the engines. Suddenly, he felt his mouth sink into his stomach as they lifted off the ground and climbed above the treetops. Zon banked a hard right, away from the highway and out toward the ocean.

Billy continued to look about in complete amazement. The sight was a joy to behold. Zon worked the levers and buttons at his fingertips, much as he had when they were on the ground, again teaching himself the feel of the converted aircraft. Once satisfied with its control, he lowered the flaps slightly, causing the jet to rise away from the treetops. As he reached eighty feet, the radar detector beeped. Zon sank back to sixty-five feet and continued cruising toward the Atlantic shore. A few seconds later, he rose again to eighty-five feet and the radar detector responded.

"Wha's dat?" Billy asked.

"Radar."

"Ain't no cops up here."

"But there's plenty of radar, from the airport, military installations, and probably White House security as well."

"Why da hell ya challengin' it, den? Ya know, day have a tendency ta shoot down anythin' day don't unda'stan'." Billy's eyes glared wide as he swung his head about, searching for missiles.

"I'm just feeling out the radar ceiling," Zon answered, without emotion. "Looks to be about eighty feet. As long as we stay below that, they can't see us."

"Haven't they already seen us?" Billy asked skeptically.

"No," Zon explained. "The cop's guns shoot the radar in tight beams, once they know where to aim it. They sweep the radar up here, so they can look at the whole sky. Those few erratic bleeps that we sent back will appear as normal background noise."

"Ya soun' awfly sho ah yo'sef." Zon didn't respond.

Within minutes, they were flying out over the ocean. Zon lowered the jet down to the water's surface.

"I'm banking left," he said, alerting Billy. As he spoke, the left wing dipped and pointed directly down at the water. The jet turned almost ninety degrees. That's when Zon righted the plane and accelerated, heading up the coast. Peering back, Billy saw water spouts shooting skyward, the air wake of the plane dragging the surface along. Noticing Billy's amazement, Zon eased the jet slightly skyward, causing the spouts to diminish, but not disappear.

"Where we going?" Billy asked.

"Rhode Island."

"Why?"

"Is your wife going to worry?" Zon asked sincerely.

"Ah . . . no . . . she's use ta me workin' ta all hours . . . in the garage."

"You mind a little more adventure? I want to see what this thing will and won't do." Billy sat pondering Zon's offer. Thinking about it, he'd just done more within the last hour than most people do in a lifetime. And here was a chance to do still more. Of course, he could die in the process. In a fit of youthful recklessness, Billy sang, "Hurt me, hurt me." Zon pressed the accelerator, once again pinning his passenger to the back of his seat.

"Banking right," Zon exclaimed moments later as the jet pivoted, then straightened and headed east, farther out to sea.

"We've got air?" he asked Billy.

"Yeah," Billy responded, "small air bottles are mounted inside the seats. Low outside air pressure will activate them automatically."

"Good."

"How's the fuel . . . ah . . . water holdin'?"

"We've only burned an eighth of one tank. It's doing about a hundred miles to the gallon." With a few small movements of his fingers, the back flappers on the wings and spoiler tilted upward. The nose of the jet rose obediently with them, until it pointed directly up. Zon gunned the engine and the jet shot straight up. Billy gasped as the G-force pulled at his guts and plastered his lips to his teeth. Instantly, he heard constant beeps emanating from each radar detector.

"Dey gonna see us now, fo' sho," he said with a taste of fear in his voice.

"That's the idea," Zon replied. Pneumatic valves zipped open and closed as the outside air was cut off and bottled air opened to maintain cabin pressure. Seven miles up, Zon leveled the jet, cruising smoothly above the partly cloudy ceiling.

* * *

"Sir, we've got a bogey!" an excited lieutenant exclaimed as he triangulated coordinates on the radar screen. Two air force officers stepped quickly over to the console.

"Have they got it at Johnson?" Captain Handrahan, the floor commander, asked. After listening intently to his headset for a moment, the lieutenant responded,

"Yes, sir. They have verified our signal. It is real."

"What the hell is it?" Sergeant Bragg, the second in command, asked as he stared at the fluorescent green blip on the screen.

"Not sure, sir," the lieutenant answered. "Judging by its flight pattern, it could be a missile, maybe fired from a sub."

"A missile?" exclaimed Captain Handrahan. "Are you sure?" "No, sir," the lieutenant replied, pointing at the screen. "It's just that we first picked it up here, out over the water, rising straight into the air. Then it leveled off at seven and a half, and has continued to fly directly south at Mach 3.2."

"Could be a missile," Bragg spoke coolly at Captain's Handrahan's side, "coming out of nowhere that fast and consistent." Captain Handrahan pondered a minute, then turned to his communications officer. "Where's the nearest point of intercept?" Sergeant Jones's fingers glided confidently across the keyboard, seeking the requested information from the computer. Instantly, he read from the screen.

"At his current heading and speed, we could intercept from Pope, in fifteen minutes."

"Scramble two Phantoms from there--on the double," he barked at the sergeant, who began immediately typing into the console. "Alert Craig at the Pentagon," Captain Handrahan ordered a second officer.

Studying the coastline in the darkness, Zon alerted Billy each time they passed from one state into another.

"You see," Zon said, his calm voice in mock contrast to the steady beeps of the radar detector, "they didn't detect us until we were off the coast of Rhode Island. They can't connect us with your shop, Richmond, nor the speed demon on I-95 . . . assuming it gets reported at all." Zon spoke casually to a silent and worried Billy, who continued to searched the sky for missiles. They were flying just off the coast of North Carolina. The sky was completely clear. To the west, a bright full moon shone beautifully. In the hour since they'd left his shop, they'd traveled over 2,000 miles.

"Nobody'd b'lieve me, even if ah tol' em," Billy whispered. Suddenly, Zon banked the jet left and headed farther out to sea. As they leveled out, the radar detectors whined at a steady, high pitch. Zon eased further down on the accelerator.

"Wha's happenin'?" an excited and scared Billy asked, trying hard not to pee in his pants.

"Couple of military jets trying to lock their guidance radar in on us."

"Guidance radar?" Billy asked, afraid to hear the answer. "To guide what?"

"Missiles," Zon said flatly. Billy's throat and mouth went instantly dry. He struggled to pull himself away from the back of his chair. Then he peered behind him and tried to spot the planes. As he stared, the screeches ceased, although the beeps continued.

"I don't see nothin'," Billy managed to say through his constricted throat.

"They're about fifty miles back."

"How you know dat?" Billy's eyes cut nervously back and forth across the moonlit horizon behind them. Only the harmonious beeps of the radar detectors responded.

"It's turned, sir," the radar officer alerted the floor commander. Captain Handrahan peered over the lieutenant's shoulder.

"It's not a missile," Bragg said, "running away from our fighters. It's a manned aircraft, and a damned fast one at that--and probably not friendly."

"Have our fighters got a lock on it?" the captain asked.

"They got an initial lock, sir," the lieutenant replied, "but that's when the bogey turned out to sea." Turning to face the captain, he added, "It's running just ahead of the fighter's radar. They're engaging to overtake him."

"Aw dey gone?" Billy asked. The radar detector beeps beat down on his eardrums like hail stones.

"No," Zon answered, trying to reassure his friend. "They're chasing us, but they can't get within range to see us or fire on us." Feeling his rectum loosen ever so slightly, Billy pulled in a slow breath of air.

"Dey cain't catch us, huh. Why not?"

"They don't have the juice, Billy Boy," Zon sang out. "They don't have the juice." Billy felt himself being pulled back into his seat again as Zon accelerated. The radar howled again, then went back to the syncopated beeps. Zon was matching their speed, staying just out of their range.

Bragg stared hard into the radar screen, shaking his head. "Damn," he exclaimed, "it can outrun us."

"Are you sure?" Captain Handrahan asked. He, too kept his eyes glued to the screen.

"Our guys are running everything, including their afterburners, and it's matched their speed--just out of their locking range."

"Let's fire on them anyway," the frustrated captain replied.

"Without a lock, there's nothing to fire on."

"Look," Handrahan barked, "that bogey's holding a steady course, and not changing speed. We can fire a heat seeker right up its ass. He'll never know what hit him."

"Those birds are flying about as fast as the missiles, Captain. Besides, the Phantom's small heat seekers would burn out before they got halfway to the bogey." Stepping back, Bragg rubbed his chin. "But we can still get his ass," he said, turning back to the floor commander. "Look, he's using the fighter's radar signal to pace himself, and it looks like that's all he wants to do, for the time being." Looking to the communications console, he shouted, "Where's the Sahara?" After punching away at his terminal, the communication's officer turned back to Bragg.

"The Destroyer's 500 miles away, sir, roughly ten degrees off the bogey's predicted flight path. They've got the bogey on their sweeps, but don't have a lock."

"Good," Bragg responded. "Have them fire a heat seeker into its path. By the time the bogey detects it on its radar, it may be too late." Turning back to the lieutenant on radar, he said, "Tell the fighters to maintain pursuit. They'll push the son of a bitch right into our line of fire."

Immediately, the Sahara fired a large surface-to-air heat seeker right into Zon's flight path.

"E. T. A., two minutes," the radar officer said as the missile's bleep appeared on the screen.

"If they see it," Bragg said, "then they should turn now." All eyes were glued to the screen as the bogey and missile bleeps raced toward each other. The bogey didn't alter course. "Good . . . good," Bragg whispered as he waited for the collision.

"Fifteen seconds," the lieutenant counted down, "five, four, three, two, one." The air in the control room froze as the two radar bleeps intersected and stood fixed over each other. Then, two bleeps showed again, set in tight together, then, one . . . two . . . one . . . two . . .

"What happened?" Captain Handrahan yelled. "Did they hit?"

"Damn! I don't know," a puzzled Bragg answered.

"Sir," yelled the lieutenant, "the Phantoms have a lock on the bogey. No . . . they've locked in on two targets."

"What's wrong with our radar?" yelled Captain Handrahan.

"It's not the fucking radar," Bragg said, staring into the screen in disbelief.

"Sheeeeit! Sheeeeit!" On board the small black jet, a bug-eyed Billy yelled as he stared through the glass dome. His eyes were locked on the firey tongue spewing out of the back of the large heat-seeking missile that was trying desperately to ram itself up their engines. Seeing it coming, Zon had aimed his jet-car directly at it. As they met, he easily flew over and past it. Instinctively, the missile turned, drawn by the heat from his engines. Zon spread his wings wide, into their tight maneuvering mode. Turning much tighter and quicker than the missile, he flew back at it. By the time it had turned about, it had to turn yet again in its pursuit. Zon tightened his supersonic circling about the missile, causing it to pursue in wide clumsy ovals. Billy watched and screamed as the missile circled spasmodically, trying its best to hit them. But it wasn't built for this type of flying, and just helplessly, awkwardly circled about the two novel pilots.

"Billy! Billy!" Zon yelled at his scared stiff co-pilot, "Relax. It can't get to us." Billy cut his eyes down at Zon, but his mouth gaped still further and his hoarse screams continued. "Billy," Zon said again, but just as Billy's screams fell silent, all four radar detectors started screeching continuously. With double the volume, Billy started yelling again, "Sheeeit! Sheeeit!" The two Phantom jets had established a lock on them and were bearing down fast. Seeking to maneuver before they fired, Zon ordered his wings back into their high-speed position, swung his circular arc wide, then whipped his ship's nose directly westward, toward the pursuing jets. The large heat seeker awkwardly fell in behind him as he accelerated. Flying toward the jets for a split second, long enough for the missile behind him to achieve top speed, Zon again thrust the wings outward and yelled at Billy.

"Brace yourself!" Instantly, he rolled the jet over, pulled the nose into a hard one-eighty and maneuvered back, past the oncoming missile, as the Phantoms fired their heat seekers. Obediently, the destroyer's missile turned again, but its engine's eastward acceleration canceled out its westward momentum, causing it to instantaneously stall, then accelerate toward its target. But as the solid burning fuel thrust the missile forward, the white hot flames drew the Phantoms' two heat seekers into its own engine. The Phantoms rocked about madly as they raced through the tremendous three-bomb explosion. The bogey skipped off their radar screens.

"It's gone, sir," the lieutenant alerted the floor commander.

"What do you mean, gone?" Captain Handrahan replied.

"Just like it came," he replied, "First due east, then straight down, into the ocean . . . and off our screens."

"You saying it crashed into the sea?"

"Probably not," Bragg suggested. "It just dove down out of our radar." With a loud sigh of disgust, he added, "It could be heading anywhere now."

"Damn!" the floor commander shouted. Looking at the communications officer, he commanded. "Have the Phantoms drop down to where we last saw it, split up, and fly north and south."

"They'll have to return for fuel," Bragg said. "We've lost it."

"Damn," Handrahan repeated, "more UFO fodder for the tabloids."

Once out of their radar range, Zon shot quickly down to skim the ocean's surface. There, he leveled out and proceeded northward, at Mach 1.

"Billy," Zon called. The mechanic didn't answer. "Billy," Still, there was no answer. Closing his eyes, he concentrated on his unconscious friend behind him. The fright, combined with the G-forces of all the high-speed maneuvering, had rendered him unconscious, though unharmed.

Deep satisfaction fueled a broad smile across Zon's face. Patting the leather console lovingly, he thrust down on the accelerator. The G-forces caressed him in loving response.

13
HAITIAN SLAUGHTER

"Who are these guys?" Yeoman Chase spoke quietly to his longtime friend, Tony Jackson.

"Who the hell knows, Chase. This is the navy, remember? Don't ask, just do it." Jackson snickered as he and Chase secured the cases holding the heavy scuba gear. Before them, submerging one by one, were six white men, each wearing heavy scuba suits that covered them from head to toe. They were also equipped with single air tanks and full face masks with radios, through which they could communicate with each other and the sub. One at a time, they eased into the pool leading out of the submarine's bottom. Each fidgeted with tank valves, adjusted masks, or checked sealed pouches they wore on their sides.

"Hey," Chase gestured to Jackson, "check out the old man." The oldest diver, and leader of the group, waited at the end of the line. He was out of shape, overweight, and appeared completely foreign in the high-tech diving suit.

"Ten bucks says he croaks before he gets back," Jackson cracked, then nudged Chase with his elbow.

"You're on," Chase replied. "Ya see his eyes? He's old and bent out of shape, but that mutha's eyes are as cold as ice." Chase placed the lock on the locker, but kept his eyes on the old man. "There's no heart behind those eyes. You can't kill a man with no heart."

"Man," Jackson sneered, "when you gonna get off that voodoo jive? Always talking that shit, when ya know it ain't real." Jackson was easily frustrated by Chase's belief in voodoo. On rare occasions, it came between them. Most of the time, however, it was just something to mock or ignore.

The last diver walked awkwardly up to the pool, sat on the edge, and allowed his stumpy legs to fall free into the water. He forced his left leg up onto his right knee, then rolled his hanging belly out of the way as he reached the flipper down to his foot. A squeak of gas eased from under him as he stretched. Allowing the leg to splash back into the cool Caribbean water, he likewise forced his right leg up to receive a flipper. Once it, too, was in the water, he fixed both hands onto the pool's side and shoved himself into the water. Chase and Jackson watched his head bob spasmodically from the unfamiliar shock of submerging into dark waters.

"Getcha money ready," Chase quipped as he pushed Jackson through the small portal and out of the room.

* * *

The five divers ahead of the general had separated, each swimming to a distant corner of the flotilla, on the surface above. By the time the general bobbed to the surface, each of the other younger and far more fit divers had boarded the ragtag boats. General Fellows swam awkwardly to the nearest diver, who helped him out of the water.

"Sir," the diver spoke through the face-mask-mounted radio, "we're checking for survivors."

"Good," General Fellows puffed as he fought to regain his breath from the brief swim. Once on board, the general looked about the flotilla. The moon's shimmer bouncing off the divers glistening wet suits slowly faded as the water evaporated. General Fellows watched as the divers quickly moved across the roped-together vessels, rolling bodies, hundreds of bodies, checking for life. He smiled to himself lightly as he watched them move silently about in the bright moonlight. He then moved in, stepping over bodies, occasionally rolling one over.

"Checked the holes," a diver relayed, after checking below deck of the larger vessels. "No survivors."

"Good," the general whispered again into his voice-activated mike. The divers paused and turned each other, noticing the eerie satisfaction heard in the general's voice.

"We count three-thousand, two-eighty-five," a diver reported, "mostly men, some women, and children." After a brief paused, he added, "Sir, it is confirmed. There are no survivors. I repeat, no survivors."

"This is General Fellows," the general said authoritatively to his reconnaissance team. "Gather here, all of you, on the double." Instantly, splashes could be heard around the flotilla as the divers hit the water in response to the general's order. Swimming around was faster than stepping over the silent, lifeless bodies. The general stepped into a boat strapped near the edge of the connected fleet of small ships and stood waiting as the five divers took up positions around him.

"Pull your weapons," he ordered. Each of the divers reached for their Velcro-sealed pouches by their sides, and retrieved what looked like ray guns from a space movie. Looking oddly at the weapons and each other, they exchanged glances. Ironically, the carnage about them, with all of the dead men, women, and children, seemed a fitting backdrop for the ray-gun weapons held in their hands. "Hold your weapons," the general ordered. "When I give the signal, I want you to fire . . . at me. Hit me in the head. Do you understand? You must hit me in the head." General Fellows looked into the five faces that stared at him through the round face masks, each responding affirmatively as he caught their eye.

Taking a deep breath, Fellows reached up to his mask and loosened the stays. His mouth went dry and his hands cold, as a shot of adrenaline rushed into his veins. Taking a quick breath and holding it, the general ripped away his face mask. With eyes closed, he pulled back his rubber hood to fully expose his balding head. Gray hair sprang wildly about his noggin. The pale light of the moon cast weak shadows on his scalp. Opening his eyes, he looked about, then drew in a deep breath of air, which smelled faintly of almonds. Reaching down to his sealed pouch, he retrieved a pair of wraparound polarized eye goggles and slid them on. As he did so, the remaining divers all raised their toylike space guns and took aim at his head. Then, looking at the surrounding men, who all still wore their breathing gear, General Fellows drew in a distressed breath, held it, closed his eyes, and hesitantly nodded his head.

Instantly, five tiny yellow dots of laser light bounced off his shining bald head. Underneath the glasses, the general opened his eyes and looked to be sure he was being hit by lasers--and that he wasn't dead. He beamed a broad smile of satisfaction, then shouted, "Everybody! Back to the sub! Now!"

Shoving their ray guns back into their pouches, the five dove, simultaneously hitting the water, back to the sub, which sat twenty yards east of the floating graveyard. As the splashing ended, General Fellows turned and surveyed the sight once more.

"Westmoreland," he said aloud, "you ass!" Fellows cast his eyes proudly up toward the moon as he thought back to his last conversation with Curtis Westmoreland, his superior, just the day before. He was senior director of the CIA and also head of the secret Inner Circle.

"Fellows," Westmoreland had said as he followed the older Marine down the clean and vacant halls of the Crast Research Building next to the Pentagon, "don't you ever get tired of these cockamamy schemes you keep dreaming up?" As usual, Westmoreland had no time for the general's projects and attempts to change the Inner Circle.

"I never tire of this, until we get this country the hell back where it belongs. And you've got to listen. It's your job." Fellows resented the younger civilian, who'd never seen combat. He didn't need civilians directing him, filtering his efforts and ideas. If they had that kind of smarts, then they'd be in the service themselves.

"I'll listen," Westmoreland replied, "but that's about all I'll do. You've been in on the effort of the Inner Circle from the very start."

"From its inception," Fellows replied, "June 20, 1963. We were commissioned and given our marching orders. But that doesn't mean that we can ignore what we're doing, or any new idea that may come along, which might be less costly or more expedient." Fellows controlled his voice to a low, even pitch, though he wanted to scream at his hardheaded superior.

"And that's why I'm listening to you now," Westmoreland replied. "Look, General. We've got our eyes and ears open. You should know that more than anyone else." Westmoreland pleaded with Fellows as they continued down the corridor, "But, even with our continual looking and searching for a more effective means, we've found nothing better than the Fifty Year Plan."

"The Fifty Year Plan . . . The Fifty Year Plan . . . , " Fellows screeched. Mere mention of the adopted tack of the Inner Circle made his blood boil. "To hell with that antiquated approach made up by a bunch of pansy civilians." Fellows turned and stuck his nose into Westmoreland's face. "Look, Westmoreland. We need to do something now. I want to see the change in my lifetime. Not for me, you understand." Realizing his rage and posture, Fellows quickly pivoted and continued down the hall. Regaining control, he continued, "I've got children and grandchildren to consider, like you. We've got to make something happen . . . right . . . now."

"But we've considered all of the short-term options," Westmoreland responded. "None of them will work."

"None of them have been tried," Fellows retorted.

"Because we're smart enough to look at each scenario, and its consequences. None yield a stable society and all of them would make this country vulnerable to attack from most any other country in the world whose got bombers and a half descent army." Westmoreland spoke slowly and deliberately, like so many times before. Still, Fellows refused to accept his truth. "You're so concerned for your children," Westmoreland continued. "Would you have them growing up in a wasteland, scared to go outside their homes, neighborhoods, or abroad?"

"It's almost that way now," Fellows replied.

"Yes, but there is a difference now and you know it." Westmoreland took some reassurance in Fellow's response. His reply meant at least he was hearing what was being said, and thinking about it. Sensing a more receptive ear, he continued. "We're into the, what is it, thirty-second year of the plan? Hell. That's well over half way. And it's working."

"The hell it is," Fellows shot back.

"Don't compare it to what it's supposed to be in the end, but rather, where it should be right now. Think back. You were there when it was first presented, modified, and adopted. A lot of people invested their lives in coming up with the plan. Still more have given up their lives for it."

"And what has it brought us?" Fellows asked.

"Exactly what it should have," Westmoreland replied. "The psychologists, historians, theologians, philosophers, doctors, all of them agreed then, and still agree now, that the plan will work and is working."

Silence filled the long hall, but for the clicking of the two sets of shoes, as the two walked on, not talking. Fellows was thinking of Westmoreland's words, not accepting them, but searching for the best counter. Westmoreland followed, hoping that his arguments for patience on the old general's part finally were getting through his thick skull.

The general was old, but had acquired a wealth of influence in the CIA, Pentagon, and even the White House. He couldn't be eliminated, but he had to be controlled. A single step out of line could expose the Inner Circle and its plans, changing the face of the United States like nothing before. The general had to be tolerated . . . humored. And if all else failed, they'd kill him. If he stepped out of line, then his more rational contacts would be far easier to deal with.

"We're here," Fellows said, as he approached a security panel outside a large door, punched in his name, security clearance code, and finally, leaned in and placed his eye on a small sight-glass for retina identification. The glowing red light on the panel quickly changed to green, and a latch could be heard releasing from inside. Westmoreland did likewise after Fellows stepped away from the panel. As the green light again popped on, Fellows reached down and spun the doorknob, then pushed the door open.

Stepping through, he said to Westmoreland, "I think you're going to see something in here that may change your mind about the plan." Without a word, Westmoreland followed him through the door. Two large tables sat across the back wall of the near empty room. The top half of each wall on three sides was glass, behind which sat tiers of empty chairs for observers. Dull white paint covered the lower walls. Etched glass darkened the surface glass, eliminating reflections. On the table sat a metal box. General Fellows walked to the table, opened the box, and retrieved what looked to be a poorly designed toy gun with a large rectangular barrel, nonmatching plastic hand grip, and thick wires running from its bottom into the box.

"This is going to save our country?" Westmoreland quipped as he approached Fellows. As he turned, he looked back at the wall containing the door through which they had entered. The wall was covered by twenty-odd small cages, each housing animals, rats, guinea pigs, squirrels, raccoons, birds, snakes, dogs, and cats.

"With a little help," Fellows grinned. Reaching up, he pressed a button in the wall behind the box. A light mist fell from the ceiling.

"Almonds," Westmoreland said, sniffing the invisible mist.

"Some have described it that way," Fellows replied.

"What is it?"

"Just watch." Without another word, Fellows aimed the gun in his hand at a small, sad-eyed beagle in one of the lower cages, then squeezed the trigger. As Westmoreland watched, a yellow dot of light appeared on the dog's side, then it instantly fell and stopped breathing. There was no whimpering, heavy breathing, or obvious pain. Its large brown eyes just rolled back into its head and it stopped living. Fellows checked his watch, then took aim at a cat and hit it with the yellow dot of light. Like the dog, it, too, collapsed, as did animal after animal as Fellows randomly shot the weapon around the room. In each death, there was complete silence, complete calm, almost as if nothing had been alive there in the first place.

"My God, man!" Westmoreland shouted, "what the hell are you doing?" Fellows dropped his aim, then again checked his watch. "What is that thing?" Westmoreland asked, pointing at the gun in Fellows's hand.

"It's a bromine laser, not very powerful at all. Couldn't burn a hole in anything, except maybe your eye." Fellows pointed the gun at an exposed wall and fired, planting the tiny bead of yellow laser light on the wall. Nothing happened.

"Then, how's it killing these defenseless animals?"

"It's not the laser," Fellows responded, "it's the almonds."

"My God!" Westmoreland exclaimed, thinking of the deadly mist he had just inhaled, "you've poisoned me! What the hell are you doing?"

"Relax," Fellows said, checking his watch yet again. With a smile, he pulled the laser up and aimed it at Westmoreland, "You're not dead . . . yet." Westmoreland step back. "You civvies, you're all alike, afraid of death, afraid to see it, afraid to face it. You got no guts, no backbone, but you still get put in charge . . . in charge of saving this country, before it's overrun with foreigners and ethnics. Who the fuck made you God anyway?" Fellows's face reddened as he spoke.

"Take it easy, Fellows," Westmoreland threw his open palms up, then spoke easily to the irate general, "You . . . you never told me what killed those animals."

"The almond smell. That light mist is a compound that we've just discovered in this lab. It's highly unstable and harmless, unless it is excited at the right wavelength."

"The right wavelength yielded by a bromine laser," Westmoreland finished.

"Exactly," chimed the general. "Once on your skin or hair, or even clothing, the compound just sits, harmless, until activated. Once activated, it instantly mutates into the deadliest compound that I've ever witnessed, attacking the central nervous system. Put simply, it instantly shuts you down. The heart stops, eyes stop, lungs, liver. All muscle control is lost instantly. There is no reaction, no screaming, vomiting, convulsions . . . nothing. Life simply dissipates." Fellows raised the laser a bit higher as Westmoreland took a step toward the door, then froze and turned to face the general.

"What are you going to do?" Westmoreland demanded.

"Prove to you that this is the perfect weapon." Without another word, Fellows pulled the trigger, activating the laser and placing a well-aimed yellow dot of light on Westmoreland's lower right arm. Westmoreland gasped, but didn't fall. Fellows began to laugh, then turned the laser on himself, placing a dot squarely into the palm of his left hand. The general chuckled again. "Like I said, it's highly unstable. The compound falls apart in four minutes, once exposed to air, whether it has been activated or not. Once it falls apart, it is perfectly harmless." Pausing a minute to allow Westmoreland's wits to return, Fellows continued. "Like I said, it's the perfect weapon. Think of it. You could expose any number of people with a simple aerosol, then selectively choose who among the number would die. Lasers are small, so are easily concealed, if need be. In a few short minutes, a small number of laser-armed men could annihilate hundreds, selectively killing. Don't you see? We could pick and choose who we kill, from any distance, among any crowd, completely anonymous."

"You planning on killing the millions among us that must be eliminated, a few hundred at a time?" Westmoreland said, finally regaining his voice.

"No," Fellows replied. "We could spray a city block or an entire city from the air, then ignite bromine-laden flares. We could kill millions that way, and yet not kill the wrong people or make the land uninhabitable for the survivors. And since death is instantaneous, with no telltale wounds, any natural disaster or industrial mistake could easily be blamed for the deaths. It will work like a charm," Fellows smiled.

"Have you tried this flare thing? Do you know that it will work?"

"Now, I'm glad you asked me that." Fellows put the gun back into the box, walked over to the exit, then invited Westmoreland to leave. "I want to try the flares out on humans, but only you can authorize it." Surprise covered Westmoreland's face. Fellows was asking his permission to perform a mass killing--as an experiment.

"You sound as if you've already got a target in mind," Westmoreland replied calmly.

"Yes, sir. My men have worked out all of the logistics. There's a flotilla of Haitians just assembled off the coast of Cuba. They are slowly steaming around the island, and will head for Miami--if we don't stop them."

"How many people are we talking about?"

"We estimate 3,000 or so men, women, and children. Does that bother you?" Fellows searched Westmoreland's face for weakness. Westmoreland fought hard to hide the sickening feeling that suddenly gripped his gut. He turned away from Fellows and walked back into the corridor as he spoke.

"You want to go down there and kill them . . . all?"

"I'll need a submarine, a small tanker plane, and clearance for a special group of my men."

"Everyone will die. No questions?" Westmoreland asked again.

"Yes, sir," Fellows responded. "We will kill all of those bastards.

My men and I will then board the flotilla and do a quick inspection, since this is the first mass killing."

"First *mass* killing," Westmoreland said. "So you've killed with this before?" Fellows didn't reply. "There'll be no evidence, nothing traceable to you, me, the navy, Inner Circle . . . nothing?"

"Nothing, I assure you," Fellows replied. "The deaths will be blamed on bad seas and drowning, just like the last three Haitian disasters. No one will question it. And even if they did, no one's got the know-how or clout to investigate."

"The perfect weapon, huh," Westmoreland reflected as he and Fellows strolled back down the long corridor.

"This could be that alternative to the Fifty Year Plan," Fellows suggested.

"What do you call this weapon?"

Fellows smiled as they neared the building exit. "Do I get the sub and tanker plane?"

"You got it. Now what do you call it?" General Fellows pushed the door open. A big grin of satisfaction rested on his face.

"We call it, ID," he said, slipping through the heavy outer doors, "Instant Death."

* * *

"Instant Death," Fellows repeated as he took a breath of fresh sea air. All traces of the almond scent had fully dissipated. Nothing but salty-sea air languished about the floating morgue. The mission had been a complete success. ID, mutated with bromine flares instead of lasers, had worked just as effectively on a mass of people. Its potency had lasted five minutes or less. And its lethal effectiveness was absolute. General Fellows stood proudly among the stacked bodies.

Fully satisfied with the mission, he pulled his wet-suit hood back over his head and pulled on his radio-equipped face mask. But as he tightened the strap, a movement off to his left caught his eye. Frantically spinning around, General Fellows peered hard out into the darkness of the open horizon. In the distance, roughly a hundred yards off, a jet black object circled, not five feet above the water, appearing little more than a shadow.

"What the hell is that?" Fellows bellowed as he squinted.

"We've just picked it up on radar," James Exum, captain of the submarine, spoke to Fellows over the radio.

"It swooped in from directly above us out of our radar range. We didn't pick it up until it hit sea level."

"It looks like a jet," Fellows said, as he rotated in place to follow the circling shadow. "Fire in its ass, small, wide-winged."

"You'd better get back down here," Exum suggested to his superior. "Even if it's one of ours, we are not here, remember?" Exum wanted the general to return so they could disappear into the depths and remain unassociated with the disaster destined for tomorrow's headlines. He, along with Fellows, had watched through the periscope, safely from the depths below, as the high-flying tanker had swooped in and crop-dusted the flotilla of black people with ID. It then turned, then launched three large flares that simultaneously ignited. Instantly, the hapless victims fell, almost in unison, as if a puppeteer had gathered their strings into his fist and cut them with one powerful swing of his blade. They fell in soft piles of flesh, atop one another. Exum had watched many ships explode and occasionally had seen sailors burn to death. But never before had he witnessed such cold and unnecessary butchery in his life. Men, women, children, infants, all helpless, all lifeless, from the ID that mutated with the flares' lightning strike.

Taking the captain's advice, Fellows turned about and plopped into the water and swam back to the sub as fast as he could.

* * *

Zon was going to take Billy safely back to Virginia after the missile encounter. But, since the master mechanic was resting calmly behind him, he'd decided instead to continue exploring the new freedoms awaiting him in his new vehicle. Turning about, he had headed south. There was still the chance that he would be detected by radar or random sighting again, and if so, he didn't want any sighting near his or Billy's home.

"The Caribbean would be nice," Zon thought as he eased down on the accelerator, pulled the nose of the plane up, and shot skyward. His jet-car had performed perfectly. With the hydrogen-powered rocket engine, he had the speed of the fastest missile. The Kaldaca Stone converter nearly eliminated the body weight, yet provided a fast and easily obtainable fuel. Automated wings and light weight yielded fighter plane maneuverability. He'd challenged missiles, fighter jets, and radar--and won. And with the ability to convert to a car, he could easily land and conceal his vehicle just about anywhere.

"I'll need a tag though," he said to himself, "a personalized one, something smooth. Shadow. No, Onyx . . . no . . . " He daydreamed as he leveled the jet off at eight miles up and Mach 3, nearly 200 miles off the coast of southern Florida.

The moon was bright and crystal clear in the blue-black sky. Suddenly, a faint flash of lightning instantaneously blanketed the heavens with gold, pulling Zon out of his star gazing. But there wasn't a cloud in the sky. The sea far below appeared calm and nearly empty. Having time, he decided to find the source of the flash.

After several silent sweeps of harmless cruise ships, he spotted the flotilla off the coast of Cuba. Diving in quickly, he inverted the jet so he could inspect the entourage as he approached.

"Boat people," he said, still several miles up, but dropping fast. "No doubt Haitian. I'll dip my wing and give them something to talk about." With a smile, he blasted down like a bullet toward the center of the small fleet. But as he approached, a haunting sense of horror engulfed him. Straining his eyes, he scanned the boats. All of the people were lying down, piled on each other, except for a single being who stood peering up, with a glass over his face.

Pulling the jet parallel with the sea and with the wings nearly touching the water, Zon circled the boats in hopes of getting a better view. While holding the plane steady in the tight fly pattern, he focused his keen vision on the people. Nausea suddenly churned his gut. Each visible face was blank, eyes fixed wide and open, mouth gaping.

"They look dead," he said aloud. "All of them . . . look dead." None of the people moved. None of the faces changed. But the person who was standing, clumsily moved to the edge and jumped into the water.

"What's a scuba diver doing out here?" he asked. "This whole thing stinks." Without another thought, he flattened the plane out against the sea and set it down on the water. "Sure hope this thing floats," he said as he shut down the engines. The jet glided to a halt on the water. As it stopped, it sank slightly. Water rushed into the hot engine casing, causing steam to bellow up. The filled engine compartment pulled the rear just below the surface, pointing the nose slightly upward. But there, it stopped. Zon struck the dome latch and the glass canopy popped open. Striking his safety belt latch, he stood up in his seat, quickly pulled off his shirt and pants, then dove headlong into the water. The canopy eased back into place automatically as the jet floated farther out of the water.

Zon quickly darted to the side of a boat and boarded. Rushing up to the nearest body, he knelt. It was a young girl, barely twelve years old. Her limp hand still clutched a homemade rag doll. Zon drew in a deep breath and fought back the rush of emotion welling up inside. She had no bruises or cuts. Except for the blank stare of death, she seemed completely normal. Zon stepped over to an older man lying next to her. The same held true. There was no visible reason for the deaths. Moving to another boat, he found more of the same. He sniffed at several of the victims' skin and clothing, but his keen sense of smell could detect nothing out of the ordinary. Tearing a piece of cloth away from one of the body's shirt sleeves, Zon stuffed it securely into his pocket.

Turning about, he saw a sight that almost wrenched his heart out. There, in the bow of the small boat, a woman lay sprawled and facedown. Underneath her, wrapped tightly in her arms, was a tiny infant, it, too, just as dead as she was. The mother had instinctively tried to protect her child even as she died, but she couldn't. Death had ignored her strength as a mother, her power as a strong woman, willing to die for her own. In spite of her will, love, and sacrifice, death had cruelly taken her child, leaving her own blissful death as its only act of satanic mercy. Zon drew in a deep breath of air, seeking the freshness of the moist ocean breeze to help clear his thoughts. Zonbolo had allowed him, had made him join with the wretched victims, one by one, experiencing firsthand the emptiness of death, the sickening madness of physical awareness with no spirit. Entering again and again into each body, he saw the horror of existence with no soul, true silence, every beat, every rhythm frozen forever.

"It is future with no dream," Idrisi had said. The old man's words made sense now, but Zon had not fully understood then. "It is past

. . . with no memory. It is, but it is not. Death is more than just the absence of life. It is the passing of spirit . . . of faith . . . of your soul." Passion engulfed Idrisi whenever he spoke of life passing. "A liberated spirit is wondrous, rhythmically joining with the universe. Yet, it is only those that remain that know the stench of death. Life is the treasure of the living, its loss, the greatest of horrors. And so it must be. We must love life and mourn its passing. Only then shall we know the enjoined splendor of its liberation."

"Water is sweetest to the man dying of thirst," Zon interpreted.

"Something like that," his mentor had responded.

* * *

"What the hell's he doing?" Captain Exum said under his breath as he peered into the periscope. The submarine commander stood in the center of the narrow bridge with the shirt sleeves rolled above the elbows. His forearms rested on the folded-down arms of the periscope. His face was glued to the periscope's site glass visor. The submarine, which rested twenty feet underneath the ocean surface and twenty yards east of the floating mass of death.

"Who is that?" First Mate Jones asked.

"Can't tell," Exum responded hesitantly. "That jet disappeared behind the flotilla. A few seconds later, this shadow pops up out of the water like a friggin' jack-in-the-box." Exum paused, but continued to stare into the scope. "Moon's giving only enough light to make out a silhouette."

"What about the nightscope?" Jones asked, referring to the infrared heat sensor built into the periscope.

"Tried it," Exum replied, "but it's no damn better. He's the only thing in sight giving off any heat over there. Straight light is better, but all I can make out is his silhouette."

Just that instant, the small watertight portal at the far end of the bridge swung open. A soggy and completely out of breath General Fellows plodded onto the bridge. Ignoring the fifteen or so men peppered about who made up the bridge's personnel, he walked right up to Exum's back.

"Is he gone?" he asked. Captain Exum didn't break his stare through the periscope.

"No," he huffed, then chuckled.

"What the fuck's he doing then?" Fellows demanded. After a brief pause, Exum said with a smirk, "Looks like the son of a bitch is praying."

"What?" Fellows replied.

"The shadow's down on his friggin' knees . . . praying."

"Let me see that," Fellows said and pulled at Exum's right shoulder. Obediently, the captain yielded, allowing the general to the periscope. Shorter than Exum, Fellows tried to hold himself up on his toes to see through the spy glass. Exum realized the general's predicament and knew his ego would never allow him to ask for help to lower the scope. Quickly, he reached up, released the lock, glided it down to meet the general, then reset the lock. Fellows made no gesture of thanks or acknowledgment. Exum stepped back beside Jones. Fellows refocused the scope on the nearest boat, where the shadow last stood. As he watched, he saw the dark figure stand, face the sub, then freeze in place.

"Well?" Exum asked.

"Looks like . . . he's staring at me," Fellows responded.

"Staring?" Exum responded, shooting a quick and silently humorous glance at his men, who stood watching. "Can you see his eyes?"

"Hell no!" Fellows shot back, "but . . . he's just standing there . . . facing this way, like . . . maybe he could see the periscope."

"Not the hell in this light," Exum retorted, "nor at this distance."

"He's moving," Fellows said.

"Look," Jones suggested to Exum, "we've completed our mission. Let's get out of here."

"Not until we can identify that shadow out there," Fellows said as he cut his face away from the scope and rested his eyes expectantly on Exum's. "This guy's an unknown. He could cause us trouble."

"My orders were to bring you out here, stand by, then bring you back," Exum replied.

"Your orders," Fellows declared, easing up to Exum, "are to take your orders from me until you've returned me and my men to base." Exum stiffened at Fellows's assault on his authority.

"Yes, sir," he replied through gritted teeth. Hair stood up on his crew's neck as well. Each felt violated by Fellows's bold show of command.

Glaring around the room, Fellows said, "We will find out who's out there. Then, and only then, will we return to base." The bridge fell silent. Fellows turned his back on Exum and his crew, then locked his face again to the periscope.

"Maybe we should surface, so we can . . . " Fellows stopped in the middle of his sentence. "He's gone." Pivoting the scope about wildly, he searched the calm ocean surface. "No sign of him anywhere."

"Maybe he's left," Jones interjected.

"Look," Exum said to Fellows, "we should return to base now. We can't risk exposure and possible link to the event that has taken place up there." He nodded upward, toward the thousands of dead bodies above. "Maybe it's good that he's gone. He never saw us. He may not even know that we're here. There's no need in us alerting him now. Our job is done." Fellows dropped his gaze to the steel floor. Exum was making sense, but he'd never liked leaving loose ends.

Just as he raised his head to concur, sounds of slow twisting metal emanated from the topside portal above their heads.

"Something's trying to open that hatch!" Jones shouted. He stared up at the portal, which opened only when the ship was on the surface. He'd secured the hatch himself and couldn't believe that something or someone was challenging the latch. Wasting no time, he charged up the ladder to check the latch again. All fell silent on the bridge, each man staring up at Jones, who stood helplessly on the ladder, watching the two-inch thick inside-latch slowly contort out of its housing.

"Secure this area!" Exum yelled. "All nonessential personnel out. If that door opens, we'll fill in seconds." Five of the twelve crewmen on the bridge scurried through the rear portal. As the last stepped through, he closed the hatch then wheeled the waterproofing latch secure. As the bolt fell home, the groaning of the twisting metal above portal fell silent. The bridge crew held its breath, each member afraid to make the next sound. Finally, out of the silence, Fellows spoke, almost in a whisper.

"The portal held."

"No," Jones said. "Whatever was turning it just stopped."

"Let's get the hell out of here," Exum commanded. Jones slid down the ladder, but as he turned to relay the commander's orders, a deafening thunder clap bounced off the inner walls of the submarine.

"What was that?" First Mate Jones shouted as he and his fellow crewmen's ears rang. No sooner had his words come out of his mouth than a second deafening strike filled the enclosed vessel.

"Sounds like a wrecking ball crashing into our hull," Exum shouted. "What the hell is that out there?" A third crash rocked the ship.

"Whatever it is," Jones said, "those licks sound strong enough to punch right through our hull."

"Was he alone?" Fellows bellowed with his hands covering his ears. "Were there any other ships?"

"None as far as we could tell," Exum answered.

"Move!" Fellows yelled at Jones, pushing the young officer aside and peering again into the periscope.

"It's dark! I can't see a thing! What the fuck's goin' on? That bast . . . no . . . no I can see. There are the boats, but I don't see . . . " The general clasped his hands to his ears as yet another thunder clap echoed about the ship. A small aftershock vibrated the bridge floor. The lights flickered.

"Jones!" Captain Exum ordered, "take her to the bottom!"

"Sir," Jones responded, then shouted the orders to dive.

"Hell! The scope's dark again," Fellows said, turning to Exum, "That . . . that . . . whatever it is must be moving back and forth, delivering those blows to the side of this ship, then returning to the glass. But what in the Sam Hill's he using out there?"

"I don't know," Exum replied, "but we've got to stop whatever it is."

The submarine shuttered as Zon slammed the end of a cold steel rod into its side. He'd wrenched it from the portal door to use as a battering ram. He'd charged himself with enormous physical power, swelling his physical energy, strength, and resilience to superhuman proportions. The people inside the sub were the only ones who could possibly know what happened to the men, women, and innocent children on the flotilla above. And he couldn't open the sub without drowning everyone on board, until it surfaced. So he was going to make it surface. Sprinting to its side, he drove the rod hard into the ship's outer casing, then swam quickly back to peer into the periscope. The repeated punch would either force them to the top or the bottom, whichever they chose.

"Friendlies would surface," he reassured himself as he struck the vessel hard enough to deliver the message, but not enough to breach the hull. But as he approached to deliver his sixth telegram, a blast of air bubbles exited from both ends of the vessel. Assured of their decision to escape to the bottom, Zon sank his fingers into the rod and drove it into the ship's side, cracking the outer hull, and punching a small water-spitting hole into its middle.

Inside, he could hear the panic as the spewing sea water sprayed about.

"Sir!" Lieutenant Pierce announced, pressing the earpiece of the small headset to his head, "we're taking on water, starboard side in Bay Three!"

"Bad?" Exum asked.

"No, sir. Repairable, but . . . " Another loud clap rocked the ship. "There's now another hole in the same section, port side."

"Get repair crews on it, on the double!" Jones shouted. Zon put his ear to the submerging sub. Inside, several seamen ran about.

"Set it here!" a seaman shouted. Quickly, two others ran in with a three-legged stand. Placing it down, the first seaman ran to its first leg, placed its foot solidly onto a metal beam running underneath the floor, placed a rivet gun to it, then fired a rivet home, locking the foot to the floor. He then quickly repeated his action at the other two feet, then moved to the other stand. Once secured, the two remaining crewmen lifted a screw-and-crank set onto the stand and mounted a flat metal plate on top of it. Aiming the flat plate at the hole on the side of the sub, the crew cranked the plate toward the spewing hole, then against it. They continued to tighten it until the leak stopped.

"Breaches secure," Pierce relayed the status report to Captain Exum. But just as two members of the repair crew sat on the floor, smiling over their successful efforts, a third hole broke through above their heads. The sound of the armor-piercing blow nearly scaring them out of their wits. Jumping to the starboard side, they quickly recomposed, then ran off to retrieve another repair stand. Returning quickly, they placed and secured the stand just below the leak. The two crewmen stood watching the spewing, finger-sized leak, wondering in fear of the terrible menace outside their ship. But just as the third rivet rang home, securing the stand, Zon, with pointed and stiffened fingers, rammed his hand through the tiny hole, right up to his forearm. In utter shock, the four crewmen below watched as the monstrously muscular fingers, hand, and forearm, ripped through the upper port side of Bay Three, flexed its black fingers, then made a fist. The hole in the hull about the arm had swollen to nine inches in diameter, yet the arm prevented any water from coming through. Out of sheer panic, one of the crewmen started toward the hand with the rivet gun. Zon, sensing his movement, rolled his fist, then pointed his finger at him. The other crewmen quickly grabbed their shipmate, thwarting the attack.

"Let me go!" the crewman yelled madly with his eyes bulged and fixed on the massive black forearm. "We've got to kill that thing!"

"Fool!" a fellow crewman replied. "What do you want to do, force him back out of that hole? The column of water that'd rush in would kill all of us."

Balling his fist, Zon began twisting his arm and easing it back out of the hole.

"He's pulling out!" a crewman yelled.

"Yeah, but he's giving us time!" another shouted, grabbing the screw-and-crank set, frantically trying to mount it while keeping his eyes fixed on the receding arm. "Somebody help me, damn it!" The others rushed to the crewman's aid and mounted a large rubber-faced plate. Then they cranked it up against the fist as it withdrew. Water started gushing in as Zon's forearm cleared, leaving the smaller wrist and fist occupying the hole. The crewmen cranked as fast as they could. Hundreds of gallons of water gushed in. Finally, the rubber pad pressed up against the hole and stopped the leak. Zon shot to the water surface, now sixty feet up, took a fresh breath, then dove again to continue antagonizing the sub.

"A what?" Exum yelled at the repair crewman, reporting the

incident.

"A black man's forearm, sir," the nervous seaman repeated aloud to the bridge crew. "Cut right through the hull like a hot knife through butter. It flexed its fingers, shot us a black power sign with its fist, then pulled back out of the hole."

"Sir," shouted Ensign Pierce, "we're at a hundred feet. Water pressure's too great for us to go any deeper with those hull patches."

"Hold her here," Jones commanded the helmsman.

Fellows looked about the ship. At the radar screen, a black crewman sat staring at his own forearm, fist clinched, and with what Fellows saw as a prideful smile on his face. Grabbing Exum's left arm from behind, he pulled the captain to the deserted upper left corner of the bridge.

"Get the niggers off the bridge," he whispered.

"What?" Exum replied, insulted by the request.

"Get these niggers off the bridge. Look around man! Can't you see what's happening?" Exum's face reddened with fury. Not waiting on a reply, Fellows continued, "You know what we've just done up above . . . killed 4,000 of their kind. They're not supposed to know that. But how do you think that would sit with them, if they found out? And now, suddenly, some black monster is punching holes in this tin can, possibly out of revenge? Think about it. You know these people can't be trusted."

"You're talking about my men," Exum growled back. "You are questioning the loyalty of my men."

"No," Fellows said, "I'm reminding you of the loyalty of race, particularly of the seven niggers standing in this room." Exum looked about the bridge. Each of the five black men on his bridge's staff, one of which was Jones, his first mate, had proven their ability and loyalty to him and this crew time and time again. Even the two additional black men from the repair crew had given no cause to question their loyalty . . . until now.

Stepping away from Fellows, Exum said, "Jackson, Jones, Mendez, Abraham, Carouthers, Flute, Stanovich, and Charity: Report to sick bay at once." The eight men turned, looked at each other, then, without uttering a word, walked to the exit portal.

"Why'd you send Stanovich?" Fellows asked.

"Sending minorities alone might cause some future repercussion," Exum said. "Stanovich was a token." Turning to Pierce, he ordered five white sailors from the sleeping B crew, to replace the dismissed seamen. Just then, another thunderous boom shook the vessel. Ensign Pierce reported a small leak in Bay Two and that the repair team was on its way.

Captain Exum ran his fingers once through his closely cropped white hair, then jammed his hands deep into his hip pockets.

"We've got to stop this or we're all going to die." "Surface . . . and . . . and we can take him out," Fellows suggested.

"There's no time," Exum replied. "Besides, we can't expose the crew to the operation above. We've got to . . . "

"I've got a fix on . . . on something," Ensign Walls, working radar and reconnaissance, interrupted. Fellows and Exum rushed over to the display screen.

"Where?" Exum asked.

"There," Walls said, pointing to a faint dot registering a hundred yards west of the flotilla, on the glowing radar screen.

"It's that bastard's plane," Fellows said. "Hit it with a torpedo."

"We're not sure what it is," Exum said. "Could be a boat broken away from the flotilla, or a whale, or . . . "

"I don't care if it's your grandmother. Hit it!"

"It's resting fairly shallow, sir," Walls interjected, "The torpedo could just glide right under it, with no impact."

"It won't matter," Exum said. "If that belongs to whatever it is punching our sides in, at least it'll have something else to worry about." Staring hard at the ensign, Exum ordered, "Fire the torpedo." Without another word, Walls punched the guidance coordinates into his console and signaled the weapons officer to fire.

Zon swam again to the starboard side of the sub. He'd found no markings of the ship, though the American accents he'd heard inside at least identified the sub's origin. The ship had stopped diving at 100 feet, but it was of little consequence. He was determined to force the ship to surface and was going to do it by punching it full of small, nonlethal, but debilitating holes.

Approaching his next chosen spot, he drew back the rod. Suddenly, a muffled whoosh pulled his eyes away from the new hole site and toward a torpedo speeding away from the ship, then up toward the surface.

"Billy!" Zon shouted, allowing a massive bubble of air to bellow forth, from his mouth. Like a bullet, he leaped from the vessel and pursued the torpedo. Guided by its programming, the torpedo shot immediately to the surface, then took bearings on Zon's ship. Zon, watched it rise, but made straight for his jet, where Billy peacefully slept.

The submarine turned about, then engaged full throttle. Zon popped up to the surface not ten yards away from his jet. The torpedo sped directly at him. Taking another fresh breath, he dove again and swam directly for the torpedo. Meeting it forty yards from his craft, he maneuvered around and grabbed it by the guidance fins, fearing that any contact with its nose cone could detonate it. Taking no chances with a timer or remote detonation, he shot his fingers into the missile's propeller, crushing the blades, then the guidance control fins. Then, like a fat javelin, he drew the torpedo around and shot it back, at the retreating sub.

"There should have been an explosion," Fellows said, "What happened to the explosion?"

"It's stopped," Walls replied, pointing at the torpedo blip on the screen.

"Blow it," Exum ordered. But as he said it, the bleep on the screen began pulsing toward them. "Blow it!" Exum ordered. Walls hit the detonation button. "How deep are we?" Exum asked.

"Still a hundred feet, sir," Pierce replied.

"Fire two more torpedoes at the target," Fellows shouted.

"In case you hadn't noticed, the first one came back," Exum retorted.

"But it got the shadow off our backs. We've found his soft spot, so let's punch it." Exum stared at Fellows, but didn't order the firing.

"Look," Fellows continued, "for all we know, the shadow's on his way back to continue punching holes in us like some kind of dartboard. We fire those torpedoes, he'll have to deal with those, giving us more time to escape. And as far as I am concerned, I'd rather have those torpedoes turned and pursuing us rather than the shadow." Exum continued staring at Fellows.

"Fire the torpedoes'" Exum ordered. "Three of them." Holding his glare on Fellows, he said, "Mr. Pierce, if you can take us away from here any faster, I'd appreciate it."

Upon Pierce's orders, the propellers of the ship spun still faster, pushing the ship northward. Three torpedoes lit off from the rear of the sub.

Floating just below the surface, not ten yards from his jet, Zon stared down into the dark Caribbean depths. The blast from the torpedo had catapulted him out of the water, but he rode the rising watery wall of energy easily enough, then settled back into the water, eager to pursue the sub. His jet rocked rhythmically with the ensuing wakes. Billy snored inside, enjoying the sensation of being rocked lovingly in a baby's cradle. Satisfied that Billy was out of danger, Zon dove into the sea. But as he focused through the clear depths, he saw the sub speeding away as three torpedoes shot toward the surface.

Wasting no time, he bolted back to his jet, climbed aboard, then reentered the cockpit, sopping wet. His entry hadn't disturbed Billy. Reaching down with his right hand, he engaged the pneumatic system, then thrust the accelerator to the floor with his right foot. He listened as water hissed away from the Kaldaca Stone in the converter. The pedal activated the igniter and he braced himself for take-off, but nothing happened. He twisted his head to the left and spotted the large wake made by the three torpedoes barreling down on him. Staring at the parting water, he remembered how the engines had flooded when he landed. The water now prevented the igniter from firing.

"The igniters are wet," he thought. "Now, with the igniters wet, the engines won't fire . . . and the oxygen-hydrogen gas mixture will build up pressure at the converter outlet." Zon's thoughts raced, but his eyes remained fixed on the approaching wake. "The converter can build up 50,000 pounds of pressure, but over a very small area." The torpedoes were within thirty yards of the jet. "It should be able to force the water out of the engines, even push the jet." The torpedoes closed to within ten yards. Water started gurgling, then rushing out of the back of the engines. Cool, dry oxygen and hydrogen gases rushed by the igniter, forcing the water out, then slowly drying away the dampness. Zon's foot remained planted to the floor, summoning the igniters to engage, demanding the rushing gases to thrust them to safety. The torpedoes closed to within ten feet. Zon suddenly felt a dull rumbling as the torpedoes charged underneath his wing, then beyond, emerged from the other side of the jet, barreling forward, still in search of a target.

But as the long cylinders of death cleared the far wing, they exploded. At that instant, the right engine's igniter engaged, lighting the unstable gases within and about. Thousands of gallons of water leaped away from the exploding torpedoes, into the air. The small black jet rose with them. Expecting the explosive push, Zon maneuvered the wings and air foils to skim along with the blast. At a hundred feet vertical, he cut away from the geyser, throttled in both engines, then blasted skyward.

14
MEDIA OF THE MIND

Charlotte, North Carolina lay picturesque in the setting autumn sun. Its landscape had drastically changed over the last ten years. Whole city blocks were bought out from under families and communities that had lived there for generations. It, like most other towns, was divided by wealth, then race, with poor and whites to the north, poor and blacks to the west, and the wealthier citizens to the suburban south and east. But unlike other cities, Charlotte was growing. Downtown was flourishing, with major investments in performing arts centers, hotels, restaurants, clubs, and shopping malls, all connected by a complex series of fifty-foot high enclosed walkways. Combined with the upgraded inner and outer loop highway system, high-dollar suburbanites traveled in and out of uptown Charlotte to high-rise offices and expensive shows without being exposed to the common man. In just a few short minutes and with small risk, they could pass from the sanctity of the suburbs, over the squalor, and into the well-guarded safety of tons of concrete and steel.

Zon sat on a cement half-wall, which bordered the high grassy slope of Tryon Park. At the corner of Tryon and Seventh, across from the park, had stood the Saint James Orphanage, where he had grown up. He sat quietly on the wall, staring. In his mind, he could still see the broken sidewalk at his feet and the old redbrick church with its heavily weathered masonry and cement joints turning mold-green toward the ground. An old wooden shack, attached to the main house, was where he and other orphans used to sleep, eat, and do most everything else. The barn's wooden planks were bowed from weather and age. Sun-baked paint peeled badly from its sides. Chips of dull-green roofing tile collected about the periphery of the building along the ground.

In his mind, Zon and the orphans still played, running laughing, and climbing about the large oak trees that stood in front of the church. Twenty, sometimes, thirty boys, ran about the streets, the park, the orphanage, just growing . . . just living.

Inside, a large kitchen in the back had been occupied by three women cooking the day away. Two old men had moved deliberately around the grounds, mending broken holes in the front fence or replacing shattered glass in the church window, which had been on the receiving end of a baseball, or rock. They all were there, in his mind, the buildings, the people, the grounds, as if nothing had changed from his youth.

And as the dinner hour approached, white motorists abandoned the streets. Black ones, coming home from the south side servant jobs, from uptown cleaning or mechanic jobs, or from nearby textile mills, took their place. Those who drove rarely arrived alone, but picked up the rest who walked and thumbed a ride from the bus stops. Some worked together on road crews, fixing potholes, or laying pavement. Many weren't related, but all were family. Their community had covered ten blocks, stretching north and west from the center of the city. Back then, it was thriving, too, like the massive metropolis of today. It was a place where people took care of each other. In this community, there were no homeless. Though many of them owned no homes, all had a place to rest with family or friends. Adults, who had to work or leave home for the day, never worried about baby-sitters or thieves. In this tightly woven world, everyone knew everyone else. Many women were there to watch one child, or six, for whatever time necessary, with no concern of feeding, bad behavior, or payment. And everyone found a meal when they needed it. Crime belonged to the rare deviant who refused to fit in, and sooner or later, left. As if in a dream, Zon viewed this utopian world before him, with no crime, no homeless, no hungry, no abuse, all real in the daytime world of his youth.

But what stood before his eyes in the reality, so glaringly

different from his past, was a monolithic fifty-story skyscraper, covering the entire block that had housed the orphanage. Its outer walls stood cold, made of shimmering stark white stones, piled high and seamless, endless, into the sky. The sidewalks were pristine. Of all that had been, only the park remained. The homeless stood and wandered in front of the building, some begging passersby for cigarettes. Others tried unsuccessfully to enter the building and pick at the complementary evening hors d'oeuvres table, set up just within for the office occupants and guarded by a small army of well-groomed police officers. Joyous laughter of playing children haunted the shadows. Hurried businesspeople scampered by, clutching packages, their eyes glued to the sidewalk, dodging each other . . . not knowing each other . . . afraid of each other. One reality had been traded for another. "Mutual love for mutual funds," Zon whispered as he reminisced on the half-wall.

Unlike the scene, the sunshine baking his back was forever the same. Whether climbing the tallest tree in Charlotte or racing along the great Beinin waterfall, the sun was always the same. Zon closed his eyes and wandered through his youth, to Beinin, then to the dismal scene in the Caribbean the night before. It loomed in his thoughts.

"All events have a purpose and place," Zon remembered from another of Idrisi's valuable lessons. "Don't allow a time to invade and dictate another. Even in tragedy, hold dear to Zonbolo. Experience your emotion, whether pleasurable or painful, as you choose, and when you choose."

A smile eased onto Zon's face as he raced around his thoughts. Suddenly, he felt a light tap on his shoulder.

"Hey!" Nikki said. She and Xia jumped down from the park's higher ground behind the half-wall.

"What's up?" Zon replied.

"We were on our way to the club," Nikki said. "This is a short cut for us." She then motioned toward Xia, her longtime friend. "I told Xia that it was you sitting over here." Zon smiled at Nikki. Though he looked into her face as she spoke, he couldn't help but notice her shapeliness showing right through her brilliant pink jumpsuit. "Care to join us?" she asked.

"Sure," he replied. "That's where I was headed anyway."

"You get lost?"

"No," he replied, rising to his feet, "I just stopped to reminisce a bit." Nodding his head toward the office tower, he added. "I use to live there."

"You've got good taste," she skeptically remarked.

"It was a long time ago. The place has changed a bit since then."

Nikki eased to Zon's right side, Xia, his left, and the three started walking down Tryon Street toward the fitness center.

"So you guys come through here often?" he asked.

"Yeah," Nikki answered. "We both live in Fourth Ward. It's pretty easy for us to walk home from work, change, then walk over to the club. It's only twelve blocks or so."

Fourth Ward was one of three housing renovation projects promoted by the city to attract the richer class back into the city. Several hundred acres of old, small single family homes on the west side, within walking distance of the city square, had been purchased, bulldozed, then replaced by high-dollar houses and condominiums.

"You left the club in a hurry the other night," Xia murmured while watching her feet pound the pavement. She sunk her hands deep into the jacket pockets of her baggy, creamy-peach jogging outfit. The tangy color beautifully accented her upswept black hair and candy smooth skin. "Did you find what you were looking for?"

"I found far more than I expected," Zon replied mysteriously.

"Oh?" she replied, casting her gaze up into his eyes. "Tell us about it."

"I'd love to. But, I'd much rather talk about you two." Nikki, feeling ignored, slid her arm around Zon's.

"Yeah, well," she chimed, intent on breaking into the conversation, "let's start with me. I'm an account executive for Peebles Bank in the Shinn Building there, on the twenty-fourth floor." She pointed to the tallest building in Charlotte, marble black, in the center of the square. "I've been there for a couple of years. It's a great job, and I'm moving up fast." Nikki cocked her head to the side. In two years, she had single-handedly shattered the glass ceiling at Peebles Bank. Before that, several black men and women had made it into the managerial ranks, most in human relations, but none in a power-wielding position. But in that short time, Nikki had moved from entry-level accountant to directing a major business unit. Of course, she hadn't been in the company long enough to develop the contacts and financial savvy to direct the unit alone, but she would learn that in time. Besides, ample help was provided by a companion unit director to whom she directly reported.

All that was unimportant to Nikki at this moment. She was quite content strolling along, arm in arm, with Zon. He was tall, strong, attractive, and couldn't keep his eyes off her. She squeezed his arm lightly as she walked, listening to herself talking about herself, her career, her life. Zon and Xia listened patiently as the three strolled.

"Xia must have heard this story a hundred times over," Zon thought. Still, her eyes shone with interest, as if hearing them for the first time. The ladies around the table had called her "shy" and "inhibited," but he saw something far more complex and intriguing. Nikki took a breath in the midst of her long tale. Zon seized the opening.

"And you Xia?" he asked.

"There's really nothing to tell," she replied with a smile. "I have an office back there on Seventh Street that I share with an accountant."

"You own your own private practice, then."

"Yes."

"Do much business?"

"Hey!" Nikki interjected. "What am I, chopped liver?" Zon squeezed Nikki's arm, turned to her, and smiled.

"I'm sorry Nikki," he said. "You'd told me so much about you. I didn't want Xia to feel left out." Xia looked into Zon's face with an expression that said 'nice cover'. Surprised by her easy read of his intentions, Zon respectfully saluted her with his eyes.

"Psychiatry, huh?" he cracked. "Read people like a book, I suppose." After a quick grin, Zon turned back to Nikki. "So tell me," he began, "how's business in the corporate world?" Grabbing the opening by the throat, Nikki slung her head high, then started talking of her life again. But this time, she kept her eyes glued to Zon's to ensure his full attention. The three walked easily along as Nikki chattered.

Occasionally, Zon stole a glance at Xia and always caught her staring back. She intrigued him, and he liked that. He was attracted to her, though he wasn't sure why or what to make of it. He knew next to nothing about her. Yet, in her childish innocence, he saw a consuming confidence. She was a mystery, to say the least. The warmness that she sparked inside of him, unlike all of his Zonbolo-distracting episodes with lust and excitation, was calming. The fatherly love that he had developed for Idrisi had been that way, enhancing his oneness of being. So, too, were the friendships that he'd developed with Boo-Boo and Billy.

But Idrisi's warning ruled women out as friends. "Maybe I'm taking the warning a bit too far," he thought as he strolled along. "Maybe I can get close to someone, some woman, these women, as long as it enhanced my . . . "

"You belong to Beinin," Idrisi's words reverberated, "as does your virginity. It is the only way that Zonbolo will exist."

"If I can be this close to this woman," Zon thought as he stole a glance at Nikki's bountiful bouncing bosom, "and not question the sanity of my celibacy, I should be able to handle just about anything." Though he joked, he decided then that he wasn't going to run from these friendships. He wanted to be close to Nikki and Xia . . . as friends, with no further connection, no passion. The decision of his celibacy was his, and he'd made it. It was not an option and needed no further consideration. But the emotional well-being of his newly found friends was a concern. He wasn't going to hurt them nor use them.

* * *

Inside the club, the three headed to the tall stools about the bar. The bartender paced rapidly back and forth on the sunken floor behind the counter. A forty-inch television screen aired the news above his head. Although the club was steadily filling with the after-work crowd, only a few patrons paid it any attention. Several empty seats remained near the center of the bar, the patrons preferring the darkened and more secluded ends to carry on their private conversations. Two waitresses, one black, the other white, both tall and leggy, scampered hurriedly back and forth between the tables and bar, filling drink orders. Bronze-and-gold trimming adorned the bar, walls, and dividers about the room. The bartender approached them quickly as the three settled on the stools.

"Whatcha drinkin'?" he asked. Zon laid a twenty-dollar bill on the glossy hardwood surface.

"Mango juice. Make it a double," he said with a smile. Then turning, he said, "Ladies, please allow me."

"I'll take a slim shake," Nikki responded.

"Cantaloupe," Xia added.

"Cantaloupe?" Nikki reacted, squinting at Xia. "Girlfriend, you eat cantaloupe. You don't drink it."

"It's okay," interrupted the bartender. "We'll juice anything you like."

"You shouldn't knock it till you've tried it," Xia said.

"Okay," Nikki responded flippantly. Turning toward the bartender, she said, "Make that two cantaloupe juices . . . since the gentleman's paying." Then she leered at Zon. Zon looked into the TV screen. It was why he had come to the bar to begin with, catch the evening news. If he were lucky, there would be some account of the Haitian deaths, or of his run-in with the sub. Either would be helpful, since he had little else to go on.

He'd flown directly to Richmond after being launched skyward by the exploding torpedoes. Billy had been safely deposited on his front step around 5:00 A.M. Flying under the guise of night, he'd brought his plane to his 100-acre home, where he had landed it easily on a small pond. Once converted to a car, he'd driven it into a cave that he and Boo-Boo had discovered while hunting the land. With the car packed safely away, he'd seen to his furry friend, who faithfully stalked the acreage, thwarting trespassers and reporting all mishaps upon his return. He and the panther then spent the bulk of the day romping about the countryside, renewing their friendship, clearing their minds.

The bartender returned with four glasses. He placed the tall container, filled with yellowish-orange mango juice and capped by a small head of foam, in front of Zon. Two of the smaller glasses contained cantaloupe juice, a thin, brownish-orange liquid. He placed one of each before Xia and Nikki. Nikki also received the tall, creamy, strawberry-flavored, appetite-squelching shake.

". . . and with the slight improvement we've seen in the slowing decline in the unemployment rate, we are convinced that this recovery, unlike the last one, will be sustained, and will prove to be the beginning of a real economic boon for this country."

The TV picture flickered as it cut from President Gunther's speech excerpt and back to the reporter.

"The President made this statement just moments after emerging from a top-level meeting with his economic advisors. Critics of his new prosperity plan commented that it was more of the same old rhetoric, with no substance."

Steve Jones, a stone-faced newscaster, sat in a navy pinstriped suit. A stack of papers sat neatly before him on a desk. Though he held one sheet in his hand, he never looked down to read it as he presented the news.

"Many on Capitol Hill anxiously await more word on the economic study done by the president's staff, so often mentioned during his election campaign. Jerry Munday has more on this from Capitol Hill."

The scene changed again, from the cozy news presentation room to the steps of the Senate building. There stood Jerry Munday, his raincoat collar whipping in the breeze as he spoke into the handheld microphone. His face displayed the same coldness as Steve Jones's, but it was rounder and warmer, adding a sense of compassion to his report.

"Steve, many of the Democrats here in the Senate are raising quite a stir over the unkept campaign promises made by President Gunther, particularly the one concerning the redirecting of the economy and social growth of this country."

Jerry stood rigidly as he spoke and rocked his body forward on key words for emphasis. He continued with occasional flashes of speech excerpts from the more flamboyant senators.

"Many say the time for think tanks, studies, and promises are over. With much of the federal and state dollars going into prisons, roads, debt service,

and pet lobbying projects, a real change in the handling of this nation couldn't happen soon enough. This is Jerry Munday reporting from Capitol Hill."

The television screen returned to Steve Jones.

"Thank you, Jerry.

Tragedy has again gripped the poor, defenseless people, caught between governments, refusing to compromise in what seems to be an unwinnable conflict."

Zon focused on the television, eager for the forthcoming details.

"From our international affairs desk in Bosnia, Pierre Lindsey reports."

Again, Steve Jones spun about and joined his audience to watch the report from war-torn Bosnia.

"It's as if the Holocaust were again upon us,"

Pierre Lindsey's heavy English accent dripped with painful compassion. The camera flashed his crumpled face, then panned behind him to several trucks stuffed full of European-looking people.

"These poor Bosnian Serbs were forced from their homes late last night as the retaliating Muslim forces ransacked their neighborhood. Hundreds of innocent women and children were forced out into the cold, desperately fleeing for their lives."

Pierre sounded almost to tears. The camera moved in on the bouncing trucks as they crept to a stop.

"As you can see, scores of desperate mothers, with nothing but the clothing on their backs, stuffed their children and themselves onto the stern of these trucks."

Pierre paused. The camera zoomed in on face after pitiful face.

"Yet mercifully, in this desperate melee, only one casualty has resulted thus far."

The camera zoomed yet again on another of the overstuffed truck beds. A small, limp body of an infant was passed from deep within the hoard. Its pale face and lifeless blue eyes filled the screen.

"Oh, my God," Nikki gasped. "That poor child."

"The world's gone crazy," Zon said.

"It doesn't make any sense to me," Nikki responded. "Those people over there should be happy. I mean, they've just freed themselves of the Soviet Union. But, instead of celebrating, they're killing each other."

"They've got a new battle cry," Xia added calmly. "Communism is dead. Long live ethnic cleansing."

"Ethnic what?" Nikki repeated.

"Cleansing," Xia answered. "These countries have far less than what they need to become fully productive democracies." Zon and Nikki peered at Xia, who stared at the TV screen. "And they're blaming their shortfall on different groups within their own ranks."

"You mean different races?" Nikki offered.

"Race, religion, origin, it doesn't matter. Growing from a Socialist to a Democratic society requires a lot of time, pain, and money. The ruling parties are simply buying time by scapegoating a group. The majority blames the minority. Then they feel better for having done something. Of course, they're no better off, but they think they are. And that allows the needed time for the transition to run its course."

"Same thing's happening in Germany, France, and Great Britain," Zon added. "Non-European-looking people are being targeted by hate groups--and sometimes, the governments themselves."

"My," Nikki said sarcastically, "you two must watch a lot of television. I bet you don't miss a clip from CNN, do you?" They both turned and laughed.

"I'll admit it," Zon said. "Ever since Connie Chung became anchor, I haven't missed an episode of the evening news." The three laughed lightly, then turned toward the bar. Assured that Zon wasn't noticing, Nikki leaned over to Xia and whispered,"Who's Connie Chung?"

Steve Jones was wrapping up the Bosnian report by the time the three returned their attention to the set. Coverage had included several shots of the fighting ground troops. Several scenes from the respective government chambers were shown, as well as three interviews from the United Nations leaders, who continued to push efforts to stop the ethnic fighting without the use of force. Then the scene returned to Steve Jones.

> *"President Gunther has stated that the U.S. government is not anxious to become involved in an extended ground war, but will not stand idly by while innocent victims suffer. 'The cause is a democratic one.' he said, 'and a moral one.' We'll be back in a moment, after a word from our sponsors."*

The newscast's theme music began as Steve stacked his papers.

Zon placed his elbows on the bar, dropped his chin onto the heel of his palms, then gently rubbed his face. A shoe commercial flashed on the screen.

"Hey,"

a deep, slow, and heavily Italian voice blurted over loud sounds of rushing wind. Zon popped his eyes open. On the screen, a white boxer shuffled around a fighting ring. He threw punches into his opponent's face, whose head jerked and hair slung away enormous beads of sweat in slow motion with every punch. Every few seconds, the scene cut to a close-up of the Italian boxer's face, then back to the ring.

"when I rock,"

the boxer said as the scene switched quickly from the flying sweat beads to his face,

"don't need no music to make um wanna run. But when I run . . . "

Again, the scene changed to show the boxer standing on a long, deserted street. He wore a gray sweat suit with the trousers cut to knee length, knee-high white socks, and bright red running shoes. Heavy sounds of blowing wind still filled the background.

"the music . . . "

he said as the scene changed again, showing him running in slow motion down the street, taking long strides, his sweat suit wet and chest muscles bouncing violently,

"makes me . . . "

he growled as the heel of his running shoe approached the pavement. The camera zoomed in to show tiny holes around the heel. As it hit the ground, the sounds of wind stopped and loud rock music blurted from the shoe until the heel of the other shoe hit the ground, where it continued to play the song. The music continued as the shoes hit the pavement and the scene cut back to the sweating boxer-turned-runner's face, who ended his pitch with,

"wanna rock."

An announcer's voice added,

"Wanna run? Get the Rock, the new running shoes with miniature CD players built into the heel."

The commercial ended with the boxer running off into the distance as rock music and rushing wind faded. The shoe manufacture's emblem flashed across the screen.

Zon looked at Nikki. "They've got to be kidding," he said.

"Honey," Nikki retorted, "those shoes cost two-hundred-and thirty-five dollars . . . and are selling like condoms." She shook her head and laughed. "The kids wear those tiny thirty-dollar CDs around their necks. It's a crazy world." Nikki stared hard into Zon's eyes as she laughed. After returning the smile, he slid his eyes back to the television, which had run a ketchup commercial, and was just returning to the news broadcast. With a semiserious smirk, Steve Jones continued with the news.

"And on this side of the globe, another episode in the continuing calamity that has engulfed the small island-country of Haiti." The crow's-feet wrinkles about his eyes deepened. "Last night, amid stormy waters just off the coast of Cuba, nearly 4,000 Haitians drowned, their vagabond flotilla capsizing in heavy waters. The U.S. Coast Guard, which maintains a protective ring around the small country, was quickly called in by Haitian authorities to assist in rescue efforts, but have yet to find a single survivor. President Gunther, responding to the news, articulated his deep regret and heartfelt sorrow over the tragedy, and repeated his plea to the Haitians for patience. Despite his warning of treacherous seas, many of the inhabitants insist on attempting the dangerous journey in makeshift vessels to the United States. To date, the Coast Guard has returned over 30,000 Haitians to their native land. Over 10,000 have perished at sea. Several hundred remain

detained in Guantanamo Bay, Cuba. No negotiations have been announced that could lead to the end of the class struggle in that small island state. Now, on a lighter note . . . "

"That's it?" Zon huffed. He had expected a biased report, but not one so blatantly detached. "Four thousand people dead," he thought, "and the news gives it twenty seconds. Where's the camera shots of the dead women and children? Where's the heart-wrenching eulogy delivered by an emotionally overwhelmed news reporter, as with the Bosnian report? Drowning," he whispered aloud. "Those people didn't drown."

"They didn't?" Xia asked, catching Zon's faint whisper. "What makes you say that?"

"Say what?" Nikki asked, noticing how Xia had slid closer to Zon. "What are you guys talking about?"

"The Haitians," Xia said. "Zon thinks they didn't drown." Zon looked calmly into Xia's probing eyes, but didn't respond. She was bright, and extremely good at gathering information from unspoken words. She'd be an excellent sounding board to use in unraveling this mystery, but involving her could be dangerous.

"Oh," Nikki replied. "Well, let's face it. They're just too many, and too black, for this country to be concerned with, let alone, open its doors to." She spoke as though the 4,000 deaths were as easily dismissed as a broken fingernail. Sipping her cantaloupe juice nonchalantly, she added, "They'll just keep returning them to their island until they finally give up." Zon turned his gaze to Nikki. Her lack of compassion for the loss of Haitian life surprised him. Just a few minutes before, she had been close to tears as she witnessed the death of a single Bosnian child. Now, she responded as if the Haitians weren't real people, just . . . Haitians.

He knew that it wasn't coldness of heart that spawned her insensitivity, but filtering and manipulation of information. The Bosnian report was intricate and personal, aimed at emotionally connecting the American viewer with human suffering, while the Haitian report was constructed to do just the opposite. Haitians were never even referred to as people. They weren't women, or children, or fathers, or mothers. Not doctors, or fishermen, or clergy, or brothers . . . just Haitians. Nikki, like most Americans, made sound judgments from the information received. But the information was tainted, leading the average citizen to the wrong, but preferred conclusion. As long as she received palatable information, she never questioned the source. And in this Age of Information, such complacency made the pen, or more accurately, the keyboard, far mightier than the sword.

"The weather report showed no storms in the Caribbean," Zon said coolly. "Yet, Jones said that the flotilla overturned amid stormy seas."

"True," Xia responded, "but overloaded vessels still sink, you know, like that ferry that capsized in the Persian Gulf during the war."

"Mmmm," Nikki murmured, slurping the last of the sweet cantaloupe juice out of the glass. "This stuff is good."

"Fifty-mile trip from Haiti to Miami . . . 4,000 drowned," Zon commented.

"Odd," Xia replied.

"Islanders, born and bred in the water . . . drowning . . . no survivors?" He held the tall empty glass in his hand and stared into the colorful light reflecting off its surface. "And no footage from the scene . . . no eyewitnesses . . . no survivors."

"So they didn't drown?" Xia contended.

"I'm convinced of it," Zon replied.

"So what now?"

"I'm . . . not sure. But since I've got nothing pressing at the moment, I'll have plenty of time to think about it."

"So you've got time on your hands, huh?" Nikki asked and eased off her stool. He spun around to face her. She stroked his forearm with her index finger. "Want to go . . . work out for a while?" Zon smiled at her offer.

"Sure. It'll give me time to think." Nikki beamed a luscious smile and began pulling at his arm.

"Could you do me a favor?" Xia interrupted before Zon could slip off his seat. Freezing in place, he answered, "Sure. What is it?"

"Xia!" Nikki screamed softly. "What are you doing?"

"Oh, it's nothing," Xia exclaimed, trying to reassure her friend.

"I need a man tomorrow. My . . . "

"Xia!" Nikki exclaimed indignantly. "Be ashamed!"

"No!" Xia chuckled. "You don't understand."

"Oh, I think I do," Nikki retorted and stepped closer to Xia. "I know you find him as attractive as I do," she whispered, "but Zon and I . . . " She slid her hands into Zon's, then grabbed them gently while sensuously casting a smile at him. Cupping Nikki's hands within his own, Zon cut her off.

"I'll be happy to do the favor," he said, "if I can. What is it?"

"Tomorrow," Xia replied, ignoring Nikki's reddening face, "it's Saturday. I've been working with a group of students at Reidmont, the alternative school. That's where kids with disciplinary problems are sent now." Xia spoke hurriedly, trying to get her story told before Nikki's ego retook the floor. "We've arranged for an overnight camping trip tomorrow night, but got not one single man to volunteer to help us. There are two women, counting me, who'll be there, along with seven girls and fifteen boys. We could sure use your help."

"I'll be glad to," Zon responded quickly. Then with a big grin, he added, "But you'll owe me one."

"Excuse me?" Xia countered.

"Yeah, excuse her?" Nikki added.

"I believe in balance," Zon said, standing up and stepping around Nikki. "I do you a favor, then you've got to do one for me."

"Okay," Xia agreed calmly. "See you tomorrow then, in my office, say, 2:00 P.M.?"

"Sounds good to me." Zon began backing away from the two as he spoke. "See you tomorrow."

"Where are you going?" Nikki pleaded.

"I'm going to lift some weights," Zon said. "I've got a lot of . . . energy to release." Seeing the dismay on her face, he added, "But we'll talk later."

"Fine," Xia exclaimed, rising from her seat to stretch. Smiling, she looked at her blushing friend.

"Yeah," Nikki said saucily, looking into Xia's eyes, but addressing Zon, "you and me, we *will* talk later." With those final words, Zon turned and walked briskly off toward the weight room.

He wanted to think and there was no better way than to let his thoughts flow with the sweat of his brow. Xia's request allowed him to part company so he could think, and at the same time, avoid Nikki's advances.

"Xia!" exclaimed Nikki as she rolled her eyes. "I'm surprised at you. We're getting a little . . . forward, aren't we?" She then stared hard at Xia, trying to insinuate first dibs on the man to her naive friend. She knew Zon had said he was spoken for, but had noticed how he enjoyed their company, and how he had returned for more of their company. He wasn't wearing a ring and there was no mystery woman in sight or ever mentioned. Even if there were such a woman and such a commitment, it must be on shaky ground to have allowed such a fine, strong, and rich man to float so far--unprotected. And if it were on shaky ground, then she might as well be the person who helped the poor man see the truth and rid himself of the situation. And she might as well be the person who helped him put a much better arrangement together. And why shouldn't that new arrangement include the one who helped him see the light? Offering herself to him in his time of loss would be the very least she could do. Besides, if his commitment was all it was supposed to be, then it could easily withstand any challenge that she or any other woman could give it. So she had to give it her best shot--for his sake.

"I wasn't being forward," Xia replied.

"Come on. That little, 'I need a man tomorrow to help with the kids. So why don't you come spend the night with me out in the woods, in a tent,' routine didn't fool me, nor him, for a minute." Nikki whined as she mocked Xia. "Your message was pretty clear." She waited for a response, but didn't get one. "Why did you cut me off like that?" She plopped down onto the stool Zon had just abandoned, then sighed lightly, feeling the pleasantly warm cushion.

"Cut you off?" Xia said in surprise. "I didn't cut you off. I merely asked him to help me with a favor. I never meant to stop you or him from . . . from . . . whatever."

"Well you did stop us," Nikki said with a slight twinge of disgust. "We were about to . . . connect."

"Oh," Xia said, "but I thought that he was committed?"

"So he says," Nikki laughed. "I think that's a line he's using to keep us all around but at bay, so he can do the choosing, you know, work his way around to all of us one at a time." Nikki paused, thinking of what she had just said. "No," she corrected sheepishly, "I . . . I think I like him. And I just wanted a chance to get to know him better, you know?" Smiling gently, Nikki searched Xia's face for understanding.

"I see," Xia responded. "Well, that's between you and him. But I really needed the help with the kids, and Zon seemed more than willing." Xia's bright round eyes beamed innocently back at Nikki.

"So you're not . . . attracted to him?" Nikki asked. Xia dropped her gaze to her empty glass on the bar and smiled. "I mean," Nikki teased, "he's such a fine thang."

Staring into the glass, with a distant look in her eyes, Xia sighed, "Yes, he is. Men are as they are."

15
A FRIEND IN NEED

Zon spent the night in Tryon Park, sleeping underneath a bench alongside a wino. He'd worked out in the weight room, cycling through each apparatus for two hours, until 8:30. Realizing his commitment to Nikki, he eased back into the juice bar, where she patiently waited. Xia was gone. After a few brief words, he offered to walk her home. She politely accepted, though he later turned down her offer to come up to her place for a drink.

He had to purchase clothing and gear for the camping trip, and be ready by 2:00 P.M., so there was no need in going home.

Next morning, before daybreak, he found a twenty-four-hour teller machine on Trade Street near the library. Placing his hands gently on the control panel, he tapped his fingers wildly and listened to the electronic responses within. He'd opened several banking accounts in several banks and placed relatively large amounts of cash in each, making money available anonymously and whenever he needed it. But he didn't want or need the burden of carrying a bank card. It was identification, and he wanted none. Manipulating the machines through rhythmic massage was almost as easy as with the slot machines in Atlantic City. Within a few minutes, he walked away with his money and receipt.

From there, he meandered about the city until the shops opened. He then bought camping apparel and gear before returning to the Body O'Gold Fitness Center to shower and dress.

By noon, he was wandering about the city again, while contemplating the Haitian disaster. There was little to go on. "The men in the sub were American," he thought as he walked. "If so, then the sub was of navy stock, so the navy was involved. But the sub had no markings and refused to surface. Their anonymity must have been more important than their survival. And the sub was unmarked," he continued, "so it had to be on a secret mission, an intentional mission, to witness the Haitians' deaths. The lone scuba diver must have been inspecting the dead," he said aloud as he remembered the figure standing on the flotilla.

"So the navy came to observe, to witness something that could kill everything. There was no pain, no warning," he continued as he strolled down Fourth Street. "No time to react, to feel pain. Everybody fell in place . . . none in the water, no last desperate attempt at escape. And what of the mysterious yellow flash," he thought, "in the clear black, moonlit sky, that had attracted him in the first place? It had to have something to do with the massacre . . . maybe a warning signal or event marker. So," he sighed while sounding out his thoughts and pacing toward Trade Street, "we've got the navy conducting illegal war games on Haitians . . . testing a new weapon, possibly . . . that appears to kill instantly, not leaving a trace of evidence behind. Chemical warfare, no doubt. Those poor people probably never saw it coming. They were alive one second and dead the next." He shook his head slightly, thinking of the callousness necessary to have killed so many of God's creatures for such a hellish reason.

"And the sub," he thought, "badly damaged, in desperate and immediate need of repair." The feel of the cold ring of violated metal about his arm returned. His thoughts wandering back to the huge hole he'd punched in the cloaked vessel. "That'll return them to port for repairs right away," he thought, "and that's where I'm going to find them." A small grin flashed across his face. "And they'll be telling one outrageous story." His grin widened as he pictured the startled faces of the sub's crewmen witnessing the "black arm of death" that plunged from the deep right through the sacred steel walls of their ship. "Wherever they dock, they'll be telling that story, probably to anyone who'll listen. And that's how I'll find them. All I have to do is to identify the naval bases on the East Coast capable of making massive submarine repairs, then just hang around, listening for the wild tale." The thought hung before his eyes. "Listening for the wild tale . . . listening," he repeated aloud. Suddenly, a satisfying thought occurred.

Content with his deductions, he turned off Trade Street onto Tryon, walking north toward Seventh. His thoughts had delivered not only a means to find the sub, but also the favor he was going to request of Xia. Hanging about a naval base, listening, wouldn't be dangerous. And he'd met no one better at gleaning unvolunteered information from people. Besides, this could cut his search time in half. There was no telling how long a repair would take or whether the crew would simply dock, take a few days of R&R, then depart on another sub. Time could be critical. And a few well-thought-out clues on what to listen for were all Xia would need to know. She'd probably deduce a bit more on her own. Even so, she still wouldn't have enough information to become involved. All in all, she'd be helping him, as he was helping her. And neither would be the worst for it.

Zon felt good about his growing friendship with Xia and Nikki. The chance meeting and idle conversation he'd had with them the day before had been more than casual, more like friendly and warm. Nikki was coming on strong to him, and he knew it. But he felt that she could easily be discouraged. And Xia made no obvious demands of their friendship. She seemed content, happy at just getting to know him and posing no threat of romantic involvement.

*   *   *

Zon eased down Seventh Street, searching the shops and buildings for Xia's office. Nikki had reluctantly given him the address while he walked her home the night before. She also volunteered Xia's numerous shortcomings, such as her poor dressing habits, introverted ways, and obviously poor upbringing. She didn't appear too threatened by Xia, but wasn't taking any chances.

Zon stood on Tryon Street, looking east. From there, he saw a small curvaceous frame dressed in a tight khaki shirt, matching pants, and a white, wide-brimmed safari hat. A khaki-colored ribbon with pink flowers adorned it. She stood several blocks away on the sidewalk, using her reflection in a large plate-glass window to apply lipstick. It was five minutes till two. As he walked briskly toward her, he noticed a large green backpack propped against the building. A heavy leather coat was draped over it. The backpack had an aluminum support frame and a bulging canvas-wrapped bedroll strapped to its bottom. Judging from the bulging straps that held it closed, it was jammed full. A large gold and brown sales tag, hanging from the metal frame, flapped gently in the breeze.

"Hi, Nikki," Zon chimed as he stepped quietly to her side. Surprised, she spun around, then smiled broadly as his handsome frame filled her eyes.

"Zon," she exclaimed. "Ah, fancy meeting you here."

"I should be saying that to you. I didn't know that you were coming along."

"Well . . . I . . . felt kind of sorry for Xia last night. You know, out there with all those kids . . . needing all the help that she could get. So I decided to take a half a day of vacation and tag along."

"Oh," Zon responded innocently. "So, you much of an outdoorsman?" He peered at her new backpack and hiking boots.

"Why? Do you like campers . . . I . . . I mean camping?"

"I prefer the outdoors," he answered, taking the time to stare into the large plate-glass window. Arched across the top were the words "Johnson Building." Underneath, scribbled in much smaller type, was a list of businesses, one of which was "Day, PA, Ph.D."

"Let me guess," he said, "this is Xia . . . Day's office."

"This is it," Nikki replied. "Poor girl does okay for herself, considering. I mean, this place is not too shabby . . . considering the rent she pays for it." Nikki's eyebrows worked up and down, and her tone turned to a whisper as she spoke of her friend. "Personally, I think that she could do better, but she likes it here. Why, I'll never understand." Pausing briefly, she stole a quick glance into Zon's face, searching for hints of growing distaste for Xia.

"Where is she?" Zon asked.

"Inside. She said she'd wait there until you showed up. Her office is in the back of the building. I think she's waiting for a phone call, some guy wanting her to check in before she leaves." Knowing she'd scored big and gotten Zon's attention, Nikki pretended to fuss over her face in the reflection, as if disinterested in her own casual comments. But just as Nikki finished, Xia emerged through the heavy metal door. Nikki tightened her lip as she and Zon turned to greet her.

"Xia," Nikki began, "Zon and I . . . we were just talking about you."

"So I gathered," Xia replied. She looked knowingly at her friend. "Hello Zon," she said as she stepped onto the sidewalk, then behind Nikki. On her back, she carried a small and tattered backpack with a bedroll tied underneath. She wore a heavy, brown-and-blue plaid long-sleeved cotton shirt over a faded yellow T-shirt. The cotton shirt was knotted tightly in front, above her waist. Her hair was pulled away from her face. It was gathered into a knot in the back from which fell her woolen curly black hair.

"Girl," Nikki commented as she eyed Xia's attire, "what size shoehorn did you use to get into those jeans?"

"Huh?" Xia responded while looking at Nikki. Then, she bent her right knee to survey her pants. "They're stretch jeans. I like the way they feel, like they weren't even there." She spoke serenely to Nikki, then broke her eyes over to Zon. She felt his eyes run over her torso like a warm ocean breeze. Zon pulled his eyes over the curves that started at her calves and ended with the molding of her breasts. She was a vision of loveliness, though dressed as if she were going to herd buffalo. Always, Xia's baggy clothing had consumed her, hiding any hint of what lay underneath. But today she stood before them, comfortable, fit, and astounding. Her clothing at the club was obviously purposeful, no doubt to dismiss her existence. Her clothing, demeanor, conversation, all seemed aimed at yielding the ultimate persona of a shrink. She was the proverbial "fly on the wall," taking in everything going on about her without altering it with her own presence.

"Stunning," Zon thought aloud, referring to the completeness of her guise--as well as the physique standing before him.

"Thank you," Xia responded.

"What happened to that shy little shapeless girl that we'd all come to know so well?" he teased.

"Yeah." Nikki interjected. Zon was staring through her to admire Xia.

"We're going camping," Xia said, smiling. "This is how I go

camping." Turning, she stared off into the distance. "The bus should be waiting for us at Reidmont a few blocks away. The school's staff promised to have the children all packed and ready to go when we arrive."

"How old are these kids anyway?" Nikki asked. Xia stood before her, looking as healthy and natural as oat bran, and it had caught Zon's eye. Trying to recapture his attention, she reached down and picked up her backpack. As she wrenched it to her shoulder, the new weight tossed her forward. Reaching out, Zon grabbed the loose strap of the pack, steadied Nikki on the other end, then lifted the overstuffed sack onto his shoulder.

"You'd better let me carry that," he said.

"Why, thank you, Zon," she smiled, then reached over and slid her fingers into his free hand.

"We'd better get going," Xia said, starting a brisk walk down the sidewalk. "These kids are fifteen- and sixteen-year-olds. They've all been in trouble at school, for one reason or another."

"What kind of reasons?" Zon asked.

"Skipping class, fighting, egging an administrator, that kind of thing," Xia answered. She faced forward, away from the two. "They're all smart, though. If you don't believe it, watch their ingenious ways of getting into trouble. Stupidity waits for something to happen. These kids don't wait for anything. It's unfortunate that trouble is so easy to get into."

"Sounds like they just need a good strong hand," Zon said.

"Exactly," Xia concurred. "They need rules and hard, consistent consequences if those rules are not followed."

"This is going to be a baby-sitting expedition, isn't it?" Nikki interjected as she sauntered along with Zon.

"In a sense," Xia responded, "that's exactly what it is. But I'd say it was more. We'll only be there overnight. So like good parents, I'd suggest that we make our rules known quickly, then stick by them until we return."

"Sounds like a plan," Zon chimed.

* * *

"Come on, Miss Day!" Donte begged the counselor. "We goan' play chicken! You be my potner!" He, the largest and strongest of the teenagers, stood before Xia, Zon, and Nikki. With hand outstretched, he eagerly coaxed Xia to oblige him. They'd driven through Charlotte's far southwest end to the local Boy Scout camp. Then, they had hiked for over a mile into the forest before reaching their campsite. Fifteen boys and seven girls had joined them, along with one vice principal, Mrs. Stevens, from Reidmont.

Upon reaching the bus, Xia took immediate charge, directing, placing, and controlling the group. The bus ride was thirty minutes, the hike thirty, and the seven tents were pitched in thirty minutes as well. After careful instructions to the young ladies, then the gentlemen, Xia allowed them to wander about the woods while she, Zon, Nikki, and Mrs. Stevens collected wood for the campfire.

Sunset approached. The air was chilly, a frosty thirty-nine degrees, but all of them had bundled up adequately, and the glowing fire eased the chill. The four adults sat about the fire, talking as the approaching darkness forced the teens back in from the forest. Zon crouched next to the fire. He felt uncomfortable with the heavy long-sleeved shirt, pants, and boots and wanted to shed them. Discretion prevailed. Orange, red, and yellow flames danced skyward from the roaring fire. Orange shards of burning embers exploded from the inferno as Zon tossed on yet another split log. Each of the ladies sat serenely about, their faces irradiated by the colorful light.

"It's hypnotizing, isn't it?" Mrs. Stevens commented as she stared into the fire.

"Yes it is," Xia said. Nikki, sitting between Xia and Mrs. Stevens, leaned over to Xia as the first of the students returned.

"Girl, how could you just let those walking hormones trip off into the forest like that? Look at the smile on some of their faces. I know the nasty's been going on out there."

"No, it hasn't," Xia replied, no concern showing in her voice. "I paired them off before they left and told them to stick to those pairs. And if something happened to one of them, it had better happen to both." Casting a confident gaze at Nikki, she added, "They've all tried me once. They'll never try me again."

"What did you do?" Nikki asked. Before she could answer, Donte had run up to Xia with his request.

"I'll play," Xia replied, popping off the oak log she'd been sitting on, "but I'll pick my own partner, if you don't mind." Donte shuffled back into the small pack of boys that had gathered to watch him ask, but now taunted him for being rebuffed. He had bragged to them of how he was going to get a good feel of her thick thighs and round hips while they were wrapped about his shoulders. Eager to be chosen, the boys quickly rushed up to Xia.

"Me! Me!" they yelled. She looked the motley crew over. Pivoting, she turned to Zon.

"Wanna play?" Caught off guard, Zon looked up, smiled, then with a large grin, answered, "Why not."

"Oh! Oh! So it's gonna be like dat, huh." Donte said. He raised his large hand and shoved it palm first in Zon's direction, the gesture showing his dismissal of the older, slightly smaller man. "Okay, okay," Donte continued, "we gonna hook ya up." Looking about, he said, "Who gon' ride? Who gon' ride?" Dashing forward, KeSandra ran giggling to Donte, who grabbed her as she approached and hoisted her easily over his head and onto his shoulders, where she locked her legs behind his back. Madly, all of the puberty-stricken boys rushed the girls in search of a partner. Quickly, four other teams emerged. Not waiting for an invitation, Zon grabbed Xia by the forearm, then lifted her skyward. She seemed light as a feather as she ascended and threw her legs wide in midair. With toes pointed and knees locked, she gracefully wrapped herself around Zon's muscular shoulders.

"Oh, my God," Nikki belched, "ballet for the baboons."

Laughing off her quip, Xia leaned down to Zon and whispered, "We'll take it easy on them. Might even let them win."

"They're a lot bigger and younger than we are," he answered aloud.

"And we gonna kick yo' as . . . butt," Donte shouted, struggling not to cuss in front of Xia as he and KeSandra clowned with the others.

"Last one standing wins," Xia said like an excited schoolgirl. A broad grin engulfed her face. Zon smiled, too, not so much in anticipation of the game, but from the warm fleshy feel of Xia wrapped around his head and shoulders. It just felt good.

Donte and KeSandra rushed their first victims. Screaming at the top of her lungs, KeSandra grabbed the smaller girl by the arm of her coat. Seizing the opportunity, Donte stepped to the side of his opponent and leaned away as hard as he could. The outmaneuvered and overpowered team of two tumbled to the soft, leaf-covered forest carpet, laughing as they hit and spun about in the leaves.

Another team reached for Xia, both the rider and carrier. Xia deflected the rider's hands, but the carrier caught her by the leg, then started pulling, while his rider struggled to grab her arm. Zon braced himself, but stood still. Xia howled with laughter, then shoved the rider backward, almost pushing the two over. With even greater laughter, she leaned toward the two. "Let's get 'em!" she yelled, urging Zon to run toward the couple. Zon faced up to the carrier, who turned to run. Xia grabbed the back of the rider's coat, then heaved backward, causing her carrier to run right out from under her. Zon laughed aloud as the girl went howling to the ground. Her carrier stumbled forward, but managed to catch himself before falling. Suddenly, Xia looked about and yelped after spotting the approach of two other teams from behind. Grabbing Zon by the ears, she wrenched his head about.

"Ow!" Zon yelled through a wide grin, "those are ears, not a steering wheel." Xia didn't hear him, but motioned him forward with her legs while staring madly at her oncoming opponents. Responding like a well-trained thoroughbred, Zon charged them.

"Lord!" Mrs. Stevens exclaimed, watching the foolery, "they're bigger kids than the kids are."

"Well, they can have it," Nikki commented. She wore a look of disgust on her face. "You won't ever catch me pouncing around in the woods like that. Look at 'em. They've got to be out of their minds."

Ten minutes later, Zon and Xia stood surrounded by the other five teams. All had remounted. Zon spun madly in a circle. Xia, having unlatched her legs, held them straight out, creating an unpenetrable wall of spinning hiking boots before their assailants. She laughed wildly while Zon yelled as he spun. The two adults-turned-teens had unseated all of them in a few short minutes. The frustrated youths had united in an effort to take their chaperons down, but they could only stand helplessly and watch the two spin.

"'At's awight," Donte said while standing patiently with KeSandra on his shoulders. "When ya stop, it's gonna be easy to knock ya drunk butts ova'."

"He's right!" Xia yelled.

"I know!" Zon screamed back, still spinning madly. Then, in the midst of the spinning, as if a choreographer had arranged the move, Xia eased herself off Zon's shoulders and into his arms. Sensing her descent, Zon wrapped her in his arms and spun downward, like a tornado winding its way into the ground. The five teams followed, collapsing on top of them into one big chuckling and screaming heap.

Buried beneath the mound of jovial flesh, Zon and Xia suddenly found themselves wrapped in one another's arms. Zon pressed his elbows hard into the ground, holding the crushing weight of the pile off her. Still, her body felt glued to his. She chuckled loudly in his ears as she squeezed his neck, her warm body baking his. They lay there laughing, consumed in the carefree and completely juvenile pleasure, waiting for the others to dismount. As the laughter slowly subsided and gave way to broad smiles, the pile of bodies dismantled, one by one and two by two, rolling across the leafy floor.

Feeling the last body lift from his back, Zon hoisted himself up, dragging Xia along. Her arms remained locked about his neck. For a split second, in the midst of the retreating youths who busily brushed themselves free of leaves, filling the evening air with chaos, and the refreshing smell of a wintering forest, their eyes met, their bodies still embraced. And in that eternity of a second, Zon felt something he'd never felt before. The warmth of her smile as she gazed upward, the closeness of her face and soft round eyes, the touch of her body, the lusciously soft cushioning of her breasts, the small cup of her waist that rested so gently in his embrace, all combined to ignite a flame deep within his gut that choked off his breath--and he didn't want to let go. So often, he had dreamed of a scene such as this, but not once had he imagined that the resulting sensation would emanate from above his waist. Feeling her loosened grasp, he unwillingly released his and she slipped out of his arms. But as she left, he felt her hands linger on his chest as they trailed away from around his neck. Her expression was intense. Her eyes never left his. Both then turned, Xia, toward the campfire, and Zon in the opposing direction, toward the setting sun.

Each walked away. Camouflaging smiles hid their newly discovered emotions. Xia rejoined the ladies and teens by the campfire.

Zon walked to a tall maple at the edge of the campsite and watched darkness creep stealthily into the forest. Delving deeply into himself, he searched his thoughts for an answer to a question he didn't know how to ask. The lump that had filled his throat had subsided, but the longing to hold Xia again in his arms grew stronger. Beams of his own thoughts, of his emotions, were scattered within and he suddenly saw no reason to collect them. But, unlike before, their golden glow possessed a red hue.

"It's happened," he thought. A twinge of sadness pinched at his gut.

16
NOT TO REASON WHY

Jake Jones, a navy E-7, and Fred Washington, an E-3, stepped heavily into the Regions Cafe, then over to a small booth in front of the pool table.

"Man," Jake started, "this working for a livin' will kill ya." The husky black man waved to the waitress for service, then plopped his muscular arm onto the table.

"Come on, Jake," Fred replied."You know it doesn't get any betta' than this."

"You sound like a commercial, Freddie."

"Truth's the light."

A waitress strolled up to their booth, lay a small blue napkin before each of them, then awaited their orders. She neither smiled nor seemed pleased at having their business. It was one o'clock in the morning, and she had another three hours to work before her shift ended. A few other late night patrons sat about the bar.

This was an odd hour for drinkers, Sunday night and two hours until military shift change. A crazy-eyed drill sergeant played pool alone in the corner with a lit filterless cigarette in his mouth. His half-filled, warm, flat beer sat on the table's corner. He shoved the pool cue mercilessly at the white ball, smashing it into the others. Small claps of thunder bounced off the walls as the balls collided within the confines of the billiard cushions. Two other navy men sat at a distant table, shuffling cards as they talked. Three women rounded out the patronage, each sitting alone, scattered about the room.

"Gin, straight up," Jake uttered, not looking up.

"Forty-Five, forty-ounce," Freddie added with a grin. The waitress didn't respond, but turned and walked toward the bar.

"You not plannin' on working tomorrow?" Jake asked.

"Nope," Freddie said, casting an eye about the room. "Just pulled two straight, and they ain't payin' overtime. So it's comp time for me."

"I pulled the double shift, too," Jake replied.

"But you old," Freddie said with a laugh. "Man's got to play hard if he plans to work hard." Freddie felt himself mellowing a bit. His words now reflected his normally jovial demeanor. The waitress set the glass of gin in front of Jake, then the forty-ounce bottle of Colt Forty-Five Malt Liquor before Freddie, with no glass, then turned and walked away. Jake raised the glass to his lips and eased down an ounce of the burning spirits. Freddie grabbed the tall clear bottle and turned it up to his lips. The bottle gurgled as air escaped into it, replacing the cold liquid that rushed down the young navy man's throat. Both sighed loudly from the refreshment.

"You know," Freddie said after half emptying the bottle, "I ain't never seen anything like that before in my life."

"Me either," Jake replied.

"What do you suppose did that?"

"Hell if I know. I've seen a lot of ships take a lot of damage, but none like that."

"Think they ran into a reef or somethin'?"

"Naw. I've seen reef damage. It tears a streak down the side of a sub. Leaves grit marks, too."

"Yeah, and we know it wasn't a joint," Freddie said, referring to a torpedo strike. "Wut'n no explosion."

"Beats the hell outta me," Jake repeated, then sipped at the glass. "I've always hated these cloak and dagger jobs. Give ya no information, won't letcha talk to nobody. Hell, they won't even letcha see who was on the ship. They just give you a piece of wreckage and expect ya to figure it all out." Jake paused for another sip. "Them holes gonna take us at least two weeks to repair."

"They ain't gonna wait that long," Freddie said before sucking down the last of the forty-ounce. "Word is they gonna ship that crew outta here Tuesday."

"Why?" Jake asked.

"Ya got me. All I hear is that Pope's had 'em locked up in da Nes' since they got here. And ain't nobody allowed to talk to 'em." The "Nest" referred to the mental wing of the base's infirmary, nicknamed after the movie.

"Pope? With I.A.C.?" Jake responded, alluding to General Pope, head of the Internal Affairs Commission.

"Yeah," Freddie confirmed. "Boys done fucked up." The commission had been completely absorbed over the last several months, trying desperately to handle the rash of suits and countersuits recently brought by gays and women over discrimination and sexual harassment in the military.

"What's that psycho got to do with them?" Jake wondered aloud.

"Who knows," Freddie responded offhandedly. "Maybe ya boys on that boat got into some heavy rump thumpin' out there under da sea." Jake threw a disgusted stare at his chuckling friend, not finding his gay joke amusing. With a tired and serious face, he turned his glass up and poured it dry.

"Ya think that's what this is all about?" Freddie asked. Jake slid toward the edge of the seat, in preparation to leave.

"Nope," he answered starkly. "Didn't no gay bashing or women's lib cause those holes--especially that big one."

"Well, what about the fist?" Freddie spouted. He hoped that the slow feeding of gossip that he'd heard would prevent his friend from leaving.

"Fist? What fist?" Jake asked, settling back to the bench.

"The black fist."

"Where did you get that shit?"

"Hey, it's what I heard. Tell me that somebody shot the black power sign, then the captain slammed all the brothers on the bridge in the brig." Freddie shot a high fist into the air, as if saluting Jake with it, then burst into laughter. With a huff, Jake rose to his feet.

"I'm going home." He tossed three dollars on the table. "I suggest you do the same."

"Ahhhh, don't go," Freddie pleaded. Ignoring him, Jake turned and walked out of the door. After watching his longtime friend leave,

Freddie motioned to the waitress for another bottle.

*   *   *

The old yellow cab jolted madly over the potholes of Tenth Street in Newport News, Virginia. Xia sat quietly in the back, directly behind the Hispanic driver. She stared intensely out of the streaky car window. The driver had been all too eager as he stuffed her suitcase into the trunk. After rushing around and opening the right rear door, he bowed across the opening, carefully placing his forearm to "innocently" brush against her hips as she got in. Noting his maneuver, Xia eased around him as she entered, then slid to the far left. She'd dressed provocatively that morning in a red short skirt outfit that showed off her taut, leggy frame. Her long black hair fell sensuously off her shoulders. If she were going to find out anything, it had to be today. There would probably be no second chance. And she'd learned well during her short tenure as a psychologist that sexually distracted men were much easier to influence.

She'd arrived in Newport News the night before, having left Charlotte by Amtrak as soon as she'd returned from the camping trip. Zon had approached her while the two hunted for firewood. He'd asked her to travel to the small Virginia military town and snoop for information. The request was strange, yet exciting, a far cry from life's situations that she normally dealt with in her own practice. And his urgency made her leave for Newport News right away.

"Damaged submarine," she whispered softly. Her stare was locked beyond the cab's dirty window, but her thoughts were lost in her imagination, trying to put together the picture that Zon had so scantily painted for her. "Odd damage . . . sea monsters . . . the hand of death . . . " Xia worked his comments over and over, pulling all that she could from them. Zon had intentionally drawn a skimpy picture of the situation, seeking to employ her help without getting her involved. But she wanted to be involved. She felt born for such pursuits, deriving immeasurable joy from the unraveling of a mystery, from facing the unknown and conquering it. With or without Zon's approval, she was going to get involved. Suddenly, a smile erupted across her face. Her assertion had ignited thoughts of Zon. After the chicken fight, the two had avoided each other. Neither seemed willing to confront what had happened, both afraid of what had happened.

Xia's mind drifted about, seeking to make sense of it all. The two navy men's comments from the night before seemed to add more to the confusion. She'd sat unnoticed in a dark corner of the bar as the two conversed. Finding the bar had been relatively easy for her since it was the only drinking establishment open after midnight, near the base. And she didn't want to waste time waiting for offices and other establishments to open the next morning. Sitting quietly in the corner, she read the second of three novels purchased before boarding the train and kept a keen ear open for anything. She'd sat there for over two hours before the two skilled mechanics walked in and unknowingly gave her a taste of the information she sought.

"Unmarked submarine," she pondered. "Strange holes in its hull . . . secluded crew . . . internal affairs investigation . . . black power signs . . . black crew men in the brig." She rearranged the bits of data over and over, but still could make little sense of it. "The mental ward seems plausible," she thought, "completely isolated, interrogation rooms, remote surveillance, drugs." Out of the night's efforts, she had received three important pieces of information. First, the crew was shipping out on Tuesday, which left only a day to get at them directly. And she knew where they were being held and by whom.

"And they're shipping out tomorrow," she said aloud.

"Uh?" the taxi driver responded, "Whacha say?"

"Nothing," Xia answered coldly. After craning his neck frantically to see her, the driver finally reached up and readjusted his mirror. Xia paid him no attention, but continued to stare through the dirty, rain-streaked glass.

Newport News was small, compared with Charlotte. The few people she'd observed were all from a few backgrounds, the military being the largest, followed by the tourist service crowd that catered to the Virginia Beach visitors, and then college students. The city was old and washed, reflecting the hazards of living on the coast.

Two- and three-story buildings passed before her as the taxi whizzed away from her hotel, out of Newport News and toward the naval base. She'd called for the cab at 6:00 A.M. to avoid the traffic and to give herself plenty of time to feel out the military infirmary.

Xia wasn't sure of what she was going to do there, but if General Pope's name could be used in any fashion to help her, she was going to use it. The two crewmen had given no other names, and probably didn't know any. The mission, crew, equipment, and outcome were all being kept secret and closely guarded, making her task even more complicated. But she needed names, something to tie people to the sub. That's what Zon had asked for. He wanted to know the people involved.

The cab eased up to the guardhouse at Camp Fault, where the driver obtained a pass and directions to the infirmary, then drove on. Stopping in front of the brown brick, three-story building, the cabbie jumped from his car, opened Xia's door, then scooted around to unload her luggage. Xia slipped the fare and tip into his large hand as he placed the heavy suitcase before her, on the sidewalk. With a smile and a tip of his hat, he jumped back into his car and drove away. Xia looked about the complex. Though it was still early, the streets and sidewalks were full of uniformed men and women, marching, exercising, cruising. Most male heads turned for the double take, and a few catcalls, as they passed. She'd never been on a military base. The feeling was surreal, almost as if it didn't exist. Cars sounded the same, as did the morning birds chirping along looking for breakfast. But the uniforms and sameness of the people, all rising together, doing different jobs but for the same purpose, delivered an atmosphere more like that of a youth camping trip rather than a place of adult business.

Xia easily lifted her suitcase, turned, and walked into the infirmary. As she entered, she noted the plaques and certificates that lined the walls of the entrance lobby. The receptionist's desk was empty. She placed her suitcase behind it, then walked around the lobby, reading all of the wall mountings. Having thoroughly inspected them, she eased over to a coffee table stacked with magazines. Pulling an issue of *Ebony* from the stack, she eased through a set of swinging doors and into a long hall of offices and inspection rooms. Pausing at each office, she noted the names on each, and all other readings that she could make out from the hall. Just beyond the third office stood a trophy case filled with golden trophies, pictures, and more certificates. While reading the inscriptions and trying to place faces with names, Xia heard voices coming from beyond the swinging doors. Quickly taking a seat by the trophy case, she opened the *Ebony* and began leafing through the pages.

" . . . with all of them. We'll reassign the three on the repair crew, but Jon . . . " Two white, middle-aged, high-ranking officers suddenly plowed their way through the swinging doors. The larger of the two caught his words in his teeth as he caught sight of Xia.

"What are you doing here?" he asked. Xia rose coyly.

"Ah, excuse me, but I'm here to interview for an examiner's position." She looked innocently from face to face. Neither broke their stare.

"You shouldn't be here. You'll have to wait outside for the receptionist."

"Sure," Xia responded. Offering her hand, she said, "I'm Doc . . . "

"You'll have to wait in the lobby," the taller general insisted. The two stepped around her and continued down the hall. Without another word, Xia hurried through the swinging doors and back into the lobby.

"What kind of operation are you running here?" she heard the same gruff voice ask as the two officers made their way deeper into the building. "Civilians roaming around like this was Disneyland . . . and fucking ears in the walls. Waiters at the damned Officer's Club last night knew more about . . ." Xia strained to hear the two, but lost them behind what sounded to be closing elevator doors. Looking about and seeing no one, she eased back into the corridor and ran to the elevator. The elevator's floor indicator stopped on three. Rushing back to the lobby, she grabbed her suitcase, stepped back through the swinging doors, and made her way to the stairwell.

* * *

"Jones," General Pope addressed the tall, middle-aged first mate, who stood saluting in the small room on the infirmary's third floor.

"Sir," Jones responded.

"At ease. Sit down." Pope stepped to the small rectangular table and threw a file down before sitting. Jones stepped behind the table, pulled out one of the high-backed chairs, and sat.

"You, ah . . . sticking with these charges?" Pope asked, holding up several sheets of paper from the file.

"Yes, sir," Jones replied. "It happened, sir. It should not have happened."

"What the hell was so wrong?" Pope suddenly shouted as he slammed the papers to the table. "Your commanding officer gave you an order. And that should have been the end of it."

"I obeyed my commanding officer, sir. But that order did not come from him." Staring intensely into the superior officer's eyes, he continued. "Sir, he would not have given such an order."

"Oh, you saying you're a mind reader now, are you?"

"No, sir. But I've served under Captain Exum for over seven years and I am proud of every minute of that service. Through those years, we've come to know and respect each other. And I know that he would not have given that order."

"And what was so wrong with that order anyway?" Pope leaped from his chair and turned his back to the crewman.

"It was racist. There was no basis for that order being given."

"You don't know that. We've spent the last two days trying to convince you of that. You know the nature of the mission will not allow us to discuss what exactly happened. You should accept that, as you always have done, for how many, thirty, forty missions in the past? You've got to believe that the order was well grounded." Pope spoke passionately, trying to appeal to the outraged navy man's sense of duty.

"And what circumstances," Jones asked, rising to his feet, "would make my captain question my loyalty to him . . . because of the color of my skin?" He paused, but no answer came forward. "You're trying to tell me that we were doing something out there that, had I fully known, I might have been racially motivated to turn against my own captain?" Jones paced to the corner of the room, where he stared into the wall. Pope stepped back over to the table, where he sat and gathered the scattered papers. Turning to Pope, Jones spoke calmly. "You served in World War II, didn't you?"

"Yes," Pope responded.

"When you fought Germans and Italians, did you lock up any white Americans?"

"Of course not."

"But after Pearl Harbor, you locked up the Orientals." Pope didn't respond. "And let's just say that we were slaughtering a bunch of black people out there the other night, like the white Allies slaughtered the Germans and Italians. Suddenly, my commanding officer looks at me!" Clinching his fists, Jones added, "He didn't see a proven loyal American, he saw a black man. Now, all of a sudden, my racial loyalties are supposed to outweigh my proven military ones. But general, it was *his* racial loyalty, not mine, that undid military protocol out there." Jones was heaving, reliving the emotional sting and humiliation when Captain Exum relieved him of duty.

"That's not the way it was," Pope argued. "We're all American . . . and American first."

"Yeah . . . as long as our differences aren't obvious," Jones added. "I am an American, and I'll stand and fight for whatever I believe that to mean. When Exum removed me from the bridge, he questioned my honor, my faith in what I thought this country stood for . . . in what I thought he stood for. It was like he put a match to the U.S. flag right there, before my eyes, to watch it helplessly burn. Yeah, I obeyed his order, because I am a soldier . . . first." After a long pause, he added,"The suit stands."

"You know that we can't allow that," Pope countered. "The navy's been getting it from both barrels, from all the gay-bashing and sexual harassment claims. Adding racial discrimination to that heap could mean the end of the navy as we know it today." After a long pause for thought, Pope added, "That's not what you want." Jones started to answer, but held his words. He'd been insulted and stripped of his faith in the navy. Doing the same to it would accomplish nothing.

"No . . . I don't want that to happen," he answered with a morbid sigh.

"What then?" Pope asked.

"I've got six years left before retirement," Jones replied. He rolled his large brown eyes to the ceiling, thinking deeply about what he was about to give up--his career, his life. A small movement to his upper left caught his eye. Spinning his head slowly about, he stared into the camera that had sat dormant in the upper corner of the small, whitewashed room for the last three long days. "I want off the sub," he said. "Let me have an assignment at Jackson until I retire. It's not too far from my home." "We'll arrange it," Pope said. "We'll train you for drug rehab." Jones didn't react, though inside, the insult deepened. He was a trained, hardened, and well-experienced navy man now destined to deal with the dregs of the service for the rest of his career. Drug rehabilitation was one of those necessary evils that the navy didn't want, but had to deal with. There would be no glory, no enemy to conquer.

"Can we tear up these papers?" Pope asked sternly. Jones turned and stared into the pile in the general's hands.

"What about the others?" he asked.

"They've all consented to drop the charges. It was a bad mistake. We know that now."

"Can I speak to Captain Exum?" Jones asked hesitantly, feeling like he'd just asked to visit a dying friend.

"That won't be possible," Pope replied, "Exum's already left. I can tell you that he feels just as badly about this as you do. He's taken a month's leave, but will return to active duty."

"Gone home to Connecticut, huh?" Jones said as a fractured glint of a smile covering his face. Thoughts of his commanding officer and longtime friend reminded him briefly of the long conversations they'd had on many nights, up on deck, as the sub cruised along on the ocean's surface. They'd promised each other home visits once they retired.

"Tear up the papers," Jones sighed. Pope ripped the stack before he finished the words. With a big smile, Pope walked over to him and offered his hand. Jones accepted the big man's hand and squeezed it firmly as they shook.

"We'll get over this . . . in time," Pope reassured him, not a hint of doubt in his voice.

"I'll never get over it," Jones replied. "The one person that I trusted more than anyone else in this world failed me. He's convinced me . . . you can't trust anyone."

"We're going to rebuild your trust in the navy," Pope responded sternly, "one day at a time."

"Tell me about it," Jones huffed. "You can't be trusted either."

"Excuse me soldier?" Pope shot back.

"You said these sessions wouldn't be recorded," Jones replied, no longer bothered by the general's rank.

"That's right . . . so?"

"The camera," Jones said, pointing to the small unit in the corner that made almost inaudible sounds when the lens focused.

"That thing's on?" Pope bellowed innocently.

"As if you didn't know," Jones replied. Leaping for the door, Pope bolted from the room and down the hall. Motioning to the guard to open the door sealing off the psychiatric corridor, he dashed around the corner, to the small recording room. Bursting in, he saw a video screen showing Jones sitting at the desk, holding his head in his hands. All of the cameras were on, recording all of the interrogation rooms. Nearly out of breath, Pope rushed back past the guard.

"Has anyone passed through here?" he demanded as he ran past, to the elevator.

"No, sir," the guard replied. The elevator door slid open and Pope leaped aboard and punched the selector panel. Exiting on the first floor, he ran for the front entrance. Bursting through the swinging doors of the lobby, he ran right past the young woman dressed in red and out onto the front steps. Looking in both directions, he saw nothing unusual. Stepping back in, he was quickly joined by the colonel who commanded the infirmary.

"Seal off this building at once," he shouted. "No one leaves until I've talked to them."

"Yes, sir," The colonel replied. Stepping up to the clerk at the desk, he asked loudly enough for Xia to hear, "How long has she been there?"

"She was sitting there when I came in," the woman ensign replied, popping to attention. "I stepped into Lieutenant Stetson's office for a few moments. She was still sitting there when I returned." Pope turned and walked to Xia, who stood upon his approach, beaming a gentle smile.

"I'm here to interview for a position," she said, and again shoved her hand at the general. Pope stared at her for a few seconds, turned, then shouted at the colonel. "Get her credentials . . . and verify them . . . you got me?"

17
THE FIFTY YEAR PLAN

The Central Intelligence Agency's Inner Circle (CIA-IC) had followed the NAACP's progress, joyously noting its slow, but sure demise. Its prominence in the sixties had been alarming, prompting an entire sector of the CIA to be charged with it. A select group of ten, made up of sociologists, psychologists, organizational strategists, and anthropologists, conferred for over two years on the organization and its potential threat to the status quo of the United State's majority-rule system.

The group's studies led to a number of conclusions. First, the organization was more of a monarchy rather than a democracy. Its leaders were dominant, in office for life, and not obligated to answer to any large elected body. Indeed, it was the charisma of the leaders in the sixties that allowed the organization to become so effective. But throughout history, monarchical rule has always eventually failed, primarily for the very same reasons. Autonomous leadership leads to rigidity, intolerance of new ideas, and the inability to adapt to new conditions. Thus, though powerful for the present, age and ownership by leaders/kings lead to eventual ineffectiveness and ruin.

Second, the group and its leadership had no long-term experience in running such a large organization. The best business strategy uses the "campaign" style of operation. This style utilizes personnel turnover every three to four years, at all operating levels, from CEO to grass cutter. Doing so yields the illusion of being in control of change. Then, as changes naturally occur, campaign organizers and strategists claim responsibility for any successes. The organization grows then to expect change, even promote it, rather than vainly trying to stop it. Change must be incorporated in order for any organization to be successful. But this knowledge comes only with experience, something the NAACP was just beginning to establish.

Change, the simplest and most inevitable factor of all, was to destroy the NAACP. Accepting this, the CIA-IC implemented actions that promoted change--in the way blacks viewed each other and the development of the black middle class. The masses would be disenfranchised, moral values broken down, and religion and sanctity of family, abandoned. The NAACP would be the first casualty for the CIA-IC.

But something had gone wrong. Unexpectedly, the NAACP's senior leader accepted early retirement, while all of the IC-groomed candidates for his replacement retreated. Suddenly, the organization was getting a breath of fresh air. Unforseen circumstances had delivered a younger group of leadership, ripened in the art of corporate organization and more in tune with society's present and ever-changing needs.

The CIA-IC could not allow that to happen.

* * *

"Take out this fresh group," General Fellows demanded, standing before a specially called meeting of the Inner Circle, "and our insiders will still prevail." He spoke arrogantly that crisp Monday morning to the group of twelve elderly white men. Just three days before he'd successfully demonstrated ID's mass murder potential. The group had assembled to discuss the results. But knowing of their small but significant concern with the NAACP, Fellows chimed in the unprompted suggestion to put his weapon to immediate use.

"We can't just wipe out the pack of 'em, at once," an elderly statesman said. "That'd be counter productive. The public won't buy it and there'd be an investigation."

"I can do it," Fellows said confidently. Curtis Westmoreland twisted uncomfortably in his seat, but didn't comment.

"This won't be like that AIDS thing, will it?" an old and balding Senator Thurston asked from the far side of the table. "That cockamamy scheme went awry, and now threatens us all. Hell, do you know how hard it is getting a good 'clean' whore these days?"

The senator guffawed and invited the rest of the table to react to the illicit humor.

"I assure you, Senator," Fellows answered, "ID polices itself. It won't be some free-floating germ that can get passed around to everybody. We control this one . . . completely."

"What about this black fist thing?" another member asked.

"I never saw a black fist," Fellows countered. "Some of those niggers on board somehow got wind of what we were doing and staged those events."

"You saw them holes in the sub, didn't ya?" Senator Thurston asked.

"Yes, sir," Fellows answered.

"And the plane, you did see the plane? And what was it that the sub fired on?"

"I was never sure of the jet plane, sir," Fellows replied. "And please remember, there were blacks on the radar, where the holes occurred, and throughout the ship. No being could have been out there like that, diving with the ship, racing torpedoes, punching holes in steel with his fist." With that comment, chatter erupted around the table. After a minute of debate, the eldest of the board slammed his hand down on the table for order.

"Westmoreland," he said, peering down the long oblong table, "you've been quiet during this whole damned meeting. Something's goin' on in your mind, and I think we should hear what it is." Fellows grimaced as Curtis Westmoreland slowly stood, gave an almost unnoticeable bow toward him, then addressed his elder compatriots.

"I've been reluctant to comment," he said calmly. "General Fellows thinks that I've been . . . well . . . less than fair in my dealings with suggested activities that step away from the Fifty Year Plan. Assuming that I have, I decided to just sit and listen during this discussion." He paused briefly, allowing the IC members time to reflect. "Personally," he continued, "I've seen what this ID can do. I know that it can strike without a trace and there's no danger of it getting out of control. But I've been listening to your comments and arguments this morning. And what I've heard confirms my own convictions." He took a long deliberate glance at Fellows. "ID will be a useful weapon in our arsenal, but not in this situation and not at this time." Instantly, a low hum filled the room as the other eleven IC members conferred. Fellows reddened and stared intensely at Westmoreland.

Without emotion, Westmoreland held up his hand to silence the group. "Gentlemen, I look at it this way. Hundreds of people in this country make countless millions of dollars killing cockroaches for a living, and they have been doing so for years. Why, with all the high tech that's gone into poison development, that bug should have been eradicated long ago. But . . . it . . . is . . . still . . . here. And probably in greater number than ever before. Ask any exterminator. They'll tell ya . . . the damned pest adapts too fast! By the time some new poison is spread sufficiently, a second or third generation of the pest has been born . . . immune to it. So the never-ending battle continues. Of course, the poison manufacturers don't mind this, and indeed, some even promote it. Now, I ask you. How many of you have roaches in your homes?" He looked around the room into each member's face, watching their reaction. The group chuckled lightly.

"Not a damned one!" Senator Thurston sang out.

"That's right," Westmoreland responded. "And it's not because you bombed your house with poison. Instead, you use poisons to keep any of these damnable creatures from getting close to your home. Think of it this way. You've formed a gauntlet of poisons and other deterrents around yourself. You don't have pests because they can't get near you." Westmoreland paused again, noting the nodding heads of agreement. "And if someone inadvertently brings in a pest, in a suitcase or clothing, that's when you use your poison." Again, the group erupted into noisy chatter. Westmoreland, feeling cocky, allowed them to stew for several minutes, before wrapping on the desk for order.

"Now, this ID is effective," the started. "And, for the record, let me say that it is the most effective poison that I've ever seen. It can kill millions at a time, or selectively kill one at a time. But it won't eradicate the minorities. If we tried now, we'd end up with pockets of them, scattered and adapting, like the cockroach, with no other purpose in this world than to survive and seek revenge . . . to pester us. That's not what we want." Again, hushed comments erupted.

Westmoreland leaned onto the table and placed his right hand on the thick bound report that sat before him. Opening it, he began leafing through the huge manual.

"The Fifty Year Plan . . . " he spoke gravely, hoping to get a response from General Fellows.

"Oh, my God!" Fellows bellowed furiously, "Not again!"

"Yes, again," Westmoreland snapped. He knew the general didn't like to be yelled at. "Again and again, General. We've all got to understand this plan, not only so we can effectively carry it out, but upgrade it as well. We're no different from you. All of us have children and grandchildren whose lives and well-being are being threatened daily by the ethnic menace." Westmoreland spoke condescendingly to Fellows. He wanted him to blow his stack before the committee. Up until now, he had been a tolerable nuisance, like a pimple. But, he'd festered to a swollen hairy boil, and now held sole possession of one of the most powerful weapons known. It was time he was eliminated. An irrational display before this group could lead to his forced retirement.

Ignoring his interruption, Westmoreland continued, louder than before, " . . . The Fifty Year Plan, once fully implemented, will first separate, then eradicate. The country that we will call home will be ethnically pure, with a small, wealthy, and easily manageable population. The ethnics will be concentrated, disorganized, and dysfunctional . . . "

"But not dead," Fellows retorted, his subdued anger brewing beneath his skin. He was disgusted with The Plan, the time it would take, its call for civil war, and civilians in control.

Oh, he'd heard it so many times before that he could almost recite it from memory. Though deeply complex, the overall plan was relatively simple. It had three major parts: unanimous ethnic distrust, threat of civil war, and finally, the establishment of ethnically divided "safe zones" or "homelands." South Africa was the original crude model, with its homeland concept. Then Russia, which pulled the greatest coup in history. Russia launched its plan for ethnic purity, controlling the population while concentrating wealth and power while using the world's hatred of communism to draw sympathy and resources to fund its effort. In one swift blow, three ethnically pure states waltzed away with most of the former country's valuable coastline, natural resources, wealth, and all of the nuclear weaponry. Meanwhile, a score of lesser countries was landlocked, poor, disoriented, and left with very little resources. Most important, each possessed at least two substantial factions to vie for power and control. With minimal investment, the wealthier states could maintain instability and control of these newly formed homelands indefinitely while the world looked on and praised their mock efforts as achievements in democracy.

Western Europe was also taking its own tack. Since it was already ethnically defined, it was busily laying blame for the poor economic conditions at the feet of immigrants. With time, the discontent of the native masses would justify complete cleansing of all ethnic groups--for the sake of survival.

And so, too, was the basis of the Fifty Year Plan for the United States, which used any and all effective means to blame poor economic performance, poor world educational and productive competitiveness, unsafe neighborhoods, et cetera, on ethnics. Once blamed, with the apocalyptic outcome well understood by the majority, the United States, too, would proceed with the controlled homeland plan.

For years, through manipulation of social order, media, and economic growth, the CIA-IC was convincing all Americans to fear the nonwhite man. The ethnic male was being painted as a crazed immoral drug addict who'd kill and rape his own mother to get his next fix. Eventually, all Americans--black, brown, red, yellow and white-- would grow to accept the ethnic male's excessively long prison sentences, beatings, and eventual removal from society.

Poverty, nepotism, and racism fueled discontent and reaction. But, whenever possible, the media placed an ethnic face on the cause before broadcasting to the public. National reports, such as the welfare population, which was primarily white, were always reported by group percentage, deceivingly giving the minority groups greater numbers.

Senator Thurston recited to his favorite anecdote every time The Plan status report was given.

"Ya see," the old, short Southern senator would start, "we raise a lotta chickens in my state." He'd smile as he'd lift his hand and draw attention to his translucent, age-blotched skin. "We'll pile fo' or five of 'em inta a small wooden cage, 'bout two foot by two foot and a foot high. That way, they don't get ta move 'round much, burnin' off the meat. Grow fast and fat that way. Problem is though, when ya pack 'em in that tight like that, ya violate theya nat'ral ter'torial instinct. So they staut eatin' one 'nother. So . . . we de-beak 'em." Always, he'd finish with a laugh and gesture with his fingers a pair of scissors snapping off the tip of his nose. "Violate a chicken's space, they tuan cannibal. Violate a man's space, same thang happen." The seventy-year-old senator's raspy laughter would then etch the walls. But he'd repeat it every time the group assembled to hear of The Plan's progress.

Everyone was sick of the story, but none denied its truth. Men, piled on atop each other in ghetto housing, had no privacy. They owned no floor space, nor any air space. Loud music and sirens constantly violated the thin walls of their world. The Plan even promoted loud sirens with city policies of blasting them whenever on call in urban developments, no matter what time of the day or night. Burglars violated their homes. Television violated their mind and morality. Necessity for day cares violated their children, their upbringing, and moral training. The streets, schools, and even garbage collection, belonged to the city, and their homes, to the landlord. And worst of all, without the teachings of a strong religion, few possessed any hope. Any one of them showing any type of impetus or ability to improve was helped to quickly escape, taking with them any ray of hope that might have encouraged another.

Under these conditions, the practice of welfare had become a tool of destruction. Children learn from birth that work has little to do with eating or earning. While there is little physical work to be done, high sugar-content food gets shipped in daily, supercharging the youth with energy that's got no positive place to go.

Then, for the masses, there is only one escape, one route that could deliver them, at least momentarily, into their own private place--drugs. That's why the "Just Say No" campaign failed in urban America. The true message of this campaign was "Say no to drugs . . . and yes to something else." For most of urban America, there was no "something else".

But the millions of poor white people were to be spared this calamity. To save the race, poor white people were steered from ghettos to small rural communities, many of which were mobile home parks. There, though just as poor and welfare dependent, a man could own the land. Most mobile homes were purchased, rather than rented. And there were still the natural pursuits, such as hunting and fishing to be enjoyed, as well as the in-between space for a man to escape to. Most important, there was rarely the violation of territory, the key to cannibalizing the minority masses.

To save money, the CIA-IC had developed crack, the cheap, potent derivative of cocaine. Illicit drug costs had become too expensive, so this was taken as a cost-cutting measure. While all ethnic groups indulged in the drug trade, a drug dealer, wishing to sell crack-cocaine to rural tenants, had to travel numerous miles to make a few sells. Meanwhile, a single dealer could score hundreds of times on a single corner in urban welfare housing.

And the true beauty of this plan was once started, it fueled itself. While social decay among defined ethnic groups raged, the media plastered the airwaves with graphic detail, blaming the group instead of the condition, blaming the symptom rather than the cause. It daily convinced the protected majority of the need to separate itself, to build bigger jails, hire more police, erect greater walls . . . separate itself for survival's sake, not from the poverty or congested living, but from the amoral debauchery of the ethnic man.

The middle-class ethnics were not to be overlooked. To justify their inclusion in the eventual cleansing effort, The Plan developed and sustained engineered backlash. Large corporations would fervently ram affirmative action efforts down the majority's throats instead of fighting the equal employment legislation. Blatant, excessive practices of racially based hiring, promoting and salary adjustments, while touted publicly as major strides toward equity, would be privately fed to the majority as evidence that their government was giving their country, their money, their very existence, away. Affluent and semiaffluent whites would watch their lives being disassembled and given away to the "less-than-deserving ethnics". This would fuel the need for a new government and new laws that served the people that put it into place, rather than the poor huddled masses yearning to take advantage of it.

These were the main points of The Plan, though there were many more subtle ones. Combined, this long-term effort would generate an outraged majority, convinced of the savagery and greed of the racially different. By then, the government, prompted by the CIA-IC, would have steadily widened the divide between the haves and the masses of have- nots to where separation of the classes--physical separation--would be inevitable. The blame for this menacing situation would rest squarely at the feet of the loathsome ethnics. This would ignite The Second Civil War. Only this time, mass communication would ensure that there would be no outraged section of the majority to resist the movement. Any inkling of morality would be abandoned when the threat of survival stood as the major issue. Battle lines would be drawn, the majority of ethnics rushing to central (and predetermined) areas for their own protection. Small skirmishes and battles would break out near the borders, like it had been in Bosnia and Somalia. Racially cleansed Armed Forces would then be called in to hold the borders.

The CIA-IC would step in at this point, proposing separate lands for the minorities who, with some coaxing and a tremendous threat of never-ending war, would accept. As with the NAACP, small monarchies would be established in each homeland, with the ruling family kept more affluent than the masses. One or two other groups who wished to rule would be supplied arms and information, enough to destabilize the government. The "safe zones" or homelands would then just creep along, near the brink of collapse, like so many African, Middle Eastern, and Pacific Basin countries. All would easily be controlled, contained, exploited, and realigned by their ethnically pure neighbors.

To make it all work, the image of the ethnic male had to be destroyed. Everyone, even his own kind, had to fear him, see him as more beast than man. And General Fellows had to admit that, after thirty-one years in the plan, this was indeed happening. Scores of well-known actors, sports figures, and other black male celebrities were being routinely stopped and harassed, appearing out of place by being both affluent and black.

The moral majority would find itself on the same side with handgun advocates and survivalist. Any talk of gun control, civil rights, voting rights, voter registration reform, or the like, would unite racists and bigots with those proclaiming their zealousness for religion, morality, and righteousness. Conservative talk shows, deriding every effort of civil rights or 'Golden Rule' philosophy-based legislation, were already growing in popularity by leaps and bounds. And news from abroad of ethnic cleansing served daily to make the idea more plausible in America.

"But not dead," Fellows repeated. His thoughts glassed over his eyes.

"That's right," Westmoreland answered. "Not dead, but alive and struggling daily for survival in their own well-designed prison of a country. Sure, we'd have to give up some land, but that will be a small price to pay to regain our old way of life and well-being. The homelands here will be well planned and managed, just like the ones in the old Soviet bloc. They'll be well managed and constantly destabilized, so they'll never be threats to us . . . ever."

"That's all a nice dream," Fellows retorted with a wild gleam in his eye, "but you can't guarantee any of this, can you?" Westmoreland bit his lip and squinted at Fellows, hoping the gesture would urge his outburst forward. "The NAACP situation has gone awry," Fellows continued. "You didn't plan it that way, did you? And what makes you think that any of the rest of your brilliant schemes will not fall apart somewhere along the way?" He drew reassurance from the silence that followed his questions. The unexpected NAACP leadership change was generating doubt in their minds about their foolproof plan. Facing the thought-filled faces about the table, he continued. "We've got our eggs in this one huge Fifty-Year-Plan basket . . . a basket with holes in it. I say that we can't afford to count solely on such a complex scheme. These dark-skinned sons of bitches . . . sure they're not as smart as we are, but like Westmoreland said, even the cockroach can adapt. Hell, niggers can, too!"

Fellows stepped away from the table like an old Baptist preacher. "Think of it," he said. "Aren't you afraid to walk the streets alone? How many different burglar alarm systems do you have? One in your home, one in your car, one in your office, one on your briefcase?" This world is unbearable . . . right now. And you've all said it . . . civil war is inevitable. I say that we strike stealthfully, now, while we can. We'll take out their leaders first, then destroy the scum-sucking masses, one region at a time. We'll cleanse God's green earth for . . . "

"You'll turn us into another Bosnia!" Westmoreland calmly interjected, a smile emanating from his face. Fellows was raving, having been caught up in his own rhetoric. "That tack will awaken the moral conscience of every being on the planet," Westmoreland added. "And you know as well as I that even an ethnically pure U.S. can't live completely separated from the rest of the world. We'll end up like South Africa was in the eighties, or worse, Ireland, ostracized from the rest of the world with sporadic attacks and counterattacks that will last for generations. Your plans to strike now . . . are stupid!" Westmoreland shouted at the general, who stood fuming at the end of the table.

"I suggest, gentlemen," Westmoreland continued, "that we congratulate General Fellow for his success with the ID trials and that we confiscate *all* of this weaponry and technology until after The Plan has fully unfolded."

"Agreed!" shouted several members from around the table. Not waiting for Fellows to cool down, Westmoreland turned to him.

"General Fellows, gather all ID, weaponry, chemicals, everything. Bring them to Fort Hood, where we'll take charge of them."

"Like hell I will! Westmoreland, I'll see you in hell first." With that final comment, the reddened general stormed out of the room.

"Gentlemen," a calm Westmoreland again addressed the group, "General Fellows is out of control."

"What do you think he'll do?" Senator Thurston asked.

"Probably go after some of your chickens," Westmoreland replied, a look of cunning about his face. "But, if my hunch is correct, I believe we can relieve ourselves of this, and the NAACP's directional change, all in one clean maneuver."

* * *

Zon stood calmly behind Xia, his hands folded casually in front of him. He'd met her at the train station early that bright Tuesday morning, wearing an olive green business suit and bright multicolored tie. After parking his camouflaged jet-car near Tryon Park, he'd taken a cab to the station. They'd agreed to meet there before she'd left for Newport News. Still, he wasn't sure how she was going to dress on her return trip, though his instincts told him that she'd dress to suit the crowd about her.

True to her nature, Xia stepped off the train wearing a tailored gray business suit, with long jacket and pants, and a brilliant red tie that dangled loosely from her neck. Untrue to their original plans, however, she had insisted on returning not to the juice bar, but to her home, to discuss her findings. Zon had agreed and now stood on the steps of her Fourth Ward residence, a single-story attached garden home with dark gray Masonite siding and burgundy shutters. Her front porch awning was nearly covered with a variety of plants, many blooming colorfully, in spite of the wintery season. Zon wondered why she had invited him there. During their cab ride from the airport, each sat on either end of the back bench. Xia had talked casually of her trip, the novels she'd read on the way, and the quaintness of Newport News. But she intentionally hadn't mentioned what she'd found.

"Come on in," she said, finally fishing the key from her suitcase and opening the wide whitewashed door. "Make yourself comfortable on the couch while I freshen up." The woman who strolled purposefully through the large, vaulted room and down the darkened hall was a far cry from the shy one he'd met that night in the juice bar. This one was so sure of herself and assertive. And she'd managed this without an attitude, retaining the greatest portion of the innocence that he'd first admired about her.

Removing his jacket, Zon hung it in the empty closet by the front door, then strolled toward the couch.

"Mind if I turn on the radio?" Zon yelled.

"No, go ahead," Xia replied. "Try the pre-sets." Zon stared into the control panel of the Onkyo stereo system that sat at eye level in a wooden corner unit. Quickly deciphering the controls, he turned on the receiver and pressed the pre-sets until he found the National Public Radio station, which was playing soulful jazz. Immediately, the four corner-mounted JBL speakers began thumping out a heavily synthesized and hypnotizing tune by Hiroshima. Zon glanced at the clock on the wall as he turned toward the couch. It was 11:15. The station aired national and local news on the hour.

Being in Xia's home bothered him. The new emotions that she had spawned in him were ever present, but didn't appear to hinder his ability to gather his thoughts, when needed. This eased his fears of strong emotions and the loss of Zonbolo. After only a minute, Xia strolled back into the room, having shed the business attire for a loose-fitting sweat suit and released her French-rolled hair to fall over her shoulders. She walked through the den where he sat and into an adjoining kitchen, turning up the stereo volume ever so slightly as she passed. Her living room was decorated in green and beige, with colorful pastels lining the walls, and several statues of African art sitting about.

"Juice?" she yelled from the kitchen amid sounds of the refrigerator door opening.

"Yes, please," Zon replied.

"Mango, right?"

"Right. Were you expecting me?" Xia ignored the question. Zon got up and walked into the kitchen. "You've got a lovely place." Xia handed him a tall malt glass full of freshly juiced mango.

"Thank you."

"Why did you bring me here?" Grabbing another tall glass of juice from the counter, Xia slipped by him and walked past the couch to a matching chair and sat.

"We have a lot to talk about," she said. Zon walked over and sat on the end of the couch next to her. The two were separated by a glass-top end table and live flower arrangement sitting on it.

"And so we have," he replied after taking a long drink of the juice. "Let's start with the submarine."

"Okay."

"What did you find out?"

"A lot more than you expected me to." Xia sat her half-empty glass down on the end table between them and swirled her finger about its cool wet rim. "The sub was there, at the shipyard . . . in for repairs. Seems like strange holes were popped into its side while it was on a secret mission off the coast of Haiti."

"It was there to observe the Haitian murders," Zon added.

"Yes," Xia responded, somewhat surprised that he wasn't trying to hide the situation from her. "A Captain Exum commanded the sub. He lives in Connecticut and is there now, on leave for a month." She spoke slowly, studying Zon's eyes, face, and every movement that might tell more than he was saying. "He's lost his crew, though. For some strange reason, he ordered all of the blacks removed from the command bridge in the midst of the exercise."

"He was afraid they'd mutiny if they discovered why they were out there. They were there to murder 4,000 people." Xia's eyes dropped to stare at the top of her glass as her mind worked to unravel the mystery.

"True," she responded, before raising her head to look again into Zon's eyes. "But none of the crew was allowed to observe, to look through the periscope, only Exum and another officer especially assigned for this mission." Xia paused for Zon's response. He gave none. "So," she continued, "if they didn't know about the massacre, then what caused the racist reactions?" Still, Zon didn't respond. "It happened after the holes were punched," she said, answering her own question.

Xia was fishing for his connection to this, and Zon knew it. Thinking quickly, he changed the subject.

"We start with Exum. He can lead us to the bottom of this."

"You don't have to," Xia replied, "I got the name of the man who assigns the special missions. He's also the one who approves them. He'll have all the answers to the massacre that you're looking for."

"How'd you get that information?" Zon asked, surprised by her achievement.

"How'd you find out about the massacre?" she countered. Zon pulled his gaze from her lovely face and stared into her reflection in the glass end table.

"Why do you ask?"

"I've had a lot of time to think about it. The navy doesn't advertise its missions, especially its secret ones. Now, the day before the massacre, you were here, in Charlotte until late, talking of going to see a friend. I've been asking myself how you managed to get to the middle of the Caribbean and back, to witness this crime . . . if you didn't already know that it was going to happen." Zon sat silently. Rising from her chair, Xia paced across the floor, where she faced the fireplace.

"You must have known about the massacre . . . before it happened," she said, more a question than an answer.

"You think I'm a part of this," Zon said.

"Now that's the puzzling part," she said. Striding over to the couch, she sat beside him. Her thigh pressed against his. Gently, she took his right hand into hers. "You're a tough read, but I just don't think you're the type. I believe that you are involved somehow with the navy, CIA, or whatever, but you've stumbled onto something wrong . . . dreadfully wrong. And now," she said, squeezing his hands firmly, "you may be mixed up in something that you just can't handle." Xia's face, like her voice, glowed with compassion. Her stare leaped back and forth, from one of Zon's large brown eyes to the other.

"You're worried about me," he said with a smile.

"To put it mildly," Xia replied seriously. "I know, now, of the people that you're dealing with. They're ruthless and don't like loose ends dangling about. And like it or not, Zon, you're a loose end. They could hurt you . . .or even kill you because of what you know. I don't think you fully understand that."

Zon couldn't help but smile because of this beautiful, distraught woman who sat caressing his hand with her hand, his mind with her compassion, and his heart with her charm. Trying to ease her concern, he spoke softly.

"You shouldn't worry. I'm a big boy. I can take care of myself."

"I believe that. But, this is much larger than you know. Let me help you."

"You have helped me already, and are helping me now," he toyed. Not amused, she threw his hands onto his lap, stood up, then turned to him.

"You know what I mean. How are you involved?" she demanded.

"I'm not involved."

"Then how did you come to be there when the Haitians were killed?"

"Look, Xia, even if I told you, you wouldn't believe me."

"Try me," she said, a small glint of a smile penetrating the seriousness of her face.

"Okay," Zon replied. He stood, then stepped away from her. "I was test flying my new plane that runs on water, that can fly at over 5,000 miles an hour, when me and my partner happened to run across this massacre." Zon shot an overexaggerated look of sincerity toward her when he finished. Incredulously, Xia stood straight-faced, staring at him, then suddenly broke forth in laughter.

"You aren't a very good liar," she said. Zon shrugged, but didn't comment.

"Ya want some more juice?" Xia grabbed the empties from the coffee table and headed toward the kitchen.

"Please," Zon said to her back as she walked away.

Sitting back on the couch, he yelled nonchalantly, "So what was the commanding officer's name?"

"General Curtis Westmoreland."

"Where'd you get that?"

"At Little Creek. It was pretty easy to move around inside . . . once I got inside." The juicer whined between their replies.

"But how'd you get that name? It must have been classified." Xia pranced back into the room with the refilled glasses of juice.

"It was. But when you tell me how you came to be there in Haiti, I'll tell you how I got the information."

"I hope that you didn't have to do anything . . . illicit?"

"Nothing that I couldn't handle," she replied, crossing her legs suggestively and cutting her eyes to mock him. "Westmoreland is a high level director in the CIA. He runs the link between the Agency and the military."

"The CIA," Zon thought aloud. An easy, steel-drum jazz beat played softly in the background. Both unconsciously tapped to the relaxing beat.

"Relatively young, a fast climber, no military background." Xia rifled off the information. "He's known for his broad thinking . . . and his ruthlessness." She sat next to Zon on the couch. Some graveness had returned to her voice. "This guy can hurt you." Not wanting to annoy her with further teasing and dismissal, Zon stared straight-faced, nodding his discernment of what she was saying.

"So what did you find out in Guantanamo Bay?" she asked, easing back on the chair and stretching her long legs out before her. Zon had told her at the campsite that he was heading for Guantanamo Bay, where the Haitian bodies had been taken for autopsy.

"The autopsy reported drowning, but the investigator's notes showed no clear cause of death."

"They were experimenting with chemical weapons," Xia said.

"That's my conclusion, too. But no traces of any unusual chemicals were found on their skin or clothing." Both paused silently, pondering the implications of such a weapon.

"The CIA's got a chemical weapon that can kill without a trace," Zon thought aloud. "And we haven't a clue as to how it works, what it looks like, or who could be a target."

"There was that flash of light," Zon said from deep within his thoughts, not realizing that he spoke aloud until the words had escaped.

"Flash of light?" Xia repeated.

"Yes. There was a huge flash of yellow light that lit up the sky, like lightning, for a split second."

"Could that have something to do with this mystery weapon?"

"I'm sure it has. Maybe it was exploded over the Haitians . . . or maybe the flash signaled the start or end of the massacre. There was a scuba diver, with his mask and headgear off, standing amid the bodies as I approached."

"So you were flying?" Xia asked cunningly.

"I told you that," Zon retorted, trying to dismiss her craftiness.

Just then, the song ended on the radio, followed by the lead-in for the midday news. It was noon. Zon stood to go.

"What are you going to do?" Xia asked.

"I'm going to start with Westmoreland," he replied, finishing off his second glass of juice.

"Start? Start to do what?"

"I'm not sure. But I've kind of gotten use to figuring things out as I go." He smiled.

"I can't let you go, Zon," Xia said, standing up and placing her hand on his chest. Her touch hadn't lost the burn it had during the camping trip.

"Look," Zon said, "you've got to believe me. I can take . . . "

The name "Curtis Westmoreland" suddenly aired on the radio. Zon and Xia froze as they listened to the news report.

" . . . spoke today from the Pentagon," a woman news reporter said.

> *"Apparently, there has been an anonymous terrorist threat phoned into Washington. From our Washington desk, here is Laura Coble."*
>
> *"Mr. Westmoreland has just alerted the media that the National Association for the Advancement of Colored People, NAACP, now into the third and final day of its annual convention in Chicago, has been threatened by terrorist. Westmoreland said that, though the call came in anonymously, the CIA has been tracking a neo-Nazi group based out of South Africa, which has been identified recently to be financially supporting the skinhead movement here in the U.S. Westmoreland says that this group has threatened a terrorist attack against the NAACP, whose complete leadership and talent pool are now conveniently gathered into one location for their convention. Leaders, of this the oldest and most influential civil rights organization in this country, were told of the threat, but elected to proceed with their final day of meetings anyway. The FBI and police are on the scene there in Chicago, hoping that their enhanced presence will deter any violent action."*

The report continued with details of changes in the NAACP leadership, then broadcast their full itinerary for the remainder of the day.

Zon stared blankly through Xia during the report.

"I've got to go," he said. Grabbing Xia by the arms, he placed her gently to the side. Then he stepped to the door.

"Zon! I'm coming with you." She fell into step behind him.

"No!" Zon shouted, hoping to shock her out of another emotional flurry. Ignoring the taunt, Xia ducked around him when he reached into the closet to retrieve his coat, then placed herself in front of the door.

"Look, Xia," he pleaded, "a lot of people could die if I don't go."

"Give me a second to change and I'll go with you," Xia pleaded, emotions brimming in her words.

"I can't wait," Zon uttered. He grabbed her by the shoulders to forcefully remove her. He couldn't take her with him, though he wanted to. She could easily get caught in a cross fire or some other danger.

But as he came closer, Xia wrapped her arms around his rib cage and drew herself to him. Zon, his Zonbolo fully centered and his senses aroused, felt her supple nipples through her clothing as they pressed against his abdomen, followed by the soft mounds of her breasts that sizzled like bacon on a hot skillet as they spread across his skin from the crush of her embrace.

"I can't let you go," she said tenderly. Her lips hovering dangerously close to his. Zon could feel his blood rushing downward, past his shoulders, through his chest, his abdomen, and into his pelvis. There, he felt himself enlarging while being nestled between two toasty thighs that spread ever so slightly, urging him on. His chest tightened, and he found it difficult to breathe.

"I can't let you go," Xia repeated hauntingly. Never so badly had he ever wanted to do two opposing things at the same time. His mind screamed at him to push her away. Idrisi's voice grew faintly from within his conscience: "Your virginity belongs to Beinin. As it goes, so, too, does Zonbolo." The faint echo of the old man's voice vacillated while a stronger and more amenable one grew from deep within his chest, urging his arms to embrace her, his lips to consume hers. Xia, incensed by the hot mass against her, fought the urge to invite this foreign pleasure in.

"Ooh," a deep guttural moan escaped her lips. Overcome by the desires within, she repeated her merciful plea.

"I . . . can't let you go," she sighed. Her hot breath blistered Zon's lips and broke what futile resistance that remained within him. Reaching down to Xia's lips, he parted them with his steaming tongue and attached himself to her . . . lips to lips, tongue jubilantly dancing with tongue, bodies intertwined. They kissed forever, neither bothering to breathe.

Falling against the door, the two finally broke their kiss, heaving for breath, still interlocked in each other's arms. "Oh, Xia," Zon moaned, his body still on fire, glued to hers, "I . . . can't . . . do this." Kissing Xia yielded his resistance, allowing the deep corner of sanity to penetrate. From deep within, it started reminding him of his commitment to Beinin . . . of the people who could suffer or die all because he'd . . . he'd . . . finally found something that could mean more to him than life itself. But it was one life . . . one life . . . that he was trading for countless thousands.

"No!" he muttered as he held on to Xia, who clung to him, her embrace far less powerful now. His sanity slowly returned, bringing with it the guilt of having to deny her, of having to walk out of that door, possibly never to return. Xia was this room, her walls holding him securely in, the decor and furnishings, her satiny smile and warm embrace. He was within her, and that's where he wanted to stay . . . but he had to go.

Drawing in a deep breath, Xia, her back against the door, looked into Zon's eyes. "I'll never let you go," she whispered. Fearful of an emotional relapse, Zon released his own embrace, pushed her to the side, and eased the door open. He began running thoughts of the Chicago convention, the bombing, the gun attacks that could take place within hours, the lifeless bodies spread about the floor, like the Haitians. The sobering thoughts straightened his stance. He eased away from her and through the door. "Zon!" she yelled as he left, then bolted from the closing door, toward her bedroom.

18
ATTACK ON CHICAGO

"O'Hare, this is Flight Five-Eighty-Five out of Dallas." An agitated Captain Davidson, pilot of the Seven-Fifty-Seven passenger jet, spoke into his mike. His eyes were glued to the ship's radar screen.

"This is O'Hare. Go ahead, Five-Eighty-Fi . . . "

Not waiting for the controller to finish, Davidson shouted, "There's something tearing dead at us, like a missile, showing up on our radar. Came out of nowhere a second ago . . . closing fast . . . it's gonna . . . it's gonna . . . " the radio fell silent.

"Five-Eighty-Five. Come back . . . are you there?"

"Ahhh . . . yeah . . . we're here," a bedazzled Davidson said. "Whatever it was . . . was heading straight for us. But, now . . . it's gone."

"Are you sure?" the air traffic controller at Chicago's O'Hare International Airport responded.

"That's an affirmative," Davidson answered. "Whatever it was, it's gone."

"Five-Eighty-Five, we've got you at 37,000 feet, two hundred and fourteen miles east by southeast of O'Hare. Please confirm."

"That's a roger."

"We've got Flight Ten-Eighty from Phoenix due west from you, bearing four-seven-victor."

"That's a roger. We've got him as well."

"We show no missile . . . or anything else on our radar in that sector."

"We don't either . . . now," a flustered Davidson answered back. "We'll have a ground crew standing by to check your radar when you land. O'Hare Ground Control, out."

"Roger. Five-Eighty-Five, out."

Zon's black jet-car cruised comfortably along, high in the clear midday sky. Not five feet below it flew Flight Five-Eighty-Five, its humongous size dwarfing Zon's jet as both airships headed for O'Hare. After spotting it in flight, Zon had flown directly at it, then straddled its back, and now flew just above the rear cabin section.

Just moments before, he'd run in a burst of mad speed toward his car after leaving Xia. Confusion had taken his mind, momentarily, but he cleared it during his short sprint.

"No one can resolve all that there is," Idrisi had told him. "One must learn to place matters away for a time. In your mind, allow space for the confused, the uncertain. Store it, hold it. In its place, it can be dealt with in your time. Out of its place . . . you shall deal with it . . . always."

"I'm getting tired of that old man being right all of the time," Zon said. He then encased his thoughts and feelings for Xia deep within the vault of his mind, where they could be held, for a time. The situation that could be unfolding in Chicago demanded that his mind be clear.

Reaching his car, he had sped off to Interstate 77, then headed north until reaching the outskirts of Charlotte. Finding a rural road, out of view, he then immediately leaped airborne. Flying along the treetops, he scanned the approaching scenery, avoiding all human eyes, until he'd reached the Appalachian Mountains at the Tennessee border. Once there, he followed the slope upward then beyond the mountain top, climbing to eight miles before leveling off and heading north by northwest, directly for Chicago. Using landmarks and his keenly accurate sense of direction and traveled distance, Zon streaked right toward O'Hare. He had spotted Flight Five-Eighty-Five 300 miles away of the airport and decided to ride its shadow into the city, hidden from midday viewers. He'd break away from the mother ship as soon as it fell beneath the radar.

Once cleared for landing, Flight Five-Eighty-Five banked east, then northwest before lowering its landing gears. Zon easily maneuvered above it, maintaining their relative position. Sensing the loss of radar, he broke from the passenger airliner and headed for downtown, where the convention was being held.

A fleet of sleek black limos sat outside the Park Plaza Hotel on Central Avenue in Chicago. Inside, the annual conference of the NAACP was in the third and final day of its convention. It had taken him an hour and fifteen minutes to get there, after leaving Xia. In his mind, he could hear the hard pounding within the vault as those debilitating thoughts struggled to free themselves.

Zon wasn't sure if anything was going to happen at the convention, nor if something did, what it would be. But the coincidence of Westmoreland's announcement and the potential presence of heartless mass murders who could kill without risk of detection was too great a combination to ignore. Dismissing discretion, Zon flew in close to inspect the hotel from above. The news reports that he'd picked up, along with the heightened ground activity, easily identified the hotel. Hopefully, his unexpected presence would disrupt Westmoreland's and the terrorist's game plan.

As he approached downtown, Zon wove his jet-car back and forth amid the tall skyscrapers. Heads turned and traffic slowed as his ominous black ship sliced its way toward the convention site. The Park Plaza Hotel was one of the newer hotels in Chicago, fifty-two stories tall, with a seamless reflective glass finish. Convention rooms, where the NAACP delegates were meeting, were located on the sixth floor. Occupying a city block, the hotel was hollow in the middle, with one large bank of twelve glass-front bullet-shaped elevators mounted on a single gigantic column in the center. Guest rooms lined the inner perimeter of the hotel on each floor beyond the eighth. Eight-feet-wide balconies and railing made up the inner perimeter of the hotel while the fifty-feet center about the elevator bank, remained empty. Guest registration was on the third floor. Utility and security occupied the lower two floors. At street level, on the first floor, shops and eateries lined each building face. The large entryways, on each face, led into long, two-story escalators, bringing cleared guests to the main floor. Utilities and maintenance were on the fifty-first and fifty-second floors. Gigantic air conditioners and heating units were mounted on the roof, which was also equipped with a helicopter landing pad.

The afternoon paper thoroughly described the hotel, as well as the well-planned NAACP itinerary and meeting locations for the full day. All in all, the hotel was fairly secure. And with the aid of the police and FBI, it offered excellent protection for the occupants within. Zon was satisfied with that, but wondered if they'd planned on the invisible threat of chemical warfare?

"All stations reporting?" Colonel Broome, a tall and muscular white ex-marine, asked as he stared at an aerial schematic.

"All teams confirmed. Activity is zero," responded Sergeant Jackson, the black communications officer. He sat toward the back of the large black van. Multiple wires ran from the console before him to radio controls mounted on his belt. Red circles peppered the schematic, which was covered in plastic, allowing the SWAT team strategists to mark and erase with ease. As the sergeant answered his superior officer, the rear door swung wide and a uniformed officer stepped in. The four SWAT officers, occupying the van, held position, but fell silent as the military officer and two others entered.

"Who's in charge?" the general bellowed.

"I am," Broome answered. Dismissing the entourage with his eyes, he turned to stare again into the schematic.

"You received your orders . . . from Washington?" The general talked to the back of the commander's head.

"Yes . . . sir," Broome answered gruffly.

"We can expect your full cooperation then?"

"Yes, sir." Colonel Broome was used to being in charge and didn't like having rank pulled on him. But he had been told the night before that the FBI was now in charge since a threatened terrorist attack was a federal affair. With dogged protest, he'd accepted his loss of control and backed away from the schematic.

"It's all yours," Colonel Broome conceded.

"This is a combined operation," answered the military general, "not the FBI, not the police." Broome stood silently, waiting for the standard lecture. "These are your men. This is your turf. You know it better than anyone. We've got the experience with terrorists; we know their methods and strategies. Our effort is best united. Is that understood?"

"Perfectly," Broome said, finally looking the general in the face.

"Good," the general replied. "I am General Sutton from Fort Hood. I've worked with navy intelligence for twenty years and provided training in covert terrorism. And I am now senior advisor to the FBI on stateside terrorism."

"I'm Colonel Broome, ex-marine of twenty-five years. Been leading the Chicago SWAT team for the last five. We've never lost a hostage nor suspect." Pride brimmed in the colonel's words.

"Very good, colonel," Sutton remarked. "Show me your setup."

Stepping back to the schematic stretched across the table, Broome pointed as he talked through each of his deployments.

"We've got four men on the roof . . . here . . . and here. They're all armed with AK forty-sevens and are the toughest individuals in my command. Nothing will get through them, without taking the roof off first."

"Good," the general replied, trying to generate some camaraderie with the older officer.

"Then on each surrounding roof, we've got two-man teams . . . here, here, here, and here. There's a sharpshooter with scope, one AK, and these two teams." He pointed to two of the buildings that sat at the diagonal corners of the Park Plaza. "They've set up missile launchers in case of an aerial assault."

"Excellent. What have you got on the ground?"

"There are four main entrances from ground level, one on each face of the building. I've got four men stationed outside each, carrying four-fifty-sevens. They're just a show of force, assisting the police in personnel movement in and out of the building. If any of the entrances is breached, the raiding force will have to climb two floors of escalators, which are completely enclosed from top to bottom. I've stationed two men at the top of each with enough machine gun fire to paint the walls. They've got orders to kill everything in the escalator tunnel, once the entryway has been breached."

"Hmmm," replied Sutton. "Any more inlets?"

"Yes," Broome replied. "There's the utility entrance, from the second floor." Colonel Broome peeled away the top sheet from the stack that lay on the table, placing it neatly on an adjacent surface.

"There's a freight elevator, here . . . and one for personnel . . . here. We've cut off the power to the smaller one. I've got two men riding the freighter and three more with repeater rifles guarding the entrance on the second floor." Broome stared into Sutton's face, looking for his acceptance. General Sutton nodded his head, then stepped away from the table.

"You've done a fine job. Your setup is by the book. Unfortunately," the general added, casting a directing eye at the two men who entered with him, "you haven't considered this from a terrorist's point of view. Anyone in their right mind would look at this fortress and walk away. But terrorists believe that there's no tomorrow. They're ready to die like ants if it will get those that follow them in behind them. Don't misunderstand. It's just that these fanatics are a different breed." Broome's jawline flexed as he struggled to accept the criticism of his commanding officer. The general waved his men toward the radio console.

Suddenly, as the radio officer rose, yielding to the federal agents, a desperate call came over his headset.

"Sir!" he shouted, "bogey spotted from Delta Building . . . coming in fast, no circling."

"Any markings?" Broome demanded.

"Markings! Can you identify?" the sergeant asked into his mike. After a second's pause, he answered, "No, sir. It's a small, smoke black jet . . . no registry or visible markings." General Sutton rushed outside the van, then stared up into the heavens. There, circling high above the Park Plaza, was the small aircraft.

"Can your men get a shot at it?" he yelled at Broome, who followed him out.

"Can we get a shot?" Broome yelled at his radio officer.

"Johnson has a bead on him with his rocket launcher,"

"Blow it out of the sky," Sutton ordered.

* * *

"What's going on up there?" General Fellows asked. He crouched uncomfortably behind a car across Central Avenue, which bordered the south side of the Park Plaza. He and eight other men, all dressed in black suits, skullcaps, boots, and face paint, had eased through the front door of the vacant Express Mail Shop and assembled in the shadows behind the large sedan. They awaited the signal to rush the utility chute across the street, which lead under the sidewalk, into the hotel basement and to the freight elevator.

"Don't know," a voiced crackled over the muffled static on the radio. "Some strange bird's flying around the hotel. It's put everyone on alert. Do we abort?"

"Negative," Fellows barked back. "We'll use this diversion instead. Either way, it's a go . . . in . . . two minutes. You copy that, Skyjack?"

"Got it," the voice on the other end answered.

"Get to that bogey and blow it out of the sky. Everyone will rush to the roof and the street. We'll rush the building, take out the guards on the freight elevator, then take it to the third floor. Skyjack will drop jumpers one and two, who'll blast the roof and bring on the rain. We'll rush the elevators and take it from there. Is that a copy?"

"Understood. We've got a go in one minute," Skyjack replied. "Wait! The jet's gone," he yelled over the radio. "It just took off into the blue heavens."

"Damn!" Fellows exclaimed, noting the too-familiar feel of an unknown aircraft intervening into his affairs. "Back to the original plan," he shouted into his radio. "We go in thirty seconds." He didn't like surprises, and there had already been two. The submarine attack had also been an unplanned event, but everything eventually worked out. He knew that the strategic thing to do now was to abort, regroup, considering the unknown, then try again. But the NAACP's schedule wouldn't allow for that. And the scathing attack he'd received from Westmoreland and the Inner Circle had mortally wounded his ego. He had to show them. He had to prove he was right, that his way was the best and way--the only way.

Fellows's collar tightened unmercifully about his neck. He ran a finger into and around it, trying to gain more breathing room. But his breathing had been restricted by the adrenaline rushing through his veins ever faster as the clock ticked down to zero. His men, all young white marines drafted into his special force after being thoroughly researched and indoctrinated, would all outrun him as they crossed the street, leaving him has the largest and easiest target to hit. But he had to be there. This event would change the course of American history. This one assault would show the huddled masses of America, that a civil war of the races could be won--without annihilating the entire population or rendering the land uninhabitable. They would be convinced when he and his men attacked the NAACP, selectively killing a well-defined group, in the midst of Chicago--in broad daylight--in spite of the best defenses in the world. Success under these conditions could ignite the world.

The eight men stiffened as they prepared to rush the guarded entryway. As the thirty seconds ticked off, the stolen jet black Pro-Nam Assault chopper rose from out of nowhere, high into the sky, three buildings to the west of the Park Plaza Hotel, then toward it.

"We've got a new one!" a frantic SWAT Team member, stationed atop the Park Plaza, shouted down to the command center. "It's an assault helicopter, heading right for us!"

"Fire on it!" Broome yelled.

"It's out of our range," another SWAT team member answered. The chopper climbed high over the hotel. Suddenly, wide doors on either side slid open. Two masked men steadied themselves in the opening. As the chopper circled the building cluster, the men in the doors took aim at the roof tops and fired grenades at the SWAT teams. Huge gushing sprays erupted as the grenades hit, spewing a fine mist of ID in every direction.

"Gas!" one of the SWAT team members yelled into his radio. Each of the members quickly dropped their weapons then struggled to don their gas masks. But after feeling the droplets on their hands and clothing, yet feeling no pain, the SWAT team members quickly relaxed, then took aim again at the assault copter. Meanwhile, the airborne assault squad dropped the launchers, grabbed flare pistols, then took aim at the rooftops.

Beating chopper blades drowned the sound of the exploding flares. But no cover was needed to conceal the sound of bodies, tumbling like large wads of soaked newspaper, to the asphalt roof.

Broome sniffed the air as he watched the chopper circle. The mist tickled his nose. "Smells like almonds," he said.

"They're using chemicals," Sutton hissed. "Tell the men to use their gas masks!" After a moment, the radio officer shouted, "I can't raise any of them, sir." General Sutton continued to take light sniffs.

Though he was familiar with most gases, he couldn't identify this one. Trying to identify it, he took in a deep breath of the inactive poison.

"Seems harmless . . . if it is chemicals," he said.

"Maybe it's a misfire," Broome responded, not taking his eyes away from the binoculars trained on the chopper, "or a breezer, to test the wind pattern. In either case, I'd suggest that we get back inside the van." Without another word, he and the other men rushed inside.

"Let's go!" General Fellows yelled. "And remember, take out everyone who's got a weapon. Any weapon! But no civilians. I repeat. No civilians. Westmoreland's sent his best to stop us. Remember. We only go after the niggers in the photos! Now, let's get this the hell over with!"

With that, the general flipped his right hand toward the Park Plaza as he held his laser pistol in the other. The lead man took aim, then launched two mist grenades toward the west entrance, where three armed SWAT team members stood along with twelve civilians. All had been looking skyward. When the grenades erupted, coating each of them with the fine mist, the three SWAT team members turned, raising their weapons as they spun. Pencil-thin beams of yellow laser light caught their eyes as they focused on the group of disguised men rushing toward them. But before they could take aim, the dancing lights found the three, and all of them instantly fell to the pavement. Three women standing near them began screaming, backing away from the falling bodies and the approaching men. Six men, dressed in civilian clothing, dug under their jackets and retrieved small, fully automatic machine guns. Their motion attracted the attackers. They, too, fell in silence as the faint yellow light beams raced over their bodies.

Three men, along with the terrified women, backpedaled from the building's entrance. Eight black-suited attackers rushed into the doors followed by a clumsy, plump and puffing ninth man. The large glass doors closed behind them. Not a single shot had been fired. Once inside, Fellows made his way to the front of the group. While heaving for breath, he checked his watch.

"We've got . . . " he said, gasping hard to catch his breath, "seven minutes and . . . ten seconds . . . to take the elevators, get to the . . . sixth floor . . . and take out the target . . . then get to the roof. Anyone gets separated . . . we meet on the roof in seven . . . minutes . . . Go!"

"Colonel Broome," the radio officer yelled. "Hanks reported an engagement on the south side. Now, he won't answer."

"Send teams six and seven," Broome barked. "Alert the rest." Grabbing a revolver holstered over a chair back, he headed again for the door.

"That's not smart," General Sutton said.

"Those are my men out there, general. If they go down, I go down." Just as Broome stepped from the van, an explosion erupted, the sound echoing off the buildings like thunder. Looking up, he saw massive chunks of debris falling toward the pavement. Ducking and dodging, he wove his way to the north entrance, where he disappeared up the escalator, shouting for his men to hold their positions as he went.

The police had cleared the streets about the hotel when Zon's jet had been spotted. Convention delegates had been alerted as well, but the police advised them to stay where they were, it being the safest and best-protected location in the city. Inside, the lobby and balconies had been cleared. People were shuffled into any room or closet that would hold them. The two SWAT team members at the top of the west escalator tunnel were waiting, their automatics trained on the bend, hiding the tunnel entrance. Suddenly, fire erupted from one of the guns; the SWAT man spotted movement deep below. A loud thump sounded, followed by an expanding sizzle as a launched grenade whined upward, toward them. The two were covered with ID mist, along with everything else within a thirty-foot radius. An exploding flare followed the grenade up the tunnel, bathing the inside of the hollow cylindrical dome with an eerie yellow glow. The two SWAT men fell where they'd crouched behind the thick wall supports just beyond the escalators. In the middle of the floor, the lifeless body of Colonel Broome lay outstretched, he, too, having been caught in the deadly ID spray. Fellows and his men eased up the escalator. Checking his watch, he radioed to the roof.

"Skyjacker."

"In place and ready with the rain," the raspy voice returned.

"Hold it till my signal," Fellows responded.

Zon had spotted the attack helicopter as it emerged from underneath camouflaging atop a parking deck west of the hotel. Feeling he'd be most effective on the ground, he blasted his ship skyward, then northward before swooping down on the north side of Chicago and back toward the hotel. Setting his jet-car down in an alley, he quickly converted it to a car, then parked it on the street. Running to the hotel, he quickly dashed around it until he spotted the dead bodies that marked the attackers' entrance. Taking a deep breath, he sensed the faint hint of almonds lingering in the air. Pulling it deep into his lungs, he noted its unnatural aroma and rapid dissipation.

"Without a trace," he whispered. He rushed toward the entrance, then froze in his tracks as a faint, almost indiscernible yellow glow filled the tower from within.

"And there's the lightning," he added. A quick glance at the pile of lifeless bodies convinced him that they'd died the same way as the Haitians.

Silently bursting through the large glass doors, he darted to the escalators, zooming past the gawking witnesses. Terror had condensed their thoughts, making them easily readable. "Eight demons" and "ray guns" leaped from their scanned minds as he passed. He spotted the eight on the escalator.

With a mighty leap, he soared upward, then landed between the fourth and fifth man in line. The assault team quickly reacted by raising their fists and reaching for weapons. But, with the stiffened forefingers of both hands, Zon struck out at the team, striking the men behind him in the throat, temple, and forehead. The fifth and sixth man on the stairs tumbled unconscious into the two behind them, sending them all rolling to the base of the escalator. Disabling the one directly in front of him, Zon used his body to shield against an attack from above. Fellows and the first two stepped quickly up and off the escalator, while the remaining man turned and threw a punch at Zon, but struck only air. The lights suddenly dimmed as the assailant felt multiple strikes about his head before he, too, fell down the escalator.

Without hesitation, Zon jumped back down the escalator to finish the three on the bottom before he pursued those at the top. As he approached, he saw the eighth man desperately fumbling with a grenade launcher, while the sixth and seventh man steadied thin yellow beams of laser light toward him. Not fully realizing the threat, Zon dodged the lasers. The terrorists swung their activated guns madly back and forth, trying to tag him as the eighth man raised the launcher to fire. Zon pivoted, then dove at the grenade launcher, grabbing the grenade by the neck just as the propellant ignited behind it. The expanding hot gas rushed from the barrel, pushing the grenade forward, with Zon's powerful hand locked to it. Like a steel claw, he held the deadly cone in his head, preventing it from launching. Using it as a rock, he hurled it into the back of the sixth man's head, knocking him unconscious, then struck the eighth man in the temple with his finger.

The seventh reached into his boot and retrieved a Forty-Five revolver. Pulling it up, he focused on the empty space Zon had occupied not a split second before. Then, the young ex-marine squealed as Zon's powerful hands cupped his rib cage from behind, squeezing the revolver from his hands.

"What's in the grenade?" Zon said to his grimacing, helpless victim.

"Go to hell!" the soldier answered. Zon squeezed still harder, forcing his middle fingers deeper into the flesh between the bones of his victim's rib cage.

"Ahhh!" the soldier screeched.

"What's in the grenade?" Zon asked again. The soldier's eyes rolled back into his head. Pain and loyalty was robbing his consciousness. His thoughts grew confused. He thought of the grenade and laser . . . how the laser was supposed to set off the poison . . . activate the chemicals . . . set off the deadly ID liquid . . . spread about . . . killing everything it touched . . . clothing or skin . . . ID, contained inside the grenade.

Zon stared at the grenade lying on the floor beside the soldier he'd hit in the head. Dropping the young soldier, Zon struck him in the head as he fell, sending him to dreamland to join his friends. Picking up the grenade, he shook it, then carefully pried it open, exposing the liquid inside.

"Fire down the hole!" Fellows ordered the point man, who carried the last launcher. After a quick look of hesitancy, the soldier stepped to the tunnel and fired a grenade. "It didn't blow," he said. He stared into the tunnel, looking for falling mist. "The grenade is gone."

"Fire another," Fellows said. "And keep firing. You!" he said, pointing to the last man. "Follow me."

The point soldier quickly reloaded the grenade launcher, while Fellows and the last of the eight assault soldiers ran for the elevator. Immediately, gunfire erupted from the inner perimeter of the hotel as the remaining Feds and SWAT personnel fired down on the two. Fellows and the soldier ducked to the side, hiding behind two great clay flowerpots by the western entrance. Both began fishing into the small pouches they wore, pulling out faceplates, rubber gloves, and small air units. The two quickly pulled on the equipment. Fellows stuck the radio to his face.

"Skyjack! Make it rain!" he yelled into the small unit. Immediately, a hole blew open at the top of the hotel, allowing the evening light to beam through. Then, a large pipe eased through, just as a heavy fog billowed forth from it, filling the entire open area, then sinking quickly to the ground.

"He's stopping the grenades!" the point man yelled from the escalator, after having fired the fourth. But as he spoke, Zon darted up the escalator. His mad dash froze the soldier in place for a split second, enough for him to approach and strike. But as the ex-marine fell, the fog settled 'round about.

Zon sniffed, smelling the now familiar almond scent. He, along with the entire lobby, had been bathed in ID. Sensing movement, he turned to his right. There, a completely masked General Fellows emerged from the shadows, though still hidden from the shooters above.

"Everybody!" Zon shouted, his mighty voice rocking the hotel. "Get out of the fog! Away from the light! Now!" He stood still and stared at Fellows, who stared curiously back at him.

"You were out there, with the Haitians, weren't you?" Fellows asked, not moving from his protected space. In his hand, he held a flare gun, the safety off, his fat finger wrapped tightly around the trigger. He stood roughly twenty feet away, with nothing but open space in between.

"Yes," Zon answered. "Why are you doing this?"

"You figure it out in hell," Fellows sneered through his mask. Zon stared hard into the madman's eyes, trying to stir his thoughts. Fellows's eyes drifted slightly. Then, a maddened grin consumed his face.

"There's not enough to go around," he said, grinning triumphantly. "And some of us want it all . . . but we can't have it." He wavered a bit, then shook his head. "This was no time to talk," he thought. "The mission isn't complete. Reinforcements must be on the way." His mind spun. "The helicopter . . . it wouldn't wait. So why talk?"

Zon stood calmly, though he tried harder than ever to ease the old soldier's mind. Once relaxed, he could rush in and take away the flare that could kill everything in sight.

"No . . . we can't have it all . . . until we get rid of the likes of you!" Fellows relaxed, feeling pleasant over thoughts of his ideal society. Zon knew it was now or never. Without crouching, he projected himself toward the old fat general who, at that instant, squeezed his fat finger around the trigger. It sent the flare streaking up the hotel's center, then exploding into brilliant, but deadly yellow light.

In a contorted lump, Zon's heavy body fell onto Fellows, breaking three ribs, but leaving him conscious.

"Get him off!" Fellows yelled. The last soldier rushed over, grabbed Zon by his massive right arm, then rolled him away. Helping the wounded general to his feet, the soldier started for the elevator.

"We've . . . got time to make the hit," Fellows grimaced.

"Forget it, General," the soldier reasoned. "This place will be crawling with backup in minutes. We're out of time."

"We can still make it," Fellows argued.

"No can do," the soldier said. Fellows argued to continue the killing as he stared down at Zon, whose Zonbolo-enhanced body shrunk back to its normal size before his eyes.

"Shit," he gasped. "What the hell was this guy?" Cautiously, he moved closer.

"Let's get the fuck outta here," the anxious soldier bellowed. Holding his laser pistol in both hands, he was ready to fire at anything that moved. But as Fellows reached to touch Zon's limp frame, a small snort erupted from the downed hero's nose, nearly scaring Fellows to death. He watched in near panic as Zon's chest rose, filled his lungs to capacity, then fell.

"That's impossible!" Fellows screamed, "The dead can't breathe!"

"Come on, General!" the soldier yelled, then sprinted toward the express elevators in the middle of the lobby. Fellows backed away, refusing to take his eyes off Zon, who lay, eyes wide, and fully dilated pupils. His mouth gaped open; his tongue hung lifelessly out at the corner. Yet, his chest rose and fell madly, like a bellows firing a locomotive. Bewildered, the wounded general, while tightly hugging his broken ribs, tripped over his own feet. He fell backward to the floor, his bald head bouncing off it like a flat basketball. Grimacing in pain, he rolled over, scooped himself up, then limped toward the waiting elevator, where the other soldier stood, waving him on.

Never before had Zon been so immersed within himself, within Zonbolo, as he was now. The ID had cut his consciousness completely away from his physical being. There was no outside. It was as if a wall had come down around his brain, cutting off every connection, every portal to the world. His memory quickly returned him to the months upon the cross, where he lay in a similar state. But the feeling was far more intense now. Nothing responded, not his legs, arms, head, or eyes. He'd noticed, too, that his heart had stopped and his lungs weren't working either. Looking about the familiar golden brown walls of his mind, now tinted slightly red due to Xia's influence, he saw them begin to turn whitish gray around him and slowly collapse inward. A message of pain emanated from them. Without the constant flow of oxygen-enriched blood, his mind was dying. And if it died, it would force him--his soul, his Zonbolo, in its purest state--out of his body.

Zon's bewilderment was disrupted by the collapsing wall of his mind. He had to get the blood enriched and flowing. From what he'd learned about ID, he knew its effectiveness was temporary. He had to stay alive long enough to let it pass. Just let it pass. Moving freely about within, he sought out his heart. The vastness and incomprehensibility of his mind were overwhelming, and would have completely consumed him had he not spent months studying and exploring it in Beinin. For an instant, he thought of the thousands who had died of the ID, trapped inside their own being. Being overwhelmed, they had no idea of the potential of their state and were able to stay there for only a moment before being cast out, forever, into the beyond.

Zon eased to his heart, visualizing the life pump lying before him, warm, full of blood, yet dormant. He had to get it pumping again, at least to his brain. Centering himself, he focused his mind force on his heart, matching its patterns and rhythms of life to his mind force. Immediately, the powerful muscles stretched, then contracted. Muscles controlling the valves moved in step to force the blood toward the brain.

Having stepped the controls through, he repeated the commands while focusing new ones on his chest muscles. A small rush of air resounded as his powerful muscles expanded the cavity, forcing air into his lungs. As he established his breathing, he broke yet another controlling beam of mind force off, sending it to the aorta and other large veins and arteries, restricting those leading downward and enlarging those moving upward. A red glow returned to his mind flesh as he worked his circulatory and respiratory systems, through Zonbolo, from within.

Once established, he was able to sustain himself in this catatonic state. But he'd lost all sense of time. Nothing connected him to the outside. So he regulated his heartbeat and breathing to a minimum, judging from the golden redness of his mind, the need for more or less oxygen. He could have been lying there for seconds or for days; he wasn't sure. Gazing about his mind, Zon caught sight of the vault he'd constructed to contain his feelings for Xia. It stood quiet in his mind's eye. But as he stared at it, it suddenly bulged, the thoughts within drew life from his notice. Looking away, he took himself back to his heart where he rode the moving muscles, up and down, flooding his guiding thoughts with their rhythm.

He'd entered the hotel minutes after the attack team, yet had noticed the quickly fading smell of almonds over the bodies strewn about at the entrance. The ID, as the soldier had called it, must last only a few short minutes. If so, he'd regain his physical control--provided no permanent damage had been done.

Suddenly, a thought hit him. Since he was disconnected from his body, could he reach out, leave his body and sustain it, yet not be trapped inside the nothingness of death while he waited for the ID to wear off? Thinking back, he remembered his visit from the "old black man of the sea" while on the freighter that had originally taken him to Africa. "Idrisi," he thought. As intensely as possible, without losing control of his life-supporting thoughts, Zon stared long and hard at the inner walls of his mind, shaping himself into a rocket . . . aiming himself at the walls . . . through the walls. Then, he fired his engines, propelling himself into them . . . through them . . . beyond them. The wall consumed him like Jell-O. His sleek body slid through on its journey upward.

Above him, the red flesh of the wall gave way to a brilliant red glow that grew lighter and thinner. Finally, he emerged on the other side, his thoughts bathed in light. Looking back, he saw himself lying horribly still but for his pulsating chest that rose and fell once a second. Wanting to test his control, Zon thought to slow the breathing. His chest froze, then rose more slowly and shallower, pulling air in as if he were sleeping rather than running a race.

Zon was outside his body for the very first time. The feeling of freedom was enormous, as it had been when he first entered Idrisi's mind. But he was free here, uninhibited by another's surroundings. Looking about, he saw Fellows and his soldier in the elevator, rising past the tenth floor on their way to the top.

"If I got close to them, maybe I could enter their thoughts, possibly even manipulate them," he thought. Willing himself upward, he felt the floor draw away, then found himself inside the elevator with the two terrorists. Just then, the elevator stopped. All of the hotel lights went out. Immediately, the eerie glow of emergency lights filled the cavernous lobby.

"Skyjack," Fellows said into the radio, "we need a ladder, and a delay." The police had cut the power to the hotel, hoping to slow their escape. Above, the tube spewing the fog retracted from the hole, and the business ends of two grenade launchers were inserted. However, instead of the smaller ID grenades, the two launchers were outfitted with large explosives. The soldiers didn't fire, but a small rope and basket came barreling through the hole, falling just above the frozen elevator.

Zon stared at the basket, then at the scrambling men inside the elevator as they fought to open the door for their escape. He then zoomed to the two men above on the roof who searched the hotel floor with launcher-mounted scopes for potential victims. But there was something else that kept pulling at his mind's eye. Glancing below, he saw small groups of people, policemen and cameramen, newsmen, the curious, emerging from each escalator entryway. All moved cautiously about the entry, but dared not to venture into the great lobby. Piles of bodies lay about them; all in sight were dead but for the two men in the glass elevator. They'd all died together in an instant, and as far as the crowd rushing in was concerned, certain death loomed for them, too, if they dared venture farther. They could die just as quickly . . . just as silently.

Zon swooped down to the crowd. Then, in a twinkling of an eye, he swooped to the elevator, then to the roof, into the chopper, then back to the elevator. His movements were as swift as his thoughts.

But something kept tugging at him. At the north entry, in the midst of the group, something else kept clawing at him, preventing him from concentrating on the terrorists. Staring deep into the crowd, Zon finally focused on a lone figure, dressed in a white bodysuit, her black hair pulled back and falling to her shoulders.

"Xia," he exclaimed mentally, in utter disbelief. "This must be a dream," he reasoned, since he had left her safely in Charlotte only a few hours before. "I've got to be making this up as I go. Still, this is all too real." He felt a sudden cold shiver from the thought of her being here, in the midst of all this death and potential dying. And he, despite all of his supernatural power, was totally helpless to protect her.

As Zon watched, Xia, following a small group of policemen, broke from the crowd toward the elevators. All of them gazed up, about the lobby walls and counted the dead bodies peppered about. Abruptly, Xia froze in place as her gaze locked to a pile of bodies strewn about the west entrance. There, she saw Zon stretched awkwardly in the midst of them. His eyes, skin, and mouth broadcast the signs of death. In his mind force, Zon cringed as he watched a visible shudder engulf her. As if frozen into slow motion from the horror of it all, she turned. Her hands rose and embraced the sides of her head, her lower jaw dropped.

"No!" she screamed, turning about to face the west entrance. Her body tightened as she ran to his side.

"Xia!" Zon cried out in his thoughts. He knew that she couldn't hear him, but was unable to stop the passionate attempt to ease her anxiety.

Attracted by Xia's scream, a grenade launcher took aim and fired directly at the small group, and Xia, standing below. Xia froze that instant, staring up . . . at him . . . through him, as if listening for some message from God. In animated horror, Zon watched her tear-filled, dazzling eyes staring up and . . . at him . . . through him, into the oncoming missile, searching . . .

"Zon!" she yelled, as the projectile raced toward her. Zon watched helplessly as the missile glided by. His hands could have stopped it, his feet, his body could have blocked it. But he had no body, no substance. All he could do was watch. The second grenade launcher fired into the northern entrance.

This dream had become a nightmare. Horror-induced anxiety had shaken him to the core, causing him to lose control of his thoughts. Instantly, as horror consumed him, he lost control and was yanked back into his body, into darkness without Zonbolo. In his thoughts, he screamed for Xia, who stood helpless, not fifty feet away in the direct path of the grenade.

Meanwhile, the poisonous ID had worn off, causing his body to erupt into spasms, the control nerves being reconnected as abruptly as they had been severed. Zon fought to open his eyes as sounds of explosions erupted in his ears.

"But the explosions were a part of the dream," he thought as he fought desperately to open his eyes from the nightmare. In spite of the convulsions, he forced himself up. The reality of the explosions jolted back some control. Gathering his thoughts, he instantly collected himself within. Small bits of hard debris pummeled his upper body. Finally, his eyes popped open, in time to deflect a large chunk of the concrete floor that came hurling at him. In that sober instant, he regained his Zonbolo, his massive body control, then popped from the floor. Squinting, he peered through the dust from the settling debris of the explosion, unsure of what he was going to find.

Loud screams erupted from the entryways, about the lobby, except the north entry. That's where the other grenade had delivered its oversized explosive payload, filling the portal with fallen concrete and steel, sealing it completely off from the lobby.

Zon rushed to the base of the elevator. There amid the settling dust was a large hole in the floor where Xia and the other onlookers had stood. Small heaps of mangled flesh lay about, fresh blood staining the concrete.

"Oh, my God," he exclaimed, searching the area madly for any clue, any reassurance that Xia was still a part of his dreams, and not plastered about the walls. "It was a dream," he repeated over and over, sickened from his close inspection of the mauled bodies about him. "It was only a dream." He stooped low, searching, trying as hard as he could not to find what he was looking for. His mind raced, fighting to differentiate dream from reality. Suddenly, a large piece of white knit fabric, streaked with rips, powder burns, and blood, floated down and fell across his head. The sweet and sensuous aroma of Xia's perfume plowed up his nose, like a race car into a brick wall.

From deep within, a guttural roar shook Zon. His heart ached as if someone had pierced it with a skewer.

"This can't be!" he screamed, clutching the torn bodysuit to his face, muffling his sobs. "This can't be!" Grasping the fabric, he crushed it to his face, pulling Xia's sensuous smell into his lungs with a deep breath. Madness raked at his mind, fueled by thoughts of her shredded body parts splattered about the walls.

With a crazed look on his face, he shot his eyes to the ceiling, where he saw General Fellows strapped in the leather harness, rising through the hole in the roof. The other soldier, still in the elevator, anxiously awaited his turn to flee. As the general cleared the hole, one of the soldiers leaned in again and fired another grenade into the hotel. This time, it struck the west entry, where Zon had been, blasting brick, steel, bodies, and the few brave souls who still dared to enter, into confetti. The shock of the exploding bomb shook Zon loose from his tormented thoughts.

"Could have stopped that one," he said, reprimanding himself for being swayed. He was enraged, but he had to stop those killers not just because of the dead that lay about, but also for those who would surely die in the future if the terrorists were allowed to escape. Grappling for control, he packed his horror tightly into the overstuffed vault of his mind.

Slinging the shroud aside, Zon jumped high onto the concrete pillars supporting the dormant elevators. His fingers sunk into the concrete as he landed at the tenth floor. Crushed cement dust spew out of the small finger holes formed by his grip. Kicking foot holes in the pillars, he then leaped skyward again, in a maddened rage, landing at the twenty-fifth level. An empty harness dropped back through the hole to the waiting soldier's hands. Loud, thunderous jolts echoed off the hotel's perimeter as Zon assaulted the stone pillars, making his way quickly to the top.

Clearly shaken by Zon's loud approach, the soldier sneaked a horrified look down while fumbling madly, before finally locking himself into the harness. Giving the signal, he rose toward the hole in the roof. But as he released the elevator, Zon reached out and grabbed his heel, crushing the bones within. The soldier cried out. Zon climbed over him, knocked him unconscious, then grabbed onto the rescue line. Approaching the hole, he lodged himself amid the exposed piping and steel beams of the roof, jolting the thick rescue line to a halt.

The tow motor in the chopper strained, trying to pull the soldier, Zon, and the hotel, up with it.

"Take off!" Fellows shouted to the pilot. "We'll drag him out of there!" The attack helicopter instantly roared, launching skyward. But the lifeline choked its ascent, jerking it to a sudden stop not ten feet above the rooftop. The pilot eased further down on the throttle, pulling the thick rope yet tighter. Inside the hole, Zon clinched the rope about his left hand. His other hand and knees were fixed to the steel girder and cracking concrete above him. The unconscious soldier dangled just below. Peering through the hole, Zon could see the chopper struggling to free itself, but was satisfied that the thick rope would hold.

"Cut the line!" Fellows yelled. "Cut the damn line!" One of the four soldiers on board leaned over and started sawing the massive nylon cord with a large hunting knife. Fellows stood up in the doorway and loaded an ID grenade to the launcher and aimed it at the hole in the roof.

"No, General!" one of the soldiers yelled, grabbing the barrel of the launcher as Fellows raised it to fire. "We're too close!" Jerking free of the soldier's hand, Fellows aimed into the hole and fired. But the grenade skewed, being blown off course by the chopper's powerful downdraft. Striking the roof, it bellowed the fine mist upward, where it was caught in the helicopter's drafting blades. They pulled it around, then down, coating the chopper and its occupants with ID.

"Shit!" Fellows screeched while reaching for another grenade. The soldier with the knife sawed madly at the rope, spitting desperately to clear the dormant poison from his lips. As he cut, taut strands twanged like guitar strings as they were set free. Fellows reached for the last ID grenade in his pouch, but something on the inside chopper wall caught his eye. Jerking his head up from the launcher, he spied a small yellow dot of light fixed firmly on the dark inner wall. Following the scant beam, he traced it back through the jagged hole in the roof. As he stared, the small dot split in two, then four. The small points of light began separating, tracking along the walls of the fuselage. Fellows's mouth fell open in shock; his hand began trembling. The chopper jerked as portions of the anchoring line popped away.

"Watch the beams!" he shouted, alerting the other soldiers except for the pilot, who couldn't hear. Down below, Zon had retrieved the laser pistol from the soldier who dangled below him. Using the shiny surfaces about, he bounced and split the lethal beam of light off the inside of the hovering craft.

"Close that fucking door! Now!" Fellows ordered, too scared to move, but hoping to stop the deadly lights. But as the soldier leaned toward the door, the rope cutter severed another cord of the rescue rope, causing the helicopter to jerk to the right. The sudden movement launched the unsuspecting soldier across a beam of light. He screamed as the beam approached his face, then instantly fell silent. His momentum threw him into the unsuspecting pilot, smashing him into the dash.

Like a large bird, diving headlong for a fish, the helicopter's nose dug into the asphalt roof. Propeller blades shredded on contact as they struck the rooftop. The chopper's body pivoted from the momentum and slammed on its side. The pilot's head was crushed into the control panel; a trickle of brain oozed out of his ear. The soldier cutting the rope was thrown out onto the landing pad, where he was stomped like a roach by the oncoming helicopter. Of the five on board, only Fellows survived.

Feeling the rope go limp, Zon swung himself up through the hole in time to see the chopper crash. Fellows, conscious but mortally wounded, was trapped in the crushed fuselage, his bald and bloodied head sticking out from the wreckage like a white-headed, puss-filled zit--in desperate need of popping.

Zon fought the sudden surge of rage that built within him, upon seeing the fat bloodied man, the man responsible for 4,000 Haitian deaths, who had so mercilessly attacked innocent people in this hotel, needlessly killing so many. This was the man who had ripped from him the essence of his dreams, a dream that he'd discovered in a woman he'd known for such a brief, eternal instant.

Xia had consumed his heart, had filled to overflowing that white void of his soul. She was that woman forbidden to him, denied him, yet whose charm and warmth he had hopelessly . . .

" . . . fallen in love with," he whispered, finishing aloud the damning thought that whirled inside his head. Though his eyes glared at Fellows, all he could see was Xia: her glowing face and hypnotizing eyes that had stared back at him so lovingly after they had kissed in her living room. "That's where she is," he thought. "That's where she'll always be . . . in that living room . . . in my arms . . . in . . ." The sight of the smoldering crash blurred before him as his tears hopelessly struggled to rinse both scenes away.

Stepping back, he shook his head sharply as he tried to clear his thoughts. He gazed down the hole into the hotel roof. His tears dove down through the gaping hole, to the floor, to join themselves to her. Yet, his heart clung to the improbable chance that she might have escaped the enormous blast that had chewed a twenty-foot hole through the three feet of mortar, leaving liberated, mangled body parts strewn about the lobby. Still, he hoped. Focusing through the glare, searching for her, he relived the floating rag of a bodysuit that had settled about him when he had first searched the hole. A stark shudder ran through him, shaking him to the core. Such pain he'd never known.

From the beginning, he'd understood the price he'd pay to possess Zonbolo. He could never touch a woman, couldn't learn to love her, or ever allow her to love him. He'd prepared himself to never love and to never let anyone close enough to get hurt. But, somehow, Xia had gotten close. She'd gotten in deep, faced the fortress he'd built around his heart and had overcome it so easily . . . before he'd realized. And she had paid for being so innocently lovable--with her life.

The lobby slowly filled with hundreds of people milling about like so many ants. Sirens of all types could be heard since the deafening whirl of the helicopter had been silenced. Bodies were being inspected and the police were fast approaching the roof. Inside, Zon stared over to the vault that had held his disabling thoughts of Xia. It stood silent, but its door swung wide as he looked on. Peering inside, he saw not the burning passion of her love. Instead, he saw a grave, dirt piled high, the marker clearly spelling out "XIA." His eyes squeezed shut, but he was unable to block out the vision in his mind. He fell to his knees in agony.

"It had to be," he sobbed aloud. "She couldn't be with me. Nobody can! What good is all of this power! It can move mountains, but it can't bring her back to me. It can't overcome my sorrow, my loneliness." Deep within, questions of his chosen fate emerged. "Is that to be my life from now on?" he asked, casting his eyes to the sky. "Befriend me . . . love me . . . and die?"

Zon covered his face with his large hands, hoping to block the hurt, but it didn't help. Just then, he perceived, in the distance, four helicopters. The sound momentarily wrenched him from his grief.

Committed to his anonymity, he leaped over to Fellows, where he grabbed the dying man's head. Fellows's dilated eyes rolled about wildly as Zon explored his thoughts, unconcerned with the mental damage he might be doing. The enraged black superman's eyes widened as he surveyed the killer's madness. ID storage . . . NAACP attack . . . Fifty Year Plan . . . engineered backlash . . . civil war . . . homelands . . . safe havens . . . ghettos . . . Westmoreland . . . ethnic cleansing . . .

He was shaken by the implications of it all. The approaching copters forced him from the wreckage to the north side of the hotel roof. As he jumped, the wrecked copter erupted into a raging inferno. In one smooth motion, he leaped to the next building, ran, then jumped again to the next roof. From there he dove into a secluded alley, where he disappeared.

19
WAR OF THE HEART

The solid brass lock easily gave way, yielding to Zon's massive right hand. Inside, soft music oozed from the stereo, as it had that morning, with mellow evening jazz.

"She must have left in a hurry," an emotionally drained Zon said to himself. He peeled his left hand tightly across his forehead, then over and around his skull. Gripping the back of his neck, his hand vainly tried to calm the storm of thoughts and emotions spinning about in his mind.

He'd flown madly about the country after leaving Chicago, finding the speed of his ship the only relief for the pain he carried inside--much as it had been in college when his friends had discovered his virginity. He couldn't face that truth either and had run madly all night around an activity field. The faster he ran, the less his disabling thoughts penetrated his wounded heart. And like then, faster flying speed required more of his thoughts, stole more of his mind away, protecting his wounded heart. But, just like then, he knew that, sooner or later, he'd have to stop. Back then, he'd run away to the Peace Corps. And now, he wanted to run away again, to escape the reality of lives lost, of Xia lost, of his own damnation to a life absent of love. But he couldn't run this time because there was simply nowhere to run. He could have flown forever in that plane, with only inevitable hunger breaking his flight. Eventually it, or something else, would have stopped him. So after flying for hours, he'd finally made his way back to Charlotte.

He wanted to go home to his farm, with Boo-Boo, but knew that he'd carry this new madness with him. No. Unlike before, he wasn't going to make a rash decision. Nor was he going to run. He was going to face it. As painful and debilitating as it was, he had decided to face the horrible reality that tore at the lining in his stomach. And there was no better place to face it than where he'd last seen Xia.

Stepping inside Xia's home, he eased the door shut behind him. The broken latch tumbled, then bouncing off the brick porch below. Though dark outside, a single lamp softly lit the room. It sat on the table at the end of the couch where he'd sat that morning, so contentedly, with Xia. It was 9:30 P.M. He'd left Chicago at 5:00. With quick and deliberate steps, he walked over to the couch where she'd sat, and sat down. A soulful love ballad by Sade thumped from the speakers, adding a mood to the room, a mood of desire and longing that wrung the blood from his heart. It conjured up memories of their passionate kiss, the long and warm embrace on the camping trip, those intense, yet innocent brown eyes that had stared so lovingly into his. Emotion welled up inside him, filled his eyes, choked off his throat. The juice glasses that they'd drunk from that morning still sat on the coffee table. He picked up Xia's and twirled it slowly back and forth in his hands above his lap as he stared into its crystalline glare, and thought of her. Huge solitary tears rhythmically splashed off its surface after trickling off the tip of his nose. Wanting to touch her, he placed the rim of the christened crystal to his lips and rubbed it gently. His mind transformed the cold, hard sensation to the sensuously soft warmth of her kiss.

Sorrow plunged him into his thoughts, lost him to his memories, oblivious to the world about him. And that's how he wanted to stay, lost to the world as it had come to be. Gaining Zonbolo was more than he'd ever imagined, making him superhuman. But it, like most panaceas, had a hefty price attached. To be super also meant that he would be forever alone. It meant that he would forever harbor enormous and constantly growing feelings and emotions of manhood that were as much a part of him as his arms or legs. He had to lock them inside forever. As great a gift as Zonbolo was, he knew now, from the pain inside, that it wasn't worth his soul.

And if Xia was still with him--if she were still alive--there would be no debate. Having her would be all the "super" he'd need or desire. "But she's not here!" he moaned aloud, his voice broken with emotion. "Get that through your head. You were chosen . . . for Zonbolo . . . for a reason." Zon spoke aloud what he thought Idrisi would say, hoping that his mentor's wisdom would help him as it had so many times before. "Your choosing . . . your quest . . . it's got to go on. Even if she were here, there would be no other choice but to turn and walk away." Zon paused. The thought of voluntarily leaving Xia rekindled subsided pains of anguish in his gut. "Turn and walk away," he recited. "Turn and walk away."

As he sat rolling and massaging the glass, a squishing noise caught his ear. Surprised, he bolted from the couch and watched as Xia, dripping wet and scantily wrapped in a towel clasped to her chest, walked briskly out of her hallway, past the stereo, and toward the kitchen, oblivious to him.

"Xia!" he shouted, his joyous heart leaping, stealing rational thought and gluing his feet to the floor. A startled Xia froze in her tracks. Turning, she stared into the ill-lit room. Her hair was dripping wet and streaked down her shoulders. Her eyes were reddened and swollen. Instantly recognizing him, she raised her hand to her gaping mouth, fell back against the outer kitchen wall, and began to sob. Zon stood motionless, watching her cry. Waves of emotions fluttered back and forth in him, from sheer ecstasy to utter disbelief. Then, as if on cue, both leaped to the middle of the room, engulfing each other in a haven of embracing arms, squeezing tightly, insuring themselves of the other's presence.

"I . . . I thought that you'd been killed," she said, her voice more sobs than words. Zon squeezed her tighter. In an instant, his heart had been mended, his soul, refilled.

"You *were* there," he replied.

"Yes, I had to come . . . to protect you. But . . . but I was too late." She struggled, trying to make sense of what was happening.

"It doesn't matter," Zon whispered. A smile dawned across his face; a wave of prickly heat washed over him. "It doesn't matter. Nothing else matters anymore." Xia didn't reply, but bathed in the joy of having his muscular arms about her, squeezing her, quenching her thirst for him. The two gently swayed in silence as they cradled each other in the middle of her living room.

"Yes," she finally replied. "Nothing else matters anymore." Grabbing Zon's elbow with her hand, she eased her head from his shoulders till she could stare into his dancing brown eyes. "Zon," she whispered, "I . . . love you." Zon's smiled touched his ears. The words rushed over him, swallowed him like the great waterfall of Beinin. He stood speechless, his heart singing as joyously as his arms and eyes, which beheld her.

Not taking her eyes from his, she slowly took a step back. Then Zon felt her wet towel fall across his feet. His breath caught in his throat. Her eyes searched his, calling him to her . . . to love her . . . to make love to her. His eyes cut back and forth between hers. He avoided the sudden and undeniable urge to cast them down onto the bare body that stood before him. Though she stood nearly a foot away, the heat of her body warmed him. Immediately, a war erupted in his thoughts, one between the fulfillment of this love that he'd been pursuing all of his adult life and the moral obligation of his pledge to Beinin. But, just as quickly, his eyes froze, no longer fueled by indecision.

"Nothing else matters," he said. Fixing his eyes on hers, he grabbed the thin black tank top and ripped it off. Xia's eyes bulged slightly, betraying her desire as they poured across the mass of rippling muscles. Seizing the opportunity, Zon sent his eyes exploring as well, down onto her beautiful, teardrop-shaped breasts.

Breathing was now next-to-impossible. His pants cut into the engorging mass contained within. Lowering his gaze still further, he followed the deep sensuous curves of her hips down to her thighs, then to the furry black mound that nestled between them, beckoning him. Breathing stopped altogether.

Embarrassed, Xia returned her gaze to Zon's eyes, catching them as they returned from her body. As she did, Zon grabbed his biker shorts and ripped them away in one clean motion. A gasp escaped from Xia's lips as she felt his freed manliness lightly thump her abdomen. Now, she, too, couldn't breathe. Seeing her tremble slightly, Zon stepped up and wrapped his arms around her, mashing their unveiled bodies together as they kissed. Instinctively, they moved with the music.

"Mmmm," he moaned. Their knotted tongues hinged their mouths together. Then, breaking their kiss but not their embrace, Zon sunk his face into her neck, where he blew gently on the fine baby hair there, sending regiments of goose pimples marching down her back. He wondered where the bedroom was.

"All the way . . . back on . . . the right," Xia gasped. Folding her legs over his right arm, Zon lifted her high and passionately kissed her as he walked to her bedroom. Laying her gently on the queen-sized bed, he eased down toward her, then stopped. Backing away, he stood erect, staring at her. She was the perfect vision of loveliness. The sensualness of her body was barely outdone by the beauty of her face, which, though great, was eclipsed by the joy in his heart of knowing that she was in love with him. He should have felt embarrassed as she stared curiously up at him, but he didn't. He hadn't wanted to stand there, but felt as if she wanted him to. His own desires were driving him downward, urging him to get to her as quickly as possible. But the instincts of his heart would not allow it. His loins screamed for satisfaction, but he wanted her satisfaction . . . more. Staring into her eyes, he searched for her feelings. In them, he saw her love, her desire, and also a slight anxiety about . . . him . . . of what they were about to do. Allowing his instincts to lead the way, he eased down into her welcoming embrace.

With the gentleness of a lamb, he sipped the nipple of her left breast into his mouth, dragging his tongue across its tip, sending a swell of ecstasy through her body. Her head sunk back against the bed, her eyes eased shut from the sensuous touch. Together, they teased and touched until neither could withstand it anymore.

"Zon, I love you," Xia gasped again as she felt his manliness beckoning to enter. Zon fought the desire to rush into her. Instead, he eased to her, then away as he felt her respond. She then rose to consume him, then, too, retreated as he eased on for more. Rolling to and fro, the two bodies worked their way closer together, the achieved portion of their union working about ever so gently . . . so satisfyingly . . . driving both to ecstasy. The rhythmic dance continued until they had completely consumed each other.

"Xia, I love you, too!" Zon suddenly shouted as together, they achieved their pinnacle of ecstasy. Exhausted, Zon fell onto her, kissing her panting mouth as both fought to inhale the hot steamy air.

The two lay spent, fulfilled, satisfied . . . united in love.

* * *

Zon sat up in the large bed, uncovered, nude, awakened by the morning sunbeams that had crept through Xia's eastern-facing bedroom window. After making love repeatedly for half the night, the two had finally fallen asleep in each other's arms. But she had rolled away in her sleep to the far left side of the bed where she now lay, her back to him, her exposed body still the vision of splendor it had been the night before.

Zon feared the morning's arrival. His decision of the night before was an irreversible one. He'd lost, no, given his virginity to Xia, cashing in his claim to Zonbolo. Though he'd expected to awaken crazed of remorse and doubt, he was surprised to find his thoughts abnormally tranquil, orderly, and all but subdued. Never before had he experienced such calm. He laughed quietly, realizing it as the impact lovemaking had on a man.

With Xia, it had been far more than he'd ever imagined, complete, with joy exploding from the satisfaction of his loins, the thrill of satisfying her, and the sheer ecstasy of loving and being loved.

Still, he had lost his power. Casting himself into his thoughts, all he could see was his contented heart and a massive river of calm with him and Xia floating happily along. His mind was aglow with thought, the interior appearing lighted from without, with a golden-red glow. But he could focus none of his thoughts into the narrow laser beams to which he'd grown accustomed. He'd tried earlier to energize himself, to peer through the window, to the treetops, to count the fly larvae on the distant leaves, but couldn't focus beyond the smooth perfect toenails on Xia's right foot. He strained to hear the air coursing through the small seam of the closed flue in Xia's fireplace, but could hear only the soft rhythm of her breathing. Though the strange bed felt wonderfully soft upon his back, he'd lost the sensation of his hair curled to his scalp. Love and satisfaction he had, but the Bolo was no more.

The loss saddened him, and he felt remorse over the things he would no longer be able to do. With time, he'd be able to fly his jet-car again, he thought, though not as well as before. And what of

Boo-Boo? Communication between them had been so easy. She'd still recognize him, but could they be as they once had? Greater still, would he want to live out there with a gigantic cat . . . and Xia? One by one, questions of his new beginning filled his mind. He pondered them all, calmly, while staring at Xia.

"I wonder if everyone goes through these changes," he said teasingly to himself. Rolling on his side, he admired Xia's exposed backside. Her rich brown skin was flawless, as smooth as silk, unblemished but for a small birthmark on her upper left thigh. Easing a bit closer, he stared at it. The mark was dark and jagged on one end.

"It's beautiful, too," he said quietly, thinking of how love had made everything about her so wonderful and familiar. The birthmark looked as if it belonged there, as if he'd known it to be there all along. Curiously, he eased to his knees and turned about, staring into the back of her thighs. Suddenly, he heard a muffled whimper.

"Xia?" he said softly. She didn't reply, but rolled toward him. The morning sun glowed as it bounced from her skin. Zon felt the itching of passion igniting within him as she rolled fully into view. But the tears in her eyes squelched his desire.

"What's the matter?" he asked, easing his hand to her shoulder.

"Did you mean it?" she asked.

"With all my heart," he answered, sensing her referral to his cry of passion from the night before. "And I'll say it again. Xia, I love you." She rolled up into his arms, embracing him.

"You're the only man that I've ever . . . known," she confessed into his right ear.

"You mean, you were a . . . "

"Yes," she answered, not allowing him to say the "V" word.

"So . . . so was I," he replied. A small grin split his face.

Violently, Xia snatched herself away from him, then stared deep into his eyes. Tears again started barreling down her face.

"I can't tell!" she shrieked. "You're lying to me!" Breaking free of him, she jumped from the bed, then stood with her back to him, her arms crossed firmly over her chest.

"I wouldn't lie, especially to you," Zon pleaded. "Until last night, I was a virgin." He sprang to his knees, but stayed on the bed.

"I . . . I gave up everything," Xia sobbed loudly, "everything that I was, everything that I had . . . and . . . and you're lying to me!"

Zon wanted to plead, but her naked form stole his thoughts. He couldn't stop staring at the birthmark. It appeared darker and bit more structured with her standing, like a small seashell . . . like a coral shell. With deep curiosity, he put his head to the bed, then pushed himself up into a headstand, wanting to stare upside-down at it. Hearing the bed squeak, Xia turned to address him face to face, only to see him in his obscene pose.

"You pig!" she shouted, then picked up a pillow and hit him with it. "You expect me to believe that a tall, dark . . . and . . . rich twenty-six-year-old guy like you has never been with a woman before?"

"Twenty-five!" Zon shouted back as he tumbled onto the bed. With her right hand, Xia grabbed the blanket beneath him and snatched it free, then wrapped herself in it before storming off toward the bathroom, still sobbing. But, before she reached the door, she heard the mirror across the room shatter. Turning, she saw Zon fall into a heap on the dresser amid a shower of sparkling glass, having been flung across the room by her powerful tug on the blanket.

"Oh, my God!" she yelled, a glint of sunshine appearing in her eye. "Zon? Are you all right?" Zon fell off the dresser and rolled onto the carpet, twelve feet from the bed. After shaking his head, he quickly jumped to his feet.

"How'd you . . . ?" he stopped midsentence. "You were a virgi . . . " he stopped again. A jumble of thoughts spun about his mind like a jigsaw puzzle. "Reading people," he recited and took a step closer to Xia. His left hand rested on his waist. She stood staring at him, growing excited from his nakedness, and from a tickling anxiety springing forth in her mind. Zon wiped his right hand across his forehead, then limply shook his finger at her. "That birthmark, on your thigh . . . I've seen it before." He stared at the carpet, afraid to believe what his thoughts suggested.

"In the jungle," Xia said softly. Zon jerked his head up and stared into her face.

"Beinin," he whispered.

"Beinin," she repeated joyously.

"Beinin!" Zon shouted. Xia flung the blanket to the floor.

"Beinin!" she answered. Zon's excitement spread below his waist. Rushing together, the two embraced, then fell to the bed and consumed each other again in the passion of rediscovered love.

20
BACK TO BEININ

The sleek, black jet-car whizzed down from the heavens, deep in the heart of Africa. Zon sat forward in the craft; Xia sat on the edge of the rear seat. Her long arms draped over the back, looping loosely around Zon's neck. Contrary to his suspicions, he had retained Zonbolo, but the unfamiliar emotions of that morning had hidden it from him. Xia's display of retained power, after losing her virginity, had coaxed him to dig a little deeper, until he regained his own.

The flight provided both of them the first opportunity to explore each other's backgrounds.

"I never knew my parents," Xia said, after recovering from the awe of Zon's craft and what it would do. "I had been brought to Africa from the U.S., as an infant. A plane crash left me the only survivor. The people of Beinin took me in and raised me. I grew up among them, learning their ways and customs, but still, I was somehow different."

"Thank God for that," Zon mused. Xia mockingly squeezed his neck.

"Anyway," she continued, "it was wonderful, during my youthful years, running, jumping in a natural playground that seemed to go on forever. But as I started to mature, I began experiencing feelings, unlike any of the other kids. And no one could explain them to me. I became curious, competitive, and at times, insatiable. But in Beinin, these feelings were foreign to everyone, except Idrisi. Somehow he seemed to have retained some knowledge of the ways of the outside. Beininians don't hide anything from each other. I guess, in their utopia, they don't have to. But I longed to hide my feelings, to not have them open and exposed. Idrisi told me, when I was just eight years old, that I'd have to leave one day."

"So when did you leave?" Zon asked.

"Just as you came in," she replied. "Idrisi sent Lindi and Zedra, my two closest friends, and me to retrieve you from the jungle. They brought you back. I couldn't return. So I made my way to Liberia, where I worked and studied geography and history. Idrisi told me of my origin in the U.S., but could tell me little else. So, after adopting the Liberian culture and language, I read everything concerning the U.S. that I could find. And I conversed with everyone I met who'd been to the States. That was how I got involved with psychiatry. One of the professors at the university there had studied in the U.S. I got from him all that I could. In all, I spent two-and-a-half years there.

You can learn about people and places from books, magazines, and conversations, but you can't learn the people themselves. I wanted to be American, so I had to learn how to think, to feel, to react, like an American. So after I learned all that I could in Liberia, I stowed away on a freighter headed for North Carolina. Arriving there and needing two names, I split mine and reversed the syllables. Daisia became Xia Day. Quickly, I made my way to Charlotte, the largest city with the most people and the most diverse culture and lost my accent in just a few days. And after a few *convenient* letters mailed to the right places, I got my certificate of psychiatry, then set up my practice. I've used it since, as a front, so I could Americanize myself."

"That's how you got to know Nikki and the others?" Zon asked.

"Yes. Plus, I still needed friends. They are good friends of mine."

"Tell me what happened in Chicago," Zon asked.

Xia chuckled lightly before beginning her tale.

"You know, now that I think about it, I thought it odd that I couldn't knock you out."

"What?" Zon retorted.

"Yesterday morning, in my living room, after we hugged. I squeezed your chest tight. Remember?"

"Yes, but I thought you were just caught up in the moment, like me."

"I was. But I was also convinced that if you went to Chicago, you were going to get hurt. So after I kissed you, and told you that I *couldn't let you go,* I tried to gently squeeze the breath out of you, to render you unconscious."

"And I thought that you'd fallen hopelessly in love with me," Zon joked as he flashed an exaggerated look of disgust.

"Oh, I had," Xia replied passionately. "I even blamed my feelings for blocking Xiabolo, preventing me from stopping you. Anyway, after you left, I quickly changed, headed for the airport, and caught the next flight out, which left not twenty minutes after I'd arrived. I'd gotten to Chicago in less than two-and-a-half hours and thought that I'd arrived in time. And you saw my horror when I realized that I was too late." Zon reached a reassuring hand to hers, showing his empathy and concern. "When I saw your dead body," she continued, "I was horrified. But as I turned to run to your side, I thought I heard you calling me . . . from the roof, so I looked up. But all I saw was that missile heading straight for me."

"So, I can communicate from that state," Zon pondered aloud.

"What?" Xia asked.

"The poison had completely liberated me from my body," Zon began. "So after I reconnected enough to keep it alive, I ventured out, spiritually I guess, and up to the roof, from where I saw you come in. When I saw your reaction to my being dead, in my thoughts, I screamed out your name. You heard me."

"Idrisi had spoken often of such ability," Xia added, "though I've never been able to do it."

"Well, I hadn't either until that poison showed me the way. But, tell me what happened next. I lost it all at that point and couldn't tell what was going on."

"Well," Xia replied, "at first, I stared up, looking for you, but saw the missile coming. I leapt out of its way, dragging as many people with me as I could, into the northern entrance. Grabbing a chunk of concrete that lay about, I ripped my white bodysuit off and used it to fling the massive chunk at the approaching missile, exploding it just before the entry. But it blew the entire structure apart, sealing closed the northern entrance. Fearing you dead, and with the host of hurt people about, I busied myself with them, trying to pretend that I hadn't lost you. By the time we'd gotten the place cleared, we heard the tremendous explosion on the roof. Hundreds of people stormed inside. I searched for your body amid the pile of the dead. All I found were stray body parts."

"You must have gone out of your mind," Zon said. "I know that I did."

"I must have," she responded. "I made my way back to O'Hare, then to Charlotte. It took me over four hours to do it. And all I could think of was the loss of you. When I got back to my place, I instinctively turned on the radio and climbed into the shower, where I'd stood for what seemed like hours, soaking in the cool water. Beinin had taught me of the healing power of falling water and good rhythm. Whenever I need to think or just chill, I head for the music and the falls. I guess that I was so caught up in my sorrow that I didn't hear you when you came in. I was going for a drinking glass when I trotted into the kitchen and saw you." Both of them smiled knowingly, the mention of the night before bringing back pleasurable memories.

* * *

"How are you planning to get in?" Xia asked. The jet slowed as it skimmed along the warm African grassland.

"I haven't quite figured that out yet," Zon replied. He scanned the area for the exact point of his exit from Beinin. "But we'll set down and try to . . . " Surprise froze the words in his mouth. From within the cockpit, both of them heard faint harmonious music. Smiles rippled across their faces. Xia tightened her hug and squeezed her face into Zon's. Before them, they watched the veil of Beinin split wide. Sailing through, they flew directly to the arena.

"Look!" Xia exclaimed, pointing down at the colorfully dressed crowd below. "They were expecting us." Zon maneuvered the jet to the middle of the field and sat it down, not ten feet from where his adopted father stood. With overeagerness, he and Xia fumbled about with their seat belts and door latch, hurriedly trying to free themselves and rejoin their lost home. Xia jumped first from the heightened craft, which was still in its flying mode. Once on the ground, she fought the urge to run to Idrisi. Instead she turned to wait on Zon, who quickly joined her on the ground. Arm in arm, they stepped up to the old man. Both bowed deeply in humbled salute, then Xia leaped forward and wrapped herself around the old man.

"Father!" she exclaimed.

"You are late, my child," Idrisi said warmly, in the ancient Beininian language while returning the hug.

"Traffic was backed up," Zon quipped as he grabbed the old man about the shoulders, trapping Xia between them. The two shoved at one another, both trying to possess the greater portion of Idrisi. Then Xia perceived a beckoning from behind. Turning, she saw Lindi and Zedra awaiting her. Breaking free of the men's grasp, she charged the two and all three united in joyful and tearful hugs.

"You knew," Zon said to Idrisi.

"We all know," Idrisi responded. "We just don't know that we know."

"Didn't we end our last conversation this way?" Zon retorted. Idrisi didn't answer, but gestured behind him. From the western entrance, four Beininians approached, carrying attire for Zon and Xia. Catching sight of them, Xia leaped with joy. Lindi and Zedra shared in her excitement.

"May I ask the occasion?" Zon asked innocently.

"Your wedding," Idrisi responded. Two women stepped to Xia and began wrapping her in the brilliantly colored garb. The two men did likewise to Zon. After they were dressed, they were led to each other, then to the middle of the field. The people seated in the arena sang softly, one harmonious melody after another. The sun stood tall and bright. Flocks of birds took turns passing over the large enclosure. Idrisi stepped up before them, then motioned the couple to kneel. While on their knees, they listened to him address them and the singing crowd.

"A day! A day! A day!" he exclaimed, his arms held high, the broad sleeves of his robe draping down like wings by his side. "From of old, these two were predestined together. Yet, separately, they were set free. And in that freedom, they have found that which can exist in no other place . . . for no other people. Their young minds said, 'We ache for one another! Let us be!' But the Wise One spoke . . . and has spoken well. Both ventured forth, finding in their path love of man . . . love of this world, and with that love, abominable suffering.

Ah, but both faced that suffering. And within it, they lost that love for the world and have found the love which passeth all on this earth. Between them now is a bond that no man can make and no man can break. We are here to salute that bond, and salute it we do!"

Idrisi floated smoothly in circles, inches above the grassy carpet, as he addressed the large audience. Zon and Xia held hands tightly, listening to the old man and realizing the truth of his words. There was no way that they could have been forced nor thrown together and still have developed the love that they now possessed. To attain it, both had explored, suffered, and sacrificed as they built an everlasting bond between them. And it all had centered around their bond of virginity to Beinin, the wall over which they had to explore, the agonizing and continual pain with which they had to live, until the ultimate sacrifice was made.

Idrisi continued his melodious speech as the crowd sang deep rhythmic tunes. After twenty minutes, he touched lightly back to the ground, saluted the couple with a deep bow, then led them to the edge of the arena, where the heartwarming multitude of Beinin rushed to greet and welcome them.

* * *

"I don't want to go back either," Zon said aloud, after reading Xia's open mind. "But we've got a lot to do." The two stood at the edge of the pool by the falls, where Zon had developed Zonbolo. The evening sun was setting atop the arena's western wall behind them. Neither wore clothing. Zon stood behind Xia with his arms draped about her, their bodies pressed together. Sunshine baked their backs. Both smiled contentedly as they stared out onto the calm waters. Beautifully soft music danced over the arena wall from the congregation finishing its farewell greeting to the sun. Across the way, the waterfall splashed forth its laughter. It echoed the joy emanating from the couple's united hearts, the joy of returning home, of finally dismissing the burden of their virtuous pledge, of finding one another, of anticipating their being in love together, forever.

"We can stay a little while." Xia said it so softly that Zon wasn't sure if his ears or minds heard the reply. "It's so beautiful here, so peaceful, so heavenly. There's not a better place on this earth."

"I know," Zon replied. "We'll stay a while." But as he spoke, he felt a tickling in his mind. Submerging, he tried to detect who had invaded his thoughts, but the culprit was in and out too quickly. Ignoring the intrusion, Zon spoke again to Xia.

"We've got to make the outside more like Beinin. We've both been given the power. And now, we've been united."

"Tomorrow," she said lazily. "Tomorrow, we'll save the world. But for now . . . " she turned and massaged her silken body into his, " . . . just love me, Zon. Just love me."

With a smile, Zon leaned down to kiss her, but buzzing erupted in their ears as their lips met. Both instinctively ducked low to the ground as a large, black lightning-fast object streaked from the sky and passed inches above their heads. Rising, they watched as Zon's jet-car did a triple barrel roll, then hovered to a vertical stop fifty feet over the middle of the tranquil pool. Inside, a wide-eyed Idrisi grinned from ear to ear, the exhilaration of the flight percolating his blood. Speaking to their thoughts, he said, "Such wonderful toys you have . . . so wonderful!" With a quick roll of his eyes, he gunned the accelerator to the floor and shot into the heavens.

"And to think," Zon said, "of all the bad-mouthing that old man put on Kaldaca for being such a thrill seeker."

"Idrisi?" Xia asked in surprise. "Now, why would he bad-mouth himself?"

"What?" he said.

"He didn't tell you?" she asked. "Kaldaca is his middle name."

About the Author

Gregory K. Morris was born and raised in Greensboro, North Carolina and now lives in Charlotte with his wife, Thalistine. They have two children, Estevon and Taronique. Greg graduated from North Carolina State University in Raleigh with a bachelor's degree in Chemical Engineering. He is considered a man of many talents and is at work on his next book.